ADVANCE PRAISE

"James Jennings's *Blue Wild Indigo* is steeped in the tradition of Southern and Southwestern writers like Larry McMurtry and Harper Lee. From the first page, Jennings whisks us away to a time, 1954, and a place, Oklahoma, that now only exists in the imagination of such talented writers. The characters become familiar to us, not because we've seen them before, but because they are so skillfully rendered."

Charles Salzberg, Three-time Shamus nominated author of *Second Story Man, Man on the Run* and *Canary in the Coal Mine*

"James Jennings is both a skilled author and a fine trial attorney. Both areas of expertise are combined to produce this marvelous novel, *Blue Wild Indigo*. As an author, Jennings weaves a fascinating tale. As a trial lawyer, he incorporates into this story the critical importance of the Rule of Law and the high price to be paid when mob rule prevails."

William G. Paul, American Bar Association President (1999–2000); Oklahoma Hall of Fame (2003); Fellow, American College of Trial Lawyers

"In his Nobel Prize acceptance speech, William Faulkner said, 'The problems of the human heart in conflict with itself alone can make good writing because only that is worth writing about, worth the agony and the sweat.' James Jennings taps into that underground stream, the heart in conflict with itself, in his new novel, *Blue Wild Indigo*."

Billy Field, Screenwriter, MGM, Warner Brothers, Twentieth Century Fox; Documentary Filmmaker, University of Alabama, Honors College; Director, TheStoryAcorn.com.

BLUE WILD INDIGO

A Novel

JAMES JENNINGS

PLUM BAY PUBLISHING, LLC
NEW YORK, NEW YORK
MORRISTOWN, NEW JERSEY

For permission requests, contact:
Plum Bay Publishing, LLC
www.plumbaypublishing.com

Library of Congress Control Number: 2024911934
Paperback ISBN: 979-8-9907945-0-4
eBook ISBN: 979-8-9907945-1-1
Hardcover ISBN: 979-8-9907945-2-8

Printed in the United States of America

Cover Image: Barbara Benton, barbarabentonart.com
Jacket Design: Sonya Dalton
Interior Design: Barbara Aronica, bookdesigner.com
Copyedited by Jeremy Townsend

Blue Wild Indigo is a work of fiction. However, some of the story it tells and some of the places, events, and persons it references are based on historical fact. All people and places and events mentioned have been used fictitiously for the purpose of telling a fictional tale. They are products of the author's imagination. Any resemblance to actual persons, living or dead, or actual businesses, places, or events is coincidental. The town of Serafina and the County of Sebastion County, as described in the novel, do not exist.

For my children and grandchildren

"When bad men combine, the good must associate;
else they will fall one by one, an unpitied
sacrifice in a contemptible struggle."

—Edmund Burke,
British statesman and philosopher
Thoughts on the Cause of the Present Discontents,
April 23, 1770

PART ONE

CHAPTER 1
Outriders

Harrison True rode straight up—back erect, head high, eyes forward. At his off side rode his lifelong friend and blood brother, Marshall Stone. Quartering south by west beneath a measureless sprawl of wild blue, with the early sun warming their backs, the horsemen followed a narrow track along the spine of a steeply pitched hogback. Slide-rock shoulders flanked them. To the right, a mantle of loose fragments, rusty gray in color, ramped down and fanned out into a brushy apron. To the left, a field of cannonball size boulders, hewn from the mother rock above by erosion and weathering, cluttered the downslope. The horses, both blooded stock—Harry's a grulla mare dark as gun metal, Marsh's a gelding the color of fire ash—picked their steps with caution. This was quarrelsome country, even for trail wise mounts and seasoned ranchers schooled in plainscraft.

Harry and Marsh had ridden out this expanse of bowleg rangeland, miles from the nearest paved road and power line, at least twice a year for the better part of the last decade. Always enjoyed it. But for Harry this time struck a different chord. On the last day of June, *Anno Domini* 1954, at three and thirty years of age he felt something gnawing at his insides. Worry burdened his heart, challenged him to hold at bay the demons that would wilt his self-assured bearing. Uncertainty rendered him wary of everything and everyone, especially the man beside him.

Still, Harry couldn't help noticing signs that some good might come of this day. Morning had broken clear despite a night unsettled by a distant peal of thunder and a quivering blue light in the western sky. Red cedar scented the air. The temperature lingered south of torrid. The wind, by its nature fretful, lay calm in draws and swags—rare for this time of year on the relic plains of western Oklahoma. And one more thing: the soaring whistle of a meadowlark. From some unseen keep came the high dulcet tones of the yellow-breasted warbler known as daybreak's joyous herald. Along with checking grass and water levels on Harry's south range, this could be a day for sorting some things out.

Harry and Marsh had come into the world days apart in the bony brush country metropolis of Serafina. Spring, 1921. The cusp of a decade later known for its roar. From day one, Marsh feared nothing. At least, he maintained a staunch will to create that impression. Rough and ready, a raconteur quick with a sharp or humorous remark, he swung a wide loop. He had a gift for spinning yarns and telling tall tales, a wry smile always on his face, holding to a firm belief the truth was fluid and, where necessary, alterable. His brother, Clayton, twelve years his junior, lived in his shadow.

Harry, a deliberate sort—not at all timid, but reserved—deported himself with discretion. Growing up as an only child, he'd been sort of a bookish boy, possessed of a certain quietness of personality. From time to time, he drifted into long reflections, what his mother called the blue devils. He could quote poetry. That set him apart from almost everyone else his age. By the time he'd come into full manhood, some said he'd earned a reputation for having a lone wolf streak. But he had a gracious and friendly manner. And no one questioned his honesty. All who knew him agreed the man was as good as his word.

From the time they could crawl, if not before, they made a pair: Harry, the boy with nut brown hair and matching eyes, and Marsh, the blue-eyed towhead. Two peas in a pod, their mothers always said. Tweedle Dum and Tweedle Dee. Both tall and lean, square-jawed, they saw themselves as tribesmen pledged to each other and to the conquest of all who might dare to stand against them. While still smooth of cheek and light of spirit, they became blood brothers. Not by mere proclamation, not by some made-up childish ritual, but by the actual shedding and sharing of blood.

For more than three decades the fealty between Harry and Marsh held. Nothing could turn one against the other. No matter what, they rode for the brand. But these days Harry could feel the braiding of their lives unraveling. And, despite an occasional glimmer of hope, he knew in the depths of his soul he could do nothing about it. Not a damn thing.

Another half hour into the ride, Marsh raised a hand in a commanding gesture, pulled up the pale horse he called Buckshot. Harry, trailing back a ways, put forward the slaty mare known as Shadow and reined to his *compadre's* left.

"What?" Harry said.

Standing high in his stirrups, Marsh rifled an arm at something off to the north of them in the middling distance.

"Lookayonder."

Harry clapped eyes on a dust-raising commotion erupting on the facing slope of a dry wash: two white-tail bucks locked in combat head-to-head. Both trophy class animals. From each ironclad skull rose an extraordinary rack of antlers—had to be twelve points, six by six. At the withers, each stood as tall as a man's chest. Together, as Harry sized them up, they would make nigh on to a quarter ton of undomesticated muscle and bone. Magnificent beasts. But he knew they were doomed.

With branched tines welded together in a fiery clash of wills, an inglorious demise awaited them. In an instant, the bucks had merged into one being and set for themselves a pitiful destiny.

Harry and Marsh watched the willful beasts dance, moving to and fro on slender legs, heads low, flags high and twitching. Thrust and parry, attack and defend. Seize the initiative, lose it. They circled, paused like boxers observing the bell at the end of a round, mouths open, saliva streaming, lungs heaving. When the air cleared, the hoofed pugilists started up again, reversing roles. The aggressor hunkering down, defender sallying forth.

Marsh let out a small mirthless chuckle that never ascended from the depths of his throat.

"Can you believe that?" he said. "Probly buttin' heads over some doe. They'll stay stuck like that till they're both dead."

"They're already dead. The fatal futility of fact."

Marsh squinched his eyes, pooched his lips, lifted his chin.

"The fatal futility of fact. Now them's some honest to goodness four-legged words. Some kind of poem? Shakespeare, maybe?"

"Novel. Henry James."

Marsh smiled.

"Figgered. How come you always gotta be so damn smart?"

The riders sat their horses, watching the savage battle harrow on. In time, Marsh drew in a long breath, emptied his lungs of air in a series of short puffs. He nodded as if he'd hammered out some kind of bargain with himself.

"Here's another little fact for you . . . while we're on the subject. Proof of the sorry times comin' down on us, I reckon. You hear what that yahoo Billy Catlett pulled yesterday?"

"No. What?"

"That sorry sumbitch. He got to hackin' on Woody Coats. Right there on Main Street, way I heard it. Rawhided him pretty good."

Harry looked hard at Marsh.

"What the hell? What got Catlett red-assed? Woody's a good kid. Never did anything to anybody."

Marsh shrugged.

"What got Catlett's blood up? General assholery, I spect. For Woody comin' out of the oven a shade dark."

"Sounds like Catlett."

"Way I heard it, he saw Woody chattin' up a little Mexican gal. Alejandra Flores. You've seen her around. Pretty little thing. Lives with her mama in a trailer out in the Mexican section. Her and Woody know each other, I guess. They wasn't doin' nothin' but talkin.'"

"And Billy got bent out of shape about that?"

"So it seems. He and some of his fellow bottom feeders was huddled up there at the corner—the regular Saturday mornin' spit and whittle club—all of 'em down on their hunkers like a committee of buzzards. They see what Woody's doin' and start pissin' and moanin'. Today it's a Mexican, tomorrow it'll be a white girl. Got themselves worked up pretty good."

Marsh allowed himself to be distracted by a streamer of granular air kicked up by the warring bucks.

"So what happened?"

"I'm gettin' there."

Marsh kept his gaze fixed on the bucks. In his own good time he went on.

"Well, Catlett couldn't leave it lay. Had to remind everybody what a pure fool he is. So, he saunters over to Woody and says, 'What's got into you, boy, pesterin' this little gal?' Woody stood right up to him.

'I ain't pesterin' nobody,' he says. Catlett jerks Woody up short. Says, 'You best watch your P's and Q's, you don't want me to take a switch to you. Learn you some manners.' 'But why?' Woody says. 'I ain't done nothin' wrong.'"

Harry could feel a wave of heat breaking over his face. "*Boy.* Woody isn't anybody's boy except his mama and daddy's. He's a fine young man. Gotta be, what, seventeen, eighteen now. Skinny as a rail, but nobody's boy."

"Well, fine young man or not, Catlett laid into him. Give him a pretty good whuppin'. Sure wudn't no Swedish massage."

"And nobody lifted a finger to help Woody? Everybody stood there and watched?"

"Not exactly. None of them chuckleheads on the corner stood up for Woody. Catlett had 'em all buffaloed. That little Alejandra went to crying and begging Billy to stop. Didn't do no good, though. But you know who did show up and actually stick up for that string bean youngster?"

"Who?"

"Buddy Pond."

"Buddy Pond?"

"You heard me. Folks say that little sawed-off feller rushed over and give Catlett what for. Offered to whup his ass. Cain't you hear 'im, with his stutter?"

"What'd Catlett do?"

"Apparently, he got so flummoxed he stopped wailin' on Woody and started laughin'. Give Buddy a shove that landed him on his backside and walked away." Marsh toggled his head. "Bud may be pony-built and have a tongue that don't work too good, but the man ain't short on gumption."

Marsh took off his hat, mopped his brow with his forearm. Put his hat back on.

"A year ago a young gentleman of color wouldn't be sidlin' up to some gal like that, though. Right there in front of everybody. If she was a darky, maybe, but not otherwise. Sign of the times, I reckon. Hear about that sort of thing everywhere these days—paper, radio."

Harry bristled. "Whadya mean that sort of thing?"

Marsh winced. "Aw, come on, you know what I mean. People used to keep to their own kind. Live and let live. Seemed to work fine. The damn Supreme Court couldn't leave well enough alone. They come along and start tellin' everybody things gotta change. No more separate but equal, they say, cause separate cain't be equal. Why cain't it? Equal's the main thing, right? Guess they never heard of 'If it ain't broke don't fix it.'"

"The country's changing. Better get used to it."

"Yeah, well, Catlett ain't gettin' used to nothin'. Unh-unh. As they say, shit don't stink less you stir it up. You can always count on Catlett for stirrin' sumpin' up."

"Waste of skin if I've ever seen one."

"You called it, pard. Him and his whole ass clown family. All a bunch of bug eaters, if you ask me."

Marsh turned his attention back to the bucks.

"At first I thought it might be better if I didn't say nothin' to you about it," he said. "But I figured you're gonna hear about it anyways. You Trues goin' back so far with the Coats family and all."

"So?"

"So nothin'. I understand family ties is all. So does Catlett. You ask me, him hidin' Woody's 'bout as close as he can get to hidin' you. You're the one he's really got it in for. Always has."

"He doesn't scare me."

"Scares me. Not for what he might do to you. For what you might do to him. Ain't worth the aggravation, old buddy. Now, I know you for bein' tough as a bus station steak, so doin' a stretch of hard time would be easy as pie for you. But if I had my druthers I'd pass on havin' to make that trip to the state pen for visitin' day ever month. Get my meanin'?"

The bucks paused again. Marsh nodded in their direction.

"Still at it. Well . . . ."

Marsh shucked his Winchester Model 1894 from the scabbard beneath the saddle fender at his right knee. Cycled the rifle's action.

"What are you doing?" Harry said, watching.

"They'll keep goin' . . . till they're both dead. Said it yourself. Might as well put 'em out of their misery."

Harry reached for Marsh's arm.

"Don't. Don't shoot 'em."

Disbelief molded Marsh's face.

"What do you mean don't shoot 'em? Why not?"

"Leave 'em alone. They might make it."

Marsh grinned.

"I swear. Lately you been—"

Renewed jousting drew Marsh's attention back to the main event. He raised himself in the saddle, craned his neck to see better. Kicking up a scud of cinnamon-colored prairie soil, the beleaguered bucks slipped into hillside scrub at the top of the grade. Marsh settled back into the saddle, lowered the hammer on the rifle.

"Well . . . too late now. They're gone."

Marsh leathered the saddle gun. He spat, wiped his mouth with the back of a hand, raising a dull hiss from the stubble of whiskers on his lower jaw. He sawed the gray about and made for lower ground. Harry hung back, hands stacked on the saddle horn. Marsh drew rein and turned.

"You comin'?"

Harry trained his eyes on the place where he'd last seen the bucks. *We live as we dream . . . alone. Joseph Conrad.* This time he swallowed his words before they escaped his mouth.

The riders descended the ridge and followed the westering sun. At midmorning they found themselves tracking the ragged rim of a narrow gyp sink canyon, russet sandstone walls inscribed with layer cake veins of the chalky white mineral. Coming into itself, the golden eye of heaven had begun to sizzle. The wind had picked up and a blue jay, known thief and homewrecker, was raising a racket. Harry could still smell the red cedar but the biting juniper scent was giving way to the heady reek of horse and sweat. Entranced by the monotonous rhythm kept by the clop of hooves, creak of saddle leather, jingle of curb chains and spurs, they withdrew into themselves.

"You're awful quiet," Marsh said after some considerable time.

"Nothing to say, is all."

But that didn't mean he had nothing on his mind. To the contrary, the drift of his thoughts had carried him to some lines from a poem by William Butler Yeats, a verse he had first read long ago in green youth:

Turning and turning in the widening gyre
The falcon cannot hear the falconer;
Things fall apart; the centre cannot hold;

Mere anarchy is loosed upon the world,
The blood-dimmed tide is loosed, and everywhere
The ceremony of innocence is drowned . . . .

Haunted by those words, Harry lapsed again into somber contempla-tion. He remained in his ruminative state until the flushing of a covey of Bobwhite Quail yanked him out of it. The muffled wingbeats of some dozen frantic gamebirds spooked the horses. They came unglued. Ears pinned, the panicked beasts flared left, edging close to the canyon rim. Turning back through themselves, they tried to bolt. With their usual aplomb, Harry and Marsh remained centered and deep-seated; they tight-reined their mounts, circled and steadied them. The ter-ror-stricken animals stamped and snorted, threw their heads, let out frenzied high-pitched cries.

"Easy, shady lady," Harry said. "Easy."

"Quieten down, Buck," Marsh scolded his mount. "Quit actin' a fool. Scared of a few damn birds. For cryin' out loud."

When the tempest passed, the men rode on. In a short time, they found themselves traversing an expanse of dead-flat desert pavement, pallid as cadaver skin. Each fall of a steel-shod hoof against the lithic carapace set off a dull clap that echoed through an invisible labyrinth below.

"Hear that?" Harry said.

"Hear what?"

"That hollow sound. Don't trust it. Step in the wrong place, you end up in China."

"You're joshin' me, right?"

Harry halted his mare and, bending down over her withers, appraised the biscuit board trackway like a detective at a crime scene.

Marsh reined up. "This ain't our first rodeo, you know. We been here before. Never had a problem."

Harry didn't look up.

"Ach. You worry too much. Always have."

Harry raised his eyes. "Maybe you don't worry enough."

"Well now . . . there's a pearl of wisdom for you. Much obliged for that. Mebbe I should oughta take up worryin'. Surely it ain't too late, not even for a rough old hide like me."

Blurting out a short laugh, Marsh put his mount forward. Hanging back, Harry hailed him with a hand held aloft and declaimed:

Forward, the Light Brigade!
Charge for the guns!
Into the valley of Death
Rode the six hundred.

Marsh halted Buck. Reined the animal around. "You 'bout done high-hattin'? Swear to God. Sometimes, you come near givin' me a case of the squeakers."

At such times Harry could usually count on Marsh to mock his erudition by referring to him as dandified, calling him Sir Harry or Master Harry or Little Lord True, or accusing him of being an aristocrat born to the purple. Of course, a Cheshire cat grin stretched from ear to ear when Marsh indulged in such good-natured ribbing. He'd learned the smile-when-you-say-that rule of the West from Gary Cooper in *The Virginian.* And he knew not so much as an ounce of truth resided in the indictment anyway. That's why he almost tickled himself to death every time he said it. If he'd said it in earnest, it would have been outright slander. More than that, it would make a surefire way to get Harry fighting mad. Nothing could move him or anyone else worth his salt to violence quicker than calling him rich—or a Republican. That, no real man could abide. Everyone they knew agreed Republicans were something you sprayed for twice a year.

Before Marsh could complete his usual harangue, Harry curdled his innards again with yet another verse:

> Cannon to right of them,
> Cannon to left of them,
> Boldly they rode and well,
> Into the jaws of Death,
> Into the mouth of hell . . .

A prickly stillness ensued. *Enough of that,* Harry thought. *No point in it. Save your breath.*

Keeping to a slow walk, the horsebackers moved on down country, each man quiet under the weight of his own thoughts. Not unusual for them. They always agreed that companionable silence served best. No need for idle chatter when you have a good horse under you and open country all around. The babble of unnecessary voices added nothing to the consonance of natural sounds. On this day, that axiom held truer than ever. For each self-possessed man, the voice of the other would do nothing but gravel the nerves.

But Marsh couldn't hold his tongue long. Aggravated on this occasion by a paucity of words, he had to say something.

"Hey, partner. I believe I hear the dinner bell ringin'. Don't know about you but I'm feelin' pure gut-shrunk. What say we make our noon camp pretty soon and throw a lip over the cornbread and beans that little darlin' Bliss packed for us."

Harry gritted his teeth. Marsh's mention of dinner didn't irritate him; his mention of Bliss did. He squirmed in his saddle like a man suffering the pain of a bad back. Feeling Marsh studying him, Harry tried to erase all expression of emotion from his face.

"Yes, sir," Marsh went on, keeping a keen eye on Harry, "that wife of mine is a woman of many talents. Heart of gold, drop dead gorgeous and, whooo-eee, one fine cook, too. And, she can quote poetry . . . like you. Her favorite poet is . . . umm . . . let's see. What's that feller's name? Robert . . . Brown . . . Brownstone."

"Browning," Harry shot back, an edge to his voice. "Robert Browning. And he's not her favorite poet. It's Elizabeth Barrett Browning. That's her favorite poet. Always has been."

Marsh nodded. "Well, thank you for bein' so well versed about my wife. I'm grateful for the schoolin'."

A troubled hush once again descended over the two men. They eyed each other for a few moments. Harry urged his horse forward, wishing he could call back the last few minutes and recraft them. Too late for that, though. And he couldn't deny the bit of a set-to with his blood brother had loosed a wind ill with tension and unease. It had gusted through his heart and, he surmised, through Marsh's, too. He could feel the chasm between them widening.

They rode on.

CHAPTER 2

Bliss

Harry first fell under the spell of Bliss Farrell as a downy-cheeked lad of fifteen. It happened one Saturday afternoon in October while he and Esau Coats, Woody's father and occasional employee of True Grocery and Produce, were offloading a day's purchases of pecans at the store. Bucking a fifty-pound bag of inshell nuts from the truck and turning to pass it to Esau, Harry laid eyes on the comely Miss Farrell—the new girl in town—strolling along the sidewalk across the street with a cadre of girlfriends. The lighthearted banter between Harry and Esau about the preceding night's high school football game came to an abrupt halt. The sight of the golden-haired beauty left him moonstruck. When she caught him looking, she gave him a warm smile. Two seconds later, she glided down the way. Harry continued watching her in the hope she might send him a parting glance. She did. And Harry sensed a hint of mutual interest in her eyes.

Witnessing Harry's rapture, Esau sidled up to his young fair-skinned swamper and said in a low voice, "You best close your mouth, son. You lible to start droolin.'"

Harry felt color flood his face. He swiveled his head to see if anyone other than Esau had observed his moment of enchantment. Seeing no one, he eased up a bit. Esau moved a half-step closer to the calf-eyed kid, his manner confidential.

"Bleve you kindly sweet on that little gal. Sure enough a head-turner, ain't she."

"Huh? What are you talking about?"

"You know good and well what I'm talkin' about. Why, it is plain as day. Blind man can see it right enough. Boy, you got the candy leg. Ain't no mistakin' it. And once you got it there ain't no help for it. Pretty soon you go tumblin' head over heels."

At a loss for a face-saving response, Harry could do nothing but lower his eyes and turn away. He went a little wobbly, but he collected himself quickly enough. He knew he could trust his old family friend. Truth be told, he didn't mind being found out . . . at least not by Esau. In fact, he sort of welcomed it.

"Well, I guess my secret's out. Candy leg, did you say?"

Smiling, Esau reached for his trusting confider with his muscular right arm and gave him a sideward bear hug.

"Yes, sir. Candy leg. But don't you get in a tizzy over it. You'cn shine right on up to that little filly all you want. Ole Esau ain't gonna let on to nobody about you two confabbin'."

He drew a fingertip from one corner of his clenched mouth to the other, made a locking motion and tossed away the key. "These old lips is sealed."

Esau's prediction of Harry's freefall proved right. Days following, Harry often found himself drinking in the sight of his new darling from a safe distance, on the streets of Serafina, in the hallway at school, feeling his heart rise within him, lodge in his throat. Bliss was a wonderment to him: fine golden hair, aquiline features, flawless skin, eyes like twin cerulean signal fires. And curves. All of it put together in her own unique way.

Harry remained a distant admirer of Serafina's leading ingenue for the next three torturous weeks. Each time they crossed paths, Bliss lowered her chin, lifted her enchanting blues, smiled, but still he made no attempt to pursue his suit. Instead, he collected facts about her, not hard to do in a town where everyone knew everyone else's business and newcomers generated much talk.

They were the same age, Harry and Bliss. Same year in school. Like him, she was an only child. Unlike Harry, whose mother had died when he was twelve, her parents were both alive. Her father, E. J. Farrell, had made and lost money as a wildcatter, dragging his wife and daughter from oilfield to oilfield until he tired of the lifestyle and found work at a refinery and bought a small frame house at the edge of Serafina. Known as a tightwad with a bad temper, he kept to himself. In contrast, Bliss and her mother, Louise Farrell, were outgoing and friendly. They appeared in town often, always with pleasant smiles and warm greetings for the neighbors. They were soon regulars at the First Methodist Church, where Bliss joined the youth group and began involving herself in churchwork: food and clothing drives, co-teaching third-grade Sunday school, helping serve and clean up at socials.

Often, Harry sneaked a peek at her from across the room as she poured coffee, sliced and handed out pieces of cake. When she caught him looking, she always offered him the same warm smile. Nonetheless, it took him the better part of a month to work up the nerve to approach her table.

"Well, finally," she said, her manner warm and inviting. "Hello, Harry."

Harry's face burned. "You know my name."

Bliss put her hands on her hips and gave him a gently chiding look, eyes twinkling. "Of course, I do."

Harry helped clean up when the social hour ended. Bliss introduced him to her mother.

"Well, I'll be heading home now to start dinner," Louise Farrell said, wiping her hands on her bib apron after delivering a tray of cups to the kitchen. "Harry, would you mind seeing Bliss home?"

Harry discovered during that first walk together that Bliss was better read than he, could quote poetry with equal facility. Didn't know as much about the natural world, couldn't identify trees and birds and flowers and cloud formations the way he could, but she exceeded him by so much when it came to care and concern for her fellow human beings that it made him feel somewhat stunted. Bliss believed that most people were good at heart, that everyone deserved to be treated with kindness and respect, that all were equal in God's eyes.

"To hate someone because their skin is a different color . . ." Bliss mused as she and Harry ambled along. "It's beyond me. How can anyone do that?"

Harry didn't have an answer, had never asked himself that question in a serious way.

"And who's that awkward boy with the bad skin who always looks like he could use a bath? Billy something."

"Catlett?"

"That's him. Billy Catlett. Why is everyone always so mean to him?"

"He's a bad seed. Bad family, bad kid."

Bliss stopped short. "I don't believe that. There's at least some good in everyone. Nobody's all bad . . . or all good."

Harry feared he'd gone too far in his harsh judgment of the Catletts. He'd have to think about that. But he was sure of one thing: Bliss Farrell had a kind and gentle heart. He wanted to know her better.

Harry needed to disclose the truth of his growing infatuation to someone, and who better than Esau Coats?

"She's kind, she's smart, she's educated, she's beautiful, and she's true-blue," Harry told Esau, who was becoming his counselor on paying court. "I think she may be the one for me."

"Well, I declare. I do declare."

With Marsh, Harry was more reticent, but Marsh didn't fail to recognize the change overtaking his friend. As Harry had feared, when the truth came out Marsh's reaction was less delicate than Esau's; it fell somewhere between snort and snicker.

"I do believe you're 'bout to come unhinged," Marsh said one day at school after watching his lovestruck friend stare as Bliss Farrell walked past. "Lawdee, boy. If you ain't somethin'. Cupid's arrow has done nailed you dead center."

Harry flushed scarlet. "I don't know what you're talking about."

"Is that a fact? OK. So, I reckon you won't mind if I go to sparkin' that little gal my own self? She is my type, you know. Bein' a real looker and all."

Harry stiffened. On this occasion, Marsh's brand of badinage didn't sit well with him. It could have been no more than the usual skylarking from his rascally friend, but something told him Marsh could also be kidding on the square. Harry had seen the way Marsh sometimes sneaked a look at Bliss. He never made a move, never even talked to her except when the three of them were together. But perhaps Marsh did have feelings for the girl who had taken up residence in Harry's heart.

At Harry's obvious discomfort, Marsh bent double horselaughing. Recovering, he patted his lovesick amigo on the back.

"Ach . . . Don't you fret none. You ain't gonna see me tryin' to ride herd on that little gal. I will stand back and watch the two of you with wonder." He put both hands over his heart and lifted a dreamy gaze to the heavens. "What a beautiful thing true love is." Harry made a fist and drew back his arm as if to deliver a Sunday punch; Marsh ducked and crossed his forearms to block the threatened blow. They both laughed.

Harry tried not to be a jealous suitor, but he couldn't help feeling protective. Bliss had a warm and amiable nature, a kind word for all. It was one of the things he admired about her, being a more reserved type himself. He worried though that, in certain cases, her belief in the basic goodness of people might be a little naïve. Take Billy Catlett, for example.

Catlett was a bony kid with hard angles and blotchy skin, ropy arms and neck, hair always untidy, clothes shoddy. He was ungraceful and knew it. Sullen and self-conscious, he was—Marsh liked to say—as ill at ease as a Baptist preacher at a dance marathon.

Catlett's old man, Ben, was a bootlegger who regarded himself highly because he could turn a dollar when others couldn't. Drunk on his own hooch most every night, he'd beat his wife and two boys until they fled into the woods and hid while he slept it off. At seven, Billy began fighting back, trying to protect his mother and baby brother. His father broke his jaw, picked him up off the floor and slapped him on the back. "At least you tried to fight like a man."

When Billy was twelve, his mother ran off for good in the dark of night with his younger brother. He thought he remembered her kissing him before she left. But it could have been a dream. After that, he pretty much had to fend for himself and learned to stay out of his father's way as much as possible and mimic his mannerisms and act the big man to mollify him when he was around. The more he pretended, the easier it became, until it wasn't pretend anymore.

It might not have been too bad if he could have stayed home, helped his daddy run moonshine. But they had to go to town from time to time, and Billy had to go to school, and he saw the way the good citizenry gave him the once over, the way kids laughed and pointed. Once, probably on a dare, a boy maybe a couple of years older than Billy went right up to him as he was heading to True Grocery, pinched his own nose and said, "Hey, stinky. You smell like a Missouri mule. You ever heard of a bathtub?" Billy punched him in the face, knocked him bleeding to the sidewalk. "Yeah?" Billy said, looking down on him. "Do I stink now?" He whirled around, puffed up, to see who'd been watching and saw handsome young Harry True and his respectable father standing together at the doorway of the family's store. Their faces showed disgust. Morris True patted his son on the shoulder and they turned away.

Catlett hated Harry in that instant with an intensity that seared his soul. *I'll show him. Someday. I'll show him.*

The year Billy turned thirteen, his dad gave him a BB gun for Christmas. A genuine Daisy, Buck Jones model. The gun took its name from the hottest cowboy movie character of the day.

Swelled up with big man fever, young Billy couldn't wait to brandish his new armament before every kid in town. He stood ready to bestow upon any obeisant whelp a look at his prized possession. Harry was one of the first to be blessed.

"New gun, uh?" Harry said, coming out of the store a few days after Christmas to find Catlett sitting on the curb polishing his new Daisy with his shirttail.

"Brand spankin' new. Only one in town."

Catlett held the gun up for inspection. Harry didn't cotton to playing into his hands when he was talking big, but his curiosity about the gun got the best of him.

"Let's see it shoot."

Exactly what Catlett hoped he'd say. He'd grown more jealous and resentful of Harry over time: his good looks, his quiet charm, his self-assurance and comfort in his own skin. This was his chance to win favor with him.

"Watch this," Catlett said.

He jacked the lever and steadied the stock against his shoulder. Laying his cheek on the polished wood, he drew a fine bead on a mongrel dog marking a fire hydrant across the street as his territory. With his hind leg cocked, the unsuspecting critter made an irresistible target. Before Harry could track Catlett's aim and stop him from shooting, Catlett nailed the mongrel right in the *cojones.* Hell could have heard the wounded critter squeal as he jumped a good three feet in the air. Leaking blood, he commenced licking himself and spinning in a tight circle. Catlett broke out laughing.

"Look at that. Tryin' to screw his ass into the ground."

The dog gimped off, whimpering, thin streaks of blood striping both hind legs.

"Now that is funny," Catlett said, grinning from ear to ear. He reached the air gun to Harry.

"Here. Give 'er a try. Pick a target."

Harry didn't move.

"Go ahead. Take a shot."

Harry put a hand up and backed away. "No. Thanks but no thanks." He wasn't about to put the stamp of approval on the wayward kid's pure quill meanness.

Catlett felt confused, stung, his fragile pride pinked by the rebuke. In the next instant the hurt he felt escalated to anger. "Suit yourself," he said, walking away. He promised himself he'd never try to curry favor with Harry True again. The golden boy of Serafina could go screw himself.

Over time, Catlett came to see cruelty and manliness as next of kin. By age fifteen, the boy was already mean as an acre of snakes. And watching Harry move so easy through life, with his winning way, best friend at his side, the most beautiful girl in town his steady, the anger he felt began hardening into hatred and an abiding desire to make him pay.

Like many boys in town, Billy was smitten with Bliss. Never tried to approach her, though. For all his swagger, he recognized his shortcomings. Plus, anyone with eyes could see Bliss had made her choice. Before long, Harry's clumsy pursuit became genuine courtship. In the span of a few months, the young sweethearts became inseparable. On Bliss's sixteenth birthday, they kissed the first time. If Harry had any doubt before that Bliss was the woman he wanted to spend his life with, he now had none.

There was no party celebrating Bliss's birthday. E. J. Farrell wouldn't allow it. The man was a skinflint and misanthrope, cold and taciturn, as niggardly with his affections as he was with his money. Parties and presents were wasteful. People should be kept at arm's length. Whatever socializing his daughter did she had to do out of the house or when her father wasn't home. He had no use for Bliss's young suitor and regarded Harry with contempt the first time he came to call to take Bliss to a Saturday matinee. Taught to respect his elders, Harry tried to time his subsequent visits to correspond with E. J.'s absences. But he didn't stop visiting. With Louise Farrell's blessing, he came often, sometimes staying for dinner, being shooed away to sit with Bliss on the porch swing while Mrs. Farrell cleaned up.

"What do you think you want to do with your life, Harry?" Bliss asked one evening as they sat, watching dusk fall around them.

"I don't know. Haven't thought much about it. Take over the store, I guess. I think my dad'd like that."

Bliss's questions made him a little uncomfortable, but they also made him feel good. Like she cared about him and wanted to know him better—better maybe than he knew himself.

"What about you? What do you want to do?"

"Teach. Maybe at the colored school if they'd have me. Seems they always need teachers." She meant the school in Black Flats, the colored part of town. "Or maybe start a school for migrant workers' children. Have you seen the way those families live? They have so little."

It was 1937, one of the Dust Bowl years, deep into a decade later dubbed the Dirty Thirties in Oklahoma. True Grocery relied on and did its best to support struggling farmers in the region. Yes, Harry had seen the suffering.

"You'd be a good teacher," he told Bliss.

"My mother was a teacher before she married my father."

"So you'll be going to teacher's college."

"If Daddy'll pay. It may take some persuading." Harry and Bliss both laughed. "But I shouldn't need a degree to teach the alphabet to kids who aren't getting any other schooling. I wouldn't even want to be paid. I'd do that for free."

Harry thought about that. "If we kept the store, you could maybe hold classes in one of the back rooms on Saturdays. Or we could drive out to the camps together and you could hold classes while I load the truck."

He clamped his mouth shut. *Damn.* He'd spoken his true feelings. He knew he wanted to build a life with Bliss. But he'd been rash. What if she didn't feel the same way? What if she startled? What if she ran? He remembered what Esau had told him about winning the heart of his lady love. "Give it time, boy. Got to have a gentle touch. Like you was holding a baby rabbit."

"I'm sorry," he said to Bliss.

"Sorry about what?" She kissed him and slipped her hand into his. "I think it sounds like a great plan."

Three months later, without warning, Bliss fell ill. Her infirmity commenced after the fashion of an ordinary transient ailment, a head cold or stomach bug, the kind that runs its course in a few days and takes its leave. Not so, this time. The girl's fever spiked and did not abate. After a couple of weeks of suffering at home, Bliss's doctor prevailed on E. J. Farrell to let him bundle her off to the hospital. What Doc Roberson labeled a virulent viremia was ravaging her unjaded body.

For weeks Bliss remained cloistered in her hospital room, keeping to her bed, day after day sinking lower. The doctor ordered every treatment medical wisdom of the day allowed, but nothing produced definitive results. Long-faced, he ushered the Farrells out of Bliss's room one afternoon and broke the grim news to them: the mysterious malady that afflicted their daughter might prove deadly. E. J. Farrell turned and left the hospital. Louise Farrell became faint and the doctor had to help her to a chair. But she collected herself and returned to Bliss's room.

From that point on, Louise Farrell seldom left her baby's side. Ever the good soldier, she kept her vigil day and night through the entire siege, sleeping on a cot in Bliss's room and leaving every other day for short visits home to bathe, change clothes, and prepare a few meals for her husband to warm for himself in her absence. If she could have, she would have breathed her own life out of her body and into her ailing daughter. She read to Bliss, brushed her hair, plumped her pillow, massaged her feet and hands, swabbed her forehead with a cool, damp cloth. She kept Bliss informed of the news of the day and made a point of encouraging her daughter by letting her know her dutiful young gallant, Harry True, was always close by—folding into her hands little notes from him, each one quoting a line or two of poetry by Elizabeth Barrett Browning. *How do I love thee? Let me count the ways.* Surprising her one day with a slim volume of her favorite poems that Harry had found at a yard sale. Louise placed the book atop the light blanket covering Bliss's chest and went to her second-floor window, parted the curtains.

"He's out there right now, you know."

"Harry?" Bliss said weakly.

"Yes, dear. He's not allowed to visit yet. So he sits out there on that bench in front of the hospital."

Bliss stirred as if to rise.

"No, darling," her mother said, coming to her daughter and with a gentle touch pressing her back down. "Not yet. You're not strong enough."

"But I'll get strong, Mama. I know I will. Can you tell him that for me?"

Louise Farrell kissed her daughter's clammy forehead, stroked her hair. "Of course."

The only thing that made it possible for Louise Farrell to claim so much as a moment for herself was knowing she had the best possible ally in the fight to save Bliss's life: Polly Coats, Esau's wife. Younger than Esau by a decade. Shorter by a foot and sturdily built with dark eyes that flashed intelligence, a no-nonsense manner and tender heart, Polly worked at the hospital as a nurse's aide during that treacherous season. She doted on her stricken young patient as if Bliss were her own blood—bathed her, fed her, encouraged her, sang to her, stood shoulder to shoulder with Bliss's mother against the relentless onslaught of an unnamed malady.

Harry visited the hospital every day. The nurses never let him near

Bliss's room, but that didn't stop him. Often, he parked himself in the waiting room, watching for Louise Farrell on her way in or out, to hand her another note or trinket to pass on, to find out how Bliss was doing—A little better? At least no worse?—or stood on the sidewalk, eyes trained on Bliss's window, hoping for a glimpse of her. At times, during the first weeks of her ordeal, he saw a shadow moving across the drawn shade. The doctor, a nurse, he had to remind himself. Never Bliss herself, for she remained abed. He could imagine the torment she was enduring. And he couldn't help wondering if she'd be the same Bliss he knew and loved when she reached the far side of this trouble . . . if she reached it. He feared she might not know him, might not care about him any longer. Worried that she never responded to his gifts and missives, no matter how much Louise reassured him. He feared her prolonged suffering might strip her of her gentleness, that she might become hard and bitter. No. She couldn't, he argued with himself. She was too staunch of spirit for that. And too good.

Harry remained a faithful watchman. One night in the fourth or fifth week, while posted on his bench, he saw the curtains on Bliss's window part. The shade rose. A frail figure appeared. Bliss. There she stood, a mere slip of a girl, pale as a bed sheet, clad in a plain nightgown. Harry leaped to his feet, watched her peer this way and that. He rushed to a patch of ground below her window and waved. She spotted him and began tapping on the glass. His heart broke at the sight of her, looking like a captive sparrow hammering at a windowpane, her hair in braids. Despite being weak as water, she smiled, lifted her arms, clasped her hands in a victorious boxer's stance, and brandished them. When Harry saw that salute, he knew she'd gained a hard-won victory over illness. She'd be back.

The next night, as Harry sat watching Bliss's window again,

hoping to catch another glimpse of her, Billy Catlett approached from the darkness. Like others in their class at school he'd been following Bliss's illness with concern and from time to time asked Harry how she was doing. Harry's first impulse was to ward him off with indifference, but knowing Bliss would want him to be kind, he greeted Catlett with a modest smile.

"How's she doin'?" Catlett said.

"Better."

"That's good. Glad to hear it. She's had a rough time, I reckon."

Harry wanted no truck with Catlett, but he couldn't help responding to his show of compassion. He searched for words of appreciation, but before he could speak, he saw Polly Coats hurrying toward them. Ignoring Catlett, she spoke to Harry.

"Hey, boy, whatchoo doin' out here?"

Startled by the redoubtable woman's stern tone, Harry rose and stood awkwardly. "Well, you know, I . . . I . . . . "

But he relaxed, realizing she was teasing.

Polly smiled, fists on hips. "I know. I know perxactly what choo doin'. You're mopin' 'round like some lovesick puppy, hopin' for a glimpse of that little ole gal up yonder."

Harry smiled. "Guilty as charged, I guess."

Polly wagged a finger at him. "A boy that wears his chin on his instep cain't see the horizon, you know."

That got another smile out of him.

"Well . . . you come on with me. She's doin' better, praise the Lord. Bet I'cn sneak you in."

Harry stood straight. "You mean it?"

"I said so, didn't I?" Polly put out her hand. "C'mon. You c'mon with me."

Harry took Polly's hand.

Young Billy Catlett stepped forward.

"Can I—"

Polly scowled at him.

"What choo talkin' 'bout? 'Course not. Shouldn't be lettin' him in and he's been settin' out here every night, aincha, boy?" She waved Billy away. "You best be gettin' on home now. Scoot!"

Billy shrank back, stung, fists jammed in his jeans pockets. Watching Polly and Harry walk away, he fell into a sulk that soured into fury. Humiliated again, this time by a lowly mammy kowtowing to Harry as if he were her lord and master.

Billy walked home cursing Harry and vowing someday he'd get even for all the insults, for always holding himself so high above. He didn't let on to his father about the latest slight he'd suffered, certain that if he did he'd get a beating for not standing up for himself. No Catlett should bear such an insult without response. His dad had taught him that, and Billy had taken the lesson to heart. He didn't know how or when, but someday he would get his retribution.

After shooing Billy away, Polly spirited Harry through a back door and hurried him up a dim stairway like a mother hen. The scent of alcohol and disinfectant scathing his nostrils, he made his way with the stealth of a burglar to the second floor. Doing as Polly did, he tiptoed down the hall to the filament of light marking the threshold of Bliss's room. Halting him at the closed door, Polly went in and helped Bliss prepare herself to receive her gentleman caller. What felt like an hour later, Polly opened the door, careful not to make any noise.

"Three minutes. No more," she whispered. "Then you outa here. Understand me?"

"Yes, ma'am."

Polly showed Harry in and went whisking off. Harry found Bliss seated in a chair, a patchwork quilt draped over her legs, hands folded on her lap. With Polly's help, she had tried to put some color back in her face with a touch of lipstick, a trace of rouge. She beamed when she saw Harry.

"You look great," Harry said. "Polly says you're getting better."

Bliss smiled back and gave a delicate nod of the head.

"She makes me say, *Every day in every way I'm getting better and better.* I think I'll be going home soon."

Harry's heart leaped.

"I thought I was going to die," Bliss said softly. "Sometimes, I was OK with dying."

Harry moved closer.

"You know what Polly says about dying," Bliss said. "Man proposes, God disposes."

Harry knelt beside her, took her hands in his.

"You can't die. You can't. I . . . I . . . ."

"Well, I'm not going to die. I have a lot of living to do yet. And I don't plan to miss out on any of it."

Harry gazed into her eyes.

"I have to tell you something."

"What?"

But before Harry could speak, Polly peeked in the door.

"Spss. Time's up. C'mon."

"But it hasn't been three minutes."

"Nurses makin' rounds. You come on with me or we both have hell to pay."

Harry stood and went to the door. Bliss raised a skinny arm to wave good-bye.

Harry rushed back to her, knelt beside her again. He pressed her hands in his. Tried to speak but couldn't. Finally, he found his voice.

"I love you, you know. I truly love you."

Bliss smiled. "Oh, and I love you."

"And you know something else?"

"What?"

"I'll love you forever." He crossed his heart. "I take an oath on it."

"And I'll hold you to it."

Bliss put her hand on his cheek and when she did he leaned forward and kissed her. He stood and disappeared through the door. Following Polly down the hall, he touched his cheek where Bliss's fingertips had been.

By the grace of God and the ministrations of Doc Roberson, Louise Farrell and Polly Coats, Bliss recovered. Youth and vitality returned. Lips, parched and cracked from fever and dehydration, became full and supple. Her complexion regained its luster. Her wealth of sun-colored hair recovered its shine and framed the exquisite features of her face. In a love poem, Harry—ever the aspiring *littérateur*—described her smile as "silken." Her eyes, the callow bard mused, were "blue as an autumn sky, inviting and full of kindness." His attempt at *belles-lettres* was overwrought, he feared. Childish, perhaps. But every word came from the heart.

In the aftermath of Bliss's illness, E. J. Farrell had little to do with his daughter, as if angry with her for getting sick. She asked him once why he stopped visiting her in the hospital. "I was in danger of dying, you know."

"What could I have done?" he muttered, not looking up from his newspaper.

A year later, Bliss's father met his maker. One Sunday afternoon, he slumped limp as a dishrag in his armchair. Stroke, Doc Roberson said. The man lingered a few days between life and death, his wife and daughter caring for him. They were at his bedside when he took his last breath.

When the will E. J. Farrell kept in a safety deposit box was read, Louise and Bliss learned he had left most of what money remained to a small college he'd attended briefly in his youth to fund a scholarship in his name. He left his wife the house and a small monthly stipend. To his daughter he left nothing, explaining that she'd benefit more from having to make her own way, as he'd done, than she would from inherited wealth.

If Bliss felt wronged or hurt, she didn't let it show. "Mama and I will manage," she assured Harry. "We're good at stretching a dollar."

"But what about teacher's college?"

Bliss sighed. "I'll get there. It'll just take a little longer." She smiled. "And look at the bright side."

"What's that?"

"Now you can visit anytime you want."

By the time Harry and Bliss had put her illness and her father's death behind them, the Dirty Thirties were nearing an end. They welcomed the return of good times. True Grocery was thriving. Louise Farrell was working as a substitute teacher to supplement her income. Bliss was earning a few extra dollars as a babysitter, and graduation was around the corner. Harry would be taking Bliss to the prom, of course. Marsh couldn't stop needling him about it.

"You gonna pop the question, old buddy?"

"What question is that?" Harry answered. But they both knew what question Marsh meant.

The answer was yes, Harry would pop the question . . . someday.

But not yet. He didn't want to rush things. For now, everything was fine just the way it was and he wanted to enjoy and be grateful for the good times. Such halcyon days could not last forever. Harry knew in his gut, despite his tender years, that good times are followed by bad. And happiness is not to be trusted.

CHAPTER 3

The Fall

The day of their June ride, as the forenoon waned, Harry and Marsh came upon a large punch bowl hollow in the earth. The ancient void, every bit of two hundred yards across, likely had formed when terra firma gave out and fell under its own weight. Nearing the rim, Harry's mare shied, whickered. Harry forked a firm hand on the animal's crested neck, shortened the reins.

"Easy now. Easy. See a booger out there?"

Harry had held up a safe distance from the verge. Marsh checked his mount at the hatchet edge, front hooves no more than the length of a stick of stovewood from the precipice.

"Just like you," Harry said to Marsh's back. "Damnfool thing to do."

Marsh touched his ear. "Eh? How's that again?"

"You heard me. Go right to the limit. Don't bother seein' how firm the ground is. How'd you ever live through the war?"

Marsh leaned around in his saddle. "War musta made you a fraidy-cat." He winked. "You can thank your lucky stars you got me here to keep you from turnin' into a old woman."

Marsh held a rapt gaze on the wide canyon surrounded by sheer-walled cliffs tinted firebrick and cool gray. Within the rockface mural lay an undulate floor of colorless, translucent crystals, packed hard in some places, duned up in others. The straight drop from the rim would equal the length of a dozen horses stretched out nose to tail tip in an equine chain. In the southwestern sky lurked a pulsating nimbus, dark as Indian corn and crazed with flashes of dry lightning.

"Could get some rain out of that," Marsh said, pointing. "Regular turd floater, maybe. Bleve I can smell the moisture."

Harry gave the living air a studying look.

"Rain? Don't think I'd count on it."

"Not countin' on it. Hopin.'"

Turning back to Harry, Marsh pulled off his hat and set it on his horse's rump. He laughed without making a sound.

"Remind you of anybody?"

Marsh took back his hat and motioned Harry forward.

"Come on. Come on up here, old son. Next by me. Double dog dare you."

Marsh fished a cigarette pack from a shirt pocket and shook out a tailor-made. He plucked a kitchen match from his hat band, struck it alight with a thumbnail. After the flare had receded and the sulfur stink had dissipated, he lit up. Waved the match flame out, licked his fingers, pinched the burnt end, discarded the charred stick. He marveled at the paradoxical beauty of the canyonscape before him.

"Ho boy, would you take a gander at that. It is the tiger shits, ain't it. So ugly it's perty. Ever time I see it, I—"

He stopped himself. Turned the gray around.

"I might as well be talkin' Chinese to a pack mule. You comin' or not?"

He launched a high-spirited smile again, one shaped by a devil-may-care attitude, the kind of look that meant *Let's see how far we can go. Let's push this sucker to the limit.* Often as not that look presaged an adventure, perhaps one fraught with danger. Harry knew it well. He'd seen it many times—in their boyhood adventures and in the nine years since they'd both returned from the war. But this time that familiar curling of the lip and arching of an eyebrow struck him as an artifact of a former era. Those days were gone. He had the sense that no matter how fast he rode he could never get the angle on them, get out ahead of them, turn them back. He told himself he didn't know how it had happened. But he knew the truth.

Relenting, Harry clucked his mount forward, but before she'd taken two steps, the natural esplanade beneath them shook. A prescient rumble sounded within the earth's honeycombed bowels. A few feet ahead of him hardpan arched and buckled. A crack the size of a plow furrow appeared and spread. A wide fissure opened. A great belching of moon gray dust came forth and after that an eruption of an inky black cloud of delirious, swarming creatures. Bats. Dozens of them. Rousted from their inverted slumber in an interior cavern by the separation of an ages old fault line, an entire terrified colony of tiny snub-nosed mammals went swirling into the air. Jolted into daylight panic, they billowed skyward like a thunderhead reeking of guano. A cacophony of shrill cries issued from the hurricane of membranous wings.

At the sudden upheaval of rock, Harry's mount blew up. Eyes showing white, she squealed and went to pitching, her feet gathered beneath her in a space no bigger than a sewer lid. Harry lost a stirrup but managed to haul back on the reins and ride out the storm.

He chided the boogerish mare. "Here! Here. Ho now. Ho."

Glued to the back of the gray, Marsh went down. Horse and rider descended upright as if by elevator. The natural calamity came so suddenly and Marsh kept his cool with such adroitness Harry half-thought for a moment he was making a joke, that Marsh had arranged it all just to aggravate him. It wouldn't have surprised him to see Marsh doff his Stetson as he disappeared. Marsh did no such thing, but he did manage to keep his seat; he rode an avalanche of crumbling rock all the way to the new canyon floor.

In a matter of seconds, the cataclysm ended. Harry got his horse under control and leaped from her back, led her to the cloven rockface and hitched her reins to a scrub oak stub standing nearby. Dropping to his hands and knees, he inched forward to the rim and peered into a twisting cloud of debris. At first, he couldn't see Marsh. He feared he might have been engulfed by rockfall.

"Marsh!" he called. "Marsh!"

No answer. He called out again.

"Marsh! Marsh!"

Harry blinkered his eyes with his hands. Dust masked his face, encrusted his mouth. It crunched between his teeth, tasted old and stale.

"Marsh!"

He heard a voice.

"Yeah. Here. Down here."

Clearing air allowed Harry to make out the dim outline of his fallen friend. At the base of the scree slope he lay on his back, right leg—from knee to boot heel—pinned by the downed horse. The animal was writhing and heaving about but couldn't rise. Marsh held the reins tight, trying to keep him from moving.

"Easy. Easy. Hold still, dammit."

Harry called out again.

"You all right?"

"Hell no, I'm not all right. My leg's under this horse. Think it's broke. I know his is broke."

"Hold on."

Harry hustled to the dark mare. He loosed the tie on the Maguey lariat at the saddle's off side, hooked his arm through the coil, resting it on his shoulder. A sinister notion stopped him. He looked back at the canyon rim. *I could ride away, make up some story. Maybe . . . maybe . . . . What's the matter with me?*

Harry shook off the treasonable wanderings of his mind. Returned to the canyon dropoff and peered over.

"Hold on. I'm coming down."

Harry unlimbered the rope and shook it out, tied the free end hard and fast to the saddle horn, lobbed the loose spirals into the canyon. He unfastened the piggin' string from the near side rear D and made a rifle sling, lashing one end of the string to his gun's barrel at the forestock tip, the other to the rifle's wrist, behind the receiver. Slung the rifle across his back.

Next, he took the cinch up a notch.

"Stand steady," he commanded the mare. "Stand. Stand."

Taking a firm two-handed hold on the hemp, he backed over the canyon lip and began working his way by abseil down the wall. The anchor horse shuffled her feet and shifted her weight against the taut rope. At the bottom Harry made his way over the incline of fragmented rock to Marsh. When he got there, the sight of his friend's face—powdered with dust possessing the pallor of gypsum mortar—braced him. Marsh roused him with a burst of sarcasm.

"About time. Whada you been doin' up there? Havin' tea? My damn leg's busted all to hell and I got a horse on it."

Harry wiped dust from his mouth and eyes.

"I could ride off, you know. Leave your disagreeable ass right here."

Harry unslung the rifle and leaned it against a rock. Grappling with the talus slide for footing, he examined the gelding's injured leg. The animal stirred and nickered. Harry patted him on the neck.

"Easy. Easy."

He saw the jagged end of the fractured cannon bone of the left foreleg protruding in a bloody mess through hide and hair. *Another life ruined by this hard country.*

Marsh had not fared much better. He tried but couldn't free his leg from beneath the horse.

"I can feel the bones rubbin'," he said.

Despite the pain, Marsh managed a tattered laugh. The fall had busted him up, but it hadn't come near taking the starch out of him.

"Man. That was one hell of a wreck. Did you see that? By God, that was somethin'. Bear cat of a fall. Did you see that?"

Harry picked up the rifle and cocked it.

"What are you gonna do, shoot me?"

"Gonna shoot this horse. I might shoot you, too. For pulling a stunt like that."

"Wouldn't put it past you. If you ever wanted to, now's the time."

"Don't tempt me. You know, I could—"

"Yeah, I heard you the first time. Maybe I got it comin'. Might be doin' us both a favor."

"Sure save me a lot of misery."

"Well, go ahead, dammit. Do it."

"Shut up, you damn tinhorn."

With the tip of his index finger Harry drew an imaginary line from the horse's left ear, across his forehead to his right eye. He drew a second line from his right ear to his left eye. With the rifle muzzle no more than an arm's length from the ruined horse's head, he took aim at the place where the two lines intersected.

"Try not to miss," Marsh mumbled, turned away and turtled his head into his upper torso. He closed his eyes, put fingers to his ears.

Harry squeezed the trigger. A shot thundered. The bullet's echo rolled away down the riven breaks. At the deafening gun noise, Harry's picketed mount hauled back against her tethered reins. Harry's ears rang.

Harry took the coiled lariat from Marsh's saddle and shook it out. For extra length, he tied the end of Marsh's rope to the free end of his own rope with a blood knot. He built a loop at the end of the two lashed ropes and dropped it over the dead horse's head. Tightened it.

"When I haul this horse out of the way, can you slide out from under it?"

"Watch me."

"OK. Let's get to it."

Using the rope again, Harry climbed with an effort of will back up the debris slope and scaled the rock palisade. He calmed the fractious mare, untied and led her about, pulled the body of the gray out of the way. Marsh freed himself from the dead weight of the carcass.

"All right. I'm clear."

Harry peered over the precipice again, cupped his hands around his mouth. "Slip that loop off the gray. Get into it and hold on."

Dragging himself over to his dead horse on his forearms, Marsh followed Harry's commands. Leading the shadowy horse, drawing the rope taut, Harry commenced towing his bulky cargo up the scabrous canyon wall. With the rope looped around his trunk at the armpits, his back against the rift, Marsh monkeyed his way to the top, digging the heel of his good leg into loose cliffside soil, hoorawing himself with grunts and curses. When he cleared the rough rim at the top, Harry helped him wrestle himself more or less upright and hobble over to Harry's horse.

"Man. That was somethin'," Marsh said. "Did you see that?"

Harry lifted the rope off him and, in an unhurried businesslike fashion, commenced coiling it.

"What a sensation. For a minute there I thought I was flyin'. Did you see that?"

Marsh grimaced with pain and caught his breath. "Don't get me wrong. I hate like the dickens to lose that gray horse. Dammit, I hate to lose him. I do. But I wouldn't have missed that ride for all the gold in California."

He slapped the saddle bow with his open hand.

"Dammit. Wouldn't have missed it."

"You want me to rig a travois to get you back home?"

"I can fork a horse."

"All right."

With Harry's help, Marsh crawled onto Harry's horse, let his injured leg hang. Biting back the pain, he made not a sound. When he'd settled in, Harry summed up what he thought of the day's adventure.

"I would have. Would've missed it all."

"Ach. I'd do it all over again right now," Marsh said.

"Yeah? You'd be doing it alone."

They spent the rest of the day making their way back to town. Throughout the trek they had little to say to each other. Marsh kept his jaws locked down tight, determined not to show the pain he was in. Harry led the slaty mare, seldom lifting his eyes from the trail ahead.

CHAPTER 4

Blood Bond

For as long as Harry could remember, he'd trusted Marsh as he trusted no man. He knew his friend was leather-tough and he could count on him when the chips were down. If necessary, he could put his life in his hands. During their long journey back to town, Harry couldn't help comparing today's misadventure to one much like it and more foolish the day they sealed their bond in blood.

It happened not long after Harry began courting Bliss. He and Marsh, both sixteen, decided to make a horseback outing through the year's first dusting of snow to Horse Thief Canyon to hunt javelina. Answering the call of their cognate visions of greatness and their mutual taste for adventure, the two young stallions stood ready to take their rightful places in the pantheon of illustrious Sebastian County hunters. Javelina would be the price of admission.

"Can you eat javelina?" Harry asked Marsh as they were contemplating their expedition.

"You better believe it. I can eat anything that don't eat me first."

"No, I don't mean *can* you eat it. Of course, you *can* eat it. I mean is it good to eat?"

"Dern tootin.' I ever tell you how to cook javelina to absolute perfection?"

Harry waited for the smart-aleck answer he knew was coming.

"Well, you skin it and dress it, do it up right, and stuff it with horse manure. Cook it till it's well done . . . then . . . and then . . . you throw away the meat and eat the manure."

Marsh busted a gut laughing. Harry cracked a half-smile, pleased with himself for denying his friend the full satisfaction of pulling his leg.

But Marsh had more than javelina on his mind. He was also hoping to get a feral hog in their sights. That would make for a true red-letter day, he said.

Having never hunted javelina or hogs, they planned their enterprise with the meticulousness of generals preparing a dawn attack. They started by seeking the advice of experienced old-timers. The mavens were known to gather on Saturday mornings, hunkered down on their bootheels at the intersection of Main and Commercial. There the boys found them, piddling away the morning, postured in what folks called the Serafina Squat, each man busying himself with reduction of a pinewood billet to curled shavings. While whittling and swapping knives, they recalled the glories of past hunts. And the boys hung on every word.

"Hogs," one liver-spotted old codger said. "They run in herds. Could be six or eight. Might could be forty-leven of 'em. Them sumbucks is vicious killers, too. Farm sow can wander off, breed with a runaway boar. In a couple of generations they're wild sure enough. Weigh four hundred pound, maybe. Know what Mescans call a hog like that? *El Diablo,* the devil."

Another old fossil chimed in, "I'm here to tell you, they's smart, too, and they can hear a pin drop a mile off. Smell out a man in total darkness. Sorry devils eat raw meat . . . eat raw meat. Can you imagine that? A hog eatin' raw meat. Damn. That orta pull your pucker string."

A graybeard with faded blue eyes, sagging red-rimmed lower lids, drew out his makin's from a shirt pocket and built a smoke. He fired it up, took a deep drag that triggered a paroxysm of coughing.

"Sounder," he managed to say in a throaty voice.

"What?" the first pontificator, hard of hearing, asked.

"Herd of hogs. You call it a sounder."

"Call it a what?"

"A sounder."

"Well, Mr. Smarty Pants, whatever you call it, they got tusks . . . ooheee do they have tusks. Best step wide of 'em. Cornered, they get mighty temperish. They'll rip you to shreds. Kill a dog in a minute, don'tcha know. They bait 'em with corn and diesel fuel. That tells you sumpin.'"

Another old mossback, mostly toothless, squinted hard at Marsh and Harry through smoke rising from the stogie lodged in the corner of his mouth.

"You daggone younkers is eat up with this hog huntin' bidness. I'cn tell. Best watch yourall's asses. This ain't no snipe hunt you're talkin' about." He snorted, swallowed. "That's my put-in."

Another wizen-faced Methuselah rearranged his chaw and wiped tobacco juice from his jowls before offering his wisdom. "Shoulders is covered with gristle. It's like armor. A bullet'll ricochet right off. To bring one down, you gotta get a shot into his vitals. I mean right into 'em. Either in front of or behind the shoulder. If you're lucky, might put one between the eyes. Might. Bullet in the spine could do it, but he might be a long time dyin.'"

"Too long by doggies," yet another wintry old jasper sounded off, slapping his knee. "I'm shootin' you straight, now. Whoooo. If they get you down, they won't leave off. No human man can whup one. You are headed for hell on a shutter. Pay heed, now. Pay heed . . . if you wanna stay on the right side of the dirt."

The boys heard it all and they took the old men's counsel to heart. But they felt the pull of the wild country and they were chockfull of grit. "We're obliged to you and we hear what you're sayin," Marsh assured them. But, with a confident head waggle aimed at Harry, he boasted, "Him and me's up to it, though." Later, Marsh said to Harry with a dismissive tone, "They're just pigs. Besides, all we're gonna find out there is little old *javaleenios*. They ain't much more than a possum." Whatever the dangers, he knew he and his friend Harry could hack it. Gainsaying old grandpas would not deter them.

The day of the hunt, the adventurers trailered a couple of trusted mounts to the border of a Sebastian County wilderness, untrammeled and untenanted. When they arrived at their destination, they tacked up. As they tightened their cinches the skittish horses pawed the ground, reeled their ears. Agitated equine grunts and groans rumbled deep within them, great clouds of steamy breath billowing from stubbly gray nostrils. They knew their riders meant business and it was time to go to work.

The backland ranged for miles. A thin welt of new snow had transformed it into an all-consuming whiteness, unmarred by hoof of beast or boot of man. The first shower of brassy sunlight glistened on the frozen crystals. Icicle bayonets, as long as a man's forearm, trimmed bare tree branches. Frigid air bore the faintly sweet scent of sumac and Judas trees.

"I figger we'll both get us a kill," Marsh said, flipping up the collar of his woolen buffalo plaid jacket, slapping gloved hands against his shoulders. "If we're lucky we might scare up some wild hogs, maybe bag one of them renegade boars the old geezers talked about. Now, there's some good eatin.'" He glanced at Harry. "I doubt that'll happen. But they're out there, Bud. They are out there. Bleve you me."

"I know they are. I know it." Red-cheeked and shivering, Harry breathed into his hollowed hands.

"It can happen. It can damn sure happen." Marsh stamped his feet against the cold. "More I think about it, the more I figger today may be the day. Betcha a dime to a donut."

"I don't doubt it. Don't doubt it for a minute."

"Yep. We'd be fixed with bacon and lard for the rest of the winter. Both families. And, we'd be the talk of the town. Heroes. We'd be legends." Marsh tugged at his hat. "Time to ride, *amigo. Listo*?"

"Past ready. If you're waitin' on me, you're goin' backwards."

The boys swung to saddle, put the rising sun to their backs and headed out. Dutiful dogs—the redbone hound Harry called Deke and Marsh's blue tick, Levi—followed along. Each boy carried in his saddle scabbard a lever action Winchester .30–30 and, in a leather sheath on his belt, a skinning knife. For meat hauling, a tarpaulin was rolled and tied with leather thongs behind the cantle of each saddle.

The hunters tramped across snowy white rolling country, along brambly arroyos, up ragged ridges. All the teeth chattering morning they hunted without success. But, along about midday they found what they were after. Topping a low rise of land that commanded a broad view of the white, vacant distance, squinting against the glare of the sun, they caught sight of their elusive quarry.

"There," Marsh said, pointing with his chin, warming his gloved hands under his armpits. He sniffed and wiped his ruddy nose with his sleeve. "Looky there. We have struck gold, my friend."

"How many you make it?"

"A good many. Better'n a dozen."

The boys lit down and each of them tightened his cinch another notch. Harry knelt and forced the dogs to their hind parts. He held them by their leather collars while Marsh dug a pair of binoculars from his saddlebag and commenced scouting the lay of the land. Marsh lowered the glasses, raised them to his eyes again and swept his gaze in a half-circle over the sun-washed snow. When he lowered them the next time, he indicated with an outstretched arm what appeared to the bare eye to be a slew of seething black specks. The dogs came to attention, moist noses twitching, dark eyes trained on the remote prey. They chafed at Harry's restraint, whining, lunging at their neckbands. The horses stamped their feet, ears pricked forward.

Marsh gave a close looking over to what he now knew was a sounder of hogs moving along a broad, grassy swale patched with snow, disfigured here and there by tussocks of wiry bunchgrass, protruding rocks and fallen brushwood branches. Harry and Marsh surmised that, having risen from the protection of some push cover thicket where they'd bedded down for the night, the hogs were hungry and on the hunt for food.

Moving in a tight formation with military precision, the hogs followed their leader, stopping often to reconnoiter, from time to time furrowing the snow with their long snouts, rooting for anything they might find to fill their bellies. They were not javelina. They were feral hogs all right, the lot of them.

At the head of the column marched a mammoth boar. The boys needed no more than a cursory glance at the leader of the pack to know they'd chanced onto the brute Marsh had hoped for. This beast was black with a red roan tint. Sure to have a bristly hide like chain mail, shoulder armor more than an inch thick. In the corners of his mouth he'd have tusks, uppers and lowers. On an animal his size, they were bound to measure a good four inches in length. And he'd have teeth, every one half as long as his tusks, each with the sharp edge of a kitchen knife. Tusks and teeth—in a fight, the boys knew they'd be deadly weapons.

"Would you get a load of that," Marsh said, field glasses pressed to his eyes once more. "That is one big son of a bitch. He'll go ever bit of four hundred pounds. And be rank as hell."

Wind favored the trackers and the hogs did not react to being observed. Marsh passed the binoculars to Harry. Harry stood. Marsh knelt, taking his turn at restraining the hounds. Harry brought the telescopic image of the fearsome chieftain into focus.

"You're right. He's a biggun. Gone wild, I reckon. Bound to be meaner'n a grizzly. Maybe we oughta—"

Marsh let loose the dogs and they took off, baying as he climbed into the saddle.

"Remember what that old coot said the Mexicans call a hog like that?" Harry said. "*El Diablo*. 'Member why? 'Cause he can kill you."

Marsh grinned. "Not if we kill him first. Let's knock on it."

Fire burning in Marsh's belly, he jammed heels into his mount. The horse responded in buck-jumps before breaking into a full gallop across new fallen snow. Harry vaulted into the saddle and set off after Marsh. Blooded by the scent of wild game carried on the wind, the dogs had taken the lead. Deke and Levi, backs roached high, ran in full cry, responding to primal instincts to pursue, to hunt, to bring down, to kill.

Alerted by the bugling of pursuing hounds and the thunder of hooves, the hogs bolted. The mounted hunters kicked after them through tangly patches of brittlebush and hoary stands of low timber, down ravines and up again, across frozen creeks. Running with tails held high and stiff as guidon staffs, the horses dodged trees and rocks, hurtled over gullies, struggling sometimes to remain upright, slipping on the ice and windrows of snow. But the gallopers, bent low in their saddles, did not let up.

The strategy was simple: the bay-hounds would run the hogs to a frazzle, haze them into a tight group and hold them until Harry and Marsh got there. From a position of advantage, they could pick them off one at a time.

When they were about to be overtaken, the tiring swine exploded through a choking sally port that led to a saw-cut canyon with a gypsum sill that glistened in the sun. Unbeknownst to the hogs, the incision in the earth coursed perhaps fifty yards, debouching into a good-sized pocket. Unscalable walls bordered the elliptical chamber on three sides. A rocky overhang ledge rimmed the top. Terrified and worn to a frazzle, the hogs turned back in on themselves. The dogs, having followed them into the narrows, commenced chivying them into a squealing cluster.

Bay-hounds now transformed themselves into kill-hounds. Barking, growling, snarling, they attacked down low, up high, withdrew, circled like untamed beasts themselves. They snapped at unprotected hocks and flanks. The hogs shrieked and flailed about in a turbulence of cloven hooves, tusks, and teeth. When they attempted to make a run for it, the dogs curbed them and reformed the gather. The red roan fought with unequaled fury. His guttural squeals thundered. Hackles on his neck and back stood like kitchen broom bristles.

The boys crossed the caprock and took their horses to the craggy rim of the slender canyon. Hearts pounding, they leaped from their mounts, each taking his rifle in hand. On foot they moved closer to the icy rimrock. What they saw when they got there exceeded their expectations. Huge and powerful, every hog. The red roan, long-tusked and ferocious, stood apart from the others. He was sure to tip the scales at four hundred pounds.

El Diablo took after Deke. In an instant, he ran a tusk into the dog's belly, sent him flying through the air like a child's toy. The gutted hound yowled in pain and when he came down he lay without moving. The stain of his blood darkened the snow beneath him.

"Take him!" Marsh cried. "It's your dog he's killed. First shot's yours. If you don't get him, he's mine."

Harry levered a cartridge into his rifle's chamber. Putting the stock to his shoulder, laying his cheek against it, he sucked in a breath. Let out half of it and tried to line up his shot. But the boar kept moving, getting entangled with Levi, who continued to press the fight alone. Tree branches and rocks obstructed Harry's view and he scoured his surroundings for a better position. Spotting one, he went for it. Gaining a small berm that offered a good line of sight, he set his boots on the icy crest. He aimed. Crooking himself to the right a bit, shifting his weight, his feet lost their anchorage and shot out from under him.

Harry went hard to his back, air leaving his lungs with a breathy groan. Finger still on the trigger, he fired a wild shot into the air, lost his hold on his rifle and sent it plunging into the abyss below. Out of control, Harry followed the Winchester, sliding down the canyon wall, nothing but blue sky in his eyes. At the mercy of sloping terrain, he headed right for the knot of raging hogs. In seconds, he found himself where the old-timers had said a man should never be: down, with *El Diablo* charging.

The boar went for Harry, squealing, grunting, plowing up dirt with his snout like a dozer. Levi pressed the attack. The boar wheeled on him, turned back to Harry.

Despite being all but KO'd by the fall, Harry managed to rise and snatch up a deadfall Blackjack limb, as stout through the middle as his wrist and half again the length of his arm. Like Samson wielding the jawbone of an ass, he met the assault of his attacker with a fierce blow to his snout. When the cudgel fractured and lost half its length, the boar seized the end of the piece clubbed in Harry's fist, wrested it from his grasp, and flung it away. Levi attacked again, spinning the beast around. Harry took a few backward steps into the dark maw of a shallow undercliff. Losing his balance when rocks rolled under his boots he fell hard to his haunches. The boar kept coming. Down again, disarmed and having no way to make a run for it, Harry would have to make this close quarters fight where he sat. His weapons would be bootheels and bare hands.

Witnessing everything from above, Marsh knew right off he had to do something fast. He shouldered his rifle, tried to draw a bead on the attacking boar. But from the rim he didn't have a clean shot. He had to move. In three leaping strides, he bounded half-way down the canyon wall until he found solid footing. He raised his rifle, leveled it and fired. But his aim was not true; he'd laid the shot low. Its impact did nothing but send a cloud of dirty snow leaping into the air, a ricochet whining through the canyon.

The boar attacked Harry, goring his calf. Harry hollered, punched and kicked. Levi drew the beast's ire. Marsh moved again, all the way down this time. At the canyon floor, he joined the melee, advancing with his rifle at hip-level. Close up, the beast's incisors resembled axe blades, tusks looked like scimitars. Marsh chambered a round, raised the rifle, sighted down the barrel, waited for Levi to circle away. He touched off the load. This time the bullet ripped into the boar's shoulder. The lung-shot beast staggered, letting out a devilish shriek.

The shot broke the boar's attack, but it did not kill him dead.

El Diablo found his feet and refocused his rage on Marsh. Head low, he charged. Marsh levered another cartridge into the rifle's chamber, sending the spent brass hull tumbling through the air. Cool and deliberate, he took aim again. With the boar no more than a dozen feet away, Marsh fired. The attacking beast stumbled and collapsed. He rolled onto his side, vermillion jets of arterial blood pulsing from his nostrils. His legs went straight. He stilled.

Marsh continued to hold the rifle to his shoulder. Through a haze of gunsmoke, his eyes remained fixed on the fallen beast, sights centered on his head. Snow around the lifeless carcass went red. The other hogs scattered and the pandemonium of shrieks and squeals quieted.

Marsh lowered the rifle and inched forward. Stood over the fallen boar, nudged it with the toe of a boot. The beast did not move. The second bullet had pierced his snout, tearing through soft tissue and cartilage, entering his chest. A perfect shot.

Kill confirmed, Marsh went to his wounded *compadre* and knelt at his side. A spatter of blood stained the snow around him. The boar's tusks had lacerated Harry's right leg in three places. Blood from defensive wounds slathered his right hand.

Marsh unsheathed his belt knife and slit Harry's trouser leg to the knee. He set the knife down and tended the wounds. While Marsh worked, Harry watched him, remaining perfectly still and speechless.

"Ain't too bad," Marsh said. "Sliced up a mite, but you'll live. A little dab of horse liniment and you'll be good as new."

Marsh looked up, saw Harry staring at him.

"What? What are you starin' at?"

Harry didn't speak or move.

"What's the matter? Are you OK?"

"That was incredible. An amazing shot. The boar . . . was . . . charging."

At first, Marsh didn't react. But in short order he collected himself. Back in character, he twitched his shoulders.

"Of course, it was amazing. What'd you expect?"

Harry picked up the knife. He took Marsh's hand in his and opened it. Ran the blade, honed to a white edge, across the palm, leaving a thin red line of blood. Marsh flinched.

Harry gripped Marsh's hand. Held it tight. The blood of two young men mixed and smeared across their joined flesh, filling to overflowing the lines and furrows of their palms. Skin on skin; blood on blood. Not Harry's blood. Not Marsh's blood. Their blood.

CHAPTER 5

Bad Seeds

Harry called Bliss from the hospital to report the news of the canyon cave-in. Gasping, she said she'd be there right away. Harry cautioned her to drive carefully, assuring her there was no need to hurry; Marsh was doing well. X-rays showed a clear fracture, but the doctor would be able to set it and it would heal.

With night coming on, Harry stepped outside the hospital to await Bliss's arrival. He lit a cigarette and stood, facing south, beneath the corrugated aluminum awning that sheltered the concrete approach to the door. Took a few paces forward and halted on the sidewalk, pondering the dimming east-west boulevard of Main Street.

Before two minutes had passed, a stir of movement somewhere to his left captured his gaze. In grainy light, he could make out a lone figure ambling toward him from the east, hands pocketed, head low. When the man drew nearer, Harry recognized him as Esau Coats.

"Evening, Mr. True," Esau said.

"Evening, Mr. Coats. Thought I might be seeing you about now. Here to meet Polly?"

"She gets off duty directly. Come to carry her home. Heard about your trouble."

"News travels fast."

"Bad news do."

"Polly tell you about it?"

"Yep. Figgered I best be seein' 'bout you and our old buddy Mr. Stone, too."

"Marsh is doing fine. Leg's pretty boogered up, but it'll heal. Won't even slow him down."

"Ach . . . I know that. Ole Marsh, he's a force of nature. He can ride the rough string. Dogged if he cain't."

"You got that right. He is a genuine twister."

"Miss Bliss on her way over, I reckon?"

"I called her. She'll be here soon."

"Marsh know yet?"

Harry tensed.

"Know what?"

"That she comin'. Prolly hep him rest easy."

"He knows."

Esau gazed up and down the darkening street. "Town look kindly peaceful now."

"Maybe. Don't think I'd trust it, though. May not be a good idea walking the streets alone at night any more than you have to. Not on this side of town . . . not anymore."

"You talkin' about what happened to my boy?"

"That. And other things. Seems white folks have taken a dislike to coloreds around here lately."

"I'm way ahead of you there, my friend. Bleve me, I got a front row seat. Everybody over in the Flats do. We got white folks drivin' around, honkin' their horns, shoutin' the ugliest kind of things you'cn think of. Why you spose that is? That Supreme Court thing we keep hearin' about?"

Harry nodded. Esau uttered a small grunt.

"Guess folks around here don't take too kindly to some fancy-ass court stickin' its nose in they bidness."

"Apparently not."

"It ain't ever been a little bit of Heaven over there, but it ain't never been like this. In my guestimation, the show ain't hardly even started yet neither."

Taking a thoughtful drag on his smoke, Harry heard the hospital doors jangle open. Over his shoulder he glimpsed a lank figure slouching toward him. Clayton Stone, Marsh's kid brother. He had no use for Clayton. Like most folks in Serafina, he'd written him off long ago as a no-account. He lived in a cheap garage apartment in town, a short walk from the hospital. Days, he worked for Marsh on the ranch. Nights, he caroused with his boon companion, Billy Catlett.

Clayton favored his big brother in looks: same honey-tinted hair, quick smile, well-proportioned physique. At twenty-one, he had the height but not the heft, having not yet filled out. He had his sibling's gift of gab, but he lacked his wit and charm, his intelligence and generous spirit. The kid's eagerness to talk didn't make him clever; it made him a loudmouth.

Marsh and Clayton had lost both their parents in a snowstorm in 1940 when the family's truck skidded on black ice and rolled. Marsh was nineteen at the time, Clayton almost eight. Relatives in California wanted to take the boys to live with them, but Marsh was of age and insisted on staying put and running the family ranch. Anyone who wanted to take his brother had better be ready to fight.

Dodgy by nature, Clayton never could walk a straight line. He commenced his chicaneries as a child with swiping candy from the five and dime. Better than half-wild at sixteen, he moved on to boozing and fast driving. The night he took the Serafina Volunteer Fire Department's one beat-to-hell old truck for a joy ride he secured his reputation as the hellraisingest kid in Serafina.

Over the years, Harry saw Clayton when True Grocery business or friendship took him out to the Stone spread. Often, he found the kid leaning on a fencepost, looking bored and watching Marsh and other hands work. The way Harry judged it, the boy decided early on he couldn't stand in the same sun as his big brother. Why try? He'd make his bones with devilment. To that, he dedicated himself.

Over beers with Harry, Marsh often described Clayton as wild as a corncrib rat and allowed as how the boy wasn't the brightest bulb in the box. Said he got fitted for a dunce hat the day he was born. But in moments of uncharacteristic openness, Marsh confessed to feeling guilty about the way he'd bullied Clayton throughout his life. Perhaps his harshness had something to do with the kid becoming Billy Catlett's heel dog. When Marsh talked like that, Harry did nothing but listen. He knew better than to agree outright. Although he never said it, Harry figured Marsh probably did bear some responsibility for the way Clayton turned out. He'd always been hard on the kid—a lot quicker to belittle him than pat him on the back. When Marsh finally gave Clayton an ultimatum—straighten up or get out—Clayton moved to town and started keeping company with Catlett.

At the hospital, Clayton stood hip-shot and insolent next to Harry, thumbs hooked in his jeans pockets. He retrieved a cigarette from behind his right ear and lit it.

"Why, evenin', Esau," Clayton said. "Couldn't hardly see you there in the dark." The kid grinned. "Out for a little stroll, are you? Lookin' for unlocked doors?"

The kid snickered. Esau and Harry paid him no due.

"Be seein' you, Harry," Esau said. "Say hey to Marsh for me. Tell 'im I come by."

"Sure thing. Thanks."

Esau went inside to wait on Polly.

Clayton snickered again. Harry gave him a cold look.

"Ahh . . . just teasin'," Clayton said, taking a quick pull on his cigarette and exhaling the smoke. "Esau's a good ole ni-" He sneaked Harry a wicked grin, put his hand over his mouth. "Oops, come near sayin' a naughty word. Post to call 'em negroes these days. Ain't that right? Pretty soon we'll be callin' chiggers chegroes."

The kid laughed out loud at his own joke. Hacked a cough. Harry stared at him.

Sensing Harry's disgust, Clayton weakened. "Ahh . . . that's the kind of thing you hear folks sayin'. You know."

"Yeah, they should know better. So should you."

The kid took another drag on his cigarette, blew out lines of smoke. He snorted again, swallowed hard.

"Marsh busted the shit out of that leg, didn't he? Bet that hurt like a son of a bitch. Doc says he's got a . . . what was it? . . . a displaced fracture, whatever that is."

"It means the bone is broken clean through and the parts are not where they're supposed to be."

Clayton shrugged, avoided Harry's eyes.

"So, you saved ole Marsh's life. Way Marsh tells it, you pulled his ass out of that hole in the ground, hauled him back to town. You a honest to goodness hero."

Harry maintained an air of indifference.

"Been hearin' them stories all my whole life. You saved Marsh's life. He saved yours. On and on. Ain't no by God end to it."

Clayton's remark caught Harry off guard. *That's right,* he thought. *There was that, too, wasn't there.* It didn't earn Clayton a pass for being an all-around no-gooder, but Harry had never thought about what growing up overshadowed by Marsh and by the blood brothers' bond would mean for him.

The revving of an engine coming from the east announced the approach of a vehicle. A moment later a pickup came screeching to a halt at the curb with Billy Catlett at the wheel. For his day job, Catlett worked at the refinery located outside of town. Nights, he served as Clayton Stone's criminal mentor. If the straw boss said frog, the wildling boy jumped.

Catlett was rangy and loose-built, but able-bodied. He had muscular arms, veiny and a little too long for a man who stood less than six feet tall. He had large, rough-hewn hands. His sinewy neck featured a prominent Adam's apple that bobbed when he spoke or laughed. When Catlett was a child, his mother explained that the unattractive protuberance originated with a piece of the forbidden fruit that had stuck in Adam's throat. Ever since, she told him, it had marked the appearance of no-account boys like him.

Full grown, Catlett made a cull of a man. His face was a study in sloppy shopwork: eyes close-set, unequal in size, the left half a bubble off level with its mate. Bat-wing ears, beak nose out of true, mouth crooked. All of this afflicted him with an abiding unease that caused him to draw his naturally narrow shoulders in and thrust them upward. He carried himself like a man wearing an ill-cut suit with trousers too short in the rise and a jacket with sleeves of insufficient length. Despite it all, Catlett the once slovenly youth had grown persnickety about his appearance, tried to improve it with the image of a bare-breasted hula girl tattooed in cobalt blue on his right upper arm. He attended to his acne-pocked neck with frequent applications of oatmeal. Kept his fingernails trimmed and clean. For his stringy dark hair he favored a duck's ass style: short on top, long on the sides, slicked back with copious applications of Wildroot Cream-Oil.

Catlett leaned to his right and peered through the vehicle's open passenger-side window, beckoned to his understudy.

"What's the holdup, boy? Get on in here, if you're comin' with me. We got us some *serio* drinkin' to do tonight."

Clayton hitched his jeans and threw in with the highbinder. Catlett gunned the engine, put the truck in gear. In a cloud of tire smoke, journeyman thug and apprentice went hot rodding away, on the prowl for trouble. Heading west, they screamed around the corner and tore south on Commercial Avenue, through Serafina's central business district. Harry followed the taillights until he lost sight of them. *More hellin' around*, he thought. *Tearin' up jack and tearin' up Jenny. Sure to end bad one of these days.*

After the rubber-burning departure of Catlett and the kid, the calm of evening returned. Harry contemplated the deserted street before him. He smoked, listening to the muffled sounds of the sleepy town stretching and yawning as it prepared to seek its nightly repose.

Harry dropped his cigarette, crushed it out with his boot. When he looked up, he saw Bliss's gray Studebaker rounding the corner from the east. She parked and hurried to the hospital's front entrance. The sight of her warmed his heart as it always did: wavy golden tresses cascading to her shoulders, slender legs, familiar gait and carriage, she walked with purpose down the sidewalk, her face painted with worry. She was wearing a simple cotton A-line dress, sleeveless, high neckline, full pleated skirt, navy with some kind of pink flowery print. The fabric hugged her body in all the right places.

When she saw Harry, she came to him and stood so close he picked up her alluring scent. She searched his face, eyes crimsoned by a mist of tears. He caressed her hair with a deft hand but harnessed the urge to go farther.

Bliss reached for Harry's hand and at her touch a gale of feelings broke within him. A barely repressible desire to take her in his arms. Like a larcenist, he searched the inrushing darkness for unwelcome observers. Seeing no one, he relaxed his guard.

"Is Marsh all right?" Bliss said.

"Yeah."

"Are you?"

"Sure."

"I was scared."

"No need. We're both OK. Marsh was drowsy with morphine when I left him but he may be more alert by now. He's got a cast on his leg. Be laid up a few weeks. Doc said the break was clean. The fibula, the outer bone in the lower leg. They'll keep him here a few days, no more."

Tears spilling onto her cheeks, Bliss wrapped her arms about herself as if to resist the force of a rising wind. Harry put his hands to her cheeks, wiped her tears away. Her lips half-parted and he leaned in. But again he checked himself.

"You better go in."

Bliss fluttered a smile and walked away. At the door, she looked back at Harry, knowing he'd be watching. "Midnight," she mouthed.

Harry nodded.

CHAPTER 6

Serafina

Harry shuddered as if the night had cooled in the aftermath of Bliss's leaving. He turned up the frayed collar of his denim jacket, gazed out at his hometown. Marsh had always described Serafina as a sorry-ass little hamlet. Called it hell's hip pocket. Harry knew he was right. Never more than two thousand souls within the boundaries of the municipality itself—no more than three times that in all of Sebastian County. Harry and Marsh thought of their native land as a toilsome place to live, not for the faint of heart. But they didn't mind that. And they thought the name Serafina had a ring to it, especially when they learned from their Sunday school teacher it was Biblical in origin. It meant *The Burning Ones.*

In high summer, semiarid Sebastian County became a colorless mosaic of dry creek beds, patches of sparse brittle grass, skillet-hot rocks. Hot and dry it was. As Marsh put it, hotter than nine kinds of hell. Old Man Winter was no less cantankerous. Without fail, at least once during the colder season a blue norther came squalling in from Colorado. Packing a wallop of blinding snow and sleet, such tempests killed stock, froze water lines, brought the whole county to its knees. In a day or two, the melt-off wiped out every trace of the white stuff. In the spring green-up, such as it was, thunderstorms sometimes raged. They made up in the southwest, stacking great masses of restless air, one on top of the other, rankled them. When a boomer cut loose it was

Katy bar the door. It roared across the countryside, spawning rain and hail, sometimes a tornado.

Whatever the season, the wind blew. Hell-snorters sent sagebrush tumbleweeds rolling and bouncing across the prairie like lost souls. The phantasmal thistles banked against barbed wire fences, hiding all but the topmost strand, and there they stayed until the wind shifted and sent them off again. A hardscrabble province of North America, Sebastian County lay in the shadow of the Hundredth Meridian, the unbending line of Oklahoma's western border, south of Route 66, the Mother Road. State Highway 9 slashed through the heart of it, running east to west.

Harry and Marsh loved their home county, knew it well. From basement rocks to surface fretwork it had played a role in the pageant of their lives as much as their own kinsmen. It birthed them, nurtured them, sometimes laid them open and bled them. They honed their spirits against its alligator skin. It lived in them, as they lived in it.

A rush of air packing a spatter of moisture roused Harry from his contemplation. He took a quick look at the heavens but saw nothing to suggest rain. He knew that on the plains of the Near Southwest, an ephemeral shower can come from nowhere. It can spill from an uncomplicated sky for no apparent reason, defy all meteorological wisdom. And as quickly as it comes, it goes. Ghost rain. Harry knew the mysterious weather phenomenon by that name. He guessed that was what had just befallen him.

He needed to walk. Smelling wetness in the air and on the brick street cobbles, he ambled down the sidewalk to the west. At the corner of Main and Commercial he paused and observed Serafina's main drag. The town's principal thoroughfare extended little more than the length of a hundred-yard dash. Earlier in the day, when people had come in from every sector of the county for their Saturday marketing, it had teemed with shoppers and vehicles, reverberated with the din of commerce. No people, no vehicles now. The street stood empty and hushed in gathering darkness. The one traffic light, hanging from sagging wires suspended from posts located on building tops on each side of the street, swayed in the breeze. The colored incandescence emitted by the robotic minister of traffic control glistened on the damp pavement.

Harry crossed the street and made his way south along Commercial, glancing at storefronts one after another. Across the street to his left, a couple of doors down from Main a small vacant lot gaped where Stegemeyer's Shoe Shop had once stood. A few months before, it had been destroyed by fire.

He passed Dawson's Appliance and Furniture Store. Words inscribed on bricks above the door advertised STOVES ••• RUGS ••• RADIOS. On a wooden sign hanging by squeaky chains perpendicular to the entrance, proprietor Dawson touted his repair service. Harry paused beneath the sign and peered in through the misty window. The shopkeeper stood in the faint interior light, sweeping the showroom floor. Looking up, he gave Harry a warm smile and waved in slow motion as if bidding farewell to a friend he'd put on a train. Harry responded in kind.

Moving on, Harry passed the Wacker's Variety Store and farther down he came to the Rexall Drug—according to the sign over the door, a place to fill a prescription or buy a Grapette or cherry phosphate. His gaze moseyed to the opposite side of the street. There stood Schaefer's Dry Goods and the Oklahoma Tire and Supply Company store—all closed for the day, all dim in meager light, mere shadows of what they'd been a few hours earlier. Harry observed the electrical distribution lines that bisected downtown Serafina, extending from east to west, fastened to knee-high rooftop stanchions at each end. Like the traffic light, they swayed in the breeze.

Farther on, Harry paused at the First National Bank, a two-story red brick building with arched windows, built in 1907 according to the inscription on the plaque over the door. A dim interior light revealed a head mount of a white-faced Longhorn steer on the lobby wall. The spread of its horns would have equaled, and perhaps exceeded, Harry's own height. Opposite, on a wall shelf, stood a lifelike mountain lion, stuffed and dried. A predatory pose suggested an imminent attack.

Gazing through the bank window again, Harry remembered the way those lifeless effigies had fascinated him as a kid. Standing in the bank lobby with his mother, he planned for the day the beasts might come to life and terrorize the good people of Serafina. It would fall to him and his friend Marsh to save the day. And in his childish fantasy they would prove themselves worthy. They had the strength and daring to do anything.

Harry chirped a laugh at the memories conjured by the sight of the taxidermied beasts, but it was a laugh shaded with sorrow. So it was with every blessed thing he saw on this night. Every wind-whipped corner of this little burg had a history. This was the place of his birth, where his ancestors had lived, where they had died. This prairie held their bones. His town, his home, his life. Where he had always fit in. Until now. These days, he couldn't help feeling like a stranger. He could see it all fading away . . . like a ghost rain.

Darkness was coming on strong now. Continuing down the street, Harry sensed someone watching him. Not far ahead he saw a man leaning against the right front fender of a pickup parked anglewise against the curb, hat raked back, arms folded, legs crossed at the ankles.

Gooseflesh prickled his neck. As he came closer, a lucifer flared yellow, sulfurous. In the fanlight, the lopsided face of Billy Catlett materialized.

Catlett lit a cigarette, blew a shaft of smoke into the match flame. With an orchestrated move of hand he flung the brittle black stick away.

"If it ain't the high and mighty Mr. Harry True," he said. "Heard you and your buddy Stone had quite a time today. Musta been somethin.'"

Catlett drew on his cigarette, issued smoke from his nostrils. He spat out a fleck of tobacco clinging to the tip of his tongue.

"Seen you and Mrs. Marshall Stone over yonder." He pointed his cigarette at the vacant space the cobbler's shop had occupied.

Harry shifted his gaze. From where they stood, he had an unobstructed view of the hospital.

"Touchin' scene," Catlett said. "'Spect that poor little thing's gonna need some lookin' after. Marsh stove up and all. Handy."

Harry did his best to show no reaction. Catlett took another drag on his cigarette and launched a skein of smoke rings aimed at Harry's chest. Harry withdrew his hands from his pockets and let them fall to his sides, fists clenched rock hard. He stepped forward.

"You got something to say, spit it out."

"Oh, no. New. No. No. No. Not me. Nothin' to say. Just bein' neighborly."

Maintaining a relaxed air, Catlett breathed in more smoke, blew it into the narrow space separating him and Harry. Tossed the smoldering butt to the concrete walk. Before the sparks died, Clayton Stone emerged from the darkness of a nearby alley. He gangled to the pickup, buttoning his Levi's.

"When you gotta go, you gotta go. Know what I mean? Hoowee. Man, I had to drain my radiator . . . in the worst way."

"The worst way?" Catlett said. "You mean through your nose?"

The kid yelped an immodest laugh.

"Hey, Billy, I thought you said we was goin' drinkin.'"

Maintaining a puerile sneer, Catlett squared his hat, aping the way he'd seen Harry do it many times. He arranged the collar of his jacket to match the way Harry wore his, strolled to the driver's side of the truck, got behind the wheel, and started up the engine as Clayton climbed in beside him. Glancing at himself in the rearview mirror, he smoothed back an errant shag of hair with a fingertip and stuffed it under his hat's sweatband. Revving the engine, he backed away from the curb, peeled out down the street. Patron and protégé riding the owl-hoot trail.

Harry took in and released a long, slow breath. He aimed a squinted gaze through the peephole created by the fiery destruction of the shoe shop to the place he'd been standing with Bliss.

Damn. The son of a bitch was watching.

CHAPTER 7

Blue Creek

When Bliss mouthed "Midnight," Harry knew what she meant. She would meet him then where they always met: at the secret place far away from city lights and spying eyes they had first visited the year after her illness. A backcountry watercourse, unknown and unmapped, Blue Creek was not on the way to anywhere. No paved road or manmade structure of any kind within a twenty-minute drive.

Harry had learned of the hidden hydrothermal spring from his old family friend Esau. The Coats and True clans had been tied together for generations. In slave times Harry's maternal ancestors had owned Esau's grandmother and grandfather. Held title to them as they did to their land, their livestock, and other chattels. After the Emancipation, Esau's grandparents stayed with their former owners. All of them, close to destitute, came west together, first to Texas and later to Indian Country. They traveled ahorseback, on a couple of Springfield draft wagons, some of them by shank's mare. Esau's people took the Coats name.

Over the course of the decades following, the relationship between Harry's family and Esau's family evolved into one of mutual respect and support. Because of their long, shared history the folk of each household always felt responsible for the other's welfare and did what they could with unequal resources to ensure it. During the Great Depression, with food in short supply, Harry's mother and father often delivered a sack of groceries to Esau's home. When Esau or Polly or the kids needed medicine, the Trues made sure they got it. When Esau couldn't find a steady job, Harry's father hired him for piecework or found someone who would. In turn, when Morris True needed help with hauling and delivering, building or repairing, Esau was always there, often waving away payment with "We're family." Esau helped out at least once a year when Harry and his dad worked the small herd of cattle they raised on the quarter section of land that had been in their family since their early days in Oklahoma. Never more than fifty head or so. Enough for Harry to get a taste of ranching and learn about roping, branding, vaccinating, and dehorning. And when Harry's mother died and he and his father were crippled by grief, Polly Coats practically moved in, cooking and tending to them until they got back on their feet.

Esau and Polly were two of Harry's favorite people. Esau had dark, swimming eyes, coarse work-hardened hands, often a stubble of graying beard. A smile usually graced his face. He had a quick wit, and laughter came easily to him. He always seemed comfortable in his own hide. Harry, in his days of childish naiveté, had no doubt that his old friend regarded the world as a kind and gentle place and accepted his station in it, whatever it might be, without complaint.

Once, when Harry was still a peach fuzz kid, as he and Esau were working in the stockroom of True Grocery, he asked Esau how he'd lived so long through such a difficult time in history without losing his smile, how he'd managed to remain such a pleasant, positive person. He must have been a lucky man, Harry said, to have avoided the hard times so many coloreds lived through.

"How'd you miss all that trouble?" Harry wanted to know. "How'd you manage to have such an easy go of it?"

The questions rolled casually off Harry's tongue. The boy had no thought whatsoever of prompting a serious discussion. He expected Esau to smile and laugh, say, "Yessir, I sure was lucky. Sure was. Hard to factor, ain't it?"

Esau did smile at first as if he might give Harry the response he was expecting. But his smile trailed away. He turned somber. He had to set the record straight. He'd taken a shine to Harry the day of his birth and cared too much for him to let him go through life not knowing the way of things in bygone times. With some reluctance and a hint of sternness, Esau took the unschooled pup to task.

"Didn't miss a thing. Where you get such a idy? I had my troubles. These eyes seen things you ain't never imagined. No sir. Didn't miss nothin'. What I wudn't witness to, I heard tell of."

Taking Harry by his skeletal shoulders, Esau seated the boy on a stack of produce crates.

"You set your skinny ass right there and give a listen. You listen close. I know the story . . . and I want you to know it."

Harry obliged, happy to humor his friend. He sat spraddle-legged and slack on his improvised seat. He knew he had no real choice in the matter, anyway.

"I was born in the year of our Lord eighteen and ninety-nine," Esau began. "Never was no slave, course. But my grandaddy was. Grandmama, too. Owned by yo mama's family. Owned. Imagine that. One man ownin' another man same as he owns a horse or a cow or a dog."

Esau drifted away in reflection.

"I declare. I do declare."

He continued.

"My grandaddy was sold off to a Georgia man when he wasn't but five years old, no bigger'n fryin' size. One day the man tore him right out his mama's arms. They both took to screamin' and cryin', beggin' and prayin', carryin' on sumpin awful. Musta been quite a scene. Didn't do no good, though. They didn't pay her no mind. They took that poor little child anyways. And that was the end of that."

Harry sat a little straighter, erased his smile. Seeing the boy was paying attention now, Esau went on talking.

"Through a chain of commerce they all ended up with your family. Best thing ever happened to 'em. Your family always treated my folks good. After the war—I mean Mr. Lincoln's war—my daddy come out here with 'em. Not a slave no more. But not what you'd call settin' in the catbird seat neither. Didn't have no other place to go. Couldn't do nothin' else. So he come."

Esau paused to collect his thoughts.

"But don't get me wrong about your family. They good folks. When we needed takin' up for, they took up for us. Why, if it ain't been for them, we'd a starved right to death. They was good to us. Some folks said too good. Called 'em . . . . Well, you know what they called 'em. In them days, that was a bad thing to call somebody. Still is."

Esau paused. "'Course, we done for your folks, too. Coupla times your mama was so sick. My mama nursed her. And when your grandaddy needed a hand clearing, building, anything, my daddy was always there."

Esau paced. He carried his chin in the crook of a hand, striking the thoughtful pose of a country barrister making his final argument to a jury. Harry was sitting upright now, back straight as a survey stake, held rapt by Esau's words.

"So you see the Coats family been here a long time, better'n fifty year, same as your family. In my days, I seen hangins, killins, all kinda meanness. All right here in this old county. Had my own brother beat up so bad he lost a eye. White folks done it. Damn near kilt him.

What'd he do to get such a whuppin? Somebody said he was uppity. That's all. Ain't supposed to be like that. No, sir."

Esau has a brother? Harry opened his mouth to ask about him but thought better of it.

Esau turned away from Harry and took a few steps, deep in thought. He shook a finger at the thin air as if preparing to make one last point. He swung back around.

"I have tried to reckon it all out. Tried for a long, long time. Best I can figger, some folks is just mean. Simple as that. They hold theirselves up by holdin' somebody else down. Cain't understand it. To save my soul, I cain't."

"Me neither," Harry muttered under his breath.

"Then, by the grace of the good Lord, Polly come along." Esau's expression softened. He shook his head. "Quite a woman. Quite a woman. Me and her . . . we buried two babies. Law-dee. Two of our own children. You imagine that?"

Harry hadn't known that either.

Esau's voice, weighted with sorrow, died out. Eyes moistened.

"No, sir. I ain't missed much. I ain't missed nothin'. And that's God's own truth."

Harry stood, head low. He fussed with the button on the cuff of his shirt sleeve, hesitant to face Esau full-on.

A forgiving smile returned to Esau's lined and weathered face. A little ragged, perhaps, but it was there. He pointed to it.

"You wanted to know about this here smile. Learned it from my daddy. Wiser than a tree full of owls, that man. He always said act like you somebody because you is. Don't ever forget that. You gotta stand tall and know your worth and let everyone else know it, too. So, that's what I done. This smile is here 'cause I chose to put it here. Coulda

 James Jennings

chose sumpin' else. Woulda been real easy. But this here's what I chose."

Harry took a step forward, looked up into his friend's kind eyes.

"I didn't know, Esau. I didn't know."

Esau put a hand on the boy's shoulder. He smiled.

"Well . . . now you do."

Esau revealed the hidden treasure of Blue Creek to Harry one afternoon not long after, in the spring of 1938. They were heading home late in the day after picking up a load of produce in a remote precinct of Sebastian County. Harry was at the wheel. Glancing over at his friend, sitting silent in the passenger seat of the rattletrap old store pickup, he could tell Esau had something on his mind.

"What's wrong?" Harry asked. "You haven't said a word for miles."

Esau shrugged off the question.

"Esau . . . what is it?"

Esau roused himself.

"All right. Reckon it's time. Gonna show you sumpin'. Turn off up yonder."

"What?"

"You heared me. Turn. Turn right yonder. C'mon."

Still a good distance from Serafina's city limits, Harry turned off the section line road onto a low-gear ranch road that cut due west.

"What are we doing?" Harry said. "Where are we going?"

"You hold your tater, boy. Do what old Esau say. We gonna follow this little bit of a road a piece. Got to have patience, son. Yessir, got to have patience."

Harry drove on.

"Come on, Esau. Where are we going?"

But Esau would not be rushed.

"Here," he said finally. "Turn here."

When he gave the word, they left the ranch road and angled onto a vague trace, little more than a cattle trail, that took them southward. It played out altogether as they neared the brink of a shallow declivity where the leafy plumage of a watermarking sash of timber came into sight. There had to be a stream bending through it.

"All right, you can stop here," Esau said. "This all the further we goin.'"

Harry stopped, killed the engine.

"What? Is this it?"

"Hear it?"

"Hear what?"

"Shh. Listen."

Harry listened.

"I don't hear anything."

"I do."

Esau pointed ahead. "Yonder way."

"What? I don't see anything."

"You will. C'mon."

Esau quit the truck and struck out on foot across a pasture of summer grass. Harry opened his door and stepped out but hesitated to follow.

"Esau, where are we going?"

Esau glanced over his shoulder, vaunted a wide smile, but kept walking.

"C'mon with me if you wanna see the finest spot for pitchin' woo in all Sebastian County. Yessir, it is sooo fine . . . finer than frog hair."

Scratching his head, Harry followed. Without knowing it, he left the undistinguished provinces of creation behind. In mere seconds he and his friend Esau arrived at a mystical place.

Standing at the skirt of the lee slope they'd seen from the truck, their eyes fell upon a stand of towering cottonwoods that shaded a run of pure untainted water dark as moonless night. Spilling over a nick point clad in smoky quartz, the flow formed an arching sheet of water as wide as the creek itself; below it, a plunge basin, calm as a mill pond. A rimming canebrake on the opposite side. High reeds and rushes up and downstream. A luxuriant growth of wildflowers Harry later came to know as Blue Wild Indigo graced the creek's banks and environs. Standing two to three feet tall, each blue-green shrub was garbed for its perennial blooming in a cloak of long-oval leaflets and violet-blue flowers, each the shape and size of a doll's teacup.

"Take a look at them flowers," Esau said with reverence. "Kindly bluish-purple. Blue of evenin'. Am I right?"

"Yes, sir. You are right."

"Blue Creek. That's what me and Polly call it. Look at it. Ain't no stock tank. That's for damn sure."

"No, sir. It's no stock tank."

"Been comin' here for years. Never seen another human soul out here. You believe that? Not a soul. Don't think nobody know about it. Reckon it some kind of lost place. Mebbe . . . you cain't see it less you got the right eyes for it."

"I can see it."

Harry understood Esau's fascination with this paradisal place. Still air smelled of moist rocks and grass, the sweetness of natural flora. Luminous bars of sunlight slanted in through cracks in the overhead latticework of soft-hued limbs. Muted light showered in a fine mist. All of it vague. Shimmery.

Esau went to the water's rim and dropped to a knee. Guileless, he dippered a handful. He examined it, splayed his fingers, letting the crystalline liquid return to its pristine provenance.

"Warm. Like a bathtub. Of a evenin', when the air cools, it give off a haze. Must be some kinda underground plumbin' carry it from a fire way down in the belly of the earth. Ain't that sumpin'?"

Harry knelt beside Esau and swished a hand in the water. More than warm, it felt heated.

The water was clear. So unclouded Harry could spy shiny pebbles on the bottom. And calm. Not the slightest disturbance of the liquid skin, save tiny ripples set in motion by an occasional falling leaf or alighting of an aquatic insect.

"Figger a crick like this here one musta ran right through the Garden of Eden," Esau said in a voice he might use to say his prayers at night. Harry smiled.

"Honest to goodness. It's true. Genesis say streams come right out the ground. You go read it your ownself. This might coulda been that place. I'cn see ole Adam and Eve theirselves out there skinny dippin'. Nekkid as jaybirds. Oooheee. Stirs a man's blood, don't it."

Harry sat back on his haunches.

"You and Polly still come here?"

"Some. Not like we used to when we was on the sunny side of our lives. More responsibilities now, you know. Get a few years older, see things different. But I 'member. Sure enough do."

"Why'd you bring me out here? Why'd you show me this place?"

"Wellsuh, that there's a good question. Been studyin' on it, but I ain't real sure I know. Maybe so's it won't be forgot. So's it can be passed on to you and your lady friend. You know, places like this . . . they don't last forever. None of 'em. Don't know the whyfor. They dry up. Somebody build a dam or something. Maybe if folks don't use it, use it right, God takes it away. Say . . . unh-unh . . . ya'll don't get to have it no more. He been known to do that kinda thing, you know. Done it to Adam and Eve. If he'd do it to them, he'd do it to anybody."

Esau touched his chin. Thought a moment.

"Figgered somebody in the family oughta know the secret. Your daddy done a lot to see us through these hard times we been havin' these last few years. This depression, President Roosevelt calls it. Figger I owe your daddy. But he too old now. I bring Woody out here sometime, do a little frog giggin'. But he cain't really appreciate it yet. Somebody your age needs to know 'bout this place. So . . . you the one. You bring your little missy out here, she think you're a regular courtin' fool."

Esau placed a hand on Harry's shoulder as they walked back to the truck. "You and Miss Bliss, you two come here often as you want. I want you to enjoy it." He turned serious. "But nobody else, you hear? Anybody else you want to bring out here, you ask Esau first. This place is special and we gotta protect it."

"I promise."

Two evenings later, Harry took his *inamorata* to Blue Creek. When she saw the secret jewel, Bliss said she felt like she'd stepped into a Claude Monet painting, with its natural light effects and loose strokes of color. In no time, the young sweethearts—both coming eighteen—lay in each other's arms on an old patchwork counterpane spread over soft green grass. Accompanied by the chittering of nightbirds, sough of wind, and sigh of creek water in motion, he pledged his love. And she pledged hers.

"You will be my Guinevere," Harry said. "And I will be your Lancelot."

Bliss smiled. "And I will send you on noble missions. You will restore justice and chivalry in Sebastian County."

"So it shall be. I'll roam hither and yon, smiting the wicked, doing good deeds. And I will love you . . . faithfully."

"You will love me, and you'll never stop loving me. It is my command."

"Yes, milady."

He reached into his shirt pocket and came out with a scrap of paper. "Listen to this. I wrote it down so I wouldn't forget it." He read:

My bounty is as boundless as the sea
My love as deep. The more I give to thee,
The more I have, for both are infinite.

"*Romeo and Juliet*," Bliss said.

"Yes. I wish I could say I'd written it for you. That's something I'd like to be someday, a poet. Maybe I'll write something as beautiful. Something everyone will know."

"You *will* be a poet. And I'll be a teacher, and maybe write novels. We'll work to support ourselves until we become rich and famous, and we'll travel the world, and our love will never fade."

Harry began stroking her golden tresses and curling a lock of hair around a finger.

"Ah ah ah," Bliss cautioned him. "'Love me for myself alone and not my yellow hair.'"

"Yeats," Harry said. Matching her one for one, he quoted the last line of the poem: "'Only God, my dear could love you for yourself alone and not your yellow hair.'"

Days to come, Harry and Bliss imagined the real life they would have together. They'd wait to marry until age twenty-one. That gave them three years to work and save money for a house. They'd design it themselves and host literary salons in their parlor. They knew their future would be different from anyone else's in Serafina, for their love was different. Other people did not feel, had never felt, what they felt. No other couple had ever loved with such intensity, burned with such passion.

Blue Creek was the place Harry and Bliss lay with bodies entwined, planning their future. They thought of it as hallowed ground and never told anyone about it. Not a soul. Not even Harry's best friend and blood brother. Harry never told him, and Bliss didn't either, not even after she became Mrs. Marshall Stone.

Two hours after leaving Bliss at the hospital, Harry stepped out of his truck at Blue Creek. Utter dark had closed in and he felt crushed by the weight of it. He felt the censure of a leering half-face moon. Slumping against the truck's left front fender, he massaged his eyes with thumb and forefinger. *What are we doing? What in the world are we doing?*

The only reply, if reply it was, came from the night itself: rustle of leaves, babble of water cascading over the spillway. Gazing through the familiar grove of cottonwoods, he could make out the creek's skinny riffles and its flowered banks. He considered drifting over to the water's edge and waiting for Bliss there, but he knew the still surface of the idyllic pool possessed reflective powers equal to those of any looking glass. The moon would pursue him and confront him there with its shimmering image. He didn't move.

But staying put provided no relief. Barely within sight from where he stood, the black profiles of a cluster of hoodoo rocks projected from the plain. In his imagination the erosional sandstone pillars—erect and inflexible—reproved him like a tribunal of stern inquisitors. He had a mind to fall prostrate before them. But an attitude of defiance boiled up within him. He had to resist an impulse to rebuke his inanimate indicters out loud.

A pair of headlights in the distance eased the stand-off. He watched the Studebaker pull off the ranch road, come toward him and stop. The lights went dark and Bliss stepped out. When she neared, Harry opened his arms to her. They embraced. They kissed. Bliss turned and put her back against Harry's chest. He wrapped his arms around her and held her close. Together, they regarded the somber plain that spread out before them, silvered by swashes of moonlight.

"You can see the blue of the wildflowers even in the dark," Bliss said in a wistful voice. "Blue Wild Indigo."

"Yes, Blue Wild Indigo," Harry said. "False Indigo. Not the real thing. They're impostors." *Like us,* he thought. "Did you get away without being seen?"

"I think so."

"You *think* so."

Bliss turned toward him. Harry knew his tone had been somewhat disputatious and he counterfeited a smile to ease the tension of the moment.

"I came directly from the hospital," Bliss said. "Told Marsh I was going home." She paused. "Medicine for the pain had him pretty loopy."

She paused again. "He was acting funny, though. Know what he said? He said, 'Say hello to Harry for me. Thank him again for savin' my ass.' I said, 'I will, if I see him, but you can tell him yourself tomorrow. You'll probably see him before I do.'"

"Well, we've become liars. Among other things."

Bliss searched his eyes. "Do you think he knows?"

"Maybe. What do you think? You're the one who lives with him."

Ignoring the coda to Harry's question, Bliss turned away. "I don't know. Sometimes I think maybe he does but that may be because I feel so guilty."

Harry's jaw tightened. "You feel guilty."

"Harry, please. Are you trying to start something? Yes, I feel guilty. Of course, I do. Don't you?"

A falling star off to the southwest seized their attention and altered the course of their conversation. The celestial ember descended like a tear of fire dripping from a Roman candle. "The sky is weeping," Bliss said. In more distant nightside reaches vague spasms of cloudbound lightning rippled. "Could be a storm is coming."

"Yes. Could be."

"We can't go on like this forever," Bliss said, sighing. "What are we going to do?"

Harry took her in his arms. "We'll worry about the future tomorrow. Tomorrow, or the day after, or the day after that." Lifting his gaze to the enshrouding darkness, he added, sotto voce, "Run slowly, horses of the night. Run slowly."

"Ovid," Bliss said. "Run slowly," she whispered. *Time. Give us time.*

Part Two

CHAPTER 8

The War

In Autumn, 1939, Britain and France declared war on Germany. Like everyone in Serafina, Harry and Bliss followed the news. But, to the young lovers, Europe's strife seemed far away and they expected the U.S. to want no part in it. They were right, until they were wrong. Before long, entire continents ignited, and the national mood began shifting. And then Pearl Harbor happened.

Marsh was the first to answer his country's call. Brash and impulsive as always, he surprised Harry and Bliss by sending Clayton to live with their relatives in California and enlisting in the Marines a week after the sneak attack. Ready to serve but not eager to leave Bliss, Harry decided to wait until Uncle Sam called him up. He received his induction notice and reported for duty in early 1942.

After six weeks of training in San Diego, Marsh shipped out to the Pacific. Harry remained stateside through basic and advanced individual training at Fort McClellan, Alabama, and Officer Candidate School at Fort Benning, Georgia. Commissioned a Second Lieutenant upon graduation from OCS, he received his permanent assignment to the newly activated 106th Infantry Division. Months of division training at Fort Jackson, South Carolina followed; after that a move to Tennessee for large scale field exercises before heading overseas.

Harry adapted well enough to army life. In him, as in most men, a trace of the ancient Spartan dwelled, a yearning to fight the good fight, to be a part of something historic. When the time came, he conjured the warrior spirit within him and breathed life into it. But he carried himself with caution. He had no intention of taking unnecessary risks. He wasn't looking for medals or glory. He wanted to do his duty with honor and survive the war. He had plans for the future.

Back in Serafina in early October 1944, on his final leave before shipping out, Harry spent almost every waking moment with Bliss.

"We could get married now," Harry said one evening as they sat rocking in Bliss's porch swing, wrapped in a blanket against the evening chill. "What do you think?"

Bliss hesitated.

Harry sensed uncertainty. "You don't want to get married?"

"No, no. Of course, I do. I feel like we're already married. I've loved you since the moment we met."

Harry smiled. "Not as much as I loved you." He tightened his arms around her. "So what is it?"

"You'll laugh."

"I won't, I promise."

The thing was, Bliss wanted a wedding. A church wedding. She wanted to be a bride, walk down the aisle to Harry wearing a white wedding dress. She wanted a minister to bless them before a gathering of friends and family. Knowing she would marry only once, she wanted it to be special.

"Is that silly?"

He kissed her.

"No, it isn't silly. If that's what you want, that's what we'll do."

So they decided to wait.

Two days later they stood together outside the bus that would take

Harry to Oklahoma City, where he'd board a train that would carry him back East to join his unit. Soon, he'd be on a troop transport ship headed for Scotland.

"Promise you'll be careful," Bliss said through a downpour of tears.

"I'll be careful."

"I'll write you every day. And I'll wait for you. As long as it takes, I'll wait. I love you with all my heart, and I'll be here when you come back. Promise me you'll come back."

"I promise."

Harry held her close.

"I have a present for you." Reaching into his pocket, he came out with a small black velvet box. "Sorry I didn't have time to wrap it."

She opened it with trembling fingers. Inside, resting on a white satin liner, lay a pendant: an oval, iridescent green and blue stone in a gold setting on a gold chain.

"It's an opal," Harry said. "Your birthstone. Something to remember me by."

"Oh, Harry, it's beautiful. I'll wear it always . . . every day . . . until—" Her voice caught in her throat.

He took her face in his hands. "I'll be back. Don't think for a minute I won't be. I will be back."

One month later, Marsh returned to Serafina. While Harry had been training, Marsh had been fighting in the Pacific, where he'd risen to the rank of sergeant. In July 1944, a Japanese bullet ripped into him during the Battle of Saipan. It turned out to be a million-dollar wound. The bullet entered below the left collar bone, passed all the way through his body without hitting an artery or piercing his lung. It tore through muscle, mangled ligaments, carved a divot out of the scapula, shattered a rib, but left him mostly intact. Infection posed the biggest threat during his initial treatment and recovery. In November, the Corps sent him home to convalesce.

"Tell Harry next time you write that I'm sorry I missed him," Marsh said when Bliss went to visit him at the V.A. Hospital in Oklahoma City.

"I will. Do you need anything while you're here?"

"Nah. I'll be out of this joint in no time. Need to work this shoulder some, build up the bicep and pec. Cain't be goin' around out of plumb."

Bliss laughed.

"I'll come by to say hidy once I'm home. Take you out for a sody pop. You can fill me in about Harry."

"I'd like that."

Bliss wrote Harry about everything and nothing. He kept every *billet-doux,* organized them by month and day, stacked and squared them like a deck of playing cards, bound them with jute twine, read them again and again, often by the illumination of a lilting Zippo lighter flame. He examined every stroke of pen, imagined Bliss's hand forming the words, tried to detect her scent on the paper. Knowing that not long before, her eyes had been on the page he was now holding warmed his heart. And tortured it. He was glad Marsh was back home, glad for his blood brother and glad for Bliss. Marsh would watch out for her, Harry knew, until he came home again.

Feeling a powerful call to do her part for her country, Bliss did volunteer work at the local Ration Board, collecting and issuing books of ration stamps, answering questions on what was and wasn't rationed and how the point system worked. On weekends, she sold war bonds in the lobby of the La Vista movie theater. When she could, she bought bonds in her own name. Everywhere she went, she wore the opal necklace Harry had given her.

When Uncle Sam came calling on Billy Catlett he turned tail and ran like a turpentined cat. Wrangling a deferment as sole support of a dependent parent, he went to Detroit and got a job in a carburetor factory. An essential industry, vital to the war effort, the old man claimed to anyone who'd listen. Not in the thick of the fighting, maybe, but the boy was doing his military service in his own way. Over drinks at Sweet Leona's, the town's leading watering hole, Ben Catlett made out like his son was involved in some top secret, non-uniform wearing kind of war effort. Something he couldn't talk about. Nobody believed it. Everyone figured it for a lie.

One night a few good old boys got liquored up and decided to let the elder Catlett know what they thought of his son's wartime activities. They painted the family's mailbox yellow. When old man Catlett cleaned it off, they painted it again. Ben Catlett complained to the Postal Service. The mischief violated federal law—you can't vandalize a receptacle of the U.S. Mail—so the Postal Service investigated. But the inspectors didn't break a sweat over it. Couldn't dredge up a single witness. Nobody in the entire county knew a thing about the dastardly deed involving the yellow paint. The government men let it go at that.

From time to time Billy Catlett showed up in Serafina. Once, he approached Bliss while she was selling war bonds in the theater and asked her if she'd like to go out for a Coke sometime.

"That's a sweet invitation, Billy," she said. "But you know I can't."

"Why not?"

"You know why not."

"You seein' somebody else?"

"You ain't wearin' a ring."

"I'm wearing this," Bliss said, fingering the pendant around her neck.

"That ain't a ring."

"Even so, I'm spoken for."

"So how come I see you with Marsh sometimes, huh?"

"He's Harry's best friend, Billy. You know that."

"So that makes him your best friend, too?"

Bliss considered that. "Yes, I guess it does. In a way."

Shot down again, Catlett's resentment and jealousy of Harry deepened. Harry and Marsh. And now—he couldn't help it—Bliss, too.

In Scotland, Harry's division readied itself to enter the European Theater of Operations. They moved from Scotland to England in November 1944, and within a few weeks, they headed for France where they joined the ongoing Rhineland Campaign. Soon, they crossed into Belgium. Harry's baptism of fire came on December 16, ten days after his arrival on the Continent. In predawn darkness, the Germans launched a surprise attack on Allied troops through the dense forest of the Ardennes region. Harry found himself on the leading edge of the Ardennes Counteroffensive in what later became known as the Battle of the Bulge, the largest and bloodiest battle fought by the United States in World War II.

Traveling in predawn darkness along an undefended stretch of road, Harry's jeep came under intense artillery fire. He suffered serious shrapnel wounds to his back and left shoulder, forehead and left cheek. The blast killed his driver. Separated from his regiment, Harry holed up with other wounded soldiers in a shelled-out house. Soon, they were overrun and surrounded by German troops. Cut off, outnumbered and outgunned, low on ammunition and supplies, the Americans were nothing but meat for the grinder. They surrendered. Harry became a prisoner of war.

The Germans marched their captives east through the snow and cold of the worst European winter in memory. Harry could barely walk. When he faltered, his buddies carried him, using a legless tabletop as a makeshift stretcher. Long torturous days of marching were followed by excruciating days and nights packed into a boxcar, traveling in a slow eastward slog to a POW camp on the east bank of the Oder River. By the time they got there, Harry was near death. Delirious from wounds, blood loss, infection, malnutrition and exhaustion he couldn't recall his name and had no dog tags. He had no sense of where he was or why.

About the time Harry arrived at his place of imprisonment, his father received a Western Union telegram from the Adjutant General stating

THE SECRETARY OF WAR DESIRES ME TO EXPRESS HIS DEEP REGRET THAT YOUR SON HARRISON F. TRUE HAS BEEN REPORTED MISSING IN ACTION SINCE SIX-TEEN DECEMBER IN BELGIUM IF FURTHER DETAILS OR OTHER INFORMATION ARE RECEIVED YOU WILL BE PROMPTLY NOTIFIED.

Two weeks later, Morris True received a letter from Harry's regimental commander, Major Marvin Sanders, saying a villager had turned in Harry's dog tags. "But we have not found your son, Mr. True. So I encourage you to hold out hope."

"The telegram says he's missing," Marsh reminded Bliss. "It don't say he's dead. They don't know where he's at. That's all. There's a whale of a difference between missing and dead."

"But they found his dog tags."

"Yeah, but they didn't find *him,* honey. All they know is he's missing. Five'll get you ten he shows up before long. You cain't trust the army for nothin'. They cain't find their ass with both hands. They gotta say somethin', so that's what they're sayin.'"

Marsh did his best to lift Bliss's spirits. He spent as much time with her as he could, mostly talking about Harry, trying to inspire hope in her that her beloved was alive and well. They avoided speculation about his fate. They recalled the good times before the war. Went to church together, to movies, to visit Harry's dad. And all the while, they grew closer, more dependent on each other.

In March, Morris True received another letter from Major Sanders expressing his regrets that he still could not confirm whether Harry was living or dead. He wrote that he'd seen the blast site and though he believed it unlikely someone could have survived the attack, he could not explain why his body had not been recovered. "I wish I had better news," he wrote. "Or lacking that, I wish I could help you find peace about your son. At present, I can do no more than wish you strength." He ended the letter by praising Harry's courage and character and assuring Morris True that, living or dead, his son had served his country and flag with courage and honor.

Bliss was devastated.

In May, news of victory in Europe arrived. Bittersweet news for Bliss. For weeks after, she hoped to hear that, like other servicemen missing in action, Harry had resurfaced as a released prisoner of war. When the news didn't arrive and still no letter came from Harry—Bliss knew he'd write if he could—somehow, it marked the death of hope that he might still be alive. Hope surrendered to acceptance that he was gone. She sank into a depression and took to sleeping all day and never leaving the house.

The Japanese surrender in August that signaled the official end of hostilities was Bliss's undoing. Louise Farrell became so concerned for her daughter that she called Marsh and asked him to pay a visit.

"She depends on you, Marsh," Mrs. Farrell said, "and she needs you now."

"I'm on my way."

Louise Farrell set a tray of cookies and lemonade on the coffee table and left the two alone in the living room. Sitting in an armchair across from Bliss on the divan, Marsh was shaken by how much Bliss had deteriorated. She was drawn, pale and thin. But she had gotten out of bed and put clothes on for him, which was something.

"So, how ya doin', honey?" Marsh asked gently. When Bliss started to cry, he went to her and held her in his arms. He'd never seen her cry before. He'd never held her in his arms before, either, didn't realize until that moment how much he had longed to do that.

It was the first time Bliss had felt a man's embrace since Harry left, and she, too, was caught off guard by how good it felt, the power of the hunger it aroused. After allowing herself a few moments of sweet comfort, she pulled away and crossed the living room to the picture window. Marsh followed, offered her a handkerchief; she dried her tears and poised herself.

She was Harry's girl. Always would be, Marsh thought, whether he ever came home or not. But Harry wasn't here now and Bliss was suffering and Marsh had promised to watch out for her. And that's what he was going to do. At that moment, he set his mind on helping Bliss recover the *joie de vivre* the war had taken from her.

"You know what you need?" he said.

Bliss shook her head.

"Well, I do."

After glancing over both shoulders in a conspiratorial fashion, he sought Bliss's eyes.

"Listen here. You need a little honky-tonkin'. And I am the guy to provide it. Go powder your nose and get your little behind in a party mood. We gonna have us some fun. Fun. Remember fun? Drinkin' and dancin' and suchlike." He gave Bliss a one-armed squeeze. "We're due. Both of us."

Bliss summoned a weary smile. "You might have something there."

"Damn right I do. Now go freshen up and let us away."

An hour later, they were sitting in a taproom one county over, downing a few beers. Laughing. Singing along with the jukebox. People celebrating the country's war victory packed the place, reveling in the return of peace and the hope of prosperity. Marsh made good on his promise. For him and for Bliss, this night was the most fun they'd had in three years. Perhaps, there was more life yet to be lived.

Walking to the car after closing time, Marsh reached for Bliss's hand. She gave it. They stopped and lifted their eyes to the star-spangled heavens.

"Lord above," Marsh said. "If that ain't a sight. But it ain't nothin' compared to you. I do believe you are the prettiest thing I ever seen."

He kissed her. A delicate kiss on the lips. But such kisses come in pairs. And pairs, if welcomed, are followed by flurries. When Bliss didn't turn away or protest, Marsh took her in his arms and kissed her again. This time, a longer, deeper kiss—the kind that declares an upheaval in a relationship.

"I ain't sure we oughta be doin' this," Marsh said, pulling back a little. "I'm feelin' a stab of guilt, kinda like I'm takin' somethin' that don't belong to me."

"Don't feel that way. We both loved Harry. And he loved us. He'd want us to take care of each other."

"Cain't help it."

Bliss took Marsh's hand. "We can't live in the past, Marsh. I'm beginning to realize that. And we can't mourn forever. Harry wouldn't want that. We have to look to the future—both of us."

Marsh nodded. "Here's to the future." He kissed her again.

Moved by gratitude, affection and genuine attraction, Marsh and Bliss were soon sharing words of love. All of them genuine. They did love each other. But not as Harry and Bliss had loved each other, and they both knew it. She was still wearing the opal necklace Harry had given her.

Kisses and warm embraces progressed to greater intimacies, the force of their physical desire overwhelming them both. Bliss and Harry had always been careful and had taken precautions. The first time she and Marsh made love, they did not. Once was all it took. Soon after, Bliss found herself in a family way.

"You're sure?" Marsh said.

She nodded.

"Well, that's it," Marsh said, dropping to one knee. Marsh had no illusions about himself, knew it might be a reach for him to make a suitable husband for a woman as fine as Bliss, but he was determined to do it.

"Bliss Farrell, will you make me the happiest man on earth?"

Tears brimmed in Bliss's eyes. "Yes, Marsh."

Three days later, in a private ceremony at the First Methodist Church with Louise Farrell, Morris True and Clayton Stone in attendance, Reverend Snowy Evans officiating, Bliss Farrell became Mrs. Marshall Stone.

Six weeks later Bliss suffered a miscarriage.

Loss upon loss for husband and wife. Marsh comforted Bliss as best he could, cooked for her, held her while she cried, concealed his own grief. One night while they held each other with tenderness in bed Marsh kissed her forehead and said, "I love you, honey. You know that. Heck, I guess I always did."

"I know. And I love you."

CHAPTER 9

Missing

On May 8, 1945, Harry and his fellow prisoners of war woke to find their German captors had left, taking most of the provisions and all the vehicles with them, and cutting the telephone and telegraph lines before departing. The compound lay hidden deep in a forest, a two-day walk from any main road, three at least from the nearest village, its existence unknown to the Red Cross. Harry and three other prisoners lacked the strength to attempt the long hike out. Two soldiers volunteered to stay with them while the rest went to find help. Seven days later a farmer arrived in a flatbed truck with two of the men who had left riding in the back. In the interim, one of the other prisoners unable to make the initial journey had died.

The farmer and the more able-bodied soldiers loaded Harry and his two debilitated companions onto the truck and took them to the village, where they were transferred to a comfortable room in a large farmhouse. The women of the house bathed them and fed them sips of broth. They called the village doctor. One of the younger women was blond and comely. In his delirium, Harry thought he was back home, being nursed by Bliss.

The clean air and country food, capable care of the farm family and local doctor, and surprising friendliness of the villagers worked wonders on Harry's health. Still, weeks passed before he and his companions regained enough strength to be transferred to the nearest hospital, and weeks more before Harry cared that no one tending him knew his identity.

August came before he had the strength and the presence of mind to say to a nurse in a strained voice, "My name is Harrison True. Hundred and Sixth Infantry. I need you to contact my commanding officer. Tell him I'm alive." A straightforward request. But nothing was simple in the aftermath of the war. The area of eastern Germany where Harry now found himself had been transferred from American to Soviet control a month before, in accordance with the Potsdam Agreement that divided Germany into four Allied Occupation Zones. Things fell through the cracks during the transition. Harry's request was never processed, but he didn't know that and took comfort in imagining his father's and Bliss's relief when they received word that he was alive.

When the Red Cross arrived weeks later, an English-speaking nurse helped Harry write letters to his father and Bliss. It puzzled him that he received no letters in return during his lengthy convalescence but he didn't worry about it too much. Delayed, he thought. The important thing was that Bliss and his dad knew he'd be coming home as soon as he regained his strength.

The second clue something might be amiss came when Harry recovered enough to be transferred to the Port of Le Havre on the coast of France to board a troop transport ship bound for New York. He dismissed this one, too.

"True, Harrison?" the processing sergeant asked.

"That's right."

The sergeant flipped pages, pulled out binders, consulted lists.

"According to this, you're MIA."

"Your list is outdated."

"Sorry, sir. If you'll bear with me, I'm sure we can get this figured out."

Harry was crossing the Atlantic when the telegram telling his father he was alive was finally sent. When he arrived at Fort Dix, New Jersey, for processing in late November, he placed a telephone call to his father first. It fell to Morris True to tell his son the army telegram had arrived only days before and his letters had never arrived at all.

"Dammit. Well, it doesn't matter. I'm back and I'll be home soon. Have to hang up now, Pop. Gotta call Bliss."

"Harry, no."

"What do you mean, no?"

"I . . . I hoped it could wait until you got home."

"Hoped what could wait?"

When Morris True delivered the news Harry had to brace himself against a wall to catch his breath. That night, outside his barracks, he threw the few letters from Bliss he'd managed to save into an empty trash can, tossed in a match and watched them catch fire. He pulled the one photograph of her that had survived the war with him out of his pocket and threw it in last, regretted the act instantly, tried to catch the photo as it fell, reached into the blaze, rescued it and pinched off the char at the corner. What was left of it he tucked away in a breast pocket over his heart.

Harry had been back in Serafina for a couple of weeks when Marsh and Bliss arrived at his door unannounced. They stood on the porch, proper and stiff. Harry answered the knock and stood shielded by the screen. A few uneasy moments passed. Marsh spoke first. Inflecting his words with frequent small chuckles, he tried to appear at ease.

"Hey, Bud. Heard you was back."

Harry felt his throat thickening.

"Damn," Marsh said. "You are a sight for sore eyes, my friend. That MIA bidness give us all a good scare. How long you been home?"

Harry felt dazed.

"Been back a while?" Marsh asked.

"Uh . . . about . . . uh . . . oh . . . a few days, I guess. Tryin' to catch my breath. You know how it is."

Marsh gestured toward the blemished flesh below Harry's left cheekbone. "Looks like you picked up a scar or two."

Harry put fingertips to his cheek.

"They'll go away in time."

Bliss remained silent, taking in the hollowness of Harry's eyes and the dark circles under them, how thin he was.

After another few moments of awkward silence, Harry collected himself and tried to smile, half-way succeeding. He opened the door, doing his best to show a relaxed manner.

"Well, come on in. Don't be standing out there on the porch."

Marsh and Bliss stepped into the living room. Marsh threw his arms around his old friend in a mighty bear hug. Laughing, he lifted him off his feet and made a full circle with him. Harry remained wooden in his blood-tied friend's embrace. When he had his feet under him again, Bliss put out her hand. He took it but for no longer than a second.

"Hey. Hey," Marsh said, forcing a smile. "Might as well get it right out there. Bliss and me . . . we . . . got married." Marsh paused, his eyes flitting from Harry to Bliss and back to Harry. "Course, you know that, I reckon. Anyways . . . we figgered if you couldn't see your way clear to come see us we'd, by God, come see you."

Harry and Marsh faced each other.

"Well," Marsh said after an awkward delay, feigning laughter and glancing again at Bliss, shrugging and turning up his palms. "Ain't you gonna congratulate us?"

It took a full five seconds for Harry to answer. "Oh. Sure . . ." He chose his words with care and when he had them he spoke in a voice that was flat but had an edge to it. "Congratulations. I know . . . I know you'll be . . . happy."

Marsh put his arm around Bliss. "We are," he said, giving her a sideways hug. "Right, honey?"

Bliss gave Marsh a small smile, let herself be squeezed. "That's right."

The conversation was brief. A few words about how good it was to be home and how fortunate they were to be alive and how ready they were to get on with their lives, how they looked forward to picking up where they'd left off a few years before. For the most part, Marsh did the talking. Harry grunted. Bliss fingered the opal necklace lying against her perfect porcelain skin. Harry noticed.

"You need to come for supper soon," Marsh said, squeezing Bliss's shoulders again. "Looks like you could use some good home cookin.'"

Harry nodded.

"We'd like that, wouldn't we, honey?"

Now it was Bliss's turn to nod. "Of course."

Marsh and Bliss took their leave. Harry had taken his first steps on the road to becoming a soft-tongued liar. And so had Bliss.

Later, Harry sat rocking on the porch swing of his family's home. A still evening—no ambient sound, save the faint moaning of a distant train hotshotting for Amarillo and the toiling of swing chains. From time to time, the subtle whoosh of a diving nighthawk. He drifted to and fro, smoking, thinking, remembering. A gray Studebaker entered the drive; he watched it pull up and park. Bliss stepped out.

She came forward, her steps hesitant. When she neared the house, Harry halted the swing. Stood. Feeling a little dizzy, he had to remind himself to breathe.

"I had to see you," Bliss said.

"No, you didn't. You shouldn't have come. Marsh won't hold with you—"

"Marsh knows I'm here. I told him I was coming."

"He didn't mind?"

"Said he didn't. Said I owed it to you."

"He lied."

"Maybe. Anyway . . . Harry, what we had—"

Harry stopped her with an upraised hand.

"Don't."

Bliss and Harry stared at each other, Harry still standing on the porch, hands now shoved into his back pockets, Bliss on the grass, girding herself with folded arms.

"After we got that first telegram and the letters from your CO," Bliss said, "I kinda fell apart. The war ended and still nothing." She searched his face for some sign of understanding. "You can't imagine the state I was in."

"And Marsh was there to comfort you. Ready and willing. You, too, I guess. Ready and willing."

Bliss sensed in him none of the love that still filled her. Only anger. And hurt. Without so much as a farewell wave, she walked back to her car, reached for the door, but didn't open it, turned back to him, tears coursing down her cheeks.

"We thought you were dead, you know."

"I wasn't."

"You didn't write. I was here, waiting. Waiting and waiting . . . for you."

"I'm here now."

She bowed her head. "Too late. It's too late now."

Harry shrugged. "Oh, well, *c'est la guerre.*"

He descended the steps.

"I have one question," he said.

Bliss looked up.

"Do you love him?"

She drew in a breath.

"Yes."

Harry stared at her. "No, you don't."

Bliss wiped her cheeks.

"Well . . . I'm glad you're home, Harry. And that you're all right."

"Am I? Is that what I am? All right?"

Bliss took a half-step toward him, opened her mouth to speak.

Harry stepped back. "No. There's nothing more to say. You're Marsh's wife now. That's all there is to it. Pretty simple. Now we get on with life. That's the way it's supposed to work. Right?"

"Yes, I guess that's the way it's supposed to work."

"Well, forget that. I'll be leaving soon."

Bliss's hand flew to her necklace. "Where will you go?"

"I don't know. California, maybe. Some place far away. I always wanted to sign on with the Tejon Ranch out there."

"You used to talk about that. I remember."

A pause.

"I'd say stay in touch," Bliss said, "but I know you won't. Will you?"

"With you?" Harry shook his head. "No."

"Well then, goodbye again, Harry. I'll check in with your dad now and then if you don't mind."

Harry shrugged.

Bliss got into her car and drove away. Harry stood alone, watching her taillights recede in the darkness.

CHAPTER 10

Tejon

Harry pulled up stakes. Like his ancestors before him he went west to make a new life. After a few weeks of wandering, he found himself at the headquarters of Tejon Ranch, located at the gateway to California's central valley, about thirty miles south of Bakersfield. He'd read about Tejon and knew the ranch had been established in 1843 as a Mexican land grant. One of the largest working ranches in North America, the outfit occupied some two hundred seventy thousand acres of oak-covered hills, rugged mountains, broad valleys, steep canyons, vast stretches of wide-open grazing land, lakes and streams. Wildlife abounded: deer, elk, antelope, wild pigs, turkey, black bear, bobcats, coyotes, and quail. The perfect hermitage for a man whose life was a shambles.

Harry entered what he took for the ranch headquarters and encountered a weather-beaten fellow with a drooping, gray moustache. The man, who had to be at least ten years Harry's senior, sat at a desk half buried under logs and ledgers. He put down the paperwork in his hands.

"Afternoon. Can I hep you?"

"Looking for work. Thought you might be able to use a hand."

"Might be we could. This here's a cow-calf operation. Can you cowboy?"

Harry nodded. The man behind the desk gestured toward a chair. Harry sat.

"You the bossman?"

"One of 'em. I ain't the majordomo as they say in these parts. More like ramrod. One of 'em anyways. Name's Branum, J. T. Branum. What name you go by?"

"Harry True."

"I like the name. Sometimes a name says a lot about the man who wears it. That go for you?"

"Hope so."

"Where you hail from, Mr. True?"

"Oklahoma."

"Oklahoma. Well, I'll be damned. Okie myself. Come out here with my folks when I's still wet behind the ears. Dust Bowl back in Cimarron County damn near ruint us."

J. T. shook his head. "Okie. Don't know why I said that. Never cared much for the handle."

"Neither do I."

J. T. looked at the ceiling, appearing to call up something from memory, lowered his gaze to Harry.

"You know what Will Rogers said about us folks that moved to California to find work. Said we raised the average IQ of both states. Funny, I guess, but not what you'd call a compliment to any of the parties concerned."

Branum smiled. So did Harry.

"What brings you to California?"

Harry shrugged. "Gotta be somewhere."

"Don't matter. Unless the law's after you. You ain't on the dodge, are you?"

"No."

"Didn't figure you was. You don't look the type."

Branum let a few seconds pass before continuing.

"Was you in the war?"

Harry nodded.

"That where you got them scars?"

Harry nodded again.

"What theater?"

"Europe. Hundred and Sixth Infantry Division."

"The Bulge, huh?"

Harry nodded.

"Me, too," J. T. said. "Second Armored."

A faraway look came over the ramrod. "Well, time marches on. 'Fore long all that'll be ancient history. Few years from now won't nobody hardly remember."

"The way it works, I suppose."

"For some folks. Not for us old boys that was there."

Harry didn't agree or disagree.

"Can you ride and rope? Thow a hoolihan? String bob-wire, fix fence?"

"Yessir."

"Gentle a horse? Pull a calf?"

"I can."

"Any objection to working long hours rain or shine, spending days on end in the saddle, a lot of it off by your lonesome?"

"That's what I'm here for."

"Job pays one hundred dollars a month and found. That suit you?"

"Right down to the ground."

"Mighty fine. Bleve you'll do to ride the river with. When can you start?"

"Anything wrong with right now?"

"Nary a thing. Welcome to *Rancho El Tejon.*"

The two men shook on it.

"Here's the rules," Branum said. "No drinkin', no gamblin', no fightin' on the ranch. What you do in town is your bidness. Cause trouble for us you'll be outa here lickety split. Any questions?"

"No, sir."

Branum raised his arm and aimed it through the front window at a long barracks-looking building a hundred yards distant.

"Bunkhouse. Head on down yonder and pick you out a bunk, stow your gear. You'll run into a feller name of Hank. Tell him I hired you. He'll put you to work."

On his way out, Harry stopped and turned to J. T.

"By the way, there is one thing."

"I'm not sure I like the sound of that. What is it?"

"The word *tejon.* What's it mean?"

J. T. smiled.

"Badger."

"Why badger?"

"We got badgers in Oklahoma, don't we?"

"A few."

"Ever seen one?"

"I have."

"So you know. They got claws and teeth. And they're about as sociable as an ulcerated back tooth. You don't mess with 'em. Savvy?"

After Harry got located, he let his father and Esau know where he was. Both of them were getting on in years and, as much as he wanted to get shed of Oklahoma, he needed to stay in touch with his family. From time to time, as he settled into his new life, he exchanged correspondence with them. On important occasions, like birthdays and Christmas, he called his dad long distance. He never asked about Marsh or Bliss; his father never mentioned them. Neither did Esau.

Working daybreak to dark, six days out of seven, Harry honed his skills as a horseman and cowman. He and his *compañeros*, full-timers and some itinerants who answered the seasonal call for staffing up, worked cattle twice a year: spring branding in May after the calving season; fall gather in October.

In the spring they sorted the newly born calves, branded and vaccinated them. They culled out the bull calves that would be kept for breeding, the rest they castrated so they'd put on weight, not burn off pounds chasing heifers. "The idea's to change their attitude from ass to grass," J. T. Branum liked to say.

In the summer, they put the breeding bulls on the cows. The entire herd spent a few months on lush pastureland, fattening up. Then came the fall works, the busiest time of year when the crew handled every feeder on the place. The cowboys gathered the cow-calf pairs, pregchecked the cows, weaned the calves, vaccinated any born in the late spring. The weaners, five or six months old and husky from feasting on rich milk and good grass, had become sturdy enough to be turned out to pasture. The bigger steers were cut out and put into the main herd, driven to the shipping pens.

Between the two works the size of the crew dwindled and the remaining ranch hands shouldered all the mundane ranch work required to keep a large-scale cow-calf operation going. They watched over the first-calf heifers, strung wire, fixed fence, baled and put up hay that would carry the livestock in the high country through winter. They busted broncs, moved cattle from pasture to pasture to avoid overgrazing, maintained rolling stock, battled pestilence and fire, made war on insects and ground squirrels who'd tear up every square inch of Tejon sod if they could. Some of the crew rode out in twos and threes from time to time to man winter camps and tend the herd.

Always working for a dollar to make a dime, the cowboys sometimes fell to bellyaching that the life they'd chosen didn't make a damn bit of sense. But after a couple of beers in town on a night off they'd laugh off their complaints and agree that every ounce of pain and misery was worth it. Despite their penury and stiff joints and sun-parched skin, they saw themselves as the exalted ones of the American West. They were, by God, cowboys. Few men could say that.

Riding for the Cross Crescent brand, drawing straight cowboy wages, Harry regained his balance and his focus. He made a top hand. More than that, he learned the business of ranching: managing the land and livestock, managing people. As J. T. put it, he learned how to "talk hoss and talk cow." He built a reputation for being an excellent horseman, a genuine cowman, and a square dealer. And he had a full immersion in the Code of the West, a body of unwritten rules of behavior crafted and handed down by generations of cowboys. Among its canons were these: act with courage, speak the truth, keep your word, talk less and say more, never pet another man's dog.

Harry and J. T. Branum became friends. In no time the foreman was passing on responsibilities to his fellow Oklahoman. They worked shoulder-to-shoulder at the spring branding, fall gather, everything in between. From time to time, they'd ride the line, inspecting fences to see if they were up and in good shape, checking grass and water levels. Sometimes they'd be out for a few days, spend the evenings by a blazing campfire. They slept under the stars or in a dilapidated line shack. They talked about horses, cattle, the ranching business, swapped war stories.

On one such night, sitting at a campfire, they fell to admiring a massive old-growth live oak. "Good God Almighty that there is some tree," J. T. posited. "Musta stood right there in that very spot since Adam was a pup."

"Four, five hundred years at least."

J. T. shifted his gaze to distant peaks bluing in the dusk. "I do love this country. It ain't Oklahoma, of course, but I love it. All four hundred twenty-two square miles inside our fences. The Lord done good work here."

He raised his eyes to the heavens. "And I love this cowboy life. Don't make no money, but we do get to see that ever night. Come morning, we get to see a eagle fly. Man can be rich as Croesus, but he cain't buy that."

Harry watched his friend as he spoke, sensed sorrow in his voice.

J. T. went on. "Won't last forever, you know. Oh, well, times change. People change. Tejon's a big outfit, but they've already got us whittled down pretty good. Time was we run a herd of twenty-five thousand head on this range. Twenty-five thousand. Now, it ain't even half that."

"Still pretty impressive."

"Well . . . ."

"How long you been here?"

"You mean on Tejon?"

"Yeah."

"Ohh, since the mid-thirties. Run off from home and sorta ended up here. Kinda like you. And . . . one thing led to another. You know. I stayed. Guess I'm the kind that stays. Seems to me like you may be cut from the same cloth."

"You ever been married?"

"Ahh, yeah, oncest. But the war put a end to that. My wife, well . . . she didn't want me to go. Bein' older and a little stove-up, I prolly coulda dodged it. But, I had to see the elephant."

He laughed a little, sobered.

"Time I got home she'd took up with another feller, 4F type. Shoe salesman. Imagine that. A damn shoe salesman. Wudn't perty."

"So it goes," Harry said, staring at the fire. "I guess it's a common story."

"That your story, too?"

"Never married. Came pretty close, but the war ruined that for me, too."

"So, you got more than a Purple Heart. You got a broken heart, too."

J. T. waited a few seconds before he spoke again.

"You're still young, you know. There's hope for you. As for me, well, I'm gettin' kindly long in the tooth for women . . . at least the marryin' kind."

"Well," Harry said, "Enough talk about women. Think I'll turn in."

Over time, Harry became convinced he wouldn't be content forever being a simple cowpuncher, or working for another man, no matter the cut of his jib. He loved the work, but he wanted it to count for something more. He wanted to have his own ranch. With that in mind, he designed his brand: a capital T with a horizontal line above it. He called it the Bar T; he'd register it with the Cattlemen's Association. Next, he applied himself to working out in his mind the kind of spread he'd have, how much start-up money it would take, how he could make a go of it from year to year. And where it would be: maybe California, maybe west Texas, maybe New Mexico. Any place but Sebastian County, Oklahoma.

Well into his second year at Tejon, Harry was back at the ranch headquarters, relaxing in his bunk after a shower and a hot meal, when another hand called his name.

"True! Phone call!"

He went out to the communal wall phone in the corridor and picked up the receiver the ranch hand had left dangling.

It was Esau Coats. Morris True had taken ill. He was doing poorly. "You best come arunnin," Esau said gravely.

The next morning, Harry headed east.

CHAPTER 11

Ruth

In three days' time Harry was back home to nurse his father through the last days of his life. Hearing his truck come up the drive, Polly Coats rushed out to greet him.

"Praise Heaven," she said as Harry came up the front steps.

"How is he, Polly?"

She shook her head sadly, took his hand and led him back to his father's bedroom.

His second day in Serafina, his old friend Ruth Blaylock showed up at the door, casserole in hand.

"Ruth."

"Harry. I didn't know you were back."

A pleasant surprise for both of them. Their parents had been close friends while Harry and Ruth were growing up, and the families often had Sunday dinner together. Harry had always liked Ruth; she was Ruth Calvert in those days. Tall and pretty with umber eyes and chestnut hair, kind and intelligent. She had introduced him to Walt Whitman and taught him to play chess. But she never held a candle to Bliss. And, besides, she was a little old for Harry, five years his senior, and everyone knew she had given her heart to Joe Blaylock.

Ruth was a war widow now. Joe, a Navy flyer, had died in the Battle of Midway. "She's a good soul," Polly whispered to Harry as Ruth took the casserole into the kitchen. "Comes by once in a while to help with your dad. Poor thing. Broke her heart all to pieces when she lost Joe."

"Good to see you, Harry," Ruth said, coming out of the kitchen. "You in town for a while?"

"Yes. Not sure how long."

"Well, maybe we could get together before you leave, catch up a little."

"I'd like that."

A week later, Harry's father died. Marsh and Bliss attended the funeral and, along with other family friends, came to the house afterward to pay their respects. It was the first time Harry had seen either of them since heading west two years before, and the sight of Bliss shook him. She was more beautiful than ever and Marsh appeared to be a proud married man.

"Sorry for your loss, old buddy," Marsh said.

"Your father was a good man," Bliss said.

Her nearness quickened Harry's heart. His eyes sought out the neckline of her demure black dress, checking for the opal pendant. She wasn't wearing it. Of course not, he told himself. Why would she?

"How long are you planning to stay?" Bliss asked to fill the ponderous silence.

"Not long."

"Don't suppose you'd like to come out for supper one night," Marsh asked. He patted his stomach, smiled at Bliss. "This wife of mine's a mighty fine cook."

"Thank you, but no, I got a lot of work to do settling Dad's estate. And Ruth and Polly are keeping me pretty well fed."

"No doubt," Marsh said. "Well . . . ." He extended a hand.

Harry hesitated, took it. He nodded to Bliss, spoke her name. She spoke his. Their eyes met for an instant. Harry saw something, or thought he did, before Bliss looked away. And the notion of staying in Sebastian County began to take root in Harry's mind.

The next day, Harry and Esau chatted about what Harry might do next. Would he return to the golden state? Start his own ranch? Go to New York to be a writer? Sail the seven seas? He didn't know.

"You took good care of your daddy these last days," Esau said. "It do you credit that you come home like you did. So, now that he gone to his reward, you can light out again. Don'tcha reckon?"

"You trying to get rid of me?"

"No, sir. Figgered you had short bidness here. Now that's done with. Lord knows how hard bein' in these parts must be for you."

"Hard?"

"You know what I mean."

"You don't think I can make a go of it here, huh?"

"'Spect not. Oh, you could make a livin' all right. But this place ain't no good for you. Not no more."

"So you think I oughta leave?"

"Prolly better had. 'Course, sometimes advice is worth exactly what it costs. In this case, nothin.'"

Esau's advice was sound; Harry knew it. But he didn't take it. He stayed.

Harry tried for a while to operate his father's grocery and feed business. But he was no storekeeper. He had promised himself he would be a cowman and a horse breeder. He sold the store, used the money and the rest of his inheritance to buy a full section of land in the southern part of the county. It was suitable cow country, as fine a spread as could be found in Sebastian County: for the most part pastureland, tall native grass, good water, a few stands of timber. He built a house on it, erected an imposing main gate of wrought iron with his brand at the center. A year later, he acquired grazing rights on a remote tract of rough range-land to the south. The latter parcel was expansive but much poorer country than the first: sparse graze, canyon-riven in places, a shallow basin of seep water here and there, a couple of dribbling streams. The back end of nowhere, but the price was right. The Bar T was growing. Harry joked to Esau that before long it would be as big as Tejon Ranch.

Harry tried to lead a solitary life. But it wasn't easy with a ranch to run and hands to manage, supplies to order and stock, friends and neighbors who kept calling and coming by, inviting him over for a meal and out for a beer.

Little by little, Harry and Marsh had no choice but to mend the rift between them. They didn't do it by airing their grievances and talking through their claims and defenses but by ignoring them, letting them stew. As it had been their duty to go to war, it was their duty to get on with life after it. Harry and Bliss forced themselves to believe that, despite everything they'd been to each other in the past, they could now be friends and nothing more. They would fake it if they had to. Festering rancor be damned.

For female company, Harry took up with Ruth Blaylock. Still pretty, full-figured, Ruth had a pleasant manner, an inviting tone of voice. But Harry sensed a great sadness about her, an emptiness that could not be filled, and a dearth of hope. The war had robbed her of the love of her life and the ability to take any real joy in it. The perfect woman for Harry. She took pleasure in the time they spent together, demanded nothing more. Whatever happened, happened. Whatever came her way, blessing or curse, she accepted.

Despite everything, though, Ruth still possessed a kind and gen-erous spirit. When Harry showed up at her house unexpected late at night, she opened the door. If he'd had too much to drink, she put him to bed, slipped between the sheets with him. When he fell ill, she nursed him. Weeks might pass with no contact between them, but that didn't matter to Ruth. She was always there when Harry called or came around.

Harry was careful never to hurt Ruth, never to take advantage of her. He respected her, and her friendship meant too much to him. Adhering to that code, he made no promises. And he never lied to her.

One midsummer morning, Harry and Ruth lay in her bed, gazing through an open window at the rose-colored dawn.

"Harry, do you love me?" Ruth said. "Sorry. You don't have to answer."

Harry considered the question. "Love. What is that . . . exactly?"

But on reflection, he judged his response insufficient. He knew that answering a question with a question was a coward's way of dodging the truth. Ruth deserved more.

"Yes . . . I do love you," he added. "But probably not in the way you mean."

"No. Not in that way. That's what I like about you, Harry. No pretense. No artifice. You are an honest man. I don't love you in that way either. The truth is . . . I sometimes try to imagine you're Joe. You don't mind, do you? It doesn't work, anyway."

"I need you, I can tell you that. I truly do."

"And I need you. No need to make more of it."

Ruth suspected Harry would disappear someday. He'd head back West or find a deeper love. One knock at her door would be the last. It had happened to her once. Why not again?

Sturdy stock, Ruth made a good show of contentment most of the time. So did Harry. Often, they went together to parties and banquets, out for a night of dancing at Sweet Leona's. They talked and laughed, enjoyed each other's company. They even pulled off double-dating with Marsh and Bliss. To the undiscerning eye, they resembled any other established couple. But from time to time, when something distracted Marsh, Harry fixed Bliss with a covetous gaze. And Ruth noticed.

Harry and Marsh seldom talked about the war. They never discussed the events that led to Marsh and Bliss being married. But there was one night, not long after Harry returned to Serafina, when Marsh came close to delivering a *mea culpa*. He and Harry were swilling down a few drinks at Sweet Leona's.

"I know how you must feel," Marsh said that night, apropos of nothing, sounding glum and wounded. "Looking back, I mean. You laid up in some Kraut hospital. Me here with Bliss. I know. Don't think I don't."

Harry sipped his beer, said nothing.

"Seems kindly crazy now," Marsh continued. "But that's hindsight. Twenty-twenty, as they say. That little gal was busted up bad when your dad got that telegram. Then the war ended, and you didn't come home . . . ." Marsh swirled his drink. "You asked me to take care of her . . . ."

"And you did."

Marsh disregarded the jab.

"Bliss . . . We . . . We thought you was dead." Marsh took a swallow of his whiskey. He wanted to explain the delicate circumstances that had prompted his proposal to Bliss but held back. No one knew about her pregnancy and miscarriage except the two of them and Polly Coats, who'd been at her side again at the hospital. Bliss had made them both swear never to breathe a word about it to anyone.

Marsh took another sip of his drink. "Point is, we didn't think you was comin' back. If I'da known, it wouldn't've . . . We never would've . . . After all, you and Bliss had—"

"We had nothing. Not a damn thing. Not really. If we did, it's over. Let it go. In the long run, none of that matters anyway. That's where we are now, right? The long run."

Marsh scrubbed his face with his palms.

"Guess I'm feelin' my liquor. Better shut up 'fore my mouth overloads my ass. If it ain't already."

There the matter rested. Marsh never again came near making an apology.

For the game Harry was playing he hewed to a rigid social construct. First and foremost, keep your distance from Bliss. Do not under any circumstances allow yourself to be alone with her. No talking about old times, no touching, not so much as hand grazing hand in the passing of a coffee cup. In a crowded room, if her scent, one you know well, happens to penetrate your olfactory sense, walk away. In group conversations act confident, satisfied with your life. Talk about the success of the Bar T. Talk about Ruth. If Bliss and Ruth are both present, pay special attention to Ruth. Whatever it takes, show Bliss, and Marsh, that you're over her. Make her think she didn't hurt you by marrying Marsh, that your separation would have happened anyway, that your youthful passion had run its course. In short, betray no sign of your true feelings. She's your friend's wife, nothing more.

Harry succeeded in keeping faith with the protocol. But he couldn't control what he felt. Every time his eyes found Bliss and she returned his gaze, he knew the feelings were still there. And, though she never let on, Ruth knew it, too. She saw it in the distance Harry kept from Bliss when the four of them were together, the care he took to avoid touching her. She took particular note of his amped-up displays of affection when Bliss was around.

Bliss didn't see what Ruth saw. She saw a man she still loved but had lost forever. He was back now, but not for her. His father's illness had brought him home, and now his new ranch and a new love kept him here. Bliss was determined not to reveal her feelings or make even the slightest attempt to rekindle his. He had no real feelings for her anymore anyway. She thought she saw something in his eyes sometimes but, more and more, she became convinced it was nothing but wishful thinking on her part. And, after all, she was a married woman. She was Mrs. Marshall Stone. Marsh wasn't Harry, but he was a good man. So Bliss kept her distance from Harry, too. Didn't give him a jot of unnecessary attention. When they were together she maintained an air of lightheartedness. She displayed extraordinary affection for Marsh, complimenting his good looks and brash sense of humor. Heaped praise upon him for his multitude of skills. "I swear," she'd say, touching his shoulder, "I don't think there's anything this man can't do." She adopted the persona of a contented, married woman. Marsh loved it. Harry endured it. Bliss knew it was all an act, and so did Ruth.

For a time, it all held. But for Harry and Bliss, the walls they'd built to contain their feelings couldn't stand forever. The first crack appeared one Saturday afternoon three years after Harry's return when he encountered Bliss in the Five and Dime. By some skullduggery of fate, at the same moment, each stepped into the housewares section at opposite ends of the aisle. Facing each other, they froze. Harry took a half-step back, turned away, turned back, froze again. Wits keened by experience abandoned him. He'd broken his own rule of decorum.

Bliss began appraising cookie tins. Harry walked right up to her.

"Bliss," he said, dissembling a benign greeting, tipping his hat.

"Harry, nice to see you."

They stood, eyes locked, close enough to kiss if either leaned forward even a little bit. Harry felt himself teeter. The laughter of children coming from the next aisle over startled them both back a step.

Harry touched his hat again. "Well, have a nice day."

"Thank you. You, too."

Still they stood gazing into each other's eyes. Everything they'd ever felt for each other was still there. And they both knew it.

On a Friday night two weeks later, Marsh and Bliss, Harry and Ruth sat down for a potluck supper at the First Methodist Church. Despite his attempt at artful dodging, Harry found himself seated on a bench next to Bliss. Her soft, well-modulated voice in his ear, her perfumed scent, the press of her shoulder against his as she reached for the salt, the water pitcher, proved more than he could bear. Late in the evening, acting on an impulse, he reached under the table as Bliss was commenting on the biscuits and, concealed by the checkered fabric cloth hanging over the edge, laid his hand next to hers where it rested on the bench, little fingers touching. She took a small breath and went on talking, didn't look at Harry, didn't move her hand. Slowly, he covered her hand with his own. A current flowed through them. It felt right.

Harry had always loved Bliss's hands. Tapering fingers, delicate skin, fine veins, slender-boned wrists. Before the war, when they would lie with bodies entwined on the grassy banks of Blue Creek, he would admire them, study them. "The work of a master craftsman," the enraptured youth once proclaimed. And on another day, word-smitten as always, holding her hand, kissing it, he summoned a line from Shakespeare: "Now join your hands, and with your hands your hearts."

Three nights after the church supper, when Marsh left town hauling a load of cattle, Harry went to Blue Creek, following a crazy feeling Bliss might be there. She wasn't. He breathed in the night air, quailed at his own buffoonery, turned to get back in his truck, and saw a car approaching. When it came to a stop, Bliss stepped out.

"You came," Harry said. "I hoped you would."

"I shouldn't have."

"But you did."

"I suppose we both knew this would happen someday."

"It was inevitable."

"Do you remember the first time we came here?" Bliss said.

"Like it was yesterday. It looks the same."

"Same creek. But not the same water."

"New water."

He took her in his arms and kissed her. And she kissed him back.

From that day forward they made no attempt to bridle their hearts—only to be discreet in satisfying their desire. A series of clandestine rendezvous followed. Harry and Bliss now had a secret to keep.

PART THREE

CHAPTER 12

Whites Only

Since World War II something folks were calling the Civil Rights Movement had been sweeping across the country. Old ways were yielding to new. During their second evening together at Blue Creek, as Harry and Bliss lay on the old scarlet and black Navajo blanket Bliss had spread out, gazing up at the stars, Harry wondered aloud about where it would all lead.

"That Supreme Court decision seems to have a lot of folks riled up," he said. "Some say they should tend to their own knittin.'" He was quoting Marsh but he wasn't going to say so.

"Times change," Bliss said. "And that's good. We have to change with them."

Harry was about to say he basically agreed when Bliss said in a dreamy whisper, "Time and the world are ever in flight."

Harry smiled. "Yeats," he said.

Sheriff Dutch Mackey couldn't quote poetry, but he had a nose for trouble. By the early summer of 1954 he could smell it beating a path to Sebastian County. An avid reader of the *Daily Oklahoman*, the state's largest newspaper, he'd been watching storm clouds gather for a long time. In 1948, the University of Oklahoma admitted its first African American student. That same year, President Truman issued an executive order ending segregation in the U.S. Armed Services. Black soldiers fought alongside white soldiers in the Korean War. In January of '53, Oklahoma writer Ralph Ellison received the National Book Award for his novel *Invisible Man,* making him the first man of color to be so honored. And in May of the current calendar year, the U.S. Supreme Court announced its decision in *Brown v. Board of Education*, striking down the separate but equal doctrine that had been the law since 1896.

Most white Oklahomans reacted to the coming of integration with acceptance, grudging for some. Often, when they talked about it among themselves they did it in a low tone, if not in whispers. Sometimes they joked about it, trying to lighten the mood. But political leaders across the South were pledging uncompromising resistance. Some vowed to fight back . . . with violence if necessary. Sheriff Mackey was hearing rumblings of that type in his county.

First elected the year after he came home from the war, Dutch Mackey had served as sheriff for the better part of a decade. Now somewhere around fifty years old, he had a great mass of steel gray hair. A bull-built man, standing over six feet tall, and square-shouldered, he had arms as big around as two on most men. On his upper lip he sported a walrus moustache with sides drooping, tips turning up in the style favored by law dogs of the preceding century. He had a booming voice and an animated method of communication. Animated—that was Harry's word. He used it because of the good sheriff's flamboyant gestures. Marsh put it more simply. He said Dutch couldn't say hell with his hands tied.

Double tough, Sheriff Mackey minced no words. When he made up his mind to do something, he brooked no contradiction. He didn't toady to anyone and wouldn't be stampeded into anything. He could take all comers. He'd turned a key on many a loutish drunk, but he sent them on their way when they sobered up, unless they'd stabbed or shot somebody. He saw no point in bringing a man up on charges for an offense no more serious than cutting the wolf loose.

Dutch and Doris Ann, his wife of more than a score of years, lived in the apartment attached to the courthouse and calaboose. Small and modest but home for them. It suited them well. They had no children and didn't aspire to the trappings of wealth and position. It wouldn't have mattered if they had. Their status derived from the badge the sheriff wore, his legendary fairness, and his wife's stouteartedness and unfailing good nature.

The sheriff tried to keep his ear to the ground and his finger on the pulse of his county. Frequently, he strolled through downtown Serafina, watching, listening, making his presence known. At least twice a week, often after dark, he and Doris Ann drove through every quadrant of Sebastian County in the sheriff's old black and white Dodge. Other times, when he needed to think, he drove out alone. In his law enforcement method, he likened himself to Marshal Matt Dillon, of the radio program *Gunsmoke.* The Old West badge-toter made nightly rounds in Dodge City; Dutch Mackey followed his example.

One more thing about the sheriff: He was known for being good to coloreds. But that didn't mean he failed to respect the boundaries set for them by the mores of the times and local Jim Crow laws. On the contrary, he saw to it that coloreds adhered to the strict admonition of the WHITES ONLY signs over the drinking fountain and the bathrooms in public buildings. But in private conversations with Sebastian County's leading citizens, including Harry True, he confided that, sooner or later, those signs were going to have to come down.

A week or so after the court ruling in *Brown,* someone had graffitied a black X with a thick-cored carpenter's pencil across one of the signs. And a couple of the bolder members of the Negro community had confronted the sheriff about them. He told Harry and Marsh about it over beers at Sweet Leona's.

The sheriff gave Marsh a sidelong glance. "And it ain't just a few grumpy members of Serafina's colored community we're talkin' about here," he said. "I been gettin' a earful from some of our own womenfolk, too."

"Bliss?" Marsh said.

"She's one of 'em, yessir." He winked at Marsh. "Women with strong opinions. Seems that's something you and me have in common."

Marsh chuckled. "Yeah. Bliss told me she'd had a word with you on the subject."

Sheriff Mackey coughed up a laugh. "A word, huh? That's how she put it?" Dutch proceeded to describe how Bliss had marched right up to him on the street one day and commenced reading the dog-law right out loud to him. "You know what she said? She said them signs have to go. She demanded it. Said we gotta do better by the children in Black Flats, too. Said we should hold a fundraiser to help out the school, buy new textbooks, hire another teacher. Told me the twentieth century is more than half over and it's high time it made its debut in Sebastian County." The sheriff widened his eyes in mock surprise. "For such a sweet little old gal, she can get hoppin' mad in a hurry. She kept a decent tongue in her head, but she come on strong. I mean strong as granny's breath, by God."

Marsh cracked a knowing smile at the sheriff's plaint.

"Don't suppose you could get her to tone it down a tad bit," Dutch said. "Take things a little slower."

Marsh snorted. "Nope. Not a gambler's chance."

The sheriff loosed a long slow sigh. "Figgered."

Sheriff Mackey and the county commissioners decided to adopt a wait-and-see attitude about the changes coming their way: wait to see how folks around the state took to the Supreme Court decision before deciding on a course of action. It made for an uncomfortable time in Sebastian County, with some members of the Negro community becoming less deferential and more resentful of whites, and some members of the white community becoming openly hostile to Negroes. The WHITES ONLY signs were being defaced with regularity. Some started disappearing. For every one that did, it seemed, a rock got thrown through a window of a home or storefront in Black Flats.

Esau confided to Harry as they sat together on Esau's porch one evening sipping some of Polly's lemonade that he was worried for his son Woody. "He looks a lot older than he is, if you understand my meaning. He's more like a kid inside. He'll say howdy to anybody, thinks he's welcome anywhere. It's partly his mama and my's fault. After losing the ones we lost, we put all our lovin' on him. Spoilt him for sure. But now I worry he ain't ready for times like these. 'Fraid he might say somethin' that don't set right with somebody, get too friendly with the wrong person, and . . ." Esau squinted into the setting sun. "I got this feelin' something's gonna happen to that boy. Cain't seem to shake it." Brow furrowed, he said to Harry. "I'd be obliged to you if you'd look out for him."

Harry wanted to tell Esau not to worry. Nothing was going to happen to Woody. But Woody had already taken one beating because of his innocent friendliness and Esau was serious. So instead, Harry agreed.

After the dust of the *Brown* decision had begun to settle, Sheriff Mackey and the county commissioners held a secret meeting to try to figure out what to do. As a stall tactic the commissioners announced they were taking the ruling under advisement and would be preparing a report on how best to comply with the Court's order that states desegregate "with all deliberate speed."

Bliss was thrilled. "I kept saying we needed to improve the school in Black Flats," she told Marsh over dinner the day she brought him home from the hospital with a cast on his leg. "But it would be even better if we built a new school, one for everybody, don't you think?"

Marsh shrugged, concentrating on his supper. So happy to be eating his wife's cooking again he could do no more than half-listen to what she was saying.

"And while they're dragging their feet on what to do about the schools, maybe now they'll get rid of those horrible 'whites only' signs. It's the least they could do, don't you think?"

Marsh put down his knife and fork, sat back.

"You are not going to let that go, are you?"

Bliss showed an impish smile as she got up to cut him a piece of her peach pie, his favorite. "No. I am not."

The issue came to a rolling boil a few weeks later. When word got around that the issue of the WHITES ONLY signs might be on the agenda for the upcoming meeting of the county commissioners. Bliss resolved to attend as an interested citizen. Marsh knew better than to try to stop her.

"You OK going without me?" he said.

"I'll be fine. Esau and Polly will be there. And Sheriff Mackey, of course."

The meeting room was filled, mostly with white folks who wanted the signs to stay in place. Along with other like-minded citizens, including Ruth Blaylock, Buddy Pond, who headed up the volunteer fire brigade, and Di Loveless, owner of Sweet Leona's since her sister Leona had passed away, Bliss waited for the chance to speak. When it appeared the meeting would end without the matter of the signs being taken up, she sprang to her feet.

"Hold on a minute," she called out, hand in the air.

The selectmen, who had failed to make the escape they'd hoped for, exchanged glances.

"Ma'am," the chairman said, acknowledging her.

"There's one more matter to deal with. The 'whites only' signs."

"What about 'em?"

"They have to go. The days of separate but equal are over. The Supreme Court said so."

The room erupted with pro and con factions yelling and waving their arms at each other. The chairman banged his gavel and shouted "Order! Order!" until everyone quieted back down.

In the end, the commissioners refused to address the matter that evening. But they did agree to take it up at the next regular meeting.

As Bliss and her allies left the meeting room and headed for their cars, other residents of Serafina who opposed removing the signs—neighbors who ordinarily smiled and said "Good Morning" when they passed on the street—pressed close around them, muttering imprecations. Bliss saw Billy Catlett with Clayton Stone, both of them leaning against a wall. Billy was grinning. Clayton averted his gaze when Bliss caught his eye. *He's embarrassed,* she thought. It didn't surprise her to see Billy there, though she continued to believe there was good in him somewhere way down deep. But Clayton had youth on his side. She hated that Billy held so much sway over him. If only Marsh weren't so hard on him. If only Clayton weren't such a lazy, mouthy kid. She loved them both and they loved her. But she couldn't seem to heal the breach between them no matter how hard she tried.

CHAPTER 13

Alejandra

A few weeks after the council meeting, on a Tuesday night in late July, Billy Catlett had something other than WHITES ONLY signs on his mind. Ambitions for a night of tomcatting had led him and his acolyte, Clayton Stone, to the invisible seam running between Serafina proper and the Mexican section. Roosted up behind the wheel in his truck like some raptor fowl, Catlett had his eye on a young girl laboring alone at a self-service laundry—the same girl he'd accused Woody Coats of hitting on the day he tore into him on Main Street. Clayton, already half-stuporous from drink, paid little attention to the girl, who couldn't have been more than fourteen years old. The lustful congress he envisioned for the night involved a bottle of snake-eye whiskey.

Foul weather threatened. Catlett had been hearing the vibratory rumble of dark-bellied clouds in the southwest for a while, but he'd counted on any stormfront taking shape in that distant territory to play out before it reached Serafina. It didn't. Without warning, a bolt of ribbon lightning zigzagged across the sky and struck nearby. Seconds later a clap of thunder and a fusillade of wind brought forth a downpour.

"My luck," Catlett groused. "We finally get rain and it has to come right now."

But soon the stormlight darkened and the rain resolved into a steady drizzle. Catlett remained focused. Through a moisture-blurred windshield and a row of open six-foot casement windows that ran the length of the whitewashed concrete building, he followed the movement of the bronze-skinned girl with predatory eyes. She bus-tled back and forth between a galvanized steel ringer washtub and a work-table that centered the room, a place for sorting and folding damp underdrawers. From afar, he studied the girl's anatomy: spread of shoulders, swell of hips, vague contours of small high breasts. What he couldn't see, he imagined.

"Mmmh, mmmh, mmmh," he said in a low, lusty voice, popping his knuckles, licking his lips. "Would you feast your eyes on that little hot tamale. Them tennis ball titties. Not what you'd call bodacious, but nice."

Slouching against the passenger door like a bored teenager, Clay-ton Stone took another jolt of tanglefoot.

"Come on. Let's get out of here."

Ignoring the kid, Catlett checked his appearance in the rearview mirror.

"Come on, Billy," Clayton whined. "Let's go."

"Hey, dingus. You can go home and lope your mule like some snot-nosed kid if you want to. Not me. No, siree. I am hornier'n a three-peckered billy goat. And that little gal's beggin' for it. Look at her. I can tell she'd love for me to plow her a new furrow."

"Hey, I'm all for skirt chasin', but you're kindly robbin' the cradle here, ain't you? You sure the juice is gonna be worth the squeeze?"

"Are you kiddin' me? Clayton, my boy, you got a lot to learn. Them little beaner girls like it. They like it a lot. And they start early."

Clayton grimaced. "Wow. Thanks for that little lesson."

"*De nada.* Here's anothern for you. You got to be careful with 'em. Now listen close to this. Them kind can lock their hips on you. Won't let go. You get stuck in 'em."

Clayton belched a laugh.

"Come on. That ain't for real . . . is it?"

Catlett winked, let out a small calculating chuckle.

"We'll sit here a minute or two. 'Fore long, that little gal'll be headin' home. See if we cain't give her a ride. Hell, you could give her a ride on Big Boy. You don't mind takin' sloppy seconds, do you?"

Catlett reached for the tongue oil. "Gimme that."

As fast as it came, the rain stopped; moon and stars broke through the remaining haze. Catlett swabbed the windshield with his palm, leaned forward to observe his prey with renewed focus.

Alejandra Flores finished folding her laundry and packing it item by item into a natural fiber basket. Toting her burden on her hip, she paused at the door in the downcast of sickly yellow illumination coming from a green gooseneck barn light fastened to the wall above the door header. After looking to her right and her left, she descended the prefab concrete steps and entered the darkness, bound for home.

"Here she goes," Catlett said. "About time. Need me some poon-tang."

Catlett slugged down the last of the whiskey and flung the bottle out the window. The sound of shattering glass caused the girl to halt and turn. Seeing nothing in the darkness, she continued on her way. Catlett and his sidekick watched the girl rush down the unlighted street and turn onto an intersecting street that loomed darker still.

Catlett switched on the engine and put the truck in gear but didn't turn on the headlights. He crept forward through dense air rife with after-rain odors of lye soap, wet grass, and dirt. He steered south and tires that had been grating on pea gravel went mute on blacktop. That's when the girl came into view. She stopped and wrenched her head in the direction of the approaching vehicle.

Catlett stopped the truck, hopped out and approached her. "Hey," he said, smiling. "How ya doin'?"

The girl took a step back.

Catlett put up his hands in a gesture of reassurance. "Hey, hey, don't be afraid. I'm not gonna hurt you. Me and my friend was passing by and saw you comin' out of the laundromat with that basket." Catlett kept walking as he talked. "That's quite a load you got there. Why don't you let me take it. We can give you a ride home."

The girl froze. Catlett smiled again, reached for the basket, grabbed her instead and clasped a meaty hand over her mouth before she could scream. Soon, he had her in the truck. At the site of the kidnapping, the girl's laundry basket lay overturned. Laundered undergarments scattered on the blacktop, a spattering of dirt clinging to damp cotton fabric.

On Catlett's orders, Clayton held the girl, arms pinned, one hand over her mouth, while Catlett drove, heading for the boondocks. She fought hard. It took all the kid's strength to keep her arms and legs under control. She kicked, clawed, tried to bite, did everything she could to get loose.

"Dammit, stop kicking," Clayton ordered her. "Hold still. Nobody's gonna hurt you. Just havin' a little fun."

When she continued to struggle and jabbed him hard with an elbow, he smacked her good across the left side of her face.

The disturbance angered Catlett.

"Cain't you keep that little bitch under control?"

"I'm tryin', dammit."

After a few minutes Catlett turned onto an unpaved road, then swung left and rampaged across the bar ditch, tore through a dense growth of chest-high switch cane, and came to a stop in a patch of ankle-high buffalo grass. He got out of the truck, came around to the passenger door, jerked it open. Yanked Clayton out of the cab and seized the girl by the legs. Handling her like a sack of horse feed, he pulled her out and dumped her to the ground. Blows to the head from the running board and hardpan left her half-senseless.

When the girl roused, she found Catlett straddling her, Clayton standing off to one side. At her attempts to free herself, her assailant's temper flared. He cuffed her with his open hand. She kept struggling, trying to push him off, and with that earned another slap.

When the girl started crying and begging for mercy, Catlett raised a bony fist and threatened to kill her if she didn't behave herself. That took the fight out of her and she collapsed, weeping. Having her under control, Catlett's manner changed. He acted as if he cared for her, as if he were doing something that would be good for her, as if he were contributing to her upbringing.

"What's your name, honey?"

The girl didn't answer.

"Come on now. What's your name?"

The girl still didn't answer. That angered Catlett and he let her have it again.

"Come on, Billy," Clayton whined, "you don't have to do that."

Catlett ignored him.

"I asked you a question, honey. Didn't your *mamacita* teach you to respect your elders? What's your name, dammit!"

"Alejandra," the girl whispered.

"Alejandra. Well now, ain't that a pretty name. I bet your folks call you Ále. Does your mama call you Ále?"

The girl nodded, her lips trembling.

"Yeah. Figgered. Don't you get all flustered, Ále. This ain't gonna hurt, not much anyway. Actually, it'll be sorta good for you. He patted her cheek, took hold of her throat. "Now, let's have a look under here."

He ripped open her blouse, exposing her teenage breasts to gray moonlight. When she tried to cover herself, he smacked her hands away. He smiled.

"Why, looky there. Boy, check out these little *chiches.*"

Clayton turned away. Catlett bunched the girl's skirt around her waist and tore off her panties. He loosened his belt, shucked his britches to his knees.

When he was done, Catlett stood in all his glory, hitching up his Levi's. The ravaged girl lay at his feet, blood smearing her thighs, tears scoring her puffy face. One eye was swollen shut. She held the back of a hand against her cheek, searching with her good eye the inscrutable dark that surrounded her. She whimpered. "Mama, Mama."

Catlett crouched on his heels again.

"Now listen, honey. You need to forget this ever happened. Put it right out of your head. If you ever, ever say anything about me or my partner here—one word, one little word—we will kill you. Don't you ever doubt it. We'll kill you and everybody in your family. It's that simple. If you're smart, you'll say you fell down the laundry steps."

Catlett gave a coldhearted snicker.

"Or . . . you can say one of them little darky boys in town done this. Uhh . . . say, Woody Coats, maybe. That boy that was bein' so friendly-like to you other day? Anybody'd believe that. Everybody knows he had his eye on you. And them kind of bucks don't count for much around here. You savvy? Savvy?"

Alejandra turned her face away, crying without making a sound.

Catlett stood, winked at Clayton.

"You're up, stud. Get down there and dip your wick in that little honey pot. And I don't mean wham bam thank you ma'am. I mean take a deep seat. She's a broncy little thing. But I figger I've rode the rough off her."

Clayton hung back. "Ahh, that's OK. This'n's all yours."

Catlett seized his arm.

"Think again, hoss. You ain't gonna crawfish on me now."

He gave Clayton a push.

"Now go to it. Let's see what kind of man you are."

The kid took a reluctant step, began fumbling with his belt buckle when a pair of headlights appeared not far away on the road. Clayton froze. Catlett saw the lights, too.

"Could be her people looking for her," Catlett said.

"Whada we do?"

"We clear outa here. That's what."

"What about her?"

"Leave her. Let's go."

They jumped into the truck, waited for the lights to disappear, and made their way back to the road.

Alejandra lay dazed, unmoving, listening for the truck to return. Finally, she mustered the strength to rise. Unsteady on her feet, she did her best to order her torn and disheveled clothing and take her bearings. Seeing headlights in the distance, she moved glassy-eyed like a sleepwalker, seeking what she thought might be a road. When she got there, she fell to the ground.

In a while, how long Alejandra had no way of knowing, another car approached, slowed and stopped. A man got out. Sheriff Dutch Mackey. Following the sweeping of the bar of light coming from his flashlight, the sheriff made his way to the girl's crumpled form. He dropped to a knee.

"My, my, my. What happened to you, darlin'? What happened?"

Alejandra tried to talk but couldn't. The sheriff skimmed bloody strands of hair away from her face, saw she was trying to whisper something.

"What's that, honey?"

"Mama," the girl said hoarsely. "Mama."

"What's your name, darlin'?"

"Alejandra."

"Alejandra what?"

"Flores."

"Alejandra, who done this to you?"

The girl took a long time to answer. She mumbled something.

The sheriff leaned to hear better. "What? What'd you say, sweetie?"

"I don't know."

"You don't know who done this to you?"

"No, no."

"Well, can you describe him?"

The girl hesitated. "Dark," she whispered.

"Dark? It was too dark?"

Alejandra shook her head.

"*He* was dark?"

She turned her face away.

CHAPTER 14

Sweet Leona's

Marsh's broken leg mended. The day he shed his cast, after six miserable weeks, he insisted Harry and Ruth join him and Bliss at Sweet Leona's Lounge for a celebration. Harry knew Marsh would not take no for an answer. And having played a key role in the bone-fracturing incident that was fast becoming Sebastian County legend, failing to attend would be impolitic.

Sweet Leona's was the only bar in Serafina—if you didn't count Imo's. A tawdry outland to some, for Marsh and Harry and other free-spirited folks it served as the preferred venue for painting their tonsils with a cold beer or a shot of whiskey. All on the sly, of course, for Prohibition held firm in the Sooner State long after the repeal of the Eighteenth Amendment. But for the most part Sheriff Dutch Mackey turned a blind eye to such trivial transgressions. As he saw his role in the community, he had a higher calling. Rousting friends and neighbors, not to mention voters, for partaking of ardent spirits made no sense to him.

Imo's held sway in Black Flats, but the more genteel members of Serafina society avoided that neck of the woods altogether. Likewise, Blacks never set foot in Sweet Leona's. In Serafina, the social order did not lack clarity: whites on top, Blacks and Indians on bottom, Mexicans somewhere in between. Everybody had a place; everybody knew his place. Simple. Or so denizens of the upper stratum chose to believe.

Leona Loveless opened her little dram shop in 1938, the year Harry and Marsh graduated from high school. But Leona didn't run the place anymore. She cashed in her chips soon after V-J Day. Doc said she smoked herself to death. He put a fine point on it by saying, "Three packs of Luckies a day for twenty years done her in." Her kid sister Dinah—Di folks called her—found her dead one morning, a cigarette burned to a stub between charred fingers. At better than three hundred pounds, it took four stout men to hoist the dearly departed onto a stretcher and haul her to the hearse for the short ride to the funeral home. Fourteen men drew straws to see who would bear the pall at her service. The six with the shortest straws lost.

After her sister's death, Di took over the bar. The slimmer of the two siblings, weighing in at about two hundred pounds, she was still imposing. She resembled her entrepreneurial big sis in many ways: same pale face and ice blue eyes, same silver blonde hair, always cut short and pin curled. She favored the same bright red lipstick and had the same cranky manner. Di Loveless. *Interesting name*, Harry thought the first time he heard it. Had to say it out loud to himself—Di Loveless. He penciled it in the spiralbound notepad he kept in a shirt pocket; he might use the name someday when he got around to writing a novel or a memoir of his adventures with his blood brother. He'd always seen himself as a wordsmith, but since Harry had been back from California he'd taken to hiding such high-flown notions from Marsh. He didn't need the grief it would bring him. Being plain old Harry True, Sebastian County rancher, presented a hard enough challenge. Trying to be Harry True, aspiring writer, would put him at risk of all manner of twitting and teasing.

Over the years, Sweet Leona's had seen roguishness of damn near every description. It stood right off the highway, south of town, a rectangular, windowless building with stucco walls the color of prairie blow sand, same inside and out. It had a belly-high hardwood bar, worktop well burnished from years of use. Brass footrail. Ranks of bottles on the backbar. Raw concrete slab floor, dappled with every kind of stain known to man. For Saturday night whoop-ups, Di kept the aggregate surface sprinkled with dance wax. Leather-soled boots and open-toe high heel shoes capering to jukebox tunes of Bob Wills and His Texas Playboys spread it around, worked it in. Left it slickrock smooth, perfect for two-stepping.

For Marsh's jubilee fandango the regular crowd times two gathered. Cowpunchers to bankers showed up for the celebration and now stood cheek by jowl. The place was jumping with excitement.

Harry and Ruth scooched in at the bar next to Harry's longtime friend Cal Barton, the druggist. Sandwiched between Barton and Ruth, Harry greeted the other men standing with Cal: Wilford Beck, the barber; Leland Cobb, a one-armed veterinarian known as Stub; Wid Isley, the lanky hardware man Marsh always called Lathy; and Oscar Tomlinson, the cotton gin manager everyone referred to as Swede.

High-steppers were dancing to Texas swing on the Wurlitzer. Like players in the round, they sashayed and do-si-doed arm-in-arm, making graceful circles, dipping, turning, throwing back their heads. The place vibrated with barroom music and the sounds of revelry. Boozy air—loud with laughter and conversation, dense with tobacco smoke—seethed with electricity. A rompin' stompin' night at Sweet Leona's.

When Marsh made his well-timed arrival, hobbling in with Bliss on his arm and leaning on a cane, the crowd erupted in a salvo of deafening cheers and applause. An explosion of whoops and hollers as if they were welcoming the return of a conquering hero. Marsh would never shirk that mantle. He beamed when he saw every head turn his way. Ever the attention-hound, he paused and accepted the adulation that was his due.

"Howdy folks. Howdy," he called out, lifting a hand in greeting. "Howdy do. Good to be back in circulation. Warms a man's heart to see all his friends like this. Sure enough does."

In high spirits, men and women left their seats and interrupted their dances to flock to the man of the hour. Patting his shoulder, slapping him on the back, they welcomed him on his return to his rightful place in Serafina society. Smiling ear-to-ear, he greeted his loyal subjects. The way he waded big-hatted through the Bacchanalian crush, exchanging hugs, shaking hands all around, he could have been a politician on the campaign trail. Bliss, his First Lady, kept to his side, but her skimpy smile betrayed reluctance. She moved as if she were stealing across a thin sheet of glass spanning a fathomless chasm.

Harry stood with his back against the bar, arms folded across his chest. He peered out from beneath the down-swept brim of his hat, watching the unwavering approach of his friend with the stove-up gait. And he watched Bliss. At his left, Cal Barton tipped back his hat and hooked his elbows on the bar. He couldn't help chortling at the vainglorious march of his friend Marsh. He nudged Harry.

"Would you look at that. The boy always was a top hand at puttin' on the dog. Bleve he could strut sittin' down."

"You got that right."

Cal Barton crossed his arms and pinched his chin.

"Hey, don't it strike you as a little bit funny he's the one gettin' all the attention? I mean, you're the one that saved his sorry ass."

Cal smiled. Harry smiled back.

When Marsh spotted Harry, he hailed him from halfway across the room, raising his voice above the hubbub.

"Hey. Hey, Harry. Hey, *amigo*, I'm buyin' you a *a-dult* beverage. Hell, I'm buyin' you ten of 'em."

When Marsh and Bliss had run the gauntlet of admiring carousers and crossed to the bar, Marsh tucked his hand under Harry's arm and held onto him. Harry's first instinct was to pull away, but Marsh had something else in mind for the man who'd saved his life. Giving his friend no choice in the matter, Marsh addressed the crowd. Standing shoulder-to-shoulder with Harry, he waved in a peremptory gesture, put fingers to lips and let fly a shrill whistle.

"Hey, everybody, listen. Listen up."

The celebratory din died down. Someone lowered the volume on the jukebox. Seizing the moment, Marsh pulled Harry close and addressed his admirers.

"I want y'all to know this man right here saved my ugly butt. I got myself in a twenty-four carat picklement and he rode to the rescue."

Revelers applauded and cheered. Harry tried again to pull away. But Marsh had more to say. He raised his right hand to quiet the room again.

"Now, if I uz bein' honest—and you know I always am—I'd have to say he mighta thought for a teensy *minuto* about leavin' me there and ridin' off. Couldn't blame him, I reckon."

A wave of hoots and laughter. Marsh put his arm around Harry's shoulders.

"But he didn't. The feller did for a fact pull my bacon out of the fire. He saved my life."

Harry felt his friend's grip on his shoulder tighten.

"I want y'all to know Harry True is the best pal a man ever had. Without a doubt, the absolute best."

Marsh gave Harry another hard squeeze and wrapped up the proceedings.

"That's it, folks. Ya'll get back to scootin' a boot. And let's do some drinkin' and bass singin.'"

On cue, the crowd applauded and cheered, and the wild wassail resumed. Once again, music blared from the Wurlitzer. Dancers took the floor. An extravaganza of noise and merrymaking broke out. Marsh leaned against the bar. Resting his right boot on the footrail, he set his cane on the counter and delighted in the whiskey bottles standing at attention in tight rows on backbar shelves like a strict regiment of fusiliers. When he'd made his choice, he called for the tavernkeeper and slapped down a crisp new ten-spot.

"Di, set 'em up. You got some thirsty folks here. Whiskey for me and my best friend, and his best gal, and my best gal. Make it the good stuff. Not that old tarantula juice. You know what I want."

"Comin' up," Di called back, finishing with other customers.

Marsh stood, favoring his game leg, one arm around Harry, the other around Bliss. Having achieved an acceptable balance, he kissed Bliss on the cheek.

"Damn. It's good to be back. Truly is."

Amidst a barrage of greetings and good wishes, Bliss smiled and slipped away. Ever watchful, Ruth caught the unspoken signal she gave Harry as she left, the way their eyes met and held. It further confirmed what she already suspected: Harry and Bliss were more than mere friends.

Ruth patted Harry's arm. "Be right back," she said, and followed Bliss to the ladies room. In the cramped interior, they stood before the mirror, arranging their hair, touching up their lipstick. For the longest time, neither said a word. Ruth spoke first.

"That Marsh . . . he's one of a kind, isn't he. Always good for a laugh, and a really good fellow to boot. Heart of gold."

Bliss gave a little laugh. "He's something else. That's for sure."

"True friendships like Harry and Marsh have are rare," Ruth said. "Takes a lifetime to build one. But you can tear one down in a minute. Don't you think?"

Bliss gave Ruth a split-second of oblique regard. "I guess so."

"Be a shame for anything to come between them. I'd hate to see that happen. Wouldn't you?"

Bliss's eyes met Ruth's in the mirror.

"What are you—"

Ruth dropped her lipstick in her bag and snapped it shut. "See you back out there," she said and took her leave.

Alone, Bliss studied herself in the mirror. What was Ruth saying? It sounded like she knew, but how could she? Harry would never . . . and the only other person . . . No, he had no reason. Harry had assured her their secret remained safe. But Ruth knew. Bliss was sure.

While the women were gone, Marsh jettisoned his festive manner and fell into a melancholy mood. It crossed Harry's mind that Marsh might be about to make a confession. He might beg for forgiveness for stealing his best friend's one true love, for being that two-timing broke dick Jody they sang about in the army. But none of that happened. The sudden presence of Di Loveless setting four glasses on the oaken bar broke the awkward silence. While pouring the drinks, full of sass as ever, she gave each of the two men a brief, but derisive, smirk. Their abrupt glooming had not escaped her notice.

"What's the matter? Ain't you boys simpatico no more? See a hoot owl in the window, or somethin'?"

At first, neither Marsh nor Harry reacted. After a moment or two,

Marsh shook off the lowness of spirit that had overtaken him and steadied himself on his good leg.

"Yeah. Matter of fact, I did see a owl. I was afraid somethin' mighta happened to you. Thought I might have to jump this bar and scrounge up these drinks my ownself."

Di chuckled. "Not hardly."

One by one, Ruth and Bliss made their way back to the bar. Marsh slid a sloshing glass across the burnished wood in Harry's direction, another toward Bliss. The third went to Ruth. Marsh picked up the remaining glass and raised it high. He inspected it as if to confirm its sufficiency to serve his epicurean taste or to view the jollification of his friends and admirers through its amber tint.

"Here's a toast," he said. "I don't want to cut this too fat. You know me. But I raise my glass to the man that saved my life. Thankee, brother."

Harry tapped glasses with Marsh and took a nip. Snatching a glimpse over his blood brother's shoulder as he drank, he caught the preoccupation showing on Bliss's face. She met his gaze with a false smile.

Marsh turned to Bliss. "And to the finest woman in Sebastian County," Marsh said. "The girl with the best and truest heart God ever made. Thank you, Darlin', for puttin' up with me. Thank you both for saving my life."

Harry and the women drank sparingly of the booze. Marsh sniffed the peaty spirit and emptied his glass in one gulp. "Ahh . . . angel's pee-pee." When his vocal cords had recovered from the forceful emission of firedrake breath, he whomped a fist on the bar. "Come on, now. Don't y'all be shy. Drink up. The night is young and the drinks are on me." He raised an arm and waved over the barkeep, pointed down at his glass. "Di, another kick of the mule, right here."

"OK. I'm comin." She was reaching for the bottle to pour the next round when a commotion erupted at the entrance. Some kind of trouble. All eyes turned.

CHAPTER 15

The Pecan Orchard

Harry zeroed in on the distraught countenance of Buddy Pond the moment he burst through the door. Pond saw him and Marsh together and made straight for them.

"Sheriff here?" he said, red-faced and panting.

Harry scanned the crowd. "No, don't think so."

Buddy turned to rush out. Harry grabbed his arm.

"Hold up. What's going on?"

"We got t . . . t . . . trouble," the smallish man gabbled, breathless and half-choking on his words.

"What kind of trouble, Bud?"

"Lynchin' trouble."

"Lynching? What are you talking about?"

Excitement started interfering with Pond's speech. Stammering, he gritted his teeth and glowered in frustration. Harry patted his shoulder.

"It's all right, Bud. Take your time."

Pond took a deep breath. "B . . . b . . . bunch of *b . . . b . . . borrachos* got Woody Coats tied up like a rodeo calf. Billy Catlett's there, railing about how Woody's the one raped that little Mexican gal. They're fixin' to haul him off and st . . . st . . . string him up."

"Hang him?" Marsh said. "Ain't that kindly illegal?"

"Not the way they see it. They said they was takin' matters into their own hands."

"Where were they taking him?" Harry said.

"Said somethin' about the p . . . p . . . pecan orchard acrost from the sale barn. Think they was headin' that way."

"We gotta find Dutch."

"Drove over there. Nobody to home. Must be out makin' his rounds. We g . . . g . . . gotta do something. Them knotheads mean b . . . b . . . bidness."

"Crazy bastards," Marsh said. "Catlett. What a no-account son of a bitch."

Buddy Pond turned to Marsh. "Your brother's there, too. I seen 'im."

Marsh grimaced. "Damn his worthless hide."

"Let's go," Harry said, motioning to Buddy.

"I'm coming, too," Cal Barton said. Wilford Beck, Wid Isley, Swede Tomlinson and even Leland Cobb put down their drinks and followed.

Marsh leaned on his cane. "Ya'll go on. I'm still kindly crippled up with this bum leg. I'll get Dutch located and we'll meet you out there." He let loose another sharp whistle. The volume of noise lowered. "Folks. Folks. Billy Catlett and his crew of good-for-nothins grabbed Woody Coats and are fixin' to string him up." A convulsion of gasps shook the room. "These men here are gonna stop 'em. Who's with 'em?"

Shouts of "I am" and "Me too" flew up. And another five or six men stood and headed for the door. Bliss and Ruth made a simultaneous move to join them. Marsh took them both by the arm.

"No you don't. You two're stayin' right here. You wanna make things even worse?"

When Harry, Buddy and the other men arrived at the pecan orchard they found a cohort of angry men clustered beneath the broad canopy of a sturdy tree. Harry saw Billy Catlett and Clayton Stone among them.

The headlights of some half dozen vehicles deployed in a half-moon formation illuminated the scene. Woody Coats had been positioned at center stage, on his knees, hands bound behind his back, rope noosed around his neck. Roughed up pretty bad by the look of him.

Before Woody, at the vanguard of the mob, stood two men with guns. Harry knew the gun-toters as Billy Ben McKinney and Homer Gene Earthman, both well known Serafina odd-job men. McKinney, a paunchy fellow, coarse-featured and swarthy, held a double barrel shotgun in the crook of his arm. He wore bib overalls under a canvas duck field coat with patched elbows and a donkey brown slouch hat, dirty and sweat-stained. At his side, Earthman, a lean and lanky sort clad in a canvas jerkin and snap-bill cap, held a revolver.

Harry signaled his backers to stand by and strode up to the men guarding Woody.

"What's goin' on here, boys?'

"Well, sir, we got ourselves a problem," McKinney said, somewhat matter-of-factly.

"That right?"

"Yessir, you see, this little *frijole* eater . . . Alejandra Flores they call her . . . got herself raped. Beat up pretty bad. This good for nothin' smoke here done it. Fixin' to string him up."

"You taking up for Mexicans now, Bill?"

Harry got no answer.

"Don't you think we ought to slow down a little bit? Sheriff's on his way."

"No need. Girl done identified him."

"Says who?"

"Well, for one, Mr. Catlett here. For another, young Clayton Stone. Bleve you acquainted with both of 'em."

Catlett stepped forward. "That's right. That's the way I heard it. Other day, I seen this boy tryin' to nuzzle up to that girl. Did my best to straighten him out. Guess it didn't take. He figgered he'd by God have his way with her. No matter what."

"That's the way you heard it, huh? Who from? You talk to the girl herself?"

"None o' your damn business where I heard it."

Harry turned to Clayton. "That the way you heard it, too?"

Clayton refused to meet Harry's gaze. "Everybody knows he done it."

"Everybody," Catlett said. "Hear that? Everybody cain't be wrong, now can they? Boy needs to learn a lesson."

"Well," Harry said, "I guess putting a rope around his neck and hanging him up in a tree is a sure way to teach him."

McKinney, shotgun at the ready, faced Harry. "Don't get in the way of this. Wouldn't be smart."

"Time to make a example," Earthman said. "Learn these people some manners. Before it's too late."

A grumble of support ran through the mob. And was met by a matching grumble of resistance from Harry's men, the sound of other guns being pulled out of hip holsters and pockets.

Paying McKinney and Earthman no mind, Harry squatted in front of Woody, spoke in a cautious undertone.

"Woody, looks like you got yourself in sort of a jackpot here."

The youngster raised his heavy head.

"Yessir. Lil' bit."

"These men say you raped a girl. You do that?"

"No sir, Mr. True. Did not. Didn't rape nobody. You know I didn't."

Woody implored Harry with his eyes.

"You know I didn't."

"Of course, you didn't."

"No sir. I don't mean that. I mean you *know* I didn't."

"I do?"

"Yessir." He darted his eyes toward McKinney. "Ask them. Ask 'em when it happened."

Harry rose and turned.

"When you boys say this happened?"

"Tuesday week," McKinney said. "Night we had that little spell of weather. About ten o'clock, somewhere around there. Ain't that right, Billy?"

"Yes, sir, ten o'clock, Tuesday week. That's what I heard."

Harry's stomach dropped. Now he understood what Woody was saying. Tuesday week. Night of the rain. Ten o'clock. On that day, at that hour, Harry and Bliss were at Blue Creek. And so was Woody.

The rainstorm had blown through about the time Harry and Bliss arrived in separate vehicles at their trysting place. Knowing their time together was stolen and brief, Harry had checked his watch: ten o'clock straight up. He and Bliss waited in his truck and when the rain slacked Harry got out and made his way around the front of the vehicle to open Bliss's door. Midway, he caught sight of a flashlight beam strafing the floor of the cottonwood bosque near the edge of the creek's catch basin. He froze. Esau? The flashlight approached. The man holding it was not Esau, but Woody.

"Well, I declare," Woody said, grinning. "Howdy-do, Mr. True. Didn't spect to see you out here."

"Woody? Didn't expect to see you either."

"Doin' a little frog gigging," Woody said, holding up the five-gallon steel bucket and long pole in his hands. "Got me a couple of pretty good croakers, but the rain kindly shut me down. I'm pretty much soaked through." He laughed a little. "Figgered I might as well call it a night. Got my daddy's old truck parked yonder way in the trees."

Still smiling, Woody threw the flashlight beam at Harry's truck. "That Miss Ruth you got with you?"

He leaned and squinted. "Why that's Miss Bliss. What's she—"

His smile disappeared. He gazed at the sky.

"Sure is dark tonight, ain't it? Misty, too. Cain't hardly see my hand in front of my face." He gave Harry a small wave. "Well, I reckon I best be gettin' on. Lible to catch my death out here. Be seein' ya, Mr. True."

"Be seein' ya, Woody."

Harry waited until he heard Woody drive away.

"Who was that?" Bliss said when Harry got back in the truck. "I couldn't see."

Harry didn't answer.

"Who was it, Harry?"

"Woody Coats."

Bliss let that soak in. "Did he . . . recognize me?"

"Yes."

Bliss was silent a moment. "Do you think he'll—"

"No. He won't say anything."

"You're sure."

"I'm sure."

Woody might be a kid in a lot of ways, Harry thought, but he wasn't stupid. Blacks had nothing to gain and everything to lose by sticking their noses in white folks' business. Harry knew it and he knew the Coatses knew it, too. Woody might say something to Esau or Polly. But they were practically family. That would be as far as any gossip would go.

Now, standing in the pecan orchard facing a lynch mob, Harry knew he could provide Woody an airtight alibi. So could Bliss. But they couldn't do it without revealing to everyone they'd been together that rain-swept night at Blue Creek. Couldn't do it without disclosing to Marsh and everyone else that they were liars and cheats. He was in no hurry to do that. Confession would come in time . . . if it had to. First, he had to make sure Woody Coats didn't get his neck stretched.

"I've known Woody Coats all his life," Harry said to the would-be lynchers as Buddy Pond and the other men who'd joined his band closed ranks behind him. "And so have most of you." He looked each man across from him in the eye. "Woody wouldn't rape anybody and you all know it. If somebody says he did, we need to let the sheriff handle it."

What he said made sense. But persuading a blood-angry mob wouldn't be that simple.

"No need for the sheriff," Billy Catlett said. "We got this little skinny-ass darky dead to rights. It don't surprise nobody you'd be takin' up for him. Everybody knows your families stick together."

Harry didn't budge.

"You men are overstepping yourselves. I'm taking Woody to the sheriff. He can deal with it. Nobody's getting hung tonight."

The gunmen and their retainers stood hard-set in anger. Harry held his ground. For the longest breath-holding time, no one moved. Billy Ben McKinney raised his shotgun and leveled it at Harry. The double muzzle glared at him like a pair of cold-blooded reptilian eyes. The men nearest Harry stepped back.

"You best stand aside, True. Folks around here got no use for your kind of highfalutin horse shit."

The sudden wail of a police siren broke the standoff. A black and white Dodge with a flashing red light on the roof pulled up and braked to a stop. Sheriff Dutch Mackey lumbered out. The passenger door opened and Marsh hefted himself to his feet. The sheriff stood to his full height and stretched as if he were working the kinks out of his back, pulled his John B. down. All eyes stayed on him as he came forward, Marsh hobbling close behind.

"What's got you boys all het up?" the sheriff said. "Feelin' sorta lynchy, are you? Need a dog to kick?"

The sheriff waited for an answer, feet wide apart, hands on the crests of his hips.

"Everybody gone deaf?"

McKinney, still toting the shotgun, spoke up.

"Caught ourselves a rapist, Sheriff. Raped a little Mescan gal. Beat her up real bad. Fixin' to hang him."

"Hang him, eh? That a fact?"

The shotgunner kept the gun on Harry.

"How about our friend Harry True? Gonna hang him, too? Or just shoot him?"

Having no interest in bandying words with some cheap gunsel, the sheriff swept his arm across the gathering of obstinate men.

"All right. Y'all get on home. If a crime's been committed, you can have your say in court."

"But sheriff," one of the militants said.

"But what? You might be interested in knowin' I been talkin' to that little gal. She don't seem to know to a certainty who done what. Could be this boy had his way with her. Could be he didn't. Could be somebody's spreadin' lies. Don't you reckon we orta kindly get the peticlars squared away 'fore we go to hangin' folks?"

The sheriff walked over to Woody and lifted the rope from his neck. Took him by the bend of his right arm and helped him to his feet.

"Let's go, son. You're comin' with me."

"But I didn't rape nobody, Sheriff."

"We'll sort all that out later. Right now, you're comin' with me."

With Woody on his left, holding him by the arm, the sheriff shifted around to face the man with the shotgun. He stood foursquare to him, not an arm's length away, watching his eyes. The sheriff lowered his gun hand to the .38 caliber revolver holstered at his hip, drummed his fingers on the checkered grip.

"You got the wrong bull by the tail, mister, and you're fixin' to get tried. Thow down on me with that shotgun, it'll come dear. There'll be some dyin' tonight. I promise you that. But it ain't gonna be this boy. And it ain't gonna be me."

McKinney's stare faltered. He lowered the gun.

The sheriff pierced the dense air with a rigid index finger aimed at Harry.

"You best come with me, too."

Woody managed to walk with the Sheriff and Harry bracing him. They put Woody in the back seat. Harry sat in the front. At the driver's door, the sheriff paused and turned.

"Oh . . . uh . . . trouble's over. You *gentlemen* best get ridin'. You've done your civic duty for tonight."

The sheriff touched the brim of his hat, exchanged almost imperceptible nods with Marsh.

"Tell Harry I'll see Ruth gets home," Marsh said.

Dutch Mackey climbed into the car and drove away.

Marsh hobbled over to his kid brother, stood inches in front of him.

"What's the matter with you? Runnin' with white trash like this. Whada you think Mama would say? Swear to God, I'm glad she ain't here to see it."

Clayton pulled his shoulders back, trying to appear defiant, but all he managed was to appear lost.

The lynchers dispersed. Marsh turned to go. In a few hobbling strides, he met up with Buddy Pond.

"Well, Bud, the Dutchman says the trouble's over. Sounds nice, don't it. But I ain't sure I'm buyin' it."

"Nope. M . . . m . . . me neither."

CHAPTER 16

The Round Pen

Sheriff Mackey drove to his office. He and Harry helped Woody out of the car and ushered him inside.

"You ain't takin me home, sir?" Woody said.

"Not tonight, son. I think you better stay here with me. Give them yahoos time to cool off. Cell cot ain't so bad. I'll have Doris Ann warm you up some supper, and we'll call your daddy to come fetch you in the morning. That work for you?"

"Yes, sir. Reckon it'll have to."

That night, Harry lay wakeful in his bed for hours. His mind tornadoed from Bliss to Marsh, to Woody Coats, to Esau. And it churned up a long-buried memory of a tale of tragedy and injustice his father had told him when he was a boy: the story of Speedy Giles.

Harry and his father were whiling away the twilight hour of a summer evening on the porch of the family home. Harry was about fourteen years old. Half-light air scented with the subtle fragrance of irises rising from edging flower beds hung cumbrous and still. Morris True sat in a metal lawn chair with a green shell-shaped back, smoking his pipe and reading the *Serafina Gazette*, the local weekly rag. Nearby, Harry lounged on the twosome swing hanging from rafters by rusty chains, his bare feet sweeping the concrete slab beneath him like bristle brushes with every arcing, a timeworn copy of *Huckleberry Finn* propped on his chest.

"Daddy," he said with trepidation.

"Uh huh."

"Daddy . . . ."

Harry hesitated. His father viewed him over the top of the reading glasses balanced low on his nose.

"What is it, son?"

"Daddy . . . Who was Speedy Giles?"

Morris True's puffing ceased.

"Where'd you hear that name?" he said, lowering the paper to his lap, pipestem still wedged between his clenched teeth.

It took all of a second for Harry to realize he'd struck a nerve. He thought to take the question back, change the subject.

"Where'd you hear it?" his father persisted, pushing up his glasses and gazing out into the distance.

"Oh, I don't know. Heard it somewhere. It doesn't matter."

"Come on now, tell me."

"Downtown. Some men were talking. I overheard them say something about Speedy Giles. I asked them who he was and they got real quiet. Said to ask you."

The elder True folded his newspaper. Bent over and laid it on the porch in a thoughtful, deliberate fashion. He stood. He took a few shuffling steps and halted, peered into the evening half-light. He took the pipe from his mouth, tapped the bowl against the heel of his hand, let cold ashes fall. He ruminated for a long time, absorbed in his own memories, as Harry sat watching and waiting. When he spoke, the words came out in a voice burdened by the great weight of sorrow.

"Speedy Giles. Oh, my. Haven't heard that name for many a year. Hoped I'd never hear it again. Not the way it works, I reckon. The sins of a man's past life don't cease to exist because the past gets to be a long time ago. Whatever you do, or fail to do, stays with you. And when you get to be my age, I think those things come back to you. Right that they should, I suppose." He paused and thought. "If old Marc Antony had it right, the evil men do lives after them. Grim prospect, ain't it?"

He glanced at his son and took a stab at making a smile. Returning to his metal lawn chair, he lowered himself onto the seat as if in the span of a few minutes he'd aged by decades, become stiff of joints, brittle of bones, vacant of spirit. With a deep sigh, he began.

"Speedy Giles was a colored kid. Skinny as a fence rail. Couldn't have been more than sixteen the day he died. Seventeen, maybe. Nice kid. Nice family. Poor like everybody else, of course, but decent people. Fastest kid in Sebastian County, folks said. Wings on his heels."

Morris True paused, let out a long sigh.

"Shirt-tail kid myself when it happened. Not as old as Speedy. Thirteen, fourteen, I reckon. Kid named Joe Tucker and I had been fishing on a chili-colored runoff creek. You know, down there south of town, off the highway a mile or so, pretty sorry place for fishing."

Morris True thought a few moments, appearing to order the images taking shape in his memory.

"Getting on toward dark. About like now. In fact, exactly like now. Joe and I were heading home. Ran into Speedy on this old dirt road that came up from the creek. There we were, three kids with cane poles—talking, laughing."

Morris True smiled. He gazed into the night. No longer a grown man with a definite past, he'd become that young boy standing on that dirt road.

"Hey, Speedy."

"Hidy, boys."

"Do any good?"

"Some. Hooked me a few mudcats."

Morris True smiled. "Those were his exact words. Remember Speedy showing off a stringer of fish. Feels like it was yesterday."

His smile faded.

"Pretty soon a truckload of gutter trash bullies pulled up. In an old Mac Brothers truck. Every one of them full of wagon yard whiskey and meanness. One of them was Billy Catlett's grandaddy, Earl Catlett. No good, rotten to the bone. I didn't recognize the others.

"They all got out of the truck, lit into Speedy. Whuppin' up on him for no particular reason. They wanted somebody to take their meanness out on. Speedy happened to be there. They didn't touch me or Joe, of course. Seemed like they didn't even see us, they were so focused on Speedy. Two scared white kids. Afraid to move."

"At first, they cussed Speedy, called him every name in the book. Bad-mouthed his mother, his father. His whole family. Hell, they probably didn't even know his family. They pushed him. Gave him a pretty good thrashing. But they didn't stop there.

"Before long, they had Speedy down, had his hands tied, had his feet chained to the back of the truck. They took off dragging the poor kid . . . I can still hear him screaming."

Morris True gazed into the gathering darkness as if it were all happening again right in front of him. He sucked in a ragged breath. "Joe and I stood there. Made no attempt whatsoever to stop it.

"Those bastards drug poor Speedy until his body all but fell apart. Found out later that when they swung out wide around a curve the boy's head hung up on a sheet iron culvert. Damn near took it off. When they were done, they strung up what was left of him in a tree."

Morris True took off his glasses and wiped his eyes.

"What happened to the men that did it?" Harry said.

His father put his glasses on.

"Nothing. Not a damn thing. Nobody ever put the law on 'em. Back in those days . . . well, nothing happened to them. I don't guess it matters now. They're all dead. Everybody that was there. Except me."

For the first time, Morris True allowed his eyes to find his son's.

"Always blamed myself. It's dogged me every day of my life since that night. I don't figure on it getting any better. Probly get worse. That kind of thing pains your soul. Shoulda done something. But I didn't."

"You were a kid, Pop. What could you have done?"

"Nothing . . . I expect. But knowing that doesn't help much. I saw it all. And . . . here's the rest of it. Maybe the worst part. Joe and I never said a word to anybody. When the sheriff came around asking questions, we kept quiet. Earl Catlett had threatened us, you see. Said if we ever told we'd end up like Speedy. 'Course it was an empty threat. He would never've touched us. I see that now. But we didn't know that then. We took him at his word. Scared us so bad we didn't even talk about it with each other. Joe and I tried to stay friends after that but we couldn't, not with something like that between us. So that was that."

"But the story got out anyway," Harry said.

"Of course. Always does."

"And they still got away with it?"

Morris True nodded.

Harry thought for a moment. "What about Speedy's family? What happened to them?"

"Left town. Couldn't hardly stay after that."

Morris True came Lazarus-like to his feet and headed for the front door. Hand on the latch, he halted, turned.

"Guess I was hoping never to tell you this story, son. Hurts something awful to remember."

"I'm sorry, Pop."

"No, don't apologize. I'm the one should be apologizing. I hope you'll learn something from my failure, make a better man than I did. I believe you will."

He smiled.

"Well, it's getting late," he said, sounding fatigued. "Think I'll try to get some sleep. Doubt I'll be able to."

Harry sat in the dark for a long time, knowing he would always remember every word his father had spoken, always remember the sadness in his voice. That night, he took an oath to himself that he would never make the same mistake his father had made. He would make up for the wrong his father had committed and redeem the pain he'd suffered for it by becoming the man Morris True wished him to be. He would never hesitate to do the right thing no matter the price because living with shame and regret was the worst price of all.

And now here he was, a score of years later, struggling through the same kind of torment that had beset his father so long ago, and glad his father hadn't lived to see what kind of man his son had become. Sleep came to him in the small hours of morning but it was a fitful kind of sleep; it brought him no genuine rest. And it didn't last long. While the morning star yet burned in the eastern sky, Harry woke with a start. After freeing himself from the bedclothes that had him trussed up like a pullet in a stewpan, it took him a few panicky moments to figure out he was at home in his own bed.

At first light, Harry made up his mind to seek merciful distraction from his troubles in hard physical labor. He'd been planning to build a new round pen and today he would do it. He needed to bow his back with annealing work, burn off some misery.

He would locate the new pen east of the house, in the northern barnlot. As he envisioned it, a train of posts set on eight-foot centers would form a perfect circle, sixty feet in diameter. Three two-by-six horizontal rails would stretch between the posts. It would be an ideal place to start a rank stud horse or blow the stink off a cranky old mare. As a horseman who knew his business, he'd be able to shape a lunging animal, even an ornery one, into a willing partner. Pushing the bronciest critter along the pen's perimeter, he could soften him, smooth out his rough edges. He'd seen the amazing quickness with which a horse will signal compliance: cocking of an ear, dropping of the head, shifting of an eye in the trainer's direction. Soon, the horse draws into the man in a noble act of submission, accepting him as his leader. Harry admired the animal's purity of instinct. Envied him his freedom from sin.

At daybreak, Harry went to work. As if he were sketching a clock-face, he laid the lumber he'd bought days before on the ground, placing a post between and perpendicular to each stack of three boards. Template in place, he bent to his task. With posthole diggers he assaulted the earth's unobliging crust, ripping up double bladefuls of dirt, heaping chunky red clods at the edge of a deepening hole.

By the time the sun had gone high he had the seminal post in place. By midday, he had a half-dozen of them set. Without so much as a mare's tail cirrus in the sky to rend the colorless noon, the blistering sun was pounding the parched earth with a relentless cadence. Sweat flooded his face. Etched his veiny arms, his chest, his back. He could feel a river of it crawling along the channel of his spine. The temperature must have already hit the century mark.

After a few hours of bone-jarring labor, Harry took a break. Lungs straining, the odor of creosote dressing on the posts singeing his nostrils, he set the two-handed implement upright in the hole he was digging and reached for the blanket-sided canteen sitting on the ground nearby. He took a long swig of the life-giving liquid, sloshed it around in his mouth. Spat. Before he could take a second drink, he caught movement off to his right from the corner of his eye. Less than the length of two fence rails away, a mangy, flea-bitten, hollow-eyed dog with a hoary muzzle stood on rickety legs. The scent of water must have drawn him in.

The slat-ribbed cur looked to be part bird dog, part half a dozen other breeds, mostly brown. A maverick strain of *canis familiaris* Harry and Marsh took to calling a Mexican Brown when they were kids. Marsh came up with the name. He reasoned that if you jumble up a dog's bloodline as much as possible, pay no attention whatsoever to breeding or pedigree, after a few generations you have a basic brown dog. Short hair, long tail, medium build, good disposition. He saw it as a way of entropy producing order, absurdity yielding logic. To him, it stood to reason that this prolific breed had reached its full state of evolution south of the Rio Grande. Hence the name Mexican Brown.

The quintessential Brown now stood in Harry's yard a few feet away. Dispossessed of everything but his anguish, barely enough of him remained to throw a snip of shadow. With caved-in flanks and prominent ribs, his hide hung on his bony frame like wet newsprint. He'd be crowbait inside a fortnight.

If Marsh had been there to describe the dog, he would have said he had the flabbin' woo woos. He would have been quick to explain, as was his wont, that the flabbin' woo woos are what you have when you're so tired and used up the cheeks of your ass hang down and touch the tops of your bobby socks. "If you got 'em," he would have said, "you're in a bad way." And he would have been right. This old mutt was in a bad way.

But desperation had emboldened him. Having a powerful thirst and nothing to lose, he'd skulked in, keeping his body low, ears laid back, head low, tail tucked between his hind legs. If he'd had a voice, it would have quivered when he begged for a drink.

Harry had half a mind to run the rangy cur off or shoot him where he stood. Why not? He'd be dead soon anyway. *You're not good for anything. Not a damn thing.* He could hear a voice in his head saying, "Get out of here. I don't need a dead dog to pull in coyotes and flies. And I sure don't need another hole to dig." But he thought better of it.

"Ahh. I'm not gonna kill you. Not today, anyway."

Taking care to avoid any threatening move, he squatted and emptied the nail can on the ground. Poured water into it from the canteen. He set the can down, pushed it closer to the dog. Eased back. The dog inched forward and sank his muzzle into the water. He lapped up every drop of it. Harry filled the can again and the dog went back to drinking.

"Look at you. You are a Mexican Brown if I've ever seen one. Descended from foundation stock, most likely."

The sunstroked dog gave Harry a beseeching look.

"What? I gave you all the water I've got."

The dog drank more. After draining the water can the second time, he raised his head. Animal alertness revived, he launched a keen stare into the distance. Harry matched his gaze to the dog's. Through shimmering heatwaves rising from the griddle hot plain, he saw the wavy form of an approaching vehicle, its rear wheels kicking up spumes of dust the color of red clay. Eyes impeded by sunglare and grit, Harry couldn't make out who'd come to pay him an unexpected visit. A moment later, he recognized the truck. It was Esau Coats. Harry glanced back at the dog as if to advise him of the imminent arrival of a longtime family friend. But the canine had vanished.

Harry returned to his work. Spiking a few nails in his mouth, he scooped up a plank, and, holding it waist-high, worked his way to the set post at what would be the twelve o'clock position on a time-piece. Like some gawky bird with wooden wings, he rested one end of the plank on a pre-driven hook on a neighboring post and leveled it, plucked a nail from the half-dozen bristling from his mouth. He fastened the plank to the post at each end, a volley of hammer blows sending forth the fervent report of steel striking steel. Standing on what would become the interior of the pen, he stood resting his arms on the new rail. Leaning forward, he watched Esau's final approach.

Esau's decrepit jalopy of a pickup trundled near, turned onto the Bar T, rattling the cattle guard. It came to a dusty halt near the inchoate round pen. Esau boosted his aging bones out of the truck and stood. He stretched. Smiled and waved.

"Mornin'."

"What say, Esau?"

"Already a hot one, ain't it. Hot and gettin' hotter."

Esau walked over to Harry. The two men stood on opposite sides of the new fence rail, Esau on the exterior.

"How you doin', Esau?"

"Well, sir, reckon I'm in pretty fair shape for the shape I'm in."

Esau surveyed Harry's work.

"This here's sure enough a mighty fine pen you buildin'. Yessir. Be hell for stout, betcha. You always been top notch at this kinda thing. Muley strong, too. You and Marsh both. And you in particular been known for bein' good with horseflesh. Yessir, you set a horse fine."

"What brings you out here today, Esau?"

"Heard what you done for my boy last night. Wanted to say much obliged. Them men was dead set on hangin' him in a tree, way I heard it. Theyda did it for sure if you hadn't stopped 'em."

"I had some help."

"Still."

Harry moved to the lumber stack to continue his work. Without being asked, Esau pitched in and helped him carry another rail.

"Well, I couldn't let 'em hang Woody. Didn't figure he did what they were accusing him of. Sheriff Mackey'll sort all that out. He's a fair man."

Harry pressed the board against the post with his body and made a small gesture with his head. Esau leaned, picked up the hand sledge and reached it over. Harry drove a nail.

"Woody doing OK?"

"Tolerable well. Fetched him home from the jailhouse this mornin'. Sheriff didn't actually have him under arrest, didn't even have the cell door locked. Keepin' a eye on him is all. Now the boy needs a little spell with his mama lookin' after him. He'll be goin' back to his little homestead this evenin'."

"Not really hurt?"

"Nahh . . . scairt though, real scarified. Second time that Catlett fellow come after 'im. But all them men done to him was peel off some hide where them ropes was. Blacked his eye."

While Esau held the board, Harry drove a nail. He moved to the far end and drove another. Now, two rails stretched between the first two posts.

"You didn't have to come all the way out here to say thanks."

The two men kept working and neither spoke. Soon, they had a third rail in place. The work went on, but manual labor became a poor substitute for conversation. Harry intuited that Esau had more on his mind than saying thanks.

"Ain't over, you know," Esau said. "Not by a damn sight. Sumpin awful happened to that little gal. Some folks still sayin' my boy done it."

Keeping his back to Esau, Harry continued to occupy himself with driving nails. He knew where this conversation was going.

"My boy didn't do it. Didn't do nothin'. I know it. That little Mexican gal know it. And you know it." Esau paused. "You and Miss Bliss."

There. Esau had spoken her name. After a moment's hesitation Harry crossed over to the other side of the rail and stood before Esau, feet wide apart.

"What exactly are you saying?"

"Sayin' you saw my boy that night. Down by the creek. You 'member."

Esau stepped closer.

"Long ways off. No way he could be in both places at the same time. So . . . I reckon you and Miss Bliss gonna be my boy's . . . alibi. Yessir. Alibi. Has to be both of you."

Harry's face hardened.

"That's right. You heared me. Gotta be both of you. If it ain't, folks gonna say you lookin' out for your own people. Stickin' up for us like Trues always done. Folks know how far our families go back."

An edgy silence followed. Harry didn't take to being backed into a corner—not by anybody. No one would force him to do anything he didn't want to do. He would not stand on his own property and take orders from somebody else, family history or not. His grip on the hammer tightened.

But he eased up, let the hammer fall to the ground. Harry ambled to the inside of the rail, a place where one day hooves would pound, where green horses would be gentled. He snaked a red bandana from his hip pocket and dabbed sweat from his forehead. He let out a long sigh.

"You are right, Esau. It is a hot one . . . for sure. Hot and getting hotter."

Esau waited for Harry to say more. He didn't.

"Told my boy I didn't know why you and Miss Bliss would be out there at Blue Creek . . . the two of ya. Didn't care. But I knew both of you'd be speakin' up to set things right. Yessir. Told my boy not to worry none. With the two of y'all backin' him up, wouldn't nobody say boo."

Harry still preferred silence.

"I told Polly and Woody we could count on you and Miss Bliss to do the right thing. Always have. Always will."

The two men found themselves divided by the rail again. It became obvious to Esau that Harry would be making no promises today. Seeing that, he headed for his truck. Before he reached it, he stopped and turned back to face the man standing inside the circular enclosure he was building with his own hands. Esau looked him dead in the eye.

"One more thing. In case you was wonderin' what the truth might be. I know who done it. Who done what that little gal say. Billy Catlett. And that skinny kid that's always hanging out with him. She didn't know his name. But I do. And so do you."

Harry jerked upright. "You don't know that. Don't know anything of the kind."

"As a matter of fact, I do. No secrets in this town. Anything you do'll beat you home. People talk. Black. White. Mescan. They all talk. White women talk on the phone and their colored help listens in. They go to the laundry and talk. They hang out the wash, talk over the fence. Heads down in their poke bonnets, they talk and talk and talk. And that's what they say."

In the heavy-hearted old man's face, Harry saw the wear of long years of experience. He saw the tracks of injustices that had trampled him all his life, the determination of a father to protect his son. When Esau spoke again, fear and worry haunted his voice.

"That little gal 'fraid of them bad men. 'Fraid of what they'd do if she tells the truth. Better to say she don't know. Let other folks spread rumors."

Harry removed his hat, held it before him by the brim. Took a long squint at the great blue dome above.

"You know, Esau. Most things fall apart if you give 'em half a chance."

Esau's manner saddened.

"This old world can be a hard place. That's for sure."

"Don't much give a damn about the world anymore. It doesn't deserve it."

"Mebbe. But my boy deserves it."

The encounter ended with Esau raising an arthritic finger to his forehead in a farewell salute.

"Reckon you need to get back to work now. We'll see ya, Harry."

He heaved himself into his truck and pulled the door to. He started the engine and put the truck in gear, but before he released the clutch, he made a final plea to his old family friend.

"'Member I said I had a feelin' sumpin was gonna happen to my boy?"

Harry remained silent.

"'Fraid I was right. They gonna hang him for sumpin he didn't do. Sure as God made little green apples, they gonna do it. His mama's beggin' him to head down Texas way, stay with some kinfolk until the sheriff sorts things out."

"Might be wise."

"Maybe. But that boy likes his mama's cookin'. Right now we cain't do nothin' but trust the Lord and trust you. I'd be obliged if you'd set things right . . . soon."

Harry put his hat back on, tugged at the forebrim, and watched the avuncular gentleman drive away. As he did, he felt a great sinking of his heart, winced at the ensnarement of a remarkable conspiracy of events. He knew Esau was right. The trouble was not over—not by a damn sight. Nor was the heat of the day. He could feel the mercury rising.

CHAPTER 17

Sleepless

A few hours after his visit from Esau, Harry found himself sitting in his truck outside the office of Sheriff Dutch Mackey. This day had missed by a mile the mark set for it at sunrise. He'd made scant progress on the round pen, his notion of absolution by hard, physical labor vanishing in a crosscurrent of guilt and indecision. After baking in the sweltering heat of late afternoon for he didn't know how long, Harry came to his decision. *It's a debt of honor. Simple as that.* He shouldered the truck door open, hesitated, closed it. Opened it again and stepped out.

When he entered the office, hat in hand, he found the sheriff dozing, a great bear luxuriating in the cool breeze of an oscillating fan. The way he had his bulk of more than two hundred fifty pounds arranged, he'd achieved a magnificent—if risky—balance. Swivel chair reclined, legs crossed at the ankles, he had a single boot heel placed on the corner of his littered desk. His massive noggin had fallen forward, chin sagging to his chest, wattling out a gorget of loose skin. The reposing man growled breathy snores in waves, bulging slack lips, rustling the moon gray bristles of his moustache, which he sometimes referred to as his cookie duster. Fingers laced, his balled hands rested against the windward slope of his mountainous belly.

From a few strides away, Harry noticed on the sheriff's desk a newspaper and a magazine. A headline on the magazine's cover read, "Integration War Looms." With a fingertip, Harry dragged the magazine closer and opened it. Lowering himself to the barrel back chair reserved for citizens seeking an audience with the sheriff, he picked up the periodical and devoured the cover story. The outrage among political leaders in the South over the Supreme Court's recent decision in *Brown* was growing. Some were promising another Civil War. The governor of Georgia, who had said in the past that school integration would lead to bloodshed and would never happen under his stewardship, warned that Georgians would fight for their right to manage their own affairs, and an Alabama state representative vowed, "We are going to keep every brick in our segregation wall intact." Ordinary people held in common the adamantine view that strict boundaries between races should be maintained. So the world had always been; so it would remain, they said. No damn Yankee court would change it.

Moving on from the magazine, Harry took from the desk the latest edition of the *Serafina Gazette*. His eyes went directly to the headline above the fold: "Locals Vow to Fight Integration." Some Oklahomans were lining up with other rebels across the country. The conclusion was now inescapable: the war between Blacks and whites would be fought on Harry's home range, too.

Lower on the page, Harry found an article about a man lynched by a mob in a nearby Texas panhandle town. In the photograph, the dead man's body hung limp from a tree branch. At first, Harry thought the image might be historical, something that happened long ago. Not so. The man in the picture had been lynched the previous week for speaking disrespectfully to a white woman. Folks might have let it pass before all this talk about civil rights, one of the townspeople said. Not now. People were scared and angry, another white resident said. He didn't condone lynching, but someone had to remind colored folk of their place.

When the sheriff cracked his heavy-lidded eyes, Harry pushed away from the desk and rose. He stepped back a safe distance from the waking bear. The sheriff drew himself up from his precarious perch, sat snorting and hacking, rubbing his cheeks. To complete his resurrectional ascent, he seized the near-empty bottle of R.C. Cola standing at the corner of his desk and drank it dry. Realized he had a visitor. He tidied up the tips of his drooping moustache with the edge of a finger, sniffed.

"Rough night," he said. "Ain't had that much excitement around here in quite a spell. Musta dozed off."

Sheriff Mackey arranged and rearranged a slapdash spread of papers on his desk, situated his sizable mass in his chair. When he had himself and the papers in proper order, he looked up.

"Oh, Harry." He built himself to his feet, scanning the room to be certain no one else was present.

"Say, I'd be obliged if you wouldn't let on about me dozin' off like this. Wouldn't do for folks to read this wrong."

The sheriff regained his official demeanor and the ursine quality of his voice.

"Now, what can I do you for, Mr. True?"

"Here to see you, sheriff . . . about Woody Coats."

"Pull up a chair."

Harry sat. The sheriff sat.

"Ahh . . . Woody Coats," the sheriff said. "Had kindly a close call last night. I want to thank you for what you and Buddy and them done. That whole situation coulda went off the rails in a hurry. Damn near had us a lynchin' and a shootin' scrape. Nothin' worse than a motley of whiskeyfied rednecks."

"Well, I didn't figure Woody'd done what they were accusing him of."

Sheriff Mackey ran the back of his hand across his mouth.

"No, I 'spect not, but I ain't got all the facts sorted out quite yet. Some folks are sayin' Woody had his eye on that little Mexican gal for a while. Wouldn't take no for a answer."

"Doesn't sound like Woody."

"No. Cain't say it does. However, ain't much that does make sense these days."

Harry shifted in his chair. "Got any other leads?"

"Hearsay's all, but cain't go arrestin' folks based on that."

The sheriff lowered his eyes to the magazine on his desk. Aimed the tip of a knotty index finger at it, tapped it three times.

"Look at this, would you. This country's gettin' to where I don't hardly know it no more."

Harry nodded.

"Trainload of trouble's comin'," the sheriff went on. "And it's comin' here like everwhere else. Shore don't need this bidness with Woody right now. No, sir."

A few restive seconds passed.

"You said you come to talk about Woody. You know somethin' about this?"

The sheriff slanted his head a little.

"If you do, you best be tellin' me."

Harry parted his lips to speak but pulled up short, thoughts of Bliss stopping him. She didn't know he was here and hadn't signed off on revealing their affair.

The sheriff studied Harry.

"Woody tells me he didn't do it," Mackey said. "I asked him point blank and he denied it. I asked him did he have a alibi witness, somebody who could prove his innocence. He kindly made out like he did.

But he wouldn't tell me who that might be. You wouldn't know nothin' 'bout that, would you?"

"I know Woody didn't do it."

"And how exactly do you know that?"

"I know."

"I'm asking you how you know."

Harry shifted.

"He's not the type. He's better than that."

"OK. Let me ask you this. Know anythin' you're not tellin' me about who mebbe did do it?"

Harry shrugged. "Just loose talk."

Mackey nodded.

Harry rose. "Well, gotta get movin'. I'll be seein' you, Dutch."

Sheriff Mackey pushed up out of his chair.

"Any time you wanna talk more about Woody, you hunt me up. I'll be all ears."

Harry reached for the door.

"Oh, by the way," the sheriff said, "you gonna be at the banquet tomorrow night?"

Harry waggled his shoulders.

"I guess."

"I know Marsh and Bliss is gonna be there. Marsh and Bliss. Fine folks, don't you think? Always figgered you and Bliss was bespoke for. Funny how things work out."

"What do you mean funny?"

"Ahh . . . funny peculiar, not funny ha-ha. You know."

Harry changed the subject back to the banquet.

"So, do you have some special interest in who's coming this year? You taking roll?"

"Newwww. Just wonderin'. Not sure about the minstrel show, though. Talk is it's a dandy, but cain't say much for the timin'. If it was up to me, we'd blow out the lamp on it. Doris Ann feels the same way. Bliss, too. She said that plain at our last meeting. Said we ought not to be doin' it now, or ever again for that matter. Imagine Ruth'd agree with that."

"Be seein' ya, Dutch."

"Yessir. Adios."

Sheriff Mackey stepped to the window and through the dusty glass watched Harry get into his truck.

"I don't know what's goin' on with you," Mackey mused aloud as Harry drove away. "But I'm gonna find out. I can promise you that."

Harry was a taut rope. At one end, his love for Bliss held tight and pulled him in her direction. At the other, his conscience and his sense of loyalty joined forces in opposition. Stretched to the limit, threads were popping.

The night following Harry's visit with Sheriff Mackey, his mind would not yield to sleep. In predawn gray, he lay in his bed conjuring up animal shapes in the random tracery of passing clouds projected in starshine and moonglow on his bedroom walls. In the interplay of light and shadow he beheld the faces of goblins: angular eyes, misshapen noses, pointy ears, mouths agape in harsh rebuke. All intent on a baleful purpose: indictment, conviction, punishment.

Through the open window Harry heard a clattering racket that seemed to be coming from behind the house. Spillage. Rummaging. Next came a grating sound from the front yard. In a lithe, one-count motion, Harry swung his long legs over the side of the bed, jack-knifed to a sitting position. Feet resting on the cool hardwood floor, he listened. Now, he heard nothing. But a moment later the noise resumed. This time, it sounded like the gnashing of teeth. Harry reached for the bedside table and, being careful not to betray himself, opened the drawer. From its unlighted interior, he withdrew the Army .45 that matched the one he'd carried during the war. He depressed the cross-hatch button with his right thumb, dropping the magazine into the cupped palm of his left hand. After checking his load, he shoved the magazine back into the pistol's grip. Being as quiet as he could be, he brought the slide back and let it go forward, carrying a live round into the chamber.

Sidearm cocked and locked, Harry crossed the bedroom in a state of hyper vigilance. At the doorway leading to the hall he paused, looked both ways. Saw nothing. But, again, he heard the menacing sound he'd heard before. Gun at the ready, he crept down the corridor and into the living room.

At the easternmost window, breathing shallow, he raised the semi-automatic. With the barrel, he parted the drapery enough to steal a look into the outer dark. That's when he identified the evildoer that had come to call: the same hag-ridden tramp that had begged for water at the round pen the day before. Perhaps thirty feet away in the ranch-yard, near the windmill tank, he lay gnawing on a bone, enjoying the spoils of his nocturnal scavenging.

At the sight of the feasting critter, Harry released his pent-up breath. He lowered the hammer on the handgun and set it on the table near the front door. His racing pulse calming, he opened the door and stepped out onto the porch. The stray's head and ears stood at atten-tion. He threw a quick glance at Harry and stiffened from head to tail tip. But he didn't bother to rise. And he didn't relinquish the rib bone held vertical between his forepaws.

At the thought of the trepidation wrought by his uninvited canine guest's clamorous presence, Harry shook his head. He couldn't help being tickled at himself and he had to stifle a chuckle. He massaged his tired eyes. Like all his woes, he'd brought this one on himself. He did it the day he gave the mendicant dog water. With a small act of kindness, he'd invited the mangy bag of bones to take up residence on his property. Now, he'd never get rid of him. *No good deed goes unpunished.*

The critter rose, trotted to the porch and sat a few feet from the bottom step.

"You. You do look a sight, don't you? Oh, well. Might as well make yourself at home. *Mi casa es su casa.* Who am I to stand in your way? The owner of this outfit, that's all."

The dog didn't move.

An idea came to Harry. He was already hub high in this dog business, anyway. Why not go with it?

"Wait," he said, raising his hand in a stay command. "You wait right there. I'll be back."

The panhandling pooch angled his head. Harry disappeared into the house, returning a short time later with a plate of meat scraps. The dog stood, nose twitching, curious. Eager for any tasty treat his reluctant host might bestow upon him.

Harry seated himself on the topmost porch step and tossed a morsel of meat to his famished guest. The dog sniffed at the food, scarfed it up. He settled himself on his haunches again. Running his tongue around his bristled muzzle, he gazed at his benefactor, ready for more.

"Pretty good, huh? Yeah. Thought you might like that. You're probably used to getting by on what a hungry coyote would gag on."

He tossed another scrap. "This is a lot better than that. Prime Bar T beef."

Again, the dog took the tendered nourishment. When he'd finished it, he sat waiting for the next course. Against his better judgment, Harry continued his descent into the quicksand of hospitality. As he sank, it was dawning on him how powerless he was to control his own destiny. How powerless he'd always been. Any sense of dominance he'd ever had always proved in the end to be nothing but illusion. No matter how hard he'd tried all his life, calculation and design had seldom steered his course. His life had been a long series of accidents. Nothing more. Everything important had come to him, or been taken from him, by some power greater than his own, or by no power at all.

"So, now you think we're best pals, huh?" he said to his watchful guest. "Well, don't misread the tea leaves. It's not up to me to take care of you. You're not mine. Not my responsibility."

Harry rose and held up the plate.

"See. All gone. You ate every bit of it. Now git. Get on out of here."

The enlivened dog didn't budge. He'd blundered on to a good deal here, and he was not about to give it up. Harry speculated about that, which led to redirecting his chastisement from the dog to himself. He, the human being on the premises, was the one who deserved it.

"Shoulda known better. Hell. I did know better. But that didn't stop me. I guess some things have to be. Right or wrong. Good or bad. For better or worse."

Harry lowered his face into his free hand and let it rest there. When he looked up, the dog hadn't moved.

"Guess I'll never get rid of you now. Well, if you're going to be hanging around here I guess I'm going to have to give you a name." He thought a minute. "Bob. I'll call you Bob. I always wanted a dog named Bob."

Bob stood, paced in a circle. That's when Harry noticed Bob was a girl.

He thought another moment or two before making up his mind.

"Well, be that as it may, I'm calling you Bob. Used to know a fellow name of Bob. Said his name was Bob, spelled backwards. Guess that'll go for you, too."

Knowing the first true light of day carried some reality he didn't want to confront, Harry watched the sun rise. Like an outrider for the firestorm of change making up in Serafina, the morning blaze was heading right for him. He could already feel the heat. He could hear the crackle and hiss of combustion. And he knew that amidst its gasping flames, Woody Coats, an innocent young man facing guilt by pigmentation, was calling out for help. Calling to him.

Miles away, Bliss was suffering her own dolorous night. She lay in her bed, eyes fixed on the ceiling, heart weighty as a creek rock within her. At her side, lay her lawful husband. She forced herself not to move, but in time she had to give up on sleep. Rising, being careful not to wake Marsh, she gathered up her dressing gown from a nearby chair and, slipping it on, padded barefoot down the hall and into the living room. There, she stood in semidarkness before the front window, gazing out at the dim light of breaking day, eyes stinging with tears. She bolstered herself with crossed arms.

Bliss had been aghast when Marsh and Buddy returned to Sweet Leona's the night of the near-lynching and told her and Ruth about the confrontation with the angry mob. She'd had to suppress a gasp when Buddy mentioned what night the crime Woody was being accused of had taken place. She'd hoped Harry would return to Sweet Leona's so she could signal him they needed to talk. But he didn't and they'd had no contact since.

Like Esau and others in town, the womenfolk especially, Bliss had heard what people were saying about who really raped Alejandra Flores, or who one of her attackers was, at least: the same person now trying to pin the crime on Woody. She rued her stubborn defense of Billy Catlett whenever Harry disparaged him, insisting there had to be good in him somewhere. She didn't believe that anymore.

Now, Bliss stood at the living room window, hugging herself, thoughts spinning. She and Harry had to come forward, tell the sheriff, tell everyone that they had seen Woody somewhere else that night. But that could cost them . . . everything.

With so much at stake she had to sort things out. First, she tried to justify doing nothing. *Surely, the sheriff knows Woody didn't rape the girl. He won't need Harry and me to clear that up for him. Surely, he's heard the rumors about Billy, too. All he really needs is for the girl to identify him. And maybe she will once she recovers more. Who's to say? Things have a way of working out. Leave it alone.* But sometimes, Bliss chastised herself, things don't work out. And keeping quiet would be lying by omission. It would be dishonest and make Harry and Bliss out-and-out cowards. She owed the Coats family more. She'd known Woody and his parents for years; Polly Coats had been like a second mother to her when she'd fallen ill years before, watching over her in the hospital and nursing her back to health—even sneaking Harry up to visit her. *They've always been there for me when I needed them. Now, I have to be there for them. But, how do I do it?*

She tried rationalizing her infidelity to her husband. *I can't go on blaming myself forever. These things happen. What's done is done. I have to find a way to live with it. Harry and I were always meant to be together. But how can we be? It's impossible. I can't do that to Marsh. He doesn't deserve it. I've hurt him too much already. I've ruined our marriage. I've destroyed his friendship with Harry. Oh, Marsh.*

At that moment, Marsh came up behind her. He plied his chest to her back, enfolded her with his arms. She startled.

"Easy. It's me," he whispered in her ear.

He tightened his embrace.

"You're trembling. Are you cold?"

"A little."

Marsh attempted to warm her arms and shoulders with his hands. He could feel her body tense beneath his touch. He swept her fine hair from the nape of her neck and kissed her there, felt her pull slightly away.

"Why don't you come back to bed?"

"I can't sleep. I'm not feeling well."

"Comin' down with somethin'?"

"I don't know. I don't think so. I'll be all right."

She turned and put a hand to her husband's cheek.

"Really. I'll be OK."

Dubious, Marsh searched her eyes.

"Is there somethin' we need to talk about?"

"Talk? No, I don't think so. Why?"

"I don't know. Never mind."

"No. There's nothing. I'm tired is all."

"I love you. I truly love you," Marsh said. "You know I do. But . . . is there something . . . I wonder if . . . ."

Bliss closed her eyes. Sensing her sadness, Marsh pulled back from the treacherous minefield of candor. Swallowing his doubts, he turned and walked away.

Bliss let him go. Again, she stood alone at the living room window. In the east, she could see a volcanic sunrise erupting. Another day was dawning and this one, like so many of its predecessors, would be nothing but a wellspring of guilt, shame, and fear. She wept. But she didn't make a sound.

Part Four

CHAPTER 18

The Burnt Cork Mask

The next night, Harry braced himself for the gathering of the Serafina elite at the annual Men's Club banquet. In the past, the highlight of the evening at the high school gymnasium had been a blackface minstrel show. White showmen, faces masked with burnt cork, would take the stage for an *opéra bouffe,* a spectacle of song and dance and skits reminiscent of Broadway's vaudeville days. This year, in response to criticisms of some citizens, including Bliss and Ruth, the planners had agreed to shorten the minstrel show and tone it down. The real headliners on the bill would be a barber shop quartet, a soft-shoe hoofer who couldn't dance a lick, and a pianist. Whether the planners would make good on their promise remained to be seen.

Members of Serafina's leading civic organization included bankers, grocers, merchants of all types, farmers, and ranchers. Veterans of the most recent world war, a few of the first. Some of them decorated for bravery, for service to country above and beyond the call of duty. Good Christian men all, they cared about their community and gave of their time and meager fortunes to make it better. The evening's proceeds would go for some worthy cause—improvement of the city recreation center, supplies for the high school or the Black Flats school. The club paid for the sign at the town's northside gateway, the one that declaimed in fancy script, *Serafina. A Good Place to Live, A Place to Grow!*

Harry would have been happy to skip the event, but Ruth wanted to go. She approved of the fundraising aspect of it and enjoyed getting gussied up and mixing with Serafina's finest. No fan of minstrel shows, she didn't know how much of it she'd be able to tolerate. But she was interested in how other members of the community would respond to it. She wanted to keep a wary eye on the guardians of the decaying past and help hold their feet to the fire.

"I might have to go out for a smoke when that part of the program starts," she told Harry as they were driving to the event.

"You don't smoke."

Ruth gave him the evil eye. He shrugged. "Up to you."

They entered the banquet hall arm in arm. Harry wore his dark Sunday suit, a starched white shirt, black calfskin boots polished to a high gloss, a crimson tie emblazoned with a hand-painted palomino horse's head. Ruth had dolled herself up, crimping and arranging her lush locks of umber hair, painting her nails, applying makeup. Her full bosom filled out her navy satin cocktail dress in the way the designer must have intended.

Marsh and Bliss arrived soon after Harry and Ruth. Mr. and Mrs. Stone were curried and combed, duded up and dolled up. A firm believer that clothes make the man, Marsh always claimed to possess more than his share of personal *élan* —a word he learned from Harry. On this night he had decked himself out in full war paint: western-cut suit, moon gray in color, smile pocket on the jacket front, stylized yoke on the back. A white pearl snap shirt and black silk string tie completed his outfit. He had slicked back his hair with a dab of Brylcreem and cologned his cheeks with Bay Rum, a concoction he called foo foo water. "Draws women like flies," he always said.

Bliss stood tall and willowy, flaxen hair coifed to perfection, cheeks brightened with a touch of rouge, lips full and red, eyelashes long and curved. At once elegant and daring, and completely seductive to Harry.

She made quite a picture in a new pink dress that became her in a way unlike anything he'd seen her wear. It had a see-through lace bodice and when she leaned forward the least little bit, the décolletage revealed a hint of the valley of her breasts. Harry's eyes kept straying to that place, despite his efforts to fix them on her face.

Harry knew what he had to do this night. An hour back, he'd assigned to himself the onerous task of maintaining a benign presence. He must do nothing to give himself away. It would, perhaps, be a fantastic feat of self-mastery but he would take great pains to avoid any manifestation of his true feelings about Bliss or the tormented nature of his thoughts. He wanted to talk to her, find out what she knew about the Woody Coats business, what she thought they should do. But he'd have to wait for the right moment, if it came. Not yet a past master at the art of lying, he'd have to be on his game.

At their initial encounter, Ruth and Bliss exchanged perfunctory greetings and pleasantries.

"I love your dress," Ruth told Bliss. "It's very flattering."

Bliss managed to smile. "Why, thank you, Ruth. You're looking lovely yourself."

Harry and Marsh howdyed and shook. As always, Marsh delivered a bone-crushing grip and a violent wag of hands. His way with all men. For Ruth he bent at the waist and made a chivalric bow. When she offered her hand, Marsh accepted it, planted a delicate kiss on it. If he could have called to mind a suitable line from Shakespeare he would have delivered it. Knowing none, he stood straight—chin tucked in, arms at his sides, feet together—clicked his heels and in his best attempt at mannered speech said, "Boy howdy, Ruth, you are pretty as a picture. I do believe you get beautifuler every day. But I think that's true for all of us. You don't have to be too smart to know who got all the good looks in this county. Somebody needs to make a Kodak of us." Everyone smiled. Marsh grinned the widest.

Marsh made no bones about counting himself and his old friend Harry as sure-enough Sebastian County grandees. And their ladies belles of the ball. Marsh reached an arm around Harry's shoulders and held him tight.

"Ooohee. This here's somethin' now. I am here to tell you. Ain't nothin' but class. Top drawer. Just look at all these folks outfitted in their best bib and tucker. Regular flock of peacocks. New York City, eat your heart out."

The young cockerels found an open table for six and seated their sweethearts. Wide-eyed, Marsh admired the elaborate banquet decorations. Crepe paper bunting and streamers in red, white, and blue. Clusters of bright-colored balloons. Splendid tables laid with the best china and silverware Serafina had to offer. A sprinkling of diamond dust glitter on the tablecloths. In the corner of the capacious room, a Hi-Fi was setting a festive mood for the evening, giving out the melodious—if somewhat crackly—tones of Rosemary Clooney singing "Hey There."

Soon, the newspaper man Ned Brett, a well-fed, ginger-cheeked gentleman with a fringe of hoarfrost hair around his bald pate, drifted over with his wife, Mildred, a silver-haired, bosomy lady whose girth rivaled her husband's.

"These two seats saved?"

"Saved for you," Marsh said. "Proud to have you. It'd be like fillin' a inside straight. Sides, you may want to put our picture on the front page of the *Gazette* next week."

Harry showed a trace of a smile but no more.

The Bretts were at least ten, fifteen years older than Harry and Marsh, but they always made good company. Publisher and editor of the *Serafina Gazette*, the only public press in the county, Ned was a hardworking newspaper man, smart and educated, articulate, curious. A news-hungry reporter, he liked to think he had his finger on the collective pulse. More than that, he had better than a passing acquaintance with the world beyond Sebastian County. And he had an appreciation of the cultural upheaval overtaking the country in the summer of 1954.

A born skeptic, Ned Brett owned the cynical manner of a blue-blooded ambassador of the Fourth Estate. He believed a statement of fact, no matter who delivered it, required verification. To him, it seemed a good bet the instinctive response of most people to a penetrating question, especially politicians, was to lie. He expected it, enjoyed it. A good lie aroused his sense of competition and piqued his own probity. It gave him the opportunity to bore in, to ferret out the truth, a treasure often given up grudgingly by those who possess it. But he managed not to take his allegiance to veracity or anything else too seriously. He maintained a healthy sense of humor about the human condition and remained philosophical when it came to his own failings. If someone lambasted the *Gazette* for misspelling a name or not getting a story right, he countered with a quick retort, "It don't cost but a nickel." An old joke, Ned admitted, but he remained loyal to it, and stood ready to acknowledge and correct any errors he made.

The Reverend Thomas Evans, known as Snowy Evans because of his unruly thatch of white hair, opened the evening's program with a blessing. According to Marsh, the right reverend, head minister of the Methodist Church and the man who had married him and Bliss, was a real glory stomper. He could preach the hell out of anybody. He opposed drinking, smoking, chewing tobacco, and everything else Marsh was for. That, for the most part, disenchanted him with churchgoing.

On the preacher's command, the folks in the now crowded gymnasium silenced themselves. Every head bowed. In a stentorian voice, the black-suited clergyman delivered a well-known two-minute homily: thanks for the bounty of their tables and other generous blessings of the Lord God Almighty, confession of sins, a plea for forgiveness, a humble appeal for continued blessings. The assembled faithful capped the invocation with a hearty amen pronounced in unison. The preacher declared dinner and a staff of dark-hued waiters and waitresses set about serving a fine feast of locally raised prime beef, with generous helpings of boiled vegetables, to light-skinned Serafinians.

Marsh stuffed a corner of his napkin into his shirt collar, let it flatten across his chest. Looking around at the plates being placed before the diners, he proclaimed it was all sure to be larrupin' good. No sidemeat and beans for this crowd. Not on this night. "And looky here," Marsh said, waving the printed menu card. "Dainties and desserts, too. A spread of divinity candies and a wedge of pecan pie." He winked at Bliss. "Bet it cain't beat yours, Darlin.'"

Harry folded his napkin in half, laid it on his lap, and watched the waitstaff work. They filled glasses with iced tea from frosty pitchers. Complemented the main course with home-baked rolls plucked from fabric-lined baskets with silver tongs. A night's work would bring short pay but enough to put new shoes on a child's feet or a week's worth of groceries in the kitchen cupboard. Harry scanned the room and spotted Esau Coats serving a table in a distant corner of the gym. This year, as always, Esau had signed on to make a few extra dollars waiting tables. Woody would have been there, too, Harry thought, if he weren't lying low somewhere, trying to avoid trouble. Harry averted his eyes before Esau noticed him.

Before their table had been served, Ned Brett, lighting a smoke, brought up the subject of the night's entertainment.

"So I understand the minstrel show will go on tonight as usual."

Marsh winced. "Now, Ned, why'd you have to go and—"

"Not quite as usual," Bliss said, cutting Marsh off.

Harry saw the women at the table exchange knowing looks.

Ned raised his eyebrows. "Oh?"

"They've kept it this year," Ruth said. "But this is supposed to be the last time."

"And it's supposed to be shorter," Bliss added. "And less offensive."

"That's what they told us, anyway, when we asked them to cancel it," Mildred Brett commented. "Might've been to placate us."

"Did you know," Ned said in a didactic manner, turning back to Harry, "the blackface minstrel show started out in New York in the 1840s, better than a hundred years ago. For a long time, it's been a tradition of civic organizations, schools, churches. Thousands of performances every year across the country. Now, seems to me, the way of things is changing. Events of this type may not be too welcome these days."

The women matched eyes again.

"Well, we know how the ladies feel," Ned said. "What do you make of that, Mr. True?"

Harry hitched one shoulder but kept mum. Ned inspected his cigarette, flicked ash into the tray.

"Our show don't differ from others," he continued. "Not a damn thing unique about it."

Mildred touched her husband's arm. "Ned."

Ned ignored her signal.

"We make sport of the darker race while they serve us supper. Coon songs, Negro hambone. Skits and jokes about darkies eating possum. Men with the big lazies. Promiscuous women. You agree with the ladies that the minstrel show is on its last legs, Harry?"

Harry declined to respond.

"Really quite remarkable, when you think about it. There's sort of an unreality about it. Folks put on that burnt cork mask and they can do and say things they'd never do and say otherwise. Gives them cover. They can be anonymous. What do you think, Harry? I always figured you for part of the intelligentsia of Serafina. That about the way you figure it?"

"I'll tell you what I think," Marsh said. "I think I need to get myself a refill on this here iced tea. Bliss, honey, you need anything?"

"No, thank you."

"Ruth?"

"I think I'll freshen my lipstick," Ruth said, rising.

"I think I'll join you," Mildred said. "Bliss? Care to join us?"

"Yes, thank you."

Alone at the table with Harry, Ned bored in.

"I don't seem to be making much progress here. Something got you sulled up?"

"Yeah. You."

Ned Brett laughed. "Well, to get anything out of you, I reckon I'd have to keep on digging for a long time, wouldn't I?"

"From now until you get religion."

"Well, that's about as likely as Reverend Evans giving jitterbug lessons tonight. Very doubtful, I'd say."

Ned had a good belly laugh at his own joke. When he quit

laughing and worked his way through the cough that followed it, he let the matter lie.

Marsh and the women returned, and the evening continued. During dinner, music wafted from the phonograph. Frank Sinatra. The McGuire Sisters. Bing Crosby. Doris Day. Beneath it, the steady clink and clatter of knives and forks striking plates, tinkle of ice cubes in glasses. Low drone of conversation. The subjects of discussion at Harry and Marsh's table ranged from politics to ranching to the weather. Table-hopping to greet friends between the main course and dessert, Harry overheard snippets of more polemic discourse about the tide of social change sweeping the country and concerns Serafina would be swept up in the craziness.

The staunchest advocates of traditional ways insisted Serafina would remain far removed from the consternation, that the social order in their little town would never change. "Our coloreds know their place," he heard a banker say. "They're well treated here and they like it fine. They tend to their bidness. We tend to ours. They keep to their part of town. We keep to ours." Harry wanted to collect Ruth and leave the nettlesome shindig right then, but didn't, couldn't. He needed to talk to Bliss.

Harry returned to his table. The evening wore on. Harry fought the bit through every minute of it. He could feel the secret he shared with Bliss scalding his insides. One moment, he was swearing to himself he'd give her up and put Serafina in his rearview mirror, keep their secret and let Woody fend for himself. The next, he was envisioning another assignation with her. Sitting opposite him, Bliss felt Harry's eyes on her, knew the effect she was having on him and, although it made her somewhat uncomfortable—Was Ruth watching? Would Marsh see?— she had to admit she liked it. As sinful as her relationship with him was, as often as she told herself they had to end it, she felt driven to nourish it, protect it. She had no right to be jealous, she knew, but seeing Harry with Ruth proved hard to endure and made Bliss want him more.

Breaking bread with both couples together for the first time, Ned and Mildred Brett didn't fail to notice that Harry and Bliss had eyes for each other. From time to time, the newspaperman and his wife exchanged knowing glances, caught Ruth studying them. Meanwhile, Marsh kept up the laughing and joking. If he took note of anything, he didn't let it show.

Well into the evening's festivities, Harry caught another glimpse of Esau. The sagacious old gentleman stood with his arms crossed at the wrists in the dim margin of the banquet room. Harry would not allow Ned Brett to draw him into a discussion of minstrel shows. But the sight of Esau standing stone-faced set Harry to thinking. Was it time to end them? He and Marsh had broached the subject over beers at Sweet Leona's a few evenings before, shaking their heads and chuckling over what their women had been up to, wanting the WHITES ONLY signs to come down and the minstrel shows to stop. After a few moments' thought, Marsh shrugged. "I dunno, mebbe they're right."

"Right about what?"

"All of it. The shows, the signs, everything. Like Bliss says, they're good enough to fight with us in a war, but they can't drink from the same water fountain when they come home? *If* they come home?" He moved his shoulders up and down again. "It is pretty insultin.'"

Harry had been surprised. It was unlike Marsh to voice a blunt opinion about most anything to anyone, even to his blood brother. He must have been thinking about this a lot. *Bliss's influence,* Harry thought. *How could her passion not sway him?* Harry wondered what

Marsh would have said if Ned had put him in the hot seat, wasn't surprised when Marsh made a break for the punch bowl. But they couldn't duck the question forever. Harry knew that. Sooner or later, they were all going to have to take a side. And what would his be? Harry had attended a dozen or more of these minstrel shows over the years. It had been an annual affair for him, part of the fabric of life in Serafina. He'd always laughed at the ribald jokes and had even participated in a few skits. Never thought twice about it. Never considered that Esau was there, watching. Never thought about Esau at all. Until now.

"I am full as a tick," Marsh said after putting away double helpings of meat and potatoes and a wedge of pie. Setting his fork on his plate, he ran two fingers inside the collar of his starched shirt, laid the flats of his hands against his distended belly. "Whoo-boy. That was one fine feed. I have damn near et enough to choke a shoat. One more bite of this fine chuck and I might founder myself."

Everyone at the table agreed.

"They had a good scald on it, I have to say," Marsh added. "Of course, it ain't no match for Bliss's home cookin.'"

Everyone at the table smiled politely, except for Harry and Bliss herself.

As the waiters and waitresses bussed tables, members of the program committee busied themselves with final preparations for the evening's entertainment. A volunteer crew had constructed a stage of plywood and two-by-fours at the east end of the gymnasium and run what would pass for a theater curtain across the room on a rope that extended from wall to wall. The flurry of backstage activity alerted the banqueters to the approach of showtime.

Along with other free spirits, Marsh repaired to the parking lot for a pre-show tipple, in this instance a quick snort of snakebite medicine from the short dog stashed in his jacket pocket. As he took his leave he touched Bliss's shoulder. Ruth saw her frown slightly. The ladies at the table excused themselves again.

The two of them alone at the table for the second time, Ned Brett crowded close to Harry. "So you never did answer me," he said. "Do you think this kind of thing has seen its day? All the bigoted doggerel and such."

This time Harry relented.

"Hard to say. My opinion, yes. No doubt about it. But I don't make the rules."

Ned sat back in his chair. "The game is afoot. The question is, do these other folks see it? They're good people, you know. Not a stumblebum among 'em. Paid hard-earned money to be here tonight. And it'll go to a good cause. Maybe fix the heater at the Black Flats school, put a fence around the playground. Ain't one of 'em thinks he's a racist, I'll bet you that. But they ain't gonna have a colored family over for dinner. Sure ain't gonna let their daughter marry a darky. Don't even want coloreds and whites attending the same school. And here they sit, smilin' and waitin' to watch a damn minstrel show."

Harry scanned the room, turned and looked Ned dead in the eye. "We're here, too, aren't we?"

Ned nodded. "So we are, so we are. Touché." He took a pack of Chesterfields from his shirt pocket, offered Harry a smoke. Harry waved it away. Ned tight-packed a cigarette and lit up. He placed the pack next to his plate and set the lighter on the pack as if he saw some virtue in maintaining an orderly table arrangement. He switched gears.

"Reckon Woody Coats couldn't make it this year. Understandable. I see Esau made it, though. His boy's hidin' out somewhere, but he's here workin' these tables. Maybe servin' steak to some of the same folks that wanted to lynch his son the other night. That's something, ain't it?"

The newspaper man sat, smoking, waiting for a reply. Got none.

"Well, reckon everybody does what he has to do to get by. You figure that's how it is?"

"You working on a story tonight, Ned?"

Ned laughed. "Mildred says I'm always working on a story. Claims she's afraid anything she says she'll read in the paper next week. Might could be right."

"Well, I didn't come here to be interviewed."

Ned didn't back off. Harsh words and a poor humor never deterred him.

"The high sheriff, Mr. Mackey, thinks you might know something about what happened to that little Mexican gal. You know, the one Woody Coats is alleged to have mistreated."

Harry bristled. "Yeah. I know who you mean."

"Dutch says he thinks you might be able to shed some light on what happened."

"He does, huh?"

A sullen hush followed. Ned took a long draft on his cigarette and exhaled a stream of smoke. With deliberate movement he stubbed out the glowing embers. He leaned back, pegged his thumbs in his vest pockets, sharpened his gaze at Harry.

"Dutch says—"

"Dutch must be getting loose lipped," Harry said. "I don't know what the sheriff's been telling you but I didn't think he was supposed to be blabbing to newspaper men about his cases."

"Well . . . I don't guess he exactly said anything out plain. I'm trying to connect the dots."

"Figured." Harry quit his chair. "I need some air."

In the lobby, he saw Bliss heading back into the gym with Ruth and Mildred. Their eyes caught and held for a dangerous moment. Harry stepped behind an open gymnasium door and watched as Bliss stopped, fumbled in her purse as if she'd left something in the powder room and gestured to her companions to go on without her. When they were a few paces away, she headed down a shadowy corridor leading to a maintenance closet. Harry followed.

"Harry, we have to talk," Bliss said, sounding worried. "What they did to Woody . . . that poor girl . . . But it wasn't Woody. Just couldn't have been Woody." She searched his eyes. "Harry, what're we going to do?"

"I don't know. Maybe nothing. Maybe we wait and hope—"

"You're not serious."

"I don't know. Maybe I am. We can't—"

"Harry," Bliss said, surprised and disappointed.

She turned and strode away. Harry started to follow but thought better of it. When he was sure she was gone he emerged from the corridor and ran headlong into Marsh.

"Hey, buddy. You lost?" Marsh said.

Harry shook his head. "Come on. They're about to crank this thing up."

"Think anybody'd notice if we made ourselves scarce?"

"'Fraid so."

Marsh's low-level inebriation had put a glow on his cheeks and primed him for the evening's entertainment. He swelled his chest and put an arm around Harry.

"Let's get this show on the road," he said. "Time to get it over with."

CHAPTER 19

Smoke

The barbershop quartet, the soft-shoe hoofer, and the pianist all had their fifteen-minute slots, offering middling performances that drew polite applause. The minstrel show capped the evening's entertainment. The mummers, rank amateurs all, faces blackened with burnt cork, mouths and eyes circumscribed with wide white circles, had donned flamboyant costumes. Outlandish zoot suits in loud colors—purple, red, yellow. Grandiose plaid panes the size of a splay-fingered hand. White spats on their feet. Long gold watch chains hooping from pockets. Fedoras with brims trimmed to no more than two inches, crowns open, standing tall, made white and brittle with plaster of Paris, all to make them resemble Harlem derbies.

Cut from more than an hour to about thirty minutes, the performance was toned down from previous years. The more overtly racist skits and jokes about lazy darkies and loose women had been dropped. But the ones that remained still made the women at Harry's table uncomfortable.

Say, Mr. Tambo, how much does a fool weigh?
I don't know, Mr. Bones.
Well, why don't you get on de scales and find out?

Mr. Bones, why were you running down the street so fast last night?
I was running to stop a fight.

Who was fighting?

Me and another feller.

The show closed with a blackface chorus singing a song called "Old Darkey Plantation Refrain."

> Thar's a happy little home down in southern Tennessee,
> War the ivy blossoms twine around the door
> And for ever fresh and green in my memory it will be,
> Though I know I'll never see it any more . . .
>
> When the autumn days had come, I would husk the yellow corn,
> In the field I was singing all the day.
> And before they made me free I had never cause to mourn,
> And around the old place everything was gay . . .

The performance ended to shouts of acclamation and thunderous applause from a good two-thirds of those in attendance, silence from the rest. Champions of tradition leaped to their feet. On stage, amateur vaudevillians took self-mocking bows, wide white smiles stretching from ear to ear on darkened faces. A curtain call followed. More cheers. More applause. Above the fleshy rumble of clapping hands soared random cries of "Bravo! Bravo!"

At Harry's table, the women sat with eyes downcast, hands in their laps. Likewise, the men. The so-called anodyne version of the show had fallen short of the mark.

"I don't think I'd call that toning it down," Ruth said.

"Nor would I," Bliss agreed.

Mildred added, "I'd say we have some work to do."

Ned scanned their faces. "What say you, my esteemed tablemates? Shall we take our leave of this establishment? And charge forth into the twentieth century before it's too late?" All rose.

When the clapping, whistling and stomping abated, patrons of every stripe collected their belongings and, amid a great tramping and shuffling of feet, funneled through the exit. The crowd fanned out on the sidewalk and lingered to say their goodnights. In the scant blue paling of the one florescent light mounted above the door, matches flared, enkindling cigarettes, signaling commencement of the inevitable postmortem of the evening's entertainment. Marsh held forth in the thick of it. Arm around Bliss, he put on his own performance, wisecracking about the good citizens of Serafina turning out in their finery. "Didn't recognize half of them with their faces washed and their hair combed." Rubbing his belly and bemoaning how much he'd eaten and confessing how a little bit of joy juice had settled his nerves before the show. "Helped it all go down a little easier. Which is a good thing, you know what I'm sayin'? I mean we ain't talkin' the Radio City Rockettes here, am I right?" His witticisms incited new laughter.

The scene galled Harry. The sound of Marsh's voice. His facial expressions. Gestures. His showing off. Was there nothing he wouldn't do to be the center of attention? It struck Harry as uncouth and swinish. And worse, as hypocritical.

From the obscure edge of the throng, Harry watched but took no part in the repartee. The sycophantic laughter of Marsh's loyal subjects, their approbation of his every word, made him want to gag. The sight of Marsh's arm around Bliss aggrieved him more. He took it as a personal affront. The false implication of a steadfast bond between loving spouses was a lie, a damn miserable lie. And Marsh knew it. He had to.

Harry swore to himself, his voice trapped in the back of his throat, "Shut your damn mouth. You sorry son of a bitch."

Ruth Blaylock did not fail to register the intensity of Harry's anger. Tracking his gaze, she understood the narrative playing out before her. It saddened her, frightened her. For Harry's sake. For Marsh's sake. For hers and for Bliss's, too. She feared one day it would all come to grief.

She tugged at Harry's arm. "It's late," she said. "Please take me home."

As if he'd forgotten she was there, Harry said, "Of course. I'm sorry. Let's go."

The crowd began to break up. Amid tailings of laughter, parting words passed between friends. Handshakes. Hugs. But the night was not over. A waning moon lurked in the firmament, its frail slip of light providing no obstacle whatsoever to man-made wickedness. And now, along the horizon, in the stead of the vanished sun, an inauspicious orange glow shimmered. An incisive breeze, snaking in from its epicenter, bore a faint odor of smoke.

"Somethin's burnin'," Leland Cobb said.

"What?" asked Wid Isley.

"Somethin's burnin'."

The crowd stilled, scented the air.

"Smoke for sure," Swede Tomlinson said. "Yeah. Smoke, by golly."

Marsh smelled it now. "Where's it comin' from?"

"West. That way yonder."

Heads turned. Men stepped into the street to reckon with the prescient reek of combustion as the one truck of the Serafina Volunteer Fire Department yawed around the corner from the east, tires squealing, siren shrilling out an alarm. A 1942 model American La France bought at auction a decade after the war with money raised by the Men's Club.

Two men sat in the open cab, Buddy Pond at the wheel and Puny Ferguson beside him. Each wore denim bib overalls, a battle-scarred leather helmet and a stained flame-resistant jacket with reflective yellow borders, all hand-me-downs from some big city fire department. A remarkable sight they made. Short-statured Buddy, who'd picked up his stutter during the war. And Puny, whose name derived from his enormous size, his prodigious gut and hams, thighs that grated on each other and jingled the change in his pockets when he treaded weightily along. Two middle-aged Caucasians, the most ordinary of men. Hardworking, salt-of-the-earth citizens ready to battle a potentially life-threatening fire with minimal equipment.

The small sea of celebrants parted and reformed around the truck as Buddy brought it to a tire-burning halt.

"B . . . B . . . Black Flats school is afire," Pond called out. "B . . . B . . . . B . . . . Burnin' like a son of a bitch. Whole damn place goin' up in flames. F . . F . . F . . . Flats'll be gone if we don't get to it."

"Let it burn," someone shouted. Harry recognized the big-talking fellow in a silverbelly Stetson and window-pane plaid sport jacket who'd laughed the loudest during the show and whistled the shrillest at the end.

"Amen," a few other like-thinking citizens chorused.

Marsh hopped onto the fire truck's running board. "Let it burn? Watch it spread? What're you folks talkin' about? 'Fore you know it, we'll lose the whole damn town."

"Marsh is right," Cal Barton said. "Cain't let it burn. Too dangerous."

"There's good people over yonder," a woman called out. Harry recognized Mildred Brett's voice. "What do you mean, let it burn? We gotta help!"

"Yeah!"

"That's right."

"Can't let it burn."

"We gotta do somethin'."

Marsh hopped from the firetruck, began rounding up the men. "Let's go. We got ourselves a fire to fight."

Husbands and wives said their goodbyes and men scattered by twos and threes to trucks and cars. Some climbed onto the fire engine's running boards and held onto the rails or clambered aboard the vehicle and hunkered down on the wood-planked bed. All aboard, the truck sped away, siren blaring.

Marsh gave Bliss a light peck on the cheek and a quick embrace.

"See you later, honey. Don't wait up. Harry and me'll take our truck. You go on with Ruth."

Bliss gave Marsh a quick, hard hug. "I'll wait up for you."

Harry kissed Ruth on the forehead.

"Y'all take my truck. I'll pick it up tomorrow."

"Be careful."

With those few words, the men and women parted. Harry and Marsh headed for Marsh's truck. Ruth and Bliss set out for Harry's.

Ruth drove. Mile after mile, she said not one word. Never let her eyes stray from the bug-spattered windshield. Bliss deported herself in like manner, staring out the passenger window into the unmitigated darkness that governed beyond the reach of low wattage city lights.

After a while, Bliss lowered her window. She put a timorous hand to her forehead, let the wind curry her hair. Silence held until she switched on the radio. Bob Wills and His Texas Playboys came across the airwaves singing "Faded Love," a tune about broken hearts.

Before the end of the second verse, Ruth had had enough. She reached over and cut off the radio with a sharp turn of the wrist.

"What are you doing?" she said, her tone severe. "What are you doing, Bliss?"

Ruth's sternness took Bliss aback.

"What do you mean? I'm listening to the radio."

"Don't play games with me. You know what I mean. You know exactly what I mean. *What* are you doing?"

"What—"

"How do you see this playing out? Who's going to end up getting hurt? Harry? Marsh? Which is it? Because somebody's going to get his heart broken. Or worse."

Bliss's eyes rounded. She felt the blood rush to her face.

"I don't know what you're talking about. I don't—"

"Please. Spare me the act. And what about *their* relationship, huh? Have you thought about that? Those two have been closer than blood kin all their lives. If something happened to destroy that friendship . . ." Ruth glanced at Bliss. "Which, of course, something will now. No way around it. I don't know if those boys could survive it. I truly don't."

Ruth's unsparing frankness caught Bliss off guard. She found herself in a muddle of confused emotions, not knowing whether to act innocent and insulted or assume the posture of a penitent and confess her sin. Acting on instinct, she tried to work up at least a particle of righteous anger, to claim the moral high ground, as if it were hers to claim.

"Who do you think you are, Ruth, talking to me like that? You are way out of line." But the brutal impact of the truth had weakened her. Her words suggested strength, but her voice trembled and she would not meet Ruth's eyes. "My private life is none of your business," she continued. "What I choose to do—"

"You are really something, you know that?"

Ruth tried to calm herself. She sat back in her seat, keeping her eyes on the darkness coming toward her at highway speed.

"I asked you a question, Bliss. I'd like an answer. How, pray tell, do you think this is going to work out?"

Bliss didn't respond.

"Come on. What's the plan? Are you and Harry going to run off somewhere and live happily ever after? He and Marsh will part friends? Everything will be fine? Is that what you're thinking?" Ruth gave Bliss a chastening look. "Are you completely out of your mind?"

Bliss quaked. Tears came. Her throat constricted and crippled her voice all the more.

"Maybe I am. Maybe we're both fools. But I know I love him. That's all I know. I've always loved him."

Ruth sighed, softened. "I know. I know you do. And he loves you. Always has and always will. I know that, Bliss. My guess is Marsh knows it, too. But you're a married woman. You are a married woman. Maybe Harry should have been your husband. But he's not. You married Marsh, and he loves you."

"You don't understand. You don't know."

Ruth restrained herself from outright mockery.

"You think I don't know? My God. I know better than any of you what it's like to lose what you love most in the world. I know how it feels to be alone."

Bliss fell silent, realizing it was time to listen.

"When I got the news about Joe, I thought my life was over. I wanted to die, too. I should have. But I didn't. Harry came along. Broken as I was. Body and mind. Heart, too. We were the walking wounded. A perfect pair."

At that moment, the truck's high beams threw into relief something in the middle of the road. A yearling doe. Not thirty feet ahead, the critter stood on delicate legs, jittery hooves contending with uncertain purchase on pavement, eyes wide with fright, shining yellow. Off her turf, she was lost in an alien land of asphalt and steel machines that move fast and come out of nowhere. Spellbound by headlights, she froze.

"Watch out!" Bliss cried.

Ruth stomped on the brake. Tires squealing, she swerved hard to the right, maintaining a chokehold on the steering wheel. Bliss braced her arms against the dash. The truck quartered the road's rocky flange, plowed through an edging of switch cane, and nosed into the bar ditch. Barreling forward with Ruth struggling to keep it from tipping sideways, the vehicle bounded and bucked along the shallow drainage, kicking up gravel and dirt, decelerating enough for Ruth to steer it out of the ditch and back onto the road.

The truck bumped and rattled to a halt. Stunned but unharmed, too shaken to speak, the reluctant traveling companions tried to collect themselves. When Ruth had her wits about her, she reached for Bliss, sitting rigid as if in shock.

"Are you all right?"

Bliss made no response.

"Look at me. Are you all right?"

"I . . . I . . . ."

"Are you hurt?"

No answer.

"Bliss, are you hurt?"

"Did we kill it? Is it—"

"No. I think we missed it."

Bliss burst into tears. She wept for all she'd done. For all she'd failed to do. For what she was, and what she was not. She wept for the elusiveness of the happiness she feared could never be hers.

Ruth put her arms around her and held her close. In an attitude of complete surrender, Bliss buried her face in Ruth's shoulder. Ruth sat peering into the enveloping night. She held Bliss for a long time, comforting her as a mother would comfort a heartbroken child. She let her cry but fought back her own tears.

"It's all right. It's all right. Shh. Shh. It's all right."

"What am I going to do? What am I going to do?"

"I don't know, Bliss. I don't know."

CHAPTER 20

Fire

Marsh drove like a man possessed. Keeping the foot feed to the floor, he raced past the fire engine and other vehicles as if they were standing still. He pounded the horn, took corners at top speed, blew stop signs like a man trying to beat a train through a railroad crossing. Damn near ran two cars off the road. For Harry, Marsh's driving constituted one more transgression for the tally book. One more irksome thing to hold against his old friend.

In his mind's eye, Harry could see Marsh flourishing onto the scene, taking command of the firefighting, shouting encouragement to the other men. Caesar and his legions. No doubt, he had the perfect pose for the occasion in mind. Before getting down to the serious business of fighting the fire, he might crack a few jokes, regale the crowd with yet another retelling of past deeds of derring-do. Every man would listen with rapt attention, laugh on cue, cheer at the correct moment. Shameless ass-kissers.

Harry came within a breath of barking out a command to Marsh to let up on the gas. The words formed in his mind. *Slow down, dammit. Are you trying to kill us?* He would suggest to Marsh in a condescending manner that if he'd ratchet down the speed a little, pay some heed to Newton's laws of motion, their chances of living until morning would rise dramatically. "Do you get it?" he would say. "Do you understand? Is this penetrating that thick brain bucket of yours?" He came close to saying that and a lot of other things. But, in the end, he managed to hold his tongue. Nothing he could have said would have made any difference anyway. At the first sign of criticism, Marsh would have stepped up the truck all the more.

Before Harry and Marsh could see the fire itself, they could hear its roar, feel its heat. Smoky air assaulted their eyes, their nostrils. A glow the color of a Halloween pumpkin loomed in the western sky, silhouetting treetops rising between them and the maelstrom. The sensorial cues they were receiving carried an unmistakable warning that they were approaching the outskirts of hell.

When they arrived at their destination, they found the schoolhouse engulfed in a frenzy of fire. The doomed structure pulsed under the unremitting assault coming at it from within. Plumes of black smoke twisted upward through fissures in exterior walls; thin curling strands of pale gray exhaust spooled out from smaller flues. Along the roof ridge, profligate flames danced about like a troupe of delirious banshees.

The primary blaze had retched out offshoots, here and there igniting a small outbuilding, a patch of dry vegetation, a few cracker box houses. Fire wreathed trees from tuberous root to leafy pinnacle. Runnels of flame ran everywhere. Black Flats residents thrashed away at them with wet tow sacks, stomped on them. Unable to crank open the one fire hydrant in the neighborhood for want of a proper tool, a desperate army of poor Black men and women and their children had formed two parallel bucket brigades stretching to ground zero from a meandering artery of water that passed nearby. Amid an outcry of frantic voices, bucketeers transferred sloshing two-gallon containers from hand to hand along the human chain in one direction, empty ones in the other, determined to save their school and homes eight quarts at a time.

Harry and Marsh leaped from the truck and stood amazed, getting their first straight-on look at the holocaust of fire. Its true dimensions astounded them. They had expected it to be bad, but they hadn't expected this. Humbled before such a pernicious monster, petty grievances and personal grudges were forgotten. Betrayal and infidelity, destruction of a marriage, loss of a friendship, all pinched down to insignificance. Harry and Marsh knew this would be a legendary burn, an epic event in the history of a runty redrock country town already struggling to stand hitched to the earth. Folks would talk about this night for as long as there was a place called Serafina. They would mark time with it. Years before the fire, years after. Life in these parts would never be the same.

"Good God A'mighty," Marsh said, not the slightest hint of bravado in his voice. "Would you look at that son of a bitch. That there is a widow-maker if I ever seen one. Sheee-yit."

For the fire combatants, the mission came clear: contain the blaze, knock it down. If they couldn't extinguish it altogether, they at least had to head it off, turn it back into itself like a herd of stampeding cattle. But it wouldn't be easy, for the conflagration already had a strong foothold and it was gaining ground.

The fire engine arrived soon after Harry and Marsh. Leaping from the truck as Buddy Pond brought it to a stop, the volunteers swung into action, offloading and assembling firehose sections. They ran the end piece to the fire hydrant and, using a steel wrench as long as a baseball bat, Buddy Pond connected the brass coupling to the outlet. A squad of men took up the assembled conduit and held it at the ready. Harry grasped the nozzle. Marsh stood behind him.

"All right," Harry called out. "Let her buck."

With the wrench Pond opened the hydrant's operating valve and unleashed a muscular arm of fire-quenching water onto the blazing school. The columnar spray arced through the air and fantailed into a tattered curtain of water. The high-pressure tubing thrashed about in the hosemen's grasp like an angry anaconda. The men fought to keep it steady and aimed.

Some of the volunteers fell in with the bucket brigade. Others helped families trying to wet down their houses with garden hoses. Some helped people evacuate their homes and salvage their meager belongings. Commands rang out. Cries of terror pierced the tumultuous roar. There were pleas for salvation. Prayers. Curses.

As Harry and Marsh struggled to hold the hose steady, a woman clad in a thin cotton night shift rushed up to them, screaming that her daughter was trapped in her burning home. The woman tugged at Harry's arm. Tears streaming down her cheeks, fire reflecting in her liquid eyes, she pointed frantically toward a house being consumed by flames.

"Help. Help me. Please. My baby. My baby."

Controlling the hose was a two-man job. Harry looked around, called out to Buddy Pond, who came running.

"Here, Bud. Take over for me. You and Marsh try to hold her steady."

With Buddy in position, Harry raced to the side of the fire truck, seized the axe secured to it with steel buckles, and ran with the frantic mother to her burning home. Finding the fire well advanced, the modicum of hope he'd harbored for a swift rescue faltered. Fear surged within him. But he didn't let it show. And he didn't let it break his resolve.

"Where is she? Where's your baby?"

"Bedroom. She's in the bedroom."

"Show me."

The woman took Harry's arm and led him around to the side of the house not yet engulfed by flames. She pointed.

"There. She's on the other side of that wall. Right there."

Harry could hear a child's faint cries coming from inside. Thin, reedy voice. Terror stricken.

"Mama! Mama!"

"Stand back," Harry instructed the mother, moving her away a few feet.

He swung the axe, tearing into the clapboard. He struck it once, twice, again and again, opening a rent big enough to squeeze through. But the fire fought back, exhaling a blast of heat and acrid breath so powerful it nearly bowled Harry over. Throwing a forearm up to shield his eyes, he retreated a few steps, dropped the axe to the ground, wheeled around, folded at the waist, hacking and spitting. He rubbed his face, brought himself erect.

Turning back to the burning house, fortifying himself to go in, Harry was wrenched around again by a bone-chilling symphony of destruction coming from the schoolhouse behind him not a hundred yards away. Timbers groaned. Bending steel brackets squealed. Trusses cracked. A window exploded, launching a tempest of flying glass shards. Harry watched the roof ridge open, a section of roof cave in, triggering an ejaculation of luminous embers and a ball of flame that extruded through the rupture like a viper's tongue, sucked itself back in. Everywhere, the rapacious blaze was gathering strength.

Harry turned to the mother. "What's her name? What's your baby's name?"

"Lucy. Her name is Lucy."

"OK. You wait here. I'm gonna go get Lucy."

Throat burning, eyes watering, Harry filled his lungs with air, cramped his shoulders and bent forward, readying to push through the breach in the wall into the unabating storm of fire within. At that instant, a powerful sense of foreboding seized him, a moment of terror and hesitation, of keen awareness of the danger and the horrors confronting him and the gut instinct to freeze or flee. The familiar beast that had dogged him and every one of his companions in arms during the war, the same tightness in the chest, dryness of the mouth, slight tremor in the arms and legs, quickening of the heart. That same feeling of having to summon all his powers of concentration and self-control to remain clear-headed and do what he had to do, even if it cost him his life. One last time, he searched every cranny of his mind for a way out, failed to find one, galvanized himself and entered the delirium of fire.

When the roof of the schoolhouse opened at the ridge, Buddy Pond shouted to Marsh, "G . . . g . . . gotta get closer."

Together, they pulled the hose to a place of better advantage, and Pond took aim at the roof opening with Marsh holding firm behind him.

"That's the ticket!" Pond cried out, not a hint of stutter. "Hold 'er steady! Pull it forward now!"

When the hose resisted, Marsh moved back a few feet to where it was snagged on a tree stump, cleared the tangle and hauled hard to give it some play. His back to the fire, he heard trusses groan again and turned to see another roof section sag and give way, knocking down an entire exterior wall and sending a tsunami of flaming wreckage crashing down on Buddy Pond.

Rushing to help his friend, Marsh took a powerful blow to the forehead by an airborne fragment of roof deck that knocked him hard to the ground and opened a gash above his right eye. He lay on his back, bleeding, stunned and disoriented, gazing at the starry sky through a haze of smoke and bewildered certainty that something was not right.

When he was able, he came to his feet and tried to get to Buddy Pond, but he couldn't. Heat and flames drove him back. With the help of other men, he pulled the hose free from the pile of burning debris and arched the spray over the blazing pyre. Together, they beat the flames back enough to dig through the smoking, sodden mess until they reached their fallen comrade. Buddy's clothes were burned away. His hair was singed down to his scalp, skin charred black over most of his body, hanging in places on his chest and arms like dirty wet gauze. When the men tried to lift him, it clung to their hands.

"Don't," Marsh said. "Don't move him. Leave him be."

Inside the burning house, Harry picked his way along a corridor of fire, daggers of flame slashing at him on all sides. Overhead, loomed a latticework of alligatored rafters and joists. All around him, lay a welter of burning roofing materials, furniture, personal belongings. A nebula of embers and filthy moist air weighed on him.

Over the sounds of riotous combustion, Harry called out to the child.

"Lucy! Lucy! Where are you? Can you hear me?"

He listened, straining to pick out the sound of a cry above the roar of the flames, but heard no answer. Holding an arm across his eyes and covering his mouth and nose with his free hand, Harry negotiated his way deeper into the inferno. He called out again. "Lucy! Lucy!" Still no answer.

When he reached the bedroom and squinted into the smoke, he saw the child. There she lay, curled up on the bed, not moving.

"Lucy! Lucy!"

But the child didn't answer.

Harry gathered her in his arms. He could tell from the limpness of her body he was too late. He felt his heart breaking.

Emerging from the inferno, Harry approached the grief-stricken mother, her dead child in his arms. At first, the woman refused to take her, as if to do so would make the tragic outcome irreversible. She stepped back, locked her arms together, shook her head. "No, no. Unh-unh, unh-unh. No, no, no." But she yielded. "Lucy?" she whispered. She searched Harry's eyes for some sign of hope. Finding none, she opened her arms and accepted her child, and sank to her knees, sobbing, "My baby. My baby. My baby."

Harry backed away. Exhausted, he shambled to join the mourners who'd pressed together around the body of Buddy Pond.

"Wall fell on him," Marsh said in a low voice. "Never had a chance."

They fought the fire all night. Hard going every step of the way. And futile. In the end, the combined efforts of residents and volunteer firefighters could do no more than confine the beast to the area of town in which it started. Beggared folk who started out the day with next to nothing now had less.

The first gray of dawn found the firefighters clustered at their truck, exhausted and filthy, faces mottled with soot, clothes disheveled, stained, torn. Rivulets of sweat and tears reamed through the grit, stinging their eyes, tracking their cheeks. Dead sky, the color of smoke, overshadowed them. Pall of sorrow. Slurries of ashes stood about, clumps of burnt sedge grass, wasted trees. Blackened timbers and charred wreckage lay smoldering. Scent of death. Harry and Marsh sat on the firetruck's running board, heads low. The place held still as a graveyard. Nearby, a fractured community of poor colored folk collected themselves in small groups, grieving, praying. Here and there, a lost soul sat alone, weeping. Others clung to each other.

A small group of men approached the firetruck carrying Buddy Pond's body on a charred door that served as a stretcher. A sooty white sheet splotched with blood covered the corpse. The weary warriors came to their feet and removed their hats. They stood solemnly, watching the stretcher-bearers place their burden in the bed of a pickup and drive away.

About the time the pickup rolled out of sight, Sheriff Dutch Mackey came forward carrying a five-gallon aluminum gasoline can. Scorched and blackened with soot. No cap. The sheriff plunked it to the ground, the empty can clanging.

"There it is. Could be what they used to fire the school. You can see the spallings on the foundation, stem wall. Somebody torched the place. That's for sure. What kind of son of a bitch would do that? Don't know what this world's comin' to."

For a long time, no one said a word. The stillness gave over to the sound of a pickup arriving. Two men stepped out of the cab, each one slamming his door. Billy Catlett and Clayton Stone. Both wore clean clothes. No dirt. No soot. No stains. Catlett produced a pint of Old Grandad from his hip pocket and belted down a drink. He passed the bottle to his partner. Eyes darting between his brother and his head honcho, the boy took a pull. Handed the bottle back to Catlett, who returned it to his pocket.

"My goodness," he said. "Somebody sure did make a mess here. And . . . peeeee . . . yew. This place sure 'nuff does stink. Smells like . . . oh, I don't know . . . like dark meat a little too well done."

Catlett laughed out loud. Clayton grinned. Regarding them with contempt, the firemen stood with backs fence post straight.

"You boys done a real fine job here," Catlett said. "They might make you honorary jigaboos if you ask 'em real nice. You're already startin' to turn."

Catlett laughed again, this time louder. Clayton joined in. Rising in a convulsion of rage, Marsh went to his brother.

"That tears it! You damn fool. Where were you? We're out here workin' our asses off trying to save this little town of ours and where were you?"

The boy opened his mouth to say something, but Marsh didn't let him.

"You are no damn good. You know that? Always have been." He made a spare gesture with his head. "Keep it up and you'll end up real trash, like him."

Catlett took a half-step forward as if to make a show of defiance. The other firefighters closed ranks. Dutch Mackey intervened.

"Hold on, boys. Ain't worth the grief."

The sheriff put himself in front of Catlett and his *segundo*.

"You peckerwoods know somethin' about this fire?"

He nudged the gasoline can with the toe of his boot. "Reckon we might find your fingerprints on this can?"

Silence.

"Cat got your tongue?" Sheriff Mackey spat. "You boys best drag on outa here. You're fixin' to get your butts whupped. Both of you."

Catlett reached into his back pocket and took out the whiskey. He screwed off the cap and took a stiff jolt. Before the bottle left his lips and his Adam's apple quit bobbing, Sheriff Mackey slapped it from his grasp.

"Drinkin' and drivin's illegal. Ain't you heard?"

Catlett's face colored. He crooked his chin at Clayton.

"Come on. Let's get out of here."

Billy Catlett and Clayton Stone sauntered to their truck. They got in and sped away, leaving a rancid flurry of dust and ash in their wake. The sheriff shook his head and spoke to his fellow firefighters.

"Well, boys, you best get on home and get some rest. I got a feelin' you gonna need it. I'm afraid the trouble's a long way from bein' over. If I don't miss my guess, it's just gettin' started."

CHAPTER 21

Skinned Knuckles

Two days later they buried Buddy Pond. Six men, including Harry and Marsh, carried his flag-draped coffin to its final resting place in Serafina's Oak Lawn Cemetery. At the same hour on the other side of town, four men including Esau Coats carried a child size coffin to its burial site in the Black Flats Cemetery. Mourners at both services wept and prayed. Same tears, same prayers. But passions were rising. Two groups of people, yoked by tragedy but divided by race, were pitting themselves against each other.

Likewise, the divide between Marsh and his brother was growing. Marsh wasn't surprised Billy Catlett didn't attend the Pond funeral; he was glad he didn't. He expected more of his own kin, but Clayton, too, was a no-show. By Marsh's lights, his brother's failure to pay his respects to a fallen hero and family friend qualified as a shameful breach of duty. And it was the last straw. The kid's chumminess with Billy Catlett had to end, especially now that it was inciting suspicions he had a role in the Black Flats fire.

Marsh spent the night following the funeral filing his teeth. *Let it lay*, he cautioned himself. *Pull in your horns.* But he couldn't do that. Hour after hour he paced and fretted, ground the fist of his right hand into the palm of his left. He talked to himself. Apologized to his dead mother and father for how their younger son had turned out, for his own failure to keep the boy on the straight and narrow. Bliss counseled him to calm down and get some sleep.

"You're hauling cattle tomorrow, Marsh. You need your rest."

"I know, I know, honey." But he kept pacing.

By dawn, he was irreversibly on the peck. "I'll be gone a few days," he told Bliss, kissing her goodbye on the porch. "I'll call you."

Bliss handed him a basket packed with sandwiches. "Drive safe."

Marsh stowed the basket in his truck, climbed in and went looking for Clayton. He'd made up his mind to teach his brother a lesson, and he was going to take the skinned knuckle approach.

Marsh found Clayton at the west pasture. Amidst a tempest of manure-soured dust and a riot of animal noise, a half-dozen of Marsh's dayworkers were loading fifty head of bawling cattle into a semitractor trailer. At a comfortable remove from the action, Clayton lounged on his horse, right leg hooked around the saddle horn, hat pushed back on his head. He was busying himself with picking his teeth. That cinched it.

Marsh got out of the pickup, slammed the door and advanced on Clayton with hard, combative strides, jaws set, nostrils flaring. When he reached the idling kid, he stood glaring at him, red-faced, feet planted wide apart, fists ready to fly. Clayton answered with a look of mock fear.

"Oh, no. I do believe my big brother is cross and out of sorts."

"I've had it with you. Goldbrickin' while these men work their asses off. Runnin' around with Billy Catlett. You cain't even carve out a little time for Buddy Pond's funeral. You are rotten to the guts."

Clayton humphed. "Looks like you got a great big old mad on at me, brother." He went back to picking his teeth. "Oh, well. I've heard it all before."

Marsh was done talking. He reached up and grabbed the kid, slapping one hand to his chest, the other to his back. Gathering fistfuls of jacket and shirt, he jerked the boy out of the saddle and threw him to the ground. The kid's hat sailed off and went cartwheeling across fetid muck, coming to rest yards away. Having gone hard to his chest, Clayton's lungs begged for air. When he had it, he pushed himself up to all fours. Marsh hovered over him.

"Get up. I'm gonna whip your ass."

The kid managed to wrangle himself to his feet. He tried to square off with his brother, to conjure a show of bravado, but he was no fist-fighter. Before he could cock an arm or let go a string of obscenities, Marsh clouted him. A right cross, flush on the jaw, stepped him back and put him down again. This time flat on his back. Consciousness started fading.

"What's wrong with you?" Marsh roared down at him. "Throwin' in with Billy Catlett, trailing along with your nose up his ass like some damn puppy dog. You oughta be ashamed of yourself. What would Mama think?"

Muddleheaded, the kid tried to stand, but lacking strength and balance he fell back to the dirt.

"If Mama was here you wouldn't be doin' this," Clayton sniveled, rubbing his jaw. "She wouldn't let you."

Marsh stomped away. Before going far he stopped and stood, hands set on hips, still steaming. When he got ahold of himself, he started thinking he might have gone too far. A strong feeling of remorse descended upon him. He went to his whimpering brother, knelt. Marsh examined his face, thumbed away the blood trickling from his split lip to the corner of his mouth.

"Are you bad hurt, Buck?"

The kid didn't answer, pushed Marsh's hands away. He rose and spat blood.

"Are you bad hurt?"

"Hell yes, I'm hurt. What do you expect?"

"All I want to know is if I need to get you to the hospital."

"Get away from me. I don't need nothing from you."

Marsh took him by the arm to steady him. Clayton jerked his arm free.

"Leave me alone, dammit. Leave me alone."

Clayton stumbled off a few feet, crying.

"You been whupppin' up on me all my life'n I'm sick of it, ya hear me? Sick of you makin' me feel like two cents worth of dog meat all the time. If I'm no account, it's cause you made me that way. You go to hell."

He stumbled to his horse and gathered the dragging reins. Leaned over and drooled a mouthful of blood.

"It's always been you and that damn Harry True," he said, wiping his mouth with the back of his hand. "Your blood brother. Blood brother my ass. He ain't nothin'. *I'm* your brother." Clayton was shouting now. "I'm your blood kin. What about me? Don't I count for anything? What about me?"

He stood at his stirrup, leaning against his horse for support, and rested his hand on his saddlebag, where Marsh knew he carried a loaded revolver.

"I oughta kill you. Blow your damn head off. You and Harry True both. Someday I will. Don't think I won't."

"You jerk that hogleg you'n me's really gonna go to fist city."

The brothers stood glaring at each other. Clayton dropped his hand from the saddlebag.

When Marsh turned to leave he found that his six hired men had been standing shoulder to shoulder, watching everything. Marsh rubbed his forehead hard as if to purge his memory of the last few minutes. But he'd be damned if he'd admit he was sorry.

Marsh jostled his head toward Clayton, chucked a thumb in his direction. "Boy's gotta learn how to do," he told the men. "Cain't spare the rod, you know. Wouldn't be doin' him no favors."

The men stood rooted.

"Ya'll best get on back to work now. Get these cows loaded. We ain't got all day."

He took off his hat and put it back on, settled it. Retrieved Clayton's hat, swept off the dirt and handed it to him. Clayton swiped it from his hand.

"I'll be gone a couple of days," Marsh said. "Maybe three. We'll sort this out when I get back."

Driving away, Marsh felt sick for the way his brother had turned out, and for the way he'd humiliated him. A dark cloud of shame and guilt enveloped him. Perhaps Clayton spoke the truth. Maybe he had put the burr under the boy's saddle.

That night at Blue Creek, a sadness hung over Harry and Bliss as they made love. With Marsh away, they had no reason to hurry home. Harry built a fire, and he and Bliss lay together on the old Navajo blanket, gazing at the night sky, letting soft breezes lull them to sleep. When Harry woke sometime later, Bliss was still slumbering. He tucked the blanket around her, rose and slipped on his jeans. Beneath a narrow slice of moon squinting from the infinite blackness of the heavens Harry stood, naked to the waist, studying the crackling fire he'd laid and banked with iron gray creek rocks. Air, weighted with mesquite smoke, pended on his shrapnel scarred shoulders. Old wounds ached.

Harry looked into the smoky dark. From within the perimeter of amber firelight that surrounded him, he could see swaths of knee-high

Indian Grass standing straight and still. Beyond it, he could make out brooding hillocks, black against the sky like billboard cut-outs. Above them in the southwest, stretched layers of clouds—pewter gray, anvil black. Although he couldn't distinguish it, he knew that close by in the solemn keep of night lurked a stand of Blue Wild Indigo.

Harry lowered his eyes to the guttering fire. He probed the throbbing coals with a stob of wood about the length of a yardstick in the manner of a man searching for something. He prodded the rubble as if he might mend back the glowing fragments of kindling or divine some meaning from them. But he did nothing but flush a gasp of incandescent embers and send them kiting away into unyielding dark. Tracing their upward course, he turned over in his mind the twists and turns in the road that had brought him to this place—the choices he'd made, the good and the bad. His own apostasy. His unreckoned sins. The coolish wind mounted. He shivered.

Bliss came to Harry cloaked in the blanket, naked beneath the woven compass of geometric patterns. Barefoot. Delicate collar bones rising in relief from her creamy shoulders. Hair tousled, cascading. She stood, inclined against Harry's back, encircling him with her arms, extending her woolen cocoon to envelope them both. He could feel her breasts nudging against his skin, and her fine cheek resting against his shoulder. Her presence warmed him.

"Did you sleep?" Bliss asked softly.

"Must have. I had a dream."

"A good one?"

"I'm not sure. It was about my father."

"Tell me."

"He was dead. At least, I think he was. It was dusk. He stood huddled with some other men. Maybe a dozen of them. Talking among themselves, making a plan, agreeing on something. I couldn't make out the words."

He paused, deep in thought.

"Go on," Bliss said.

"I passed them by. Didn't go near them. Knew I couldn't. Wasn't supposed to. Don't know how I knew it, but I did. My dad saw me. He smiled, but he didn't say anything. Didn't come to me. Didn't motion me over. I kept my distance. Moved on."

Harry resumed rummaging through the heart of the fire.

"That's all. Nothing more to it."

He gazed into the night sky, black as a celestial ink spill, replete with starfire.

"I know the points of light and the dark spaces between them form shapes. A bear, a scorpion, eagle, flying horse. But I can never quite make them out."

"Neither can I," Bliss said. "But I know they're out there."

"The question is what's beyond them."

"God, I guess. . . . Yes, I'm sure of it."

Harry drove the wooden stake into the ground and let it stand upright by the fire. He snugged the blanket around Bliss's shoulders. Took her in his arms and held her.

"I love you, you know. I've always loved you. Can't help myself. There's never been a time when I didn't love you. And there never will be."

"I know. And I love you. I've never loved anyone the way I love you."

Harry sighed.

"But what we're doing now, it should never have started. We should have . . . ."

"Too late for that. Besides, it wasn't possible. It was just a matter of time. It was always a matter of time."

Harry relented. He and Bliss stood, gazing into the flames.

"Woody Coats didn't rape that girl," Harry said.

"I know."

Harry's face showed surprise.

"You thought I didn't know?"

"I . . . How did you know?"

"I'd know it from knowing Woody. He'd never do such a thing. But it's not just that. The night they tried to lynch him, when Marsh and Buddy came back to Sweet Leona's, Buddy told us everything." Bliss looked up at Harry. "He mentioned what night the rape happened."

"Ahh. . . and you remembered."

"Of course I remembered." Bliss fell silent, stared into the fire. "So, who do you think did rape that girl?"

"Esau says it was Billy Catlett."

"That's what I've been hearing. Sadly, it doesn't surprise me."

"And it wasn't Catlett alone. Someone was with him."

"I've been hearing that, too. But nobody seems to know who it was."

"Esau thinks he does."

"Oh? Who?"

Harry didn't answer.

"Who does Esau say was with him, Harry?"

"He says it was Clayton."

Bliss stiffened, pulled away.

"No, that can't be true. Clayton?"

Harry remained silent.

"You don't believe that. You can't."

"Afraid I do."

Bliss stared at him.

"Why? Because Esau says so? Esau's a good man, but he wasn't there. From what I hear, even poor Alejandra doesn't know who the other man was." She took Harry's arm. "Look. I know Clayton for what he is. But surely he wouldn't do that. Billy Catlett might. But not Clayton."

"Oh, yeah. Down deep he's a good kid, huh? A little misunderstood, maybe. You're going a little easy on him, aren't you?"

"No, I am not. Being my husband's brother doesn't mean . . ."

Now Harry backed off a step. She had spoken that word, that terrible word. It burned in his ears.

"Your husband. Oh, yes. You have one of those, don't you. That is a rather uncomfortable little fact. And worse, it's *your husband's* brother we're talking about. Your *husband's* brother. Now that is a bit of a complication, isn't it?"

Bliss felt stung. She shed the blanket and started putting on her clothes. Harry slipped on his shirt.

"Not to put too fine a point on it," he said, "but how does this work exactly? I've been wondering. You come out here and make love to me, tell me you love me, you go home and do the same thing with *your husband.* That's it, right? Has to be. How else could you hide the truth from him?"

"Harry, don't."

"Oh well, I guess you still have your marital duties, don't you. And, you've got to keep up a good front."

"I could say the same thing about you and Ruth, you know."

"I'm not married to Ruth. I don't lie to her."

"No? So you've told her about us?"

They turned away from each other.

"Why are we doing this?" Bliss said.

Harry paced.

"Why? I'll tell you why. An innocent kid damn near got strung up because of something *your husband's brother* and his useless buddy did. Sorry, but that doesn't sit too well with me."

"You can't be sure of that. Billy, maybe. But not Clayton."

Harry struggled to contain his anger. "Well, whether it was Clayton or not—"

"It wasn't. It couldn't have been."

"Let me finish. Whether it was Clayton or not, the fact remains that Catlett's spreading the word that Woody did it, and unless Alejandra comes forward, which it doesn't look like she's going to do—"

"That poor child."

"—Woody has no one to defend him."

"Except us," Bliss said calmly.

"Yes, except us. We're his alibi. You and I. We are the two people who know where Woody was that night."

"Do you think Alejandra knows about what happened to Woody? Maybe if she did . . . ."

Harry shook his head. "Don't think it'll be that simple."

"No. No, of course not. That poor girl has been through enough already. She's probably afraid to say anything."

"That's what Esau said."

"They might have threatened her."

"Maybe."

Bliss took a deep breath, exhaled slowly.

"So, we have to tell Dutch, tell him the truth. Tell him we saw Woody at Blue Creek. The two of us. That's what we have to do."

"Right."

"But even if we come forward, that doesn't help Dutch catch the real perpetrators. And Dutch isn't even the one we have to worry about. He knows Woody didn't do it. I'm sure he does. It's all the people willing to believe Billy's lies. They're the ones we have to convince. And the only way to do that is—" Bliss broke off. "Harry, what are we going to do?"

"I don't know. I do not know."

Bliss hugged herself, raised her eyes heavenward.

"Do you think God will punish us for what we've done?"

"Yes. He already has. And I suspect there's more yet to come."

Bliss seemed to collapse in on herself. She lowered her gaze.

"The hills look so peaceful. So quiet. You could lose yourself in them. They'd never find you out there."

Harry returned to the fire. Bliss followed him. They gazed out into the misty *cordillera,* as if in its ridges and shadows they might find a way to sort things out.

"My, my," Bliss whispered. "How did life get to be such a mess?"

"Our own doing, I'm afraid."

"Yes. Our own doing. This can't go on, can it?"

Harry didn't answer. He picked up the stob of wood and thrust the tip into the glowing coals, worked it around. When the fire had rekindled itself, he dumped the brand onto the flames and let it burn. He drew Bliss close.

"I'm not giving you up. Not ever."

He put his lips to hers, kissed her with all the passion he'd ever felt, all he ever would feel. He kissed her, knowing his own life depended on having her, knowing that every powerful force in the universe opposed them, knowing the desperation of his chosen way. But he could imagine no life apart from this woman. He would never yield. If his promise to himself and to Bliss meant no life at all, so be it.

CHAPTER 22

The Second Man

Bliss had to know the truth about Clayton. Had to know whether he had anything to do with the rape of Alejandra Flores. To get the answer, she knew she'd have to put the question to Alejandra herself. She didn't want to cause the poor girl more hardship than she'd already suffered, but there was no other way. The next morning she baked a batch of ginger snaps, packed them in a tin, and headed over to the Mexican section.

Alejandra Flores lived with her widowed mother in a singlewide trailer nestled in a motte of cottonwood trees a short distance east of Serafina and a little south of the main highway. It was one of a dozen manufactured homes clustered together and occupied by local Mexicans, as well as migrant workers and their families.

Turning into the *barrio* Bliss came upon a young boy, maybe ten years old, riding a rusty red push scooter. When she stopped, he stopped. She asked if he knew Alejandra Flores. *"Sí,"* he said and pointed to the Flores home. Bliss said *gracias* and drove to the trailer. She got out of the car and stood, holding the cookies, strengthening her resolve. When she was ready, she proceeded to the door and knocked.

After the second knock the door opened a crack, wide enough for Bliss to see standing on the other side a Mexican woman in her middle years. She had her gray-streaked raven hair bound in a single husky braid that hung over her shoulder to her waist. She wore a white blouse, sky blue skirt, and a gray kitchen apron, dusted with flour. Alejandra's mother.

"Good morning. Mrs. Flores?"

"*Sí*," the woman said, looking from Bliss to the cookie tin she was holding.

"*Buenos días, Señora Flores.* My name is Bliss Stone."

"Stone?"

"Yes. I was hoping to talk to your daughter, Alejandra. Is she home?"

The woman turned sullen. "*No. No está aquí.*" She started to close the door.

Bliss took a half step forward. "No, please wait." She held out the tin. "I . . . baked these for you and Alejandra. I hope you like ginger snaps."

Mrs. Flores didn't respond. She peered at Bliss around the aluminum edge of the door.

Bliss's eyes moistened. She put a hand over her heart.

"Please, Mrs. Flores, I'm very sorry for what happened to Alejandra. Truly I am. Very sorry. And I hope whoever did this terrible thing to her gets caught. That's why I'm here. I need to know if someone . . . I mean, people are saying all kinds of things, and if I could talk to Alejandra . . . ."

"No." The woman started to close the door. But Alejandra appeared behind her, a slender girl with large dark eyes and long shiny black hair, her oval face still showing bruises.

"*Está bien, Mami.*"

The mother gave her daughter a questioning look. Alejandra nodded. Her mother sighed and opened the door and with a graceful sweep of hand invited Bliss inside. She accepted the cookies and showed Bliss to a divan in the living room. Alejandra sat in a chair at her right. Mrs. Flores put the cookie tin on the coffee table.

"*Quiere un café?*"

"*Sí, gracias.*"

Mrs. Flores went to the kitchen and returned with three cups of coffee. Setting the tray on the coffee table, she settled in on the divan next to Bliss.

"I'm so sorry for what happened to you, Alejandra," Bliss said softly.

Alejandra lowered her head. Bliss tried again.

"Sheriff Mackey took you to the hospital, is that right?"

Alejandra nodded.

"And they took good care of you there?"

"*Sí.*" She spoke in a low voice.

Bliss opened the cookie tin and held it out.

"*Gracias.* Thank you for the cookies, Miss, Miss . . ."

"Stone. Mrs. Stone. But please, Alejandra. Call me Bliss."

Alejandra nodded. "Thank you, Bliss."

"Did Polly Coats help take care of you? While you were at the hospital?"

"Oh, yes," Alejandra said. "She is such a kind woman." Alejandra said something in rapid Spanish to her mother. Bliss caught the mention of *Señora* Coats.

"*Oh, sí, sí. Ella es un ángel,*" Mrs. Flores said, crossing herself.

Bliss smiled. "Yes, she is a saint. She took care of me, too, years ago when I was sick."

"Oh?" mother and daughter said in unison.

And so the ice was broken, and Bliss, showing great compassion, was able to coax Alejandra into talking about what had happened to her. In the conversation that followed, Bliss confirmed what she already knew: Woody Coats had nothing to do with the crime. Bliss could see that Alejandra and her mother didn't know about what had happened to Woody. She didn't tell them. It would serve no purpose, Bliss decided, except to upset them and make Alejandra feel worse than she already did. Instead, Bliss inquired about the color of the man, or men, who had hurt her. Was she able to tell? Were they black? White?

"*Blanco.*"

"One man? More than one?"

"Two."

"But you don't know who they were . . . ."

Alejandra and her mother exchanged worried looks.

"He said he will kill me, kill my mother . . . ."

"Who did? Who told you that?"

"If I say, you will tell—"

"No, Alejandra, I won't." She wouldn't, either. It wouldn't help. The truth had to come from Alejandra herself.

With her eyes, Alejandra implored her mother for guidance. Her mother nodded.

"*Lo promete?*" Alejandra said. "You promise? You will not tell?"

"I promise," Bliss said, crossing her heart.

Alejandra laced her fingers in her lap. "The one with the oily hair and the truck," she whispered. "And the tattoo." She pointed to her right arm. "He is called Billy."

"Billy. There are a lot of—"

"Catlett." Alejandra's eyes filled with tears. "Billy Catlett."

"I'm so sorry, Alejandra."

"You won't tell."

"No, I won't tell." She paused, took a deep breath. "And the other man?"

Alejandra frowned. Yes, there had been a second man. A younger one. He didn't do to her what Catlett did, but he let it happen and he helped. He hit her and subdued her and held his hand over her mouth and watched as Catlett violated her.

Bliss listened. *Please,* she prayed. *Please don't let it be Clayton.* She took a breath. "This . . . younger man. You don't know who he was."

"No." Alejandra had seen him before, she was sure of that, but she didn't know his name.

"Do you think you would recognize him if you saw him again?"

Alejandra didn't answer. Bliss waited.

"He was afraid, too."

"Who was?"

"The other man."

"Afraid of what?"

"Of Billy. He watched Billy hurt me, and when Billy told him to . . . he said no, but Billy said yes. And he would have. He would have . . ." Alejandra paused. "Because he was afraid, you see? But a car . . . ."

Bliss felt a wave of nausea. She reached into her shirt pocket and extracted a photograph of the two brothers, folded so Marsh's face didn't show. She creased it again, handed it to Alejandra.

"Is this him? Was this the second man?"

Alejandra examined the photograph, closed her eyes, her face etched with pain. She put the photograph on the coffee table.

"*Sí,*" she said, tears coursing down her cheeks. "That is the man." She lowered her head into her hands and sobbed.

Mrs. Flores went to her daughter and held her against her breast, stroked her hair. "*Mija, mija.*"

Bliss pressed a hand over her mouth. In tears, she retrieved the photo.

"I'm sorry. I'm so sorry. Thank you for . . . I'm sorry. So very sorry."

Mrs. Flores led her daughter out of the room. Bliss saw herself out.

During a phone call the day before, Marsh had told Bliss about the licking he'd given Clayton and how bad he felt about it. He asked her to check up on the kid, have him over for a meal to see how he was doing, and she agreed. When she got home from her visit with Alejandra Flores, she called Clayton and invited him over for noon-day dinner.

Clayton was sullen at first, but he appeared to relax when Bliss made a fuss over his fat lip and bruised cheek. He calmed even more when Bliss set a bowl of beef stew, a plate of cornbread, and a cup of coffee before him. He shoveled it all in like a field hand.

"More stew?" Bliss refilled Clayton's bowl and sat down at the kitchen table with him as he ate.

"Woody Coats had nothing to do with the attack on Alejandra Flores," she said calmly. "You know that, don't you?"

Clayton sipped his coffee. "Way I heard it, he did," he said.

"But you know that's not true."

He lowered his cup to the table and gave its dregs a studious look.

"You know it's not true because you were there."

Clayton froze. His eyes twitched in Bliss's direction and held in an icy gaze. He worked his jaw; the muscles rippled.

Bliss took a deep breath.

"You and Billy Catlett kidnapped Alejandra Flores. You beat her up. You took her out in the country and Catlett raped her."

Clayton sat back. "That's a damn lie."

"It's not a lie. It's the truth and you know it."

"I don't know any such thing."

Bliss leaned in closer and lowered her voice. "Yes, you do, Clayton. You know it, and I know it, and other people know it, too."

"Oh, yeah? Like who?"

They stared at each other.

"I didn't rape her."

"Doesn't matter. You helped. You're as guilty as Catlett."

Beads of sweat broke out on Clayton's forehead. His eyes darted around the room. He fidgeted. Bliss put her hand on his arm.

"You have to go to the sheriff, Clayton, and tell him what happened. Every bit of it."

The kid jerked his arm away.

"You mean turn myself in? Even though I didn't rape her?"

"Yes. You have to tell the truth."

Clayton focused on the bowl of stew before him, shook his head.

"No, no, no. They'll put me in prison."

"Maybe. But if you testify against Catlett, they might go easy on you."

Clayton gave a toss of his head. Rolled his eyes.

"Here we go again. I shoulda known. You and Marsh . . . gangin' up on me, tryin' to put the screws to me. Ain't no end to it."

"No, Clayton. We're not doing anything to you. You did this to yourself. Now, you have to do the right thing. That's what you're going to do."

Clayton laughed. "The hell I am." He leaned forward and narrowed his eyes at Bliss. "Know what? I don't believe you anyway. You're bluffin'. You don't know nothin'."

"I know it wasn't Woody."

"You do not."

"Yes, Clayton, I do."

Clayton readjusted himself in his chair. "Oh, yeah? And how do you know?"

Bliss took a deep breath. "Because I saw him somewhere else that night."

Clayton snorted. "You're lyin.'"

"And I wasn't alone. Someone else saw him, too, and if we have to—"

Clayton blew up. He bulldozed the bowl of stew off the table onto the floor with his forearm, pushed back and vaulted out of his chair.

"You're all the same. Cain't trust any of you. You tricked me to get me over here."

Clayton headed for the door. Bliss rose and reached for his arm. He jerked away and shoved her against the wall, held her there by her shoulders.

"Stay away from me," he growled. "I'm tired of bein' fooled with."

He released her and stormed out the door.

Frightened by Clayton's violent explosion, heart hammering, Bliss remained frozen in place. When she'd steadied herself, she went to the telephone and instructed the operator to ring Harry's number.

PART FIVE

CHAPTER 23

Powder Keg

While Bliss was trying to get Harry on the phone, Harry was striding down the gravel drive from the main house at the Bar T headquarters to collect the mail. Bob followed at a casual trot. She'd been enjoying ranch life for days. Harry kept her fed and watered and she belonged to him now, like it or not.

In the tin newspaper delivery tube adjacent to the mailbox he found a special midweek edition of the *Serafina Gazette*. Returning to the house, he browsed the headlines. Sprawling across the entire width of the front page a headline in bold black letters screamed out: ARSON! MURDER! SHAME!

Lowering his eyes to Ned Brett's editorial, he read:

Evil has come to our little town. And it didn't come from the outside world; it came from within. We, the good people of Serafina, bred it and birthed it ourselves. Looks like we are what the Bible says: *The burning ones.* Our handiwork is ARSON. Our crime is MURDER. The mantle of SHAME lies heavy on our shoulders.

First it was the heinous attack on an innocent young woman by unknown assailants who remain at large. Then the attempted lynching of a young man by a coterie of self-appointed vigilantes acting outside the law. And now the Black Flats fire will forever be a blight on our souls.

Perhaps only a small gang of vandals poured the gasoline, perhaps one blackguard alone put a torch to it. Perhaps the same person or persons are tied to all three crimes. We cannot say. We do not know. But one thing is undeniable: All of us share the blame. We all have blood on our hands. For far too long we have turned a blind eye to intolerance and injustice. We, members of the so-called superior race, have much to atone for.

Ned Brett went on to opine that he was speaking a hard truth but a truth that must be told. Hatred, pure and simple, had killed Buddy Pond and several Negroes. He didn't identify the latter by name. Likewise, he didn't name Woody Coats when he expressed outrage that a young Black man had come within an inch of losing his life because of a crime he likely had not committed. But he held nothing back when he avowed that the time for change had come. Now, four years past its midpoint, the twentieth century had come knocking at the door of Sebastian County. And the good people of Serafina could answer that knock by agreeing on two things: 1. This year's Men's Club minstrel show would be the last ever staged in Serafina. 2. It was time for the WHITES ONLY signs to come down.

"What the hell," Harry said. "What the hell."

He knew in an instant how white folks would react to Ned Brett's broadside. They'd be mad as a swarm of hornets. The inkslinger had not spared them and they would not spare him. They'd brand him as moralistic, sanctimonious, and self-righteous. People who were shocked by the rape, attempted lynching, and suspected arson would declare in two shakes they had no part in any of it and if they'd known what was going on they would have tried to stop it. They would raise their voices in a cry against injustice—not only on behalf of Alejandra Flores, Woody Coats, and the victims of the Black Flats fire, but on behalf of themselves. They would resent bitterly being accused of a crime they did not commit, sidestepping their past enjoyment and tacit support of the minstrel shows and whites-only policies. Some would argue that, even if what Ned Brett said was true, he shouldn't have said it. It would do nothing but fan the flames of civil unrest. And meanwhile, Billy Catlett and his gang of jackals were still walking around free—ready to put flame to fuse and watch Serafina erupt like a powder keg unless somebody stopped them. And no one but Sheriff Dutch Mackey could do that.

Harry respected the sheriff but knew Dutch could have a slow way of working. Add to that the fact that he had no deputy, and Harry concluded that no one was going to get Catlett off the streets anytime soon. Harry couldn't do much about that but he knew he had to do something. And the one thing he could do was try to protect Woody Coats. He'd start by coming clean with the sheriff.

After reading Ned Brett's editorial, Harry went straight to his truck. When he opened the door, Bob jumped onto the seat.

Harry motioned the dog out of the truck. "Not a chance. Git."

Man's best friend refused to budge.

"Beat it."

Harry hauled the dog off the seat. "Go guard the house or something."

Bob retreated to the porch. There, she made a circle, dropped and curled.

Some guard dog.

Harry climbed into the truck and headed for the sheriff's office, plenty ticked at Ned Brett for stirring up trouble. Maybe he'd go by his office and have a word with him, too.

Turning onto Commercial, he found the street deserted. *Not good,* he thought. He parked across the street from Dutch Mackey's office and switched off the engine. Feeling like a man caught between two wind-driven wildfires, he remained in his truck for a long time. He couldn't move. One moment he saw himself flinging open the door and appearing before the sheriff like a penitent, spilling his guts, providing Woody Coats an ironclad alibi and begging that Bliss be kept out of it. The next, doubt and dread paralyzed him. He began asking himself what his father would do, what his father would expect him to do. The answer was clear: He had a blood debt to pay. If he did nothing, he would live out his days loathing himself for his cravenness. He already had a crawful of that.

Harry took a deep breath, opened the truck door and stepped out. He crossed the street. On the sidewalk, he viewed the deserted thoroughfare, up and down. He saw no moving thing, save a splayed-out newspaper blowing down the street. Twisting and turning in the wolfish wind, it came right for him, plastered itself around his ankle. He peeled it from his boot vamp, balled it in his fist and threw it aside.

"Damn you, Ned."

Harry found the sheriff at his desk, a cigar stub in his mouth, the *Gazette* flattened out before him. Harry closed the door and stood before the man with the badge. Without raising his eyes, the sheriff took the cigar stub from the corner of his mouth and set it in the ash-tray. He spoke in a tired voice.

"I guess the sumbitch has gone absolutely, stark-ravin' mad. Gotta raise some hell. Bleve he's about to get 'er saucered and blowed."

The sheriff peered at Harry over the tops of dusty reading spectacles perched low on his prodigious nose.

"Seen you out yonder. Wondered how long it was gonna take you to make up your mind to come in."

The sheriff lowered his eyes to the paper again.

"Arson. He calls it what it is. At least, he got that part right. That's rare for a newspaper man. Somebody damn sure torched the place. Kilt them people. Pure evil. I do believe this country's goin' to hell on a fast horse. Yessir. I surely do."

The sheriff motioned toward the chair across from his desk.

"Have a seat."

Harry sat. He corrected the crease of his hat and hung it on his knee.

"We need to talk."

The sheriff looked up.

"About Woody."

The sheriff folded the newspaper to the size of a café menu and pushed it to the corner of the scarred oak surface of his desk, a sort of no man's land stretching between lawman and petitioner. He set his leathery hands flatwise on the desktop, patted it, swept them back and forth as if to whisk away a film of dust. He put his hands together, steepled his fingers, looked up.

"I'm all ears."

Harry eyed him.

"Woody didn't rape that girl. I think you know that."

The sheriff struck a thoughtful pose.

"I suspicioned that's what was on your mind. Go on."

Before Harry could get his next words out the blast of an explosion rocked the room. A godawful noise rumbled in from somewhere to the south, down Commercial Avenue.

"What the hell?" The sheriff pushed up from his desk with a strident scraping of chair legs. "What the . . . ."

The sheriff and Harry made for the door. Looking out, they could see smoke billowing through what had been the front window of the *Serafina Gazette*'s office at the end of the street.

"Grab the extinguisher," Sheriff Mackey commanded, pointing. "By the door."

Harry stepped inside as the sheriff's wife, Doris Ann, came rushing into the office from the residence.

"What the—"

"An explosion in Ned's office."

"Oh, my Lord—"

Doris Ann headed for the door.

"No, stay here. Call the fire truck."

Carrying the fire extinguisher, Harry caught up with the sheriff who was already racing toward the blast. Up and down the street, doors flew open and people rushed into the street, shielding their eyes with their hands, covering their mouths in shock. Cal Barton and Wid Isley fell in behind Dutch and Harry.

"What happened?" Wid asked.

"Don't know yet."

"That's Ned's office, ain't it?"

"Yeah."

There, they found a scene of wanton destruction. Shattered glass everywhere. Sidewalk. Street. Venetian blinds bent, hanging askew. Furniture and office equipment overturned. Dust and smoke thick in the air. Bits of paper churning from floor to ceiling. The smell of plaster dust. Pungent reek of some high explosive. A small bum fire in a corner.

"Ned!" the sheriff called out. "Ned. You in here?"

Harry opened up on the blaze with a pressurized discharge of white powder. The two men advanced into the chaos, fragments of broken glass grinding under their boot soles, waving their hands to cleanse the air before their eyes of dust and debris.

"Ned, where are you? Dammit, where are you?"

A thready voice answered.

"Here. Over here."

They found Ned on the floor under a table in a far corner. Head bloody, arms cut, glasses crooked on his face. One lens spiderwebbed. The sheriff and Harry knelt and helped him sit up. He was addled, but he had no life-threatening wounds. His wits appeared to be returning.

"You all right?" the sheriff asked.

"What?"

"Are you all right?"

"Yeah . . . I . . . I think so. Ears are ringin'. Cain't hear thunder. What was it?"

"Couldn't say."

"What?"

"I don't know what it was," the sheriff said more loudly. "What about you? What'd you see?"

"Heard something come through the window. Had a split second to dive for cover before everything sorta went black."

"Musta been some kind of bomb. Not a very big one, thank God. Homemade prolly. Maybe a hand grenade. Somebody mighta stoled it from over to Fort Sill. It happens."

Harry and the sheriff helped Ned to his feet. The newspaper man leveled his glasses and tried to ream out his ears with a blunt fingertip. Assessing the shattered window, the sheriff shook his head.

"Hand grenades in Serafina. Can you imagine that?"

"What?"

"Hand . . . never mind."

Now at himself again, Ned Brett assessed the damage.

"Well . . . I'd hazard I got somebody's attention."

"Yessir," the sheriff said. "Bleve you did."

"What?"

"You damn sure got somebody's attention."

Ned went straight to the printing press. Without giving a thought to his own injuries, he checked every part of the half-century old sheet-fed offset printer. Examined it like a doctor examining a patient. When he'd satisfied himself it had survived the blast, he patted it, pronounced it well. He did everything but kiss it.

"At least the sonsabitches didn't get my press. She may be bloodied, but she's damn sure unbowed. Another extry'll be hittin' the streets this time tomorrow evenin'. These boys we're up against are mean, Dutch, but they're good for bidness."

The sheriff waved dust from the air, hacked a cough.

"You know it wouldn't do no harm to kindly lay low a day or two."

"Can't do that. No, sir. Not a chance. Getting after these bastards is like jacking off a hyena. If you stop, he'll eat you alive. I'm not stopping."

Heralded by a screaming siren, the fire truck arrived. A small cadre of helmeted men in overalls dismounted and entered the shambles. D. C. Grubbs, a refinery worker, led the way.

"Anybody hurt here, Sheriff?"

"No, don't guess so. Ned's banged up pretty good. But he's all right, I reckon."

"What about Mildred? Where's she at?"

"Home. She's OK."

"Better check the gas and electric," Grubbs said to one of the other men. "Might could be some kinda leak."

"Mebbe," Dutch said. "Not likely."

Doris Ann appeared in the doorway, breathing hard. "Dutch. Dutch, honey. You best get over to the Flats. Call come in. Big trouble out that way. People runnin' around with guns."

"Colored or white?"

"Both, apparently. Caller sounded real scared, like folks were fixin' to start shootin' each other. If they haven't already."

The sheriff turned toward Harry.

"I could prolly use some back-up. Might be kindly overmatched alone. I got you, I figger, and some of these men here. You think you can locate Marsh?"

Harry shook his head. "No. He's gone. Hauling a load of cattle."

The sheriff turned to Doris Ann. "Darlin', you tend to Ned here. He needs a little lookin' after. Harry, you ride with me." To Grubbs, "Think you can round up a few more men, come help us out?"

"Sure, Sheriff."

Harry headed out after the sheriff, stopped, turned. "Doris Ann, do me a favor. Could you call Bliss and Ruth, make sure they're OK? They're both home alone. Tell 'em there's trouble all over and to stay put, lock their doors. Could you do that for me?"

"You bet."

"And . . . tell 'em I'll call when I can. This could be a long night."

CHAPTER 24

Black Flats

The first shot had been fired before they got there. When they approached the invisible boundary that separated white and Black worlds, they found a Black man lying crumpled at the margin of the road like some stray dog hit by a car. Dutch pulled over.

"You wait here," he told Harry. He stepped out and, hand on holster, walked closer and squatted over the body for a moment. He stood, checked his surroundings. Street quiet and deserted.

"Damn shame," Dutch said, returning to the vehicle and climbing behind the wheel.

"You know him?"

"Yeah. So do you. Dick Rawlins."

"What? No." Dick Rawlins. Handy man, yard mower. About as ordinary and harmless as a man can be. Decent human being.

No sign of struggle or altercation. The scene told a simple story: somebody with a gun had encountered him on the wrong side of the dividing line by chance. A lone Black stray carrying an armload of groceries. The gunman shot him to rags.

"What are we going to do?" Harry said. "We can't leave him there."

Dutch hunched over the steering wheel, squinted at something ahead.

"'Fraid we're gonna have to for now. What's that up yonder?"

A little farther on Harry and the sheriff discovered another casualty. This time, Ernest Hennessey, a septuagenarian grandfather to a passel of kids who knew him as Poppy. After they'd shot him, the killers had put a rope around his neck and strung him up in a tree. His arms and legs hung straight as arrows. His head lolled, mouth agape, swollen tongue protruding. His eyes, foggy and red lined, bulged.

A crude sign stood propped against the tree trunk. Lettering scrawled in runny black paint on a rectangular offcut of gray sheet metal shrieked out: *Black man, don't let the sun go down on you in the streets of Serafina.*

The sheriff angled the Dodge to the side of the road again and stopped.

"Oh, my," he said. "Oh, my."

Harry and the sheriff got out of the car, leaving their doors open, and inched forward as if they were entering the lair of some wounded wild animal. Standing in the shadow of the hanging corpse, they gazed upward. For them, any remaining doubt about the death spiral of humanity evaporated.

"Lord, Lord, Lord," Harry said.

The sheriff removed his hat. Shook his head.

"If that ain't just pitiful. Absolutely pitiful."

The sheriff squinted up at Hennessey's hanging corpse. "He musta been dead already when they done that to him."

"Yeah. This was no lynching. The killers meant to use him as a scarecrow."

At that moment, the sheriff felt a presence at his back. Heard a snuffling sound. Scuffing of shoes on gravel. The sheriff and Harry realized at the same instant that they were hearing the sound of human grief, the lamentations of an aching heart.

They turned. Before them, stood a man they knew as Tom Hennessey, firstborn son of the man hanging in the tree. Oxblood eyes with agate pupils brimmed to overflowing. Tears sluiced down his umber cheeks. He stood, choking back sobs. In his outstretched trembling hands, he held a revolver. For the longest time, no one moved or made a sound. Tom Hennessey tried to speak. He moved his lips, but the words disintegrated in his mouth.

"That's my daddy in that tree, Sheriff," he finally said, his voice trembling. "You post to stop this kinda thing happenin'. Where you been? Whatchoo been doin'?"

The sheriff lowered his hand to the pistol holstered at his hip.

"I'm sorry, Tom. Sorry about your daddy. Truly I am. We need to get him took care of. How 'bout you 'n me doin' that . . . together?"

"Too late," Hennesey said, gripping the gun. "Too late fer everthin'."

"So, what're we gonna do, set to cuttin' each other in two with bullets? Don't believe that'll do. Come on, Tom."

Harry kept still.

The sheriff took a step forward.

"Come on. Come on, Tom. All you're gonna do with that gun is buy more pain for your family. I'd take it as a kindness if you'd put it down. Let's get your daddy in the house."

Slowly, Tom Hennessey lowered the gun, dropped his head, tears dripping from his cheeks. The sheriff reached for the revolver and lifted it from Tom Hennessey's hand. The grieving man relinquished it without protest. The sheriff touched him on the shoulder. When they'd collected themselves, they tended to the grim business at hand . . . together. And a small retinue of neighbors arrived to help Tom Hennessey carry his father away.

By the time the sheriff and Harry reached Black Flats the frenzy had abated, but evidence of the general uprising was everywhere. Windows shattered by bullets and rocks. Signs and fenceposts torn down, shoes and bonnets littering the streets where people lost them as they fled to safety. Garbage cans overturned.

Sheriff Mackey and all the level-headed men he could turn out to help him restore order, Black and white, had to douse a few fires, break up an armed group of Black Flats citizens, send some self-styled white vigilantes packing, scatter two opposing armies of young hellions, hollering and waving sticks—one side insisting to the sheriff that the other had come to kill every man, woman, and child in the Flats; the other insisting they were there to head off an all-out attack on the white section of town. "They're plannin' it, Sheriff, I swear," one white ruffian protested as Dutch Mackey grabbed him by the collar, booted him back the way he'd come. "A whole army of 'em. A hundred or more. They're comin' for us, you mark my words. And they all have guns."

By the end of the day the sheriff and his ad hoc crew of deputies had, more or less, restored order, but it hadn't come easy. The sheriff had to bust a few heads, show his weapon a couple of times, which he seldom did. A feint in the direction of his holster usually sufficed. Telling people to go home and not cause any more trouble sometimes did the trick. The sheriff couldn't do much more than that. Couldn't lock up half the town.

When quiet had returned, the sheriff sent his deputies home and drove back to his office with Harry.

"Call if you need me," Harry said as he got out of the sheriff's car.

"Hope not to, but thanks."

Dutch watched Harry drive off, thinking about what the young tough he'd booted down the road had said about an army of Black men planning to attack. Where had the kid heard such a crazy story? Maybe it was his own wild imaginings. Or maybe it was a harbinger of more and worse to come: more tensions and fear, more panic and hysteria. More hatred. More violence.

Not ten minutes later, as Sheriff Mackey stood at his window, sipping an R.C., lost in thought, a pickup truck pulled up in front of the jail. Billy Catlett at the wheel, four of his henchmen standing behind the cab, a tarp-covered load in the bed of the truck. Catlett stepped out, reached through the open window, laid the heel of his hand on the horn. The other men dismounted the truck and lined up next to it. Catlett joined them. The sheriff came through the door and stood looking down at them. At a signal from Catlett, the men pulled away the tarp to reveal their cargo: the bodies of three dead Black men laid out on the truck's bed. Clothes soaked with blood.

Mackey's stomach turned. "Good God Almighty," he whispered.

Catlett jerked a thumb toward the truck.

"These here are your troublemakers, Dutch. Worst of 'em, anyways. They done everything. These here ones and that little girl diddler Woody Coats. Figgered you wouldn't wanna have to pick this garbage up off the streets so we did it for you, didn't we boys?"

The other men grunted and nodded.

Catlett swelled out his chest, ready to take in the praise he seemed to think he and his sidemen deserved. But Dutch Mackey was of no such mind. He stepped forward and narrowed his eyes at the dead bodies. He hadn't felt such rage and disgust since the war. Hadn't witnessed rows of bodies since the liberation of Dachau. Never thought he'd see such a thing again . . . never in his own hometown. He came down the steps, spoke without taking his eyes off the laid-out corpses.

"Well, I guess someone sure taught 'em a lesson. You takin' credit? You figger we oughta pin a medal on you?"

Loud laughter and hoots waxed from Catlett's possemen.

"Somebody needs to teach these darkies a lesson," Catlett said, sneering. "If it ain't gonna be you, us ordinary folks gotta take the law into our own hands."

In an explosion of fury, Dutch Mackey caught Catlett in the jaw with his ham-sized right fist. A perfect haymaker punch, the full force of his considerable weight behind it. The blow twisted Catlett around and knocked him off balance. Before he could recover, the sheriff shoved him face-first against the truck fender and cuffed him. He grabbed a hank of greasy hair and slung Catlett to the pavement, stood over him, shaking with anger. He reached for the pistol at his hip as if he intended to skin it and put an end to the man's very existence, but he got hold of himself. He raised an arm, swung it in an arc at the other men standing in front of him, mouths hanging open.

"I know who y'all are. Ever man jack of you. I know where you live and I know who your people are. So listen up. This ain't over. Whoever did this will pay. I promise you that. Ever last one of you sonsabitches. And don't even think about runnin' because I will hunt you down. You hear me? Now get out of here. And get them . . . people . . . over to the undertaker."

"But Sheriff," one of the men protested. "He won't take 'em."

"He'll take 'em. You tell him I said to take 'em. Do it now."

He snatched Catlett up by his belt at the small of his back and his shirt collar at the nape of his neck. He heaved him up the steps, pushed him inside. Under the sheriff's prod Catlett lurched down the jail corridor to one of the two cells. The sheriff threw him onto the slab floor, clanged the steel barred door shut, and ran the hasp bolt home. He dug the key out of his pocket and secured the lock.

"I ought to let you rot in there. You are a no good son of a bitch, if I ever seen one."

Catlett spat on the floor. "Ahh . . . come on now, Sheriff. You know I ain't the one that needs to be in jail. You need to get that little coon cat kid in here. Woody Coats. He's the one that—"

"You can save your breath. I ain't buyin' it. Ain't nobody buyin' it 'cept you and your pack of dogs. Woody Coats wouldn't hurt nobody. You know it. I know it." The sheriff scorched Catlett with his eyes. "Got a pretty good idea who did do it, though."

"Oh, yeah. Who?"

"Truth has a way of getting out, Mr. Catlett. Let's leave it at that."

The sheriff walked away, displeased with himself for saying even that much to Catlett about what he knew but couldn't yet prove.

Catlett cursed under his breath. The sheriff was bluffing. Had to be. The girl wouldn't talk. Unless she'd forgotten what he said would happen if she did. Maybe he needed to pay her a follow-up visit, refresh her memory. But first, he had to get out of jail. With Clayton Stone still on the loose, he didn't figure that would take too long.

CHAPTER 25

Revelations

Bliss had seen Ned Brett's editorial and had received the call from Doris Ann about the trouble in Serafina. Home alone and unable to reach Harry by telephone, she could do nothing but worry. When the phone rang, she jumped for it.

"Harry?"

"No, it's not Harry," Marsh said. "It's me. Were you expectin' a call from Harry?"

"Oh, um, yes. There's been some trouble in town. He's there with the sheriff and had Doris Ann call Ruth and me to warn us. I thought he might be calling with more news."

"What kind of trouble? Are you in danger, darlin'? Do you need me to come home?"

"No, no, I'm fine. There was an explosion at Ned Brett's office and some trouble in Black Flats."

"Explosion. What kind of explosion?"

"Doris Ann says they're not sure yet. But Ned wrote an editorial that angered a lot of people. She thinks there could be a connection."

"Shit." A brief silence. "But you're OK? You're safe?"

"Yes, I'm fine, Marsh."

"You're sure? I don't know. You don't sound fine to me."

"No, really. I'm fine."

A lull.

"Well, I think I best get on home. I'll be there tomorrow."

"All right, Marsh. Whatever you think is best."

Marsh had hoped for another response. Perhaps "Oh, thank you, honey." Or "I'll wait supper." Or "Yes, hurry please."

"I love you, Darlin'," Marsh said.

Another lull.

"I love you, too. Be careful on the road. See you soon."

She hung up the phone.

Marsh hung up, too. He pulled open the louvered door of the phone booth and took in the wind-scoured plain, replaying in his mind the restive tone of Bliss's voice when she answered the phone expecting Harry, the way it flattened when she found out it was him. Something twisted in his gut. Yes. He had to get home.

Minutes later, Bliss's phone rang again. This time it was Harry.

"You're there," Harry said. "Good. Are you OK?"

"I'm fine. Are *you* OK? Where are you?"

"I'm home."

"Oh, thank goodness. I was so worried. What's the situation in Black Flats?"

"Not good. We got things calmed down . . . for now. But I don't know how long it's going to last." Harry paused. "People died, Bliss."

"Oh my God."

"Have you heard from Marsh?"

"Yes, he called. He'll be home tomorrow."

"Good. You gonna be OK there tonight?"

"I . . . I think so."

Harry heard the hesitation.

"What's wrong?"

"Nothing. It's . . ."

"What, Bliss?"

"I went to see Alejandra Flores."

"You what?"

"I went to see Alejandra Flores today."

"Why on earth . . . . No. Let me guess."

"I had to know if Clayton was involved, Harry. I had to know if he had anything to do with what happened to her."

"And?" Harry held his anger in.

"She told me everything." Bliss paused. "For what it's worth, Clayton didn't rape her. That was Catlett."

"But Clayton was there."

"Yes. He didn't rape her, but he was part of everything."

"How was she able to identify him?"

"I showed her a photograph and asked if it was him. She said yes."

"So now what? Is she going to talk to the sheriff?"

"No. Oh, no. She's terrified Billy will kill her. She made me promise not to say anything, either."

"So we're right back where we started."

"Not exactly."

"How do you mean?"

"I had Clayton over for dinner after I got back. Marsh asked me to keep an eye on him."

Harry waited.

"And I asked him about it. Accused him, really. I told him I knew he'd been there. I didn't tell him how I knew because I promised Alejandra I wouldn't. But he knew I knew something. He tried to pin it on Woody again and I told him I knew that was a lie, too, because I'd seen Woody somewhere else that night and that I wasn't the only one."

Harry winced. "Did you tell him you were with me?"

"No. I wouldn't do that without asking you. But I didn't have a chance anyway. He lost his temper and pushed me against the wall. I thought he was going to hit me."

"That son of a—"

"He didn't, Harry. He didn't hit me. He ran off. But I've never seen him like that before. It was scary."

"Where is he now?"

"I don't know."

"And you're there alone."

"Yes."

Harry thought for a moment.

"OK. Look, why don't you come stay with me until Marsh gets back. He'll understand. With all the trouble in town, I don't think he'd want you being alone anyway."

"No, he doesn't. That's why he's coming home. But I'm not sure he'd like me staying with you any better. He sounded a little funny on the phone. He's never said anything, but sometimes I wonder if he doesn't suspect."

Harry often wondered, too. Marsh was a lot of things, but he wasn't stupid.

"He'd still want you safe, Bliss. That would be his priority, and he knows he can count on me to watch out for you no matter what."

"True, but . . . I don't know."

"OK. How about I see if Ruth wants to come over. She's alone, too. You can have the spare bedroom, she can take my room and I'll take the couch."

"You think she'd go for that?"

"I can ask. The worst that can happen is she says no, you come over anyway and we get you home early tomorrow before Marsh gets back."

No immediate response.

"Really, Bliss. I don't think you should be alone tonight. I'm not sure it's safe."

Bliss hesitated. "OK. Let me grab a few things."

"Good. I'll call Ruth."

Ruth declined Harry's invitation. She thanked him for his concern but insisted she'd be fine.

"I've been on my own for a long time, Harry. I can take care of myself."

"I know you can, but I worry about you."

"I appreciate that but there's no need."

"Well, call if you change your mind. We'll be here."

Tears pricked Ruth's eyes. *We.* She and Harry had never been *We.*

"Thanks, Harry."

At the Bar T later that evening, Harry and Bliss made supper together, both aware it was the first time they'd been alone anywhere but Blue Creek since before the war. It felt awkward and intimate at the same time.

"Where do you keep your utensils, Harry?"

"That drawer over there. How do you like your steak?"

"Medium, please."

"I'm not the best cook, I'm afraid," Harry said, sliding a well-done steak onto Bliss's plate. He put the frying pan back on the stove, wiped his hands on a dish towel. "I've got candles around here somewhere."

Bliss smiled. "That would be lovely."

Over supper Bliss talked more about her visit with Alejandra and her quarrel with Clayton.

"You have to tell the sheriff that the girl knows who attacked her, Bliss."

"I can't, Harry. I promised."

Harry thought as he chewed his steak. "Do you think you could persuade her to tell the sheriff herself?"

"I don't think so. She was awfully frightened."

"Maybe if you went with the sheriff. She and her mother know you now."

Before Bliss could respond, the phone rang.

"Maybe it's Ruth," Bliss said as Harry sprang to his feet.

 It was Doris Ann.

"Harry. Dutch needs you. We got trouble again."

"Where?"

"Here. At the office. It's a mob, calling for him to come out. Can you get here?"

"Leaving now."

"Hurry, Harry. I think they mean business."

"What is it?" Bliss asked as Harry went for his hat and holster.

"Sheriff's got trouble. I gotta go."

"I'll go with you."

"No, it's too dangerous. You stay here. And lock the door. I'll be back as soon as I can."

CHAPTER 26

Hanging Fever

Earlier that evening, Clayton Stone had made his way to Sweet Leona's on the hunt for Billy Catlett.

"Seen 'im? Nope cain't say's I have," Di Loveless said, toweling glasses behind the bar. "But I know where you can find 'im." She waved her towel in the direction of the courthouse. "He's enjoying the hospitality of Sheriff Mackey, behind bars, where he belongs."

Clayton felt a chill. "Behind bars? What for?"

"You didn't hear?"

"Hear what?"

As Di filled him in on the day's horrific events, Clayton leaned on the bar, weak with revulsion and relief. At least he hadn't been there this time. He'd had nothing to do with this one. But what should he do now? He got a beer and made a slow retreat to a dark, back table to think.

Sweet Leona's began filling up, first with the usual patrons and later a smattering of Serafina's elite, the class Di Loveless liked to call the highbrows. Everyone was in a dither about the trouble in Black Flats. When a crowd had assembled, hotspurs Billy Ben McKinney and Homer Gene Earthman began fomenting unrest. And anyone who hadn't heard the rumor about an army of Black men with guns getting ready to attack heard it now.

"We gotta do something," McKinney exhorted the crowd. "If we don't, what's to come of this little town of ours? I'll tell you what. It's gonna die. Pretty soon it'll be deader'n hell."

"That's right," the woman standing beside him put in. "Our homes will be broke into. Burned to the ground. We white women won't be safe. Our kids neither."

In normal times, the more strait-laced members of Serafina society present that night would have had little use for these kinds of people and this kind of talk. But on this occasion they found themselves hanging back, listening and deferring to a deputation of the local underclass, loudmouthed men and women who spoke with passionate intensity and angry voices. They were setting the tone, and they were out for blood.

"Enough is enough," Earthman said. "To hell with what the Supreme Court says. We gotta hold the line."

"You ain't just awoofin'," Earthman's female companion added. "If we don't it'll be more than the schools integratin'. This time next year we could be overrun with half-breed pickaninnies."

Mutterings of agreement, spiked with foul curses, coursed through the assemblage of malcontents. The less vocal members of the crowd feigned agreement with head nodding and tongue clucking. A few people showed distress at what they were hearing, but no one made any loud protest or stomped out in disgust.

Smelling trouble, Di Loveless positioned herself behind the bar, in easy reach of the saw-gun she kept under the counter.

Clayton Stone saw his opportunity and stepped up to make his contribution to the rising tide of unrest. "We gotta have justice, and we gotta have it fast," he said. "Why, Billy Catlett's sitting in jail right now 'cause he tried to get justice. And what happened to him? Sheriff locked 'im up."

Angry shouting.

"Young Stone here's right, by God," Earthman said. "We cain't count on the sheriff no more. He's got one of our own in jail. Meanwhile, the Coats kid is still out there roamin' around free as a bird. Ain't no tellin' what he might do next. All Billy Catlett was tryin' to do was set things right. If we gonna have law and order in Sebastian County we gonna have to take care of it our ownselves in our own way."

More shouts, this time louder, more fever pitched.

"Hold on there a minute." The one bold voice rising in an attempt to stamp out the fires of hysteria belonged to Di Loveless.

"Justice," the tavernkeeper said, twisting the word. "What a load of bullshit. It ain't justice you want. It's blood. Y'all got a bad case of hangin' fever. The whole damn lot of you. That's the short of it."

"Aw, Di, that ain't true," Clayton Stone said. "We ain't like that."

"Yeah, come on, Di," McKinney said. "You got us wrong."

"The hell I do. You don't give a tinker's damn about law and order. Catlett sure don't. He wants to showboat around. Kill somebody. Since when you boys hold a fellow like that so high?"

A flare-up of choleric voices supported the agitators. A few of the diffident folks in the corners of the room tried to urge caution but a blare of catcalls and jeers drowned them out. Some rousers cursed them for cowards. Others ordered them to keep quiet or get out. Afraid to say more, the dissenters muzzled themselves.

Di Loveless remained staunch.

"Bill, you got all these tight-assed tea-sippers and handwringers browbeat. They're afraid to open their mouths. The fear in this place stinks to high heaven. Pee-yew." She held her nose. "That's what you deal in, right? Fear. You say you're afraid of this, that, and the other. You love bein' afraid. You want everybody else to be as pussified as you."

McKinney glared at her and the quislings who had the temerity to urge calm. "We got no time for lily-livered types," he said, wagging an index finger in the air. "And no use for girly men, either." He addressed the room. "Billy Catlett's sittin' in jail right now for doin' what he had to do to protect our way of life. Meanwhile, a criminal, a rapist—let's call 'im what he is—is still out there somewhere plannin' his next attack on one of our own sweet little gals for all we know. Seems to me somethin's bad wrong with this picture."

Answering the call of tribal passions, the clamor of the crowd grew louder and took on a more sinister tone.

"Ach," Di said, batting away McKinney's words with the flick of a wrist. "You boys is working yourselves into a lather . . . and for what? You ain't nothin' but a damn lynch mob tryin' to grow balls enough to do something."

"This ain't no lynch mob," McKinney said.

"No? Well, what do you call it?"

"It's a vigilance committee."

Di let out an expectorating laugh. "Oh, yeah? Since when?"

"We just now formed it."

Di laughed again, this time from the depths of her copious gut. "Vigilance committee. Like hell you are. Ain't a swingin' dick in here cares a monkey's fart about that little Flores girl or any other Mescan. We ain't even sure what actually happened. Way I hear it, Dutch Mackey ain't sorted that out yet."

"Don't need no sortin' out," Earthman said. "That little chili bean gal said the Coats boy done it. That's what I heard and I believe it. We don't need no more proof."

Clayton Stone piled on.

"That's right. I heard the same thing and I believe it, too.

Everybody believes her. What reason would she have to lie? It ain't the kind of thing you lie about." The crowd grumbled its agreement.

"You believe that, do you?" Di said, looking straight at Clayton Stone. "Hell, you never even talked to her. Wouldn't know her if you passed her on the street. Same goes for the rest of y'all. And the Coats kid ain't out there plannin' to do nothin' to no one. Y'all know that. He ain't never hurt nobody in his young life. Any of you yahoos even seen him since you tried to string him up? I figger he's gone to ground. I would if I was him and I'd stay there."

"Yeah? Well if he ain't got nothin to hide, why's he hidin'?" Earthman called out. "Don't make no sense to me."

Di's mouth fell open. "Oh, my Lord. If that ain't stupid, I ain't never heard stupid. And I promise you I've heard plenty of stupid in this bar."

Shouts of resentment toward the adversarial barkeep rolled across the room. Hisses and boos.

Di didn't weaken.

"Come on now, folks. Why don't y'all simmer down and have a drink. Let the law take its course. That's what we got a sheriff for."

"We ain't waitin' on the sheriff no more," McKinney said. "We are the law, Di. You got that? *We* are the law."

McKinney, the man with the loudest voice in the room, was galvanizing the crowd.

"This ain't no time to show yeller," he admonished the seething throng. "We gotta stick together on this. Do the right thing. Sheriff's got the wrong man in jail and he's letting the wrong man run loose on the streets of Serafina. If he ain't gonna do nothin' about it, we will. Are you with me?"

A roar erupted and a forest of upraised arms, each as rigid as a hoe handle and capped with a fisted hand, shot up.

"We're with you," Clayton Stone called out. "Free Billy! Free Billy!"

"Stretch that little rapist son of a bitch," someone shouted.

"Free Billy! Free Billy!" Other voices took up the chant.

The conservative citizenry occupying the corners of the room shrank back. The rest of the mob headed for the door. Di Loveless moved quickly to the entrance and tried to block their way, throwing up her arms as if to prop up a collapsing wall.

"Hold on. Hold on now. You don't want to do this."

Shouts of affirmation from the incensed vigilantes filled the room, the volume rising.

"Stop," Di pleaded. "Go on back and have a seat. Drinks on the house. Don't be stupid. Let the sheriff do his job."

A collective cry of "Free Billy! Free Billy!" from the men massing at the doorway answered her plea for restraint.

"Step aside, Di," McKinney said. "We mean bidness."

The belligerents pushed forward, shunting Di Loveless out of the way, spewing curses and vulgarities. The identity of each individual rowdy having merged into one surging mass, the mob poured into the night like a gusher of Oklahoma Crude.

A phalanx of rageful men and women, some twenty strong, marched to the jail, Clayton Stone carried along with them. Shouting and brandishing weapons retrieved from their trucks—long guns, pistols, rakes, axe handles—they thronged in front of the courthouse, cursing and shouting epithets, their faces illuminated by the jaundiced glow of nearby streetlights and the fluorescent fixture over the door.

A blustering voice surmounted the rabble noise. "Sheriff, get on out here. We got bidness!" Billy Ben McKinney, armed with a shotgun, came forward. "Ya hear me, Sheriff? Come on out."

Fists pumping, the mob began to chant, "Come out. Come out. Come out!"

At the same moment the mob made its first move toward storming the Sebastian County Bastille, the door opened and Sheriff Dutch Mackey appeared. He stood on the steps, feet wide apart, chin tucked in, hands on hips, cigar clenched in his teeth.

At the imposing sight of him, every dissident tongue stilled.

The sheriff took the cigar from his mouth and inspected the smoldering tip. Clamping the cheroot between his hard-set jaws again, he gave the mob the once-over.

"Evenin', folks. What the hell y'all doin'? You bunch of muttonheads decide to come down here and make complete idgits out of yourselves? Packin' iron. All tooken more than a little drunk. Good God Almighty."

"This here's a vigilance committee," Billy Ben McKinney shouted. "We want Billy Catlett."

The mob took up the demand. "We want Billy! We want Billy!"

"Vigilance committee. Like hell it is. You're talkin' through your hat. You know that kinda thing don't cut no ice with me."

"We want Billy Catlett," Homer Gene Earthman said. "You got no bidness thowin' him in jail. He ain't done nothin'. That Coats kid, he's the one raped that little girl. Time to get somethin' done around here."

The sheriff threw his cigar away.

"Get somethin' done. I tell you flat out what's gonna get done. You're gonna call off your dogs right now. Any man tries to take my prisoner gets a bullet in his beef section. That's what's gonna get done. You hear?"

"Forget that," McKinney said. "We want Catlett and we want 'im right now."

Homer Gene Earthman tried to put an end to the palaver. "This ain't no time to go flabby, Dutch. Now, get out of the way."

"Why don't y'all go on home," the sheriff said, planting his feet a little wider apart and resting a hand on his holster. "Give it till mornin'. Folks see straighter in daylight."

"We're seein' fine right now, Sheriff."

That's when the uncivil parley ended. Not with a bullet but with a rock about the size of a man's fist. It came flying in from the shadowed periphery and struck Dutch Mackey hard in the head near the left temple, dropping him to the pavement like a sack of flour. A scrum of men overwhelmed him. Before he could get his pistol out of its holster, a blizzard of fists administered another half dozen blows to his head and belly until he lay sprawled unconscious on the concrete steps, khaki sheriff's shirt ripped at the shoulder, face bloody, eyes blackening.

When Clayton Stone saw what was happening, he lost his nerve. No longer a blustering gasbag, he was now a scared kid who was having trouble catching his breath. Backstepping, glancing around to see who might be watching, he pulled to the rear of the mob and faded into the surrounding darkness.

Doris Ann came barreling out the door. "Get off him! Get off him, you monsters!" she shouted, wielding a baseball bat that one of the men caught hold of before she could land a blow. Three other men forced her back inside and sat her down hard in a chair as McKinney knelt over the unconscious sheriff and rifled through his pockets until he found the ring that bore the cell key. He also relieved the sheriff of his gun.

With three armed men standing over her, Doris Ann could do nothing as McKinney and Earthman went back to the jail, unlocked Catlett's cell and escorted him out the door, stepping over the still unconscious sheriff as they made their way down the steps to the cheers of the vigilantes waiting to welcome him. McKinney handed Catlett the sheriff's gun. "Here's a little present for you from the sheriff."

Catlett smiled and stuck the gun in the waistband of his jeans.

"Good work, boys," Catlett said as the men gathered around him, congratulating him and patting him on the back, telling him again and again how he had no business being in jail in the first place. "You done good bustin' me out. Much obliged. Now we got more work to do."

An ensemble of vigilantes raised a chorus of approval.

"We gotta take care of that Coats kid now," Catlett declared. "He's the one raped that little Mexican gal. We all know it. Dutch Mackey knows it."

Wild shouting and brandishing of weapons.

"We know where he lives. In that little shotgun house south of the sale barn. I say we go get him, string his sorry ass up for all them wooly-heads to see. Won't be no mistakin' we mean bidness."

"Yeah! Yeah!"

Catlett surveyed the faces of the men surrounding him. "Where's my righthand man at?" He spotted Clayton half-hidden behind his truck. "There you are." He went to him and clapped a firm hand on his bony shoulder. "Come on. You ride with me." He turned back to the mob. "Whadaya say, men? Are you with me?"

The mob roared.

"All right. Let's go. Somebody get a rope."

Woody Coats should have left Sebastian County and gone to stay with Texas kin the way his mama kept begging him to do. But he didn't. He liked his little place at the edge of the Flats, liked being close to his folks and liked his mama's cooking. Even after his brush with death he had trouble believing people could want to do him harm. To his mind, if he stuck close to home he'd be fine until the sheriff got things sorted out. Maybe the sheriff didn't know yet who hurt that girl but Woody was confident the sheriff knew it wasn't him. Harry and Miss Bliss would've seen to that by now. Woody was sure of it.

But Woody was mistaken. He was sitting at his wooden dining table enjoying a plate of his mother's chicken and dumplings when a mob of roughs and bullyboys, inspirited with rage and fueled with redeye whiskey, kicked in his door and jumped him. One of the men brained him with a cut-down billiard cue while another tied his hands behind his back with a length of twine. They dragged him outside amidst cheers and vile imprecations and slammed him against the trunk of a hanging tree.

As Clayton sat frozen in the passenger seat of Billy Catlett's truck, Catlett climbed out, took the lariat one of his accomplices provided, fashioned a crude noose at the end and looped it around Woody's neck. Pulled it tight.

Stunned and confused, unable to fight or flee, Woody could do nothing but plead for his life. "Please, please, please. I didn't do nothin'. I swear it. I didn't do nothin.'"

As Woody sank to his knees, pleading and begging, McKinney took the hangrope from Catlett and lofted the end of it over a stout branch of suitable height.

"No! Please! I didn't do nothin'! I—"

Catlett took up the dangling end. At his signal, he, McKinney and two other men hauled back on the line, hoisted Woody into the air, pumping his legs and gagging. His eyes bulged, blood-red specks freckling each creamy white sclera. His tongue thickened in his mouth.

McKinney and Catlett tied the loose end of the rope to the stub end of a lower branch worthy of the load and let their noosed victim dangle. It didn't take long for Woody to stop moving and go slack. Gravity, the pertinent law of nature, elongated his skinny neck. Walleyed, frothing at the mouth, he swung from the gallows tree like a pendulum, trousers wet with urine.

The hangmen stood back and fell still. There was no cheering. No back slapping, no claims of victory, no declarations of justice served. Nothing but silence.

Their thirst for blood sated, the mob began dispersing. One and two at a time, men peeled off from the group, slunk away to their vehicles and departed the scene. As they left, Billy Catlett shouted after them.

"You done the right thing, boys. Don't you fret about it. Folks gonna thank us."

Catlett climbed into his truck, started it, felt Clayton's eyes upon him.

"What? You got something to say?"

"Why'd you have to go and do that, Billy? You ain't killed enough darkies already?"

"Hey, that's the one that raped that little Mescan gal, remember. Only got what he deserved."

"Nah, nah, that don't solve nothin'. Don't matter he's dead. She knows he didn't do it. She knows it was us, Billy."

"Of course, she knows, you moron." Billy put the truck in gear and backed away to turn around. "But that little gal ain't talkin'. She ain't that stupid. Or if she is, she's gonna be changin' her tune after tonight. You'n me're gonna make sure of that right now."

"I ain't talking about her," Clayton said, slamming his hand on the dashboard in frustration.

Startled, Catlett stopped the truck.

"Not her? Whadya mean not her? Who then?"

CHAPTER 27

Loose Ends

"Bliss, that's who," Clayton said. "She knows. She knows it wasn't Woody."

Catlett stared at the kid. "What are you talking about?"

"I'm telling you she knows Woody didn't do it. She knows it was you and me."

"That's crazy. She don't know nothin.'"

"Dammit, will you listen to me for once?"

Surprised by Clayton's show of temper, Catlett shut up.

"She tricked me. While my asshole brother's out of town she invites me over for dinner. She has all this food, she says, and it'd be a shame it goin' to waste. So, fine. I'm sittin' there all natural like finishin' a bowl of beef stew and that's when she hits me with it."

"Hits you with what?"

"That you'n me done it. She wasn't bluffin' neither, Billy. I'm tellin' you. She knows it for a fact. I don't know how she knows, but she knows. And that's not all. She knows Woody Coats didn't do it, too. Says she saw him somewhere else that night. Says she'll testify to it if she has to."

Catlett sneered. "She's lyin.'"

"No, she swears. Her and somebody else saw him somewhere."

"Her and who?"

"I dunno. What difference does it make?"

"What difference does it make?" Catlett reached over and smacked Clayton across the back of the head. "You stupid . . . . You didn't ask?"

Clayton rubbed his head, shot Catlett an aggrieved look. "No, I didn't ask. I got the feelin' she wouldn't tell me anyway."

Catlett stared out the windshield. What Clayton was telling him didn't make any sense. If Bliss had seen Woody somewhere else that night, she'd have told the sheriff by now for sure. They both would've, she and anyone with her. Marsh sure would've. Why keep it a secret? And then Billy flashed on the tender scene he'd witnessed between Bliss and Harry outside the hospital the night after Marsh broke his leg. And he understood. Bliss wasn't with Marsh that night. She was with Harry.

Catlett twisted around in his seat.

"You say Marsh is outa town?"

"Yeah. Why?"

"Out of town," Catlett said. "Well, well, well, ain't that interesting."

Catlett smiled, hunched forward. Maintaining a death grip on the steering wheel, he aimed a stern gaze at Clayton.

"You listen to me, hoss. This here's ticklish bidness we into. Better get your big boy pants on. We got ground to cover."

"We? What do you mean we? I've had enough, Billy. I'm done."

"'Fraid not, buddy boy. We got our ass in a sling and you are in this deep as me. That there is a calcified fact, mister. Sooner you get that figgered out, better off you'll be. There's folks out there that'd be happy seein' you and me in the state pen. Twenty years of bustin' up rocks with a sledgehammer prolly sounds about right to 'em. That or worse. Well, it don't sound so good to me."

Talk of doing hard time jarred the kid.

"But . . . I . . . I . . . d . . . d . . . ."

He bungled his words. Tried again.

"I . . . I didn't do nothin'. You better look to your ownself. I was just there, same as now. Didn't do nothin' to nobody."

"That don't mean pig pee, my boy. Mr. John Law won't give a hoot about that. Nobody will. You're what they call a accessory. That means you're as guilty as me. If I have to, I'll be spillin' my guts about you. Tellin' how you mounted that little piece of tail, laid the wood to her. Hoooeee. You was lovin' ever minute of it."

"That ain't true, Billy. And I don't think anybody's gonna give a rat's ass about that anyway after what you done in Black Flats and . . . and . . ." Clayton threw a thumb at Woody's dangling body without turning to look, ". . . and after this here." He leveled accusing eyes at Catlett. "You killed people, Billy. That's what the sheriff's gonna come after you for. And you're gonna fry."

Catlett displayed his best lawbreaker curl of lip and squint of eye. "Ain't nobody gonna come after me for nothing. You hear me? Dead men don't talk." He leaned in close. "And neither do my associates. Cause they know if I go down, they're going down with me. And that includes you. Savvy?"

Clayton cringed.

Catlett leaned back and smiled, watching the kid become the malleable invertebrate he knew he could count on. He had him where he wanted him.

"So, you see, we don't have to worry about any of this bidness. What with all this hell goin' on around here, nobody'd ever point the finger of blame at you and me. We got a coupla hundred smokes we can blame for anything we want. That is our ace in the hole. You can bet your boots on it." Catlett furrowed his brow. "Way I figure, we got a clean shot out of this. All we gotta do is tie down loose ends."

The kid's legs trembled. Hands, too. A nervous tic chinked his left lower eyelid.

"Loose ends? What are you drivin' at, Billy?"

"I mean Harry True and his best squeeze."

"Ruth Blaylock?"

Catlett smirked.

"No, not Ruth Blaylock. I do believe you are stupid as you look. I mean Bliss. Mrs. Marshall Stone. Remember her? Bad as I hate to do it, I'm gonna let the cat out of the bag here. Harry True's been hosin' her since who laid the chunk. You must be the only dumb bastard in town that don't know it."

"Well, I don't know it. And I don't want to know it. What's that got to do with anything?"

"This. That's why Bliss didn't tell the sheriff about seeing Woody somewhere else that night, and that's why she didn't tell you who she was with. She was with Harry True."

"She was not."

Catlett skulled Clayton again. "Shut up. And now you're telling me she's threatenin' to go to that jerkwater sheriff."

"Well, she didn't exactly say that."

"And you say she knows for sure we're the ones who did it."

"She could be bluffin'."

"Mebbe. Mebbe not. One way to find out."

Catlett started the engine. Clayton grabbed his arm. "We ain't gonna do nothin' to her, are we, Billy? I mean hurt her? Come on, she's my brother's wife."

Catlett shifted into gear. "Nah. We ain't gonna hurt her. Just gonna talk to her. Put the fear of God in her. Make sure she sees things the right way. Let her know we'll keep her little secret if she keeps ours."

"I don't know, Billy. I don't need no more trouble."

"Look, shithead, we in this together. Don't you ever forget it. This ain't no time for a limp dick. You stick with me, or you gonna have more trouble than you already got."

"I don't know. I . . . I . . . . "

Catlett opened his jacket wide enough to reveal the wheel gun wedged in the waistband of his jeans.

Clayton's eyes widened. "Where'd you get that?"

"Borrowed it from the sheriff, you might say."

"Whada you gonna do, shoot me?"

"If it comes to that."

Clayton's mouth fell open. Catlett winked.

"Nah. Would I do such a thing? No way. You and me's buds. You know that. But I don't bleve I'd push it if I was you. I say we swing by, pay Bliss a little visit, see what's what."

As they drove, topkick and sidekick kept their own counsel, each of them. Catlett, conspiring with himself, envisioning the enterprise ahead. He became eager to see it through now that the wheels were in motion and there was no going back. Unfettered by any notion of consequences, he played out in his imagination how he'd find Bliss alone and put the fear of God in her. He would pace himself, have some fun. Why not? He had nothing to lose. And she owed him. She'd always carried herself mighty high, looking down on people like him. He chuckled. *Imagine that. Miss Goody Two Shoes screwing her husband's best friend. She deserves any punishment that might come her way.*

Clayton Stone slouched in the passenger seat, fidgeting, gazing out the window at the obscured expanse of land. Convinced Catlett would shoot him if it came to it. But too wrought-up to curb his tongue.

"What are we gonna do?" he said in a sniveling voice. "Billy, what are we gonna do?"

Catlett let the question hang.

"Pull over," the kid demanded. "Lemme out."

Catlett still didn't react.

"Billy, let me out."

Catlett kept driving. The kid kept talking.

"Billy, I got a bad feelin' about this. Man. Oh, man. I . . . I . . ."

Catlett snickered. "What's the matter with you? You got a case of worms?"

"Bill-lly—"

"You don't know whether to shit or go blind, do you? Why don't you just shut up. You gonna do what I tell you to do. You let me do the thinkin'."

"I'm not gonna shut up. I can tell you that right now. I'm not—"

"Shut up!"

Catlett pulled off the road and cut the headlights. He put the truck in reverse and backed into a brake of blackjack oak. Stopped. Nerves keyed-up, the kid came forward in his seat, searched right and left.

"What? What are you doin'? What's goin' on?"

Catlett sat, conning a broad sweep of low rolling country before him. Across the road and down the way, stood a house, front side perforated with yellow squares of windowlight. The Bar T homestead. Catlett's dry lips drew back and thinned over stained teeth.

"Well, looky there. I do believe somebody's home."

"Now what? What are we doin'?"

Catlett leaned in.

"Now we get out of the truck, real easy-like. And don't slam the door."

"Then what?"

"Then we go have us a little look-see. Find out if Mr. True is entertainin' a guest tonight. I'm bettin' Bliss is with 'im right now. Bet they're both there."

"So what? So what if they are?"

"We pay 'em both a visit, have a little talk."

"But what if they don't wanna talk?"

Catlett patted his gun. "We persuade them." He opened his door. "Now come on."

The subaltern kid followed his orders. He got out of the truck and stood next to Catlett at the front bumper. Catlett dipped his chin toward the house. When the kid didn't respond, Catlett seized his arm and pushed him forward.

"Let's go."

Like *bandidos* they crept across moon-blanched open ground. When they neared the house, they stopped and crouched behind the trunk of a towering elm. There, they watched and waited. Nervous anticipation and the incessant trilling of insects heated Billy Catlett's blood. Tonight, he would not wallow in resentment of Harry True as he always had. He would not be intimidated. He would act. He'd get the drop on Harry, make him beg for mercy and, if he had to, put a bullet in his head. The time for payback for all the insults and slights Harry had dealt him over the years had arrived. Tonight, he would square accounts.

Clayton squinted at the large picture window, wringing his hands, sweating from every pore of his body. The open curtains offered an unhampered view of the house's interior.

"There ain't nobody there, Billy," the kid said. "And I don't see Harry's truck. He musta gone to town and left the lights on. Come on. Come on. Let's get out of here."

"Shh. You learn to whisper in a sawmill?"

"Billy, come on. There's nobody there."

Catlett grabbed the kid's arm, squeezed hard to make him hush. A light flickered. A figure passed by a window. Female.

Snoozing on the porch, Bob woke, came to her feet and began barking. The door opened and Bliss came out.

"What is it, Bob?" she said, putting a hand on the dog's head. "You see something?"

Bliss squinted into the distance. Listened. Heard and saw nothing. Probably a coyote or a possum. She patted Bob's head. "It's OK." Not wanting the dog to run off after whatever she'd seen, Bliss brought Bob inside. She came reluctantly, whining. Intent on coaxing and calming her, Bliss closed but forgot to relock the door.

Catlett relaxed his hold on the kid.

"Nobody there, huh? She's treed, boy. She's treed."

The kid broke, raised himself soundlessly and bolted. Catlett reached for him. Grabbed a fistful of sleeve but the kid pulled free and took off. Catlett cursed him through clenched teeth. "Damn yellowbelly. You sorry son of a . . . ." But he could do nothing about it now. The kid had scarped out. He'd have to go it alone.

Catlett dropped to one knee, wiped his oily forehead with the back of his hand. He could see Bliss bustling back and forth, carrying plates, wiping the table, cleaning, straightening. She stopped at the distant sound of a vehicle starting and driving away—Clayton taking off in Catlett's truck. She came to the window.

Catlett froze. Held his breath. He didn't let it out until Bliss drew the curtains and became a vague form on the other side. *OK, honey. Time for you and me to have a little talk.*

Catlett advanced on the house, saw Bliss's Studebaker parked around the side. At the corner, he found the telephone line. He dug a folding lockback knife from a jeans pocket, unlocked the blade, slid it under the line and cut it clean. He pocketed the knife.

Catlett prowled to the front porch. Through the semi-sheer window dressing, he observed Bliss's blurry form. She stood at the kitchen sink drying dishes.

Heart banging in his chest, Catlett placed a big-knuckled hand on the door's silver knob and tested it. It clicked. He pushed the door open.

Curled up on the floor and thrown off by the natural way the stranger entered, Bob lifted her head and gave him a quizzical look. Friend? But as Catlett closed the door, she jumped to her feet, hackles high. She growled. Bliss turned, plate and dish towel in hand. When she spied the intruder, the color drained from her face. She tottered backward a step, catching herself on the counter and dropping the plate. Bob snarled, bared her teeth, went for the intruder. And Catlett shot her dead.

"No!" Bliss cried out.

Catlett fixed his eyes on Bliss. He smiled.

"Well . . . well . . . well. Fancy meeting you here."

PART SIX

CHAPTER 28

Coming Clean

At the sheriff's office, Harry found Dutch Mackey in his living quarters, reposed full length on the made bed, still in his wear-scarred rough-out boots and bloodstained shirt, upper lip split open, left eye battered shut. A heavy bandage around his temples, a damp washcloth stretched across his forehead. Doris Ann sat, daubing his wounds with tincture of iodine.

"My Lord," Harry said. "What happened here?"

Doris Ann glowered at him, tears streaking her face.

"That mob. Those bastards done this to Dutch. It's a wonder they didn't kill him. Pert near did. They busted that scut Billy Catlett out of jail. Dutch tried to stop 'em. Done everything he could. Didn't nobody offer to help."

"Where'd they go?"

"Don't know, don't care. They were plenty riled up, though. I can tell you that."

"Back to Black Flats?"

"I said I don't know," Doris Ann snapped. "Just glad to be rid of 'em. Look what they did to Dutch."

Dutch groaned and tried to lift himself on his elbows. "I'm OK. They didn't hurt me none."

"Whoa, there," Doris said, firmly pushing him back. "I ain't done with you yet."

Without argument, the sheriff lay back down.

Harry removed his hat, pulled a chair to the bedside and sat. Lowering his head, he ordered his rumpled hair with his fingers and let his hand rest at the back of his neck. From his bed, Dutch Mackey watched him through purple eye slits.

"Woody had nothing to do with what happened to that little Flores girl," Harry said finally. "Nothing. Not a thing."

Dutch didn't respond. Doris Ann continued nursing his wounds.

"I know because I saw him somewhere else that night. He was miles away from all that sorry business. I saw him. And Bliss saw him. She was with me."

Doris Ann paused her ministrations. She and her husband exchanged a look.

"Figgered you knew more than you was tellin'," the sheriff said. "Way you been mopin' around here like you was wrestlin' with some private demon."

Dutch peeled the damp cloth from his forehead. "Help me up," he said to his wife. Doris Ann protested, tried to restrain him, but Dutch wouldn't have it. Sighing, she helped him pull himself upright and bring his legs over the side of the bed. He patted her on the arm.

"I'm all right, Honeybunch. I'm all right."

"No, you're not. You're beat all to hell and you need to lie down. You're bein' pigheaded."

Doris Ann sat back in frustration. There was no use in arguing and she knew it.

Dutch rotated his head, exploring the limits of his mobility. He winced. He touched his bruised and swollen cheeks with his fingertips and exercised his jaw. Took in a deep breath, let it out.

"Hoo boy, I wish I could say I gave as good as I got, but I don't bleve

I ever got a lick in. They knocked the pee-waddin' outa me. Guess I'm gettin' too old to cut the mustard."

"Don't be ridiculous," Doris Ann grumbled. "Musta been a dozen of 'em beatin' on ya . . . or more." She glanced at Harry. "Them kind hunt in packs, you know. They busted Catlett out of jail and took off."

"Yeah, I got that part."

Doris Ann glared at him again but bit her tongue.

Dutch gazed at Harry with weary eyes. "Look, I appreciate you vouchin' for Woody. You and . . . Miz Stone. She knows you're here talking to me I take it."

Harry wasn't sure how to answer. "She knows I'm here."

"Well, you can thank her for me, too, I guess. But you'd have to be crazy to think Woody had anything to do with it. Flores girl never actually accused him. Never accused anybody. Catlett and his bunch been talkin' that up. And, yeah, OK, it's helpful someone can say for sure Woody didn't do it. But that don't help us nail whoever did."

"I think you know who did it."

"Dammit, Harry," the sheriff said, trying to gain his feet. He grimaced in pain, sat back down. "No, I don't know. That's the thing. I heard rumors, sure. I got me a pretty good idea who done it. But that don't amount to a bucket of spit. I know who delivered them black bodies to my door, sure. But that don't mean I know who kilt 'em." He shook his head. "No, no sir. That ain't the way it works. I need me some eyewitnesses, or a confession. Some kind of proof. And I ain't got that. I ain't got squat."

Harry leaned forward, elbows on thighs, hands clasped. "Maybe if you talked to the girl again. Maybe if you took Bliss with you."

"Bliss," Doris Ann said, sounding offended. "Why would he do that?"

"She paid Alejandra a visit today."

The sheriff folded his arms, lowered his chin. "Did she now? And why did she do that?"

"Let's say she heard the rumors, too. About who raped that girl, and who was with him. You know Bliss. She always wants to believe the best about people, especially family. So, when she heard who the second man was supposed to have been, she decided she had to find out for herself."

"So she went to Alejandra," the sheriff said.

"And after that she confronted Clayton."

Harry expected Dutch and Doris to show surprise when he dropped Clayton's name, but they didn't. Seemed he hadn't told them anything they didn't already know, or at least suspect.

"Catlett's the one that raped that girl," Harry continued. "Clayton Stone was right there with him. I know that for a fact, too."

"Uh-huh. And by 'a fact' you mean what exactly?"

Harry heaved a frustrated sigh. "OK. Look, I know. It doesn't matter what I say or what Bliss says. But I'm telling you Bliss talked to the girl, and if the two of you visited her together, she might be more inclined to talk to you." Harry turned to Doris Ann. "Maybe you could go, too. You have a comforting way about you. I think Alejandra's mom might feel better if you were there."

Doris Ann gave Harry a disgusted look. "Don't you go tryin' to butter me up, Mr. Harry True. What I want to know is how you know so much about what Mrs. Stone was up to today. Marsh tell you? Oh, no, that's right. He's out of town, ain't he?"

"Now, Mama," the sheriff said. "Mind your tongue."

"Oh, foot. You know what I'm sayin' is true."

Harry looked away.

"Fairly amazing," the sheriff said. "What gets into folks sometimes. Them boys that opened up a can of whup ass on me ain't bad *hombres.* Not really. Most of 'em's ordinary folks. Normal times, they don't do like that. They kindly locoed—all of 'em, all simultaneous. When that happens, there ain't no help for it."

The sheriff mulled his own words.

"Can they go back now? After all this foolishment that's taken holt of the whole damn town, can they go back to bein' who they was? Can this town? I ain't so sure."

Harry studied his hands.

The sheriff studied him. "Catlett know you and Miss Bliss are ready to alibi the kid?"

"Don't think so. Bliss told Clayton she's ready to do it and she wasn't alone, but she didn't tell him she was with me. I don't think Catlett knows anything yet. Bliss says Clayton took off after she confronted him. Nobody's seen him since."

"I have," Doris Ann said, sitting straight-backed. "He was out there with that bunch of jackasses beatin' you up," she said to Dutch. She turned to Harry. "He was hangin' around in the background like the little weasel he is, but he was there. The two of 'em took off in Billy's truck."

"So Catlett prolly knows about Bliss by now," the sheriff said. "I 'spect that'd get him spooked. Or maybe he just don't give a damn. Prolly figgered killin' a few colored folks in these sorry times would be easy enough to get away with. Mebbe he's right. Mebbe raping a little Mexican girl won't count for much either. Hard to know what a jury of his peers might do with him. Hell, his peers busted him outa jail."

Bliss. At the thought that Clayton could have told Catlett about his confrontation with Bliss, a feeling of near panic flared in Harry. He stood.

"I need to use your phone."

The operator tried to make the connection to Harry's ranch but couldn't.

"Call won't go through," she said. "Must be some problem with the phone or the line out your way."

"Keep trying."

"I am trying. It's not working. I'm not surprised, the way things are—"

Harry slammed the receiver into its cradle. Dutch Mackey was on his feet, teetering at his side.

"Sumpin' wrong?" the sheriff said.

"Yeah. Bliss is at my place. Line's dead."

"You best get on out there."

Harry turned toward the door.

"Wait."

Dutch hobbled over to a tall wooden case standing against the wall. Opened it and took out a 12-gauge pump riot gun. He jacked the slide, chambering a shell. Lowered the hammer, pitched the shotgun to Harry.

"Take that with you. Could get a little western out there. Go on now. I'll be along directly. Soon as I ain't seein' two of everthing."

Shotgun in hand, Harry rushed out and jumped into his truck. Speeding past Sweet Leona's, he spotted Clayton Stone closing on him from the opposite direction in Billy Catlett's truck. When he blew by, Harry stood on the brake, swerved to the right, wheeled the truck around and stepped hard on the foot feed. He overtook the kid as he turned into the parking lot at Sweet Leona's, cut him off and angled him over in a metal-crushing meeting of front fenders.

Clayton and Harry leaped from their trucks and, bringing the wrath of God with him, Harry descended on the kid. Clayton tried to run, but Harry extended a foot and tripped him. The kid went sprawling into the gravel, arms extended, heels of his hands plowing furrows as he came to a hide-peeling stop. Harry hauled him up and chucked him against the truck.

"Lay off, man," the kid protested. "I didn't do nothin'. I wasn't gonna hurt nobody. It was Catlett's idea. I swear. He made me go. He made me."

"Made you go where?" Harry gave Clayton another shove. "Where is he?"

"Your place."

"My place? Bliss is at my place."

"Yeah. I know."

The kid snickered. Harry slapped him hard. The kid yelped like a dog. Harry backhanded him, grabbed him by the shirtfront with both hands.

"How long's he been there? When did he get there?" Harry cocked an arm as if to go to school on him again, this time with a fist. Clayton ducked and tried to shield his face with his hands.

"He's there now," he whimpered. "I run off. Didn't do nothin'. Swear to God I didn't."

Harry grabbed the kid by the shoulder and wrenched his arm behind his back. "If anything happens to Bliss," he growled, force-marching Clayton to the entrance of Sweet Leona's. "I mean if he touches one hair on her head, he's dead meat and so are you." He kicked the door open, noise reverberating through the now vacated establishment, and shoved the kid inside at the moment Di Loveless came up with the shotgun she kept under the bar.

"What's goin' on here?" she exclaimed. She lowered the gun when she saw Harry.

"Di, do me a favor and march this son of a bitch over to Dutch. The sheriff's had a rough day. If the punk tries to run, let go with that scatter gun."

Harry threw Clayton into a chair, held him there until Di came around the bar holding the gun.

"Proud to," she said.

Harry raced to his truck, jumped in, and gave it the gas.

CHAPTER 29

Gone

Harry studied the house with misgivings. He didn't like what he was seeing at all: door ajar, curtain hanging askew, lamplight cast along a bizarre azimuth against the living room wall. Bliss's Studebaker gone.

Heart banging, he opened the truck door and stepped out. Took the shotgun in hand, thumbed back the hammer. Carrying the gun waist high, finger on the trigger, he made his way to the steps, mounted them, catfooted across the porch to the door. Peering inside he beheld a scene of violence and disorder. Chairs overturned. Shards of broken dishes on the kitchen floor. Standing lamp knocked askew and leaning against a footstool. Bob dead on the floor in a bloody heap. No sign of Bliss.

Harry searched every room, raced to the barn, checked it and went back to the house. Standing in the living room, thoughts racing, he saw the sheriff's car speeding up the driveway, Doris Ann behind the wheel. Riding shotgun, the sheriff wore his hat catawampus on his head, tilted to the right by the bandage wrapped around his skull. He horsed his big-shouldered body out of the car, stood stiff as a tin woodman seized up with rust. Instructing his wife to wait there, the sheriff heaved himself up the steps and across the porch. Leaning against the open doorjamb to catch his breath, he saw Harry surveying the room, shotgun in hand.

"Catlett's got Bliss," the sheriff said.

Harry jerked to attention.

"Where?"

"Not sure. Di Loveless was marching Clayton over to the jail when Catlett came tearin' into town in Bliss's car. Had Bliss in the back seat. Cold-cocked Di, snatched up Clayton and drove like sixty. Soon as Di got her head screwed on right she come to tell me. Said looked to her like they had Bliss tied and gagged but she couldn't be sure."

"Di know where they were headed?"

"South, she thinks. Heard Catlett say somethin' about border country. They're prolly highballin' it for Old Mexico, figurin' on holding Bliss hostage till they get across."

Harry charged past Dutch and out the door. Halted on the porch, forced himself to think.

"What are you fixin' to do?" the sheriff said, coming to his side.

"Go after them," Harry answered in a carefully controlled voice. "I'm going to get Bliss back. And I'm going to kill Billy Catlett and Clayton Stone."

"You gotta find 'em first. Big country out there. Man can lose hisself in all that empty, slip on into the hell and gone. Trail can go cold before you know it."

"I'll find them."

"They got a right smart of a lead on you," the sheriff said. "And you don't know where in perdition they've went."

"My bet is Di's right. They'll head south. Take the town road, cut off soon as they can. I know that country."

"I'll get on the horn to the Highway Patrol and the Texas Rangers when I get back to the office. See if they cain't mebbe close the back door on these sumbitches."

Harry waved his thanks and started for his truck. The sheriff tried to work his hat into place as he came down the steps. Pulling it low across his forehead, he lost his balance and had to reach for the porch column to steady himself. Doris Ann hurried to help him sit down.

"Hell fire and damnation," Dutch said. "Help me up. I gotta get to the office."

"You ain't goin' nowhere till you catch your breath."

"I got sheriffin' to do, woman."

"It'll keep."

Harry drove his truck around to the barn and hitched up a tandem axle two-horse trailer. He threw a double-rigged saddle with breast collar and bridle on Rocky Red, a three-year-old sorrel gelding, and loaded him in the trailer on the high side. He caught up a buckskin he called Blazer, slipped a rope halter with a braided cotton lead shank on him and over that a headstall with a snaffle bit. Tied the split reins short. The spare mount, close-coupled and stout-built, he loaded bareback. Both animals were serious horseflesh. They had a nice, even gait. And they had bottom. They were sure to need it.

Harry pulled to the front of the house and rushed back inside past Doris and Dutch, came out again three minutes later, carrying a Winchester lever action rifle and saddlebags bulging with a couple of boxes of .30–30 shells. Over his shoulder hung a pair of binoculars and a canteen. In a russet leather cross-draw shoulder holster of the military type he carried his Army .45. On his belt, he had an ammunition pouch of olive drab cotton webbing that held two loaded pistol magazines.

"You best give me a chance to get hold of the Highway Patrol," the sheriff suggested again. "This ain't no cotillion you're goin' to. Catlett's rattler mean and now he's scared. He'd as soon gun you as look at you."

Harry stowed his gear on his saddle, closed and bolted the tailgates on the trailer.

"No time. Trail'll go cold."

He climbed into his truck and headed out. What he had to do, he would do alone and he would do it now.

An hour later, Marsh came home to a dark house. Didn't see Bliss's car. He opened the door and called for her. No answer. He flipped on the lights, checked their bedroom. Bed unoccupied and unslept in. He checked every room; no one there. He searched for a note. Found nothing. Bliss had mentioned the trouble in town. Maybe she'd gone to stay at Harry's place until Marsh could come fetch her. She'd be safe there; Marsh had no doubt about that. He tried to call Harry, couldn't get through. Trouble with the line, the operator said. Been like that all night. Thinking Clayton might know something, Marsh called him. No answer. Marsh got back in his truck and headed for Sweet Leona's. Like as not, the kid would be there. He wasn't, but Di was, stretched out with her feet on a chair, holding an ice pack to the left side of her face.

"What happened to you?" Marsh said.

"Never mind me. He took Bliss."

"Whadaya mean, he took Bliss? Who took Bliss?"

"Catlett."

Marsh wheeled and stormed out, heading for the sheriff's office. There he found Dutch Mackey in the living quarters, lying in bed, Doris Ann sitting in a chair close by.

"What happened? Where's Bliss at?"

The sheriff spoke without rising.

"Catlett and the boy took her. Headed south prolly. Harry went after 'em."

"Whadaya mean, the boy? You mean Clayton? That's crazy. Why would Clayton take off with Catlett? What's Catlett want with Bliss?"

"You don't know."

"Know what?"

The sheriff reached for his wife. Doris Ann helped him rise. He hung his legs over the side of the bed, rubbed the back of his neck.

"Catlett's the one that raped that little Flores gal. No surprise there, I reckon." He looked at Marsh. "Your little brother was right there with him when he done it."

Marsh exploded.

"That's a damn lie. My brother would—"

"Bliss went to see the girl today," Dutch continued. "Not sure what was said, but when she got back, she confronted your brother. Said she knew it was him and Catlett who done it." Dutch paused. "Told him she knew it wasn't Woody, too, 'cause they saw him somewhere else that night and they'd swear to it if they had to. Your brother musta told Catlett and—"

"Wait a minute. Who's they?"

Dutch and Doris Ann glanced at each other. Dutch heaved a sigh.

"Bliss and Harry. They seen Woody somewhere else that night."

"Bliss and Harry? Together?"

The sheriff nodded.

"Where?"

"Not sure. Somewhere a far piece from the scene of the crime's all I know."

Marsh tried to process what Dutch was telling him.

"When did all this happen?"

"Month ago Tuesday. Night that squall rolled through."

"While I was still laid up at home."

"That's right."

"That don't tally. Cain't be. Bliss was at a meeting with Ruth and

Buddy and them folks who want the 'whites only signs' to come down. I remember 'cause it ran late and—"

At that moment, Marsh knew. The harsh truth he'd suspected but refused to believe now punched him hard in the gut. He took off his hat, slumped into an armchair. The sheriff watched him.

"You already knowed, didn't you? I ain't tellin' you nothin' you didn't know."

Marsh stared at the floor. He drew in a deep breath, exhaled through his nose.

"I ain't blind, am I? I ain't stupid. I've seen how they look at each other, heard a few whispers. But I didn't think . . . I mean . . . ."

Marsh shook his head.

"Well, if that don't beat all. Guess that's what passes for loyalty these days. Your wedded wife and your best friend, your blood brother . . . ."

He rose.

"Well, I'm done with that," he said, regaining his grit. "I ain't playin' the fool no more."

He put his hat back on.

"What are you gonna do?" Dutch asked.

"What do you think? Gonna fetch my family in."

"Harry figgers they're headin' south, makin' a run for the border. You reckon you can find 'em?"

"I'll find 'em. I'll find my wife and my brother. And I'll find Harry."

"He's aimin' to kill Catlett and Clayton."

"He ain't killin' my brother. He'll have hell gettin' that done."

CHAPTER 30

Down Country

Harry drove through the remains of the dark hours. He took the main highway back to Serafina, and on the west side of town turned south onto a washboard county road. After a while, he struck out on a quilt-work of unpaved arterials. Catlett's true purpose defied all reckoning, but Harry had a hunch he was thinking he could work his way along the backroads and disappear into the wildlands before anybody could get a rope on him. Harry knew those roads well. He'd driven them in daylight and dark as a kid, buying produce for his father's business. And he knew the surrounding west country. He had a pretty good idea of where Catlett might be headed, and how he'd get there. With any luck, he would run him to ground.

By dawn, Harry had reached the *rincón,* a parsimonious stretch of untenanted Dust Bowl country failed homesteaders thought of as the end of all roads. A common hell. That's how a toothless old goat of bygone days had once described it to Harry. For him, this sun-seared stretch of withered prairie had come to that name by rights in the depths of the Dirty Thirties. In those days, he'd been one of a sorry lot of worn-out nesters—next year people, orphans of a vanished land of promise. Plow chasers like him were the storied folk of a sad era, people betting on the come, trying to prove up no-account ground, counting on the land's increase, hoping spring rains would break the drought and moderate temperatures would return. But for such folk disaster was their natural lot. The drought went on for a decade. The heat never abated. For most of them it was root hog or die, so they abandoned their homes and farms, moved on without notice or ritual. A few diehards hung on in that derelict land. The *mal país,* badlands.

That's where Harry came upon Bliss's Studebaker, abandoned at the side of the road. The doors stood open, giving the vehicle the appearance of a dead bird with splayed wings. Not a soul in sight. He got out of his truck and approached the car on foot. Up close, the metal hulk resembled a brittle cicada husk. Dun colored dust coughed up by the desiccated prairie had begun cloaking the seats and floorboards, dash.

Harry found the key in the ignition. He cranked the starter, but it produced nothing but a dry, scratchy sound. The gas gauge showed empty. He got out and lifted the trunk lid. Nothing there. He stood at the drift line of dirt along a sagging barbed wire fence that paralleled the road. Looked past the dried-out carcass of a coyote strung by its heels on the wire to the forlorn country beyond it. A cross breeze had set a brace of tumbleweeds rolling before him. His gaze tracked their movement and settled on a wind scowl homestead standing a quarter mile off at the end of a twin-rutted track. House with a steep-pitched roof, walls chipped and scaled to gray wood. A small breaker of skeletal trees on the north side. Wind and sun-racked corn rows in a destitute field to the east. No sign of life except a thin spire of smoke tapering upward from the stone chimney. On the sandy loam between the road and the house, Harry could cipher a trail of vague footprints. Three sets of them.

Harry unloaded the horses. He had gentled the spirited Rocky horse in his new round pen, but the animal was no more than greenbroke. Harry knew him to be a tad ill-mannered, so he untracked him and walked him around in a circle a couple of times before tightening the cinch and mounting. He dallied the buckskin's halter lead rope to the saddle horn and unsheathed his rifle. He booted his mount forward and rode out at a walk, sitting the horse high, holding the rifle upright, stock resting on his thigh. If Catlett and Clayton were holing up inside with Bliss, they'd have spotted him, but Harry figured he'd be dodging bullets by now if that were the case.

He crossed the yard but before he could halloo the house, a shave-tail kid in raggedy bib overalls, a boy slat-thin and worn to a nub, came running around a corner, brandishing a hoe at high port.

"You git on outa here," the kid hollered, planting himself before the family stronghold in the stance of St. Peter guarding the gates of Heaven. "We don't want no more trouble. Git!"

The boy couldn't have been more than thirteen, fourteen years old. A bruise purpled his left cheekbone; the eye above it swollen. He wore dust like dark face powder, and he was sweating mud.

"You git on outa here. Go on. Git."

"What happened here, boy?"

The bobtail was in no hurry to answer. He swiped a ratty swatch of straw-colored hair from his forehead, and after several moments tried to speak. But he couldn't get the words out. Harry softened his tone.

"What happened?"

When the boy found his voice, the words came out wet with tears.

"Who are you? Whadaya want?"

"I'm looking for a woman. And the two men that took her. That's her car yonder."

"You the law?"

"Have you seen 'em?"

"They was here. We all howdy'd and shook. Daddy give 'em water from the well and then one of them daggone fellers poleaxed him, whomped him up 'side the head when he wudn't lookin'. Stove in his skull. Liked to kilt him."

"Which one?"

"Older one. One with the short gun. Other one popped me, give me this shiner. Caught me a beaut. Next thing I knowed, they'd gotten theirselves three horses out of the pen. Stoled 'em. Ever last one of 'em. Poor as all git out, nothin' but jerk-line hayburners. But all we had on the place."

"Where's your mama?"

"Dead. Lung fever took her."

"What's your name, boy?"

"Hightower."

"Thought so. I know your people. How's your daddy?"

"Cain't say. Don't act like he wants to wake up."

Harry shook his head.

"I'm sorry to hear that, son. Can you tell me which way they went?"

The kid smeared dark smudges of tears across his cheeks. He spoke as if he were in a daze and didn't quite understand what he'd been asked.

"Thowed some old hulls on 'em. Dusted outa here. Them jughead plugs cain't carry 'em far, though. Pert near done in already."

Harry asked again which way they'd gone. Coming to himself, the boy pointed south into the hell-scuffed distance.

"Yonder way. Ain't nothin' out there 'cept rough country till you make the river. Jackrabbits and mountain boomers. Sidewinders. Prairie dogs."

"Was the woman OK?"

"'Spect so. But she looked kindly hard used."

Harry gazed off into the unwelcoming expanse of the *mal país*. A wave of distress tempered with anger and cold resolve overwhelmed him. When he looked back at the boy, the sight of a dutiful scion reduced to a frazzled, filthy urchin softened his heart.

"How come you folks never left out of here along with everybody else?"

The boy became speculative. Fresh tears reddened his deep-set eyes. He raised a hand against the morning glare, shooed a fly from his face. Shuddering, he spoke as if the question had caused him to exhale the last of the spirit within him.

"Oh . . . my daddy was a member of the Last Man Club. He give his word back in the thirties like all them others. Took a oath he'd be the last man here. Bleve he is. They all quit off, but not him. Folks said he had a head like a rock. Guess they was right." The kid nodded. "Hope they was right."

"You can take your daddy to town in my truck over there if you've a mind to. Might do him some good to have some doctoring. Key's in it."

The Hightower boy spat and wiped his mouth. Stiffened his back.

"Ahh, I 'spect we'll make do," he said, voice bell-clear.

"You sure?"

"We don't need no help."

"Suit yourself."

"I aim to."

Harry touched his hat brim with a finger.

"Much obliged," he said.

"You goin' after 'em?"

Harry nodded.

"Well, shouldn't oughta take you too long to run 'em down. You're better mounted by a damn sight. And ain't nary a one of 'em much shucks as a horseman. Don't know how much water they're carryin'. Didn't see no canteens."

"How much of a start do they have on me?"

"Couple hours." The kid took in a deep breath.

"They's one more thang you might orta know. They's packin' heavy artillery now. Made off with Daddy's lever action and a box of cartridges. And I 'spect that older feller has the craw to use it."

Harry touched the brim of his hat again. He reined the Rocky horse about, jigged him into a brisk trot and, with the buckskin keeping pace, set off down country.

CHAPTER 31

Mal País

The outlaws had a good lead on Harry. But they lacked the skill and wisdom to maintain it. They drove their spavined horses without letup, seldom giving them a chance to rest and blow, Catlett on a flea-bitten gray gelding, Bliss on a rawboned claybank mare, Clayton on a blood bay. The rough country they were traversing squandered no pity on the animals; heat and dehydration were taking a toll. By noon, they bordered on being unsound of wind and limb.

The riders fared no better. Beneath an immense vault of blue sky, unmitigated by even a scrap of cloud, every stretch of ground they covered had become an ordeal. Eating and breathing dust for hours, their throats rawed, nostrils dried, spirits drained. Not once did they strike an upright cross fence or encounter so much as a hairline trace of water. Time was, they would have run on to some rangy bush cattle. Not anymore. They kicked up a few steer skulls that lay bleaching in the sun but saw nothing on the hoof. Not even any chips. They skylined an occasional coyote studying them from some faraway rampart. In the absolute distance, well beyond gun range, they thought they could make out a herd of pronghorn. Nothing more, save a watchful squadron of black, long-winged turkey vultures that circled overhead, waiting for someone to die.

The riders pushed on through the horse-killing part of the day. They skirted patches of prickly pear cactus, some two, three acres in size, spiny green paddles as big as dinner plates rising stirrup-high in places. If they tried to pick their way right through, the commandeered farm nags paid for the folly with their own blood.

They wormed their way through catclaw thickets, threaded a path through tangles of arthritic mesquites, every branch armed with menacing thorns. They limped across beds of hoof-splitting rock scrabble. Crashed through tie-ups of chaparral, cheatgrass and snakeweed. When they were alert enough, they stepped wide of sword-shaped Yucca leaves with stiletto tips. Relief came when they were able to follow an age-old game trace or chanced upon a patch of sparse short grass—buffalo, blue grama. Likewise when an infrequent salt flat formed a pasty lesion on the prairie.

Deep cut gulches bedeviled them. No use in trying to judge distance as the crow flies, for the rugged terrain often didn't allow traveling in a straight line. After keeping to the caprock a while, they would have to slip off and work their way along interlocking spurs. For the most part, they were climbing and descending, climbing and descending. Every time they crested a rise, hope faded as their eyes fell on yet another ripsaw landform.

Long into their tribulation, Catlett called a halt. He ranged his squinted eyes across his entire field of vision. With his fingertips he tapped his right cheek. Grimed with an amalgam of sweat and dust, inflamed with sunburn, it stretched tight as an orange peel. Nothing he saw promised any relief. The kid hove up beside him.

"Sorry old country," Catlett said, swatting a deerfly that had been hectoring his neck. "Ain't nothing out here that don't have a thorn or a sharp edge on it."

"Wouldn't give two bits for a full section of it."

"Two bits. This whole piece of redneck country ain't worth a bucket of dog squeeze."

"Yeah. I'd rather be in hell with my back broke."

At that moment, something glittering on the ground fifteen, twenty yards out caught the kid's eye. With the reins, he quirted the bay into spiritless motion.

"*Ándale,* you son of a bitch."

"What's up with you?" Catlett called. "Get on back here."

But the kid kept on. When he reached the source of the dancing light he went goggle-eyed, shot out an arm.

"Mine!" he exclaimed, like some schoolboy finding a shiny new dollar on the playground. "Mine! Would you look at that."

Sliding off his horse, he wobbled forward, knelt before his find. The neck of a cut-glass whiskey decanter—intact, stopper and all—peeked out from the scaly ground. Despite its semi-internment the exposed geometrical panes threw off an acute reflection of sunlight. The kid unearthed the treasure. Grinning, he held it aloft. It tossed another glint of light.

"Hey, look. Lookeehere."

Catlett rested a censorious gaze on his sidekick.

"Yeah boy. You cut a fat hog, didn't you. What are you gonna do with that out here?"

"I don't know."

"You don't know. Answer's nothin'. Ain't gonna do nothin' with it. Get rid of it."

"Unh-unh. Look at it."

"Yeah. Part of the loot some *desperado* got rid of on his run to the river. Or somethin' some tornado blew in from the panhandle."

"But this thing's gotta be worth somethin'."

"If it had water in it. But it don't. Use your head, dammit."

The kid held up the glasswork, turned it in the sun, marveling at the way it bent and broke impacting light beams into a prismatic spray of hues and tints.

"Wish it did. Wish it did have water in it."

Catlett hawked up a noxious laugh.

"You wish. Wish away, boy. While you're at it, I'll go you one better. I'll wish us up a pitchfork rain, too. And I could do with a cold beer. That'd be nice."

Catlett spat dryly.

"Get on back here, numb nuts. We ain't got time for toys."

The kid went to Bliss, sitting slumped on the mare, wrists bound. He lifted the decanter. "Wanna see?"

Bliss turned her face away.

"Never mind then," Clayton muttered. He took a last look at his treasure and tossed it to the ground, footslogged to his horse and climbed laboriously into his saddle.

They toiled on. Catlett set a course for some vague destination that had not yet congealed in his head. Away. He was getting away. He figured the law, or Harry True, or Marshall Stone, or all of them were on his trail. He could think of nothing to do but put distance between himself and them, try to make it across the Red River into Texas and figure out the rest on the fly.

If it came to it, he might be able to use Bliss as a bargaining chip. Trade her for a head start on a run to the border. Get his pursuers to drop their guns, let him go. He turned to check on her. Stupid bitch. Wouldn't say how she knew what she knew even with a gun pointed at her. Either she was a hell of a bluffer or the Flores girl talked was the way he figured it. If she'da just said so, he mighta let her go and gone after that little chili gal instead. Shut her up for good and struck out alone. Let Clayton spill his guts to the sheriff. Wouldn't have mattered.

He'd've been gone. The kid wasn't any use to him now except maybe as a spare bargaining chip. He looked back at the two stragglers. Maybe he'd just kill them. He'd think about that. For now, all he could do was keep moving.

A couple of miles to the rear, Harry kept hard on their trail. As he rode, he caught the play of light on the kid's tossed decanter out of the corner of an eye. Reining up the Rocky horse, he fixed his eyes in the direction of the glint and groped in his saddlebag for his binoculars but by the time he came out with them Catlett and company had dropped into another gully. Glassing the scope of the desolate waste before him, he saw nothing but a stir-up of dust. Still, it heartened him. The sunglare had to have been manmade. The dust must have been raised by horses' hooves. He took up the slack in the lead rope and touched up the red horse. He pressed on.

Marsh was following. He, too, had tacked up and trailered Buck-shot to the *rincón*. Like the others, he'd stopped at the Hightower place. Grave news there. The shaggy-headed boy gave Marsh the same report he'd given Harry about what Billy Catlett and Clayton Stone did to him and his daddy, but this time with a different ending. Grief-stricken and barely able to form words, he managed to tell Marsh the Lord had called his daddy home. Marsh could do nothing but say he was sorry and much obliged for the help.

Marsh could proceed by dead reckoning now. He could read signs, cut the outlaws' trail, ride them down. With Harry and his two horses following the three stolen animals, there'd be hoofprints aplenty and fresh droppings. Such markers would augur well for making better time than his old friend and closing the gap. Pressing his advantage, he paced his mount at a brisk clip.

Marsh knew how to give chase the horse cavalry way. Walk, trot. Walk, trot. Get off and lead, track on foot. Do it over and over again. Maintain an even gait, make good time, but husband the animal's strength. It remained for him to run the fugitives to earth and when he'd done that, he'd still have a horse under him.

The drudging monotony of the day wore on. The merciless sun climbed, searing everything beneath it, pounding the earth with the force of a blacksmith's hammer on an anvil. Here and there, barren scabland sneezed a random dust whirl to haunt the null distance and give it a spirited, if malign, quality. The long riders and their captive forged on at a walk, heads low, listless, verging on unconsciousness.

Come midafternoon, Clayton was a near goner. Drawn up like a raisin, he slumped in the saddle under his filthy hat, his body aching for moisture. He'd tried to oppose his thirst with a pebble in his mouth, but the plainsman's method of creating saliva offered little relief. The wilting heat had baked the dross out of his system, leaving his body dehydrated and his clothes vile with sour perspiration and filth. From time to time, Catlett berated him for smelling high, complaining that he stunk like an overripe gourd.

Worse, Catlett chastised the kid for having a bad case of the bum-fidgets. He watched his backtrail without respite and gabbled nonsensical admonitions to himself. Sometimes, in an interior monologue, he appeared to be making a plea for mercy to some invisible overlord. Other times, his lips moved but he made no sound. Often, he engaged in idiotic conversations with hallucinatory companions.

The horses, lathered at the chest and flanks, were blown, too. Thick-necked draft stock, they were not cut out for criminal life. And recent years had been as hard on them as on their hapless overseers.

Their ribs could be counted one by one. The hollows above their eyes had deepened from dehydration and meager rations. And now, the lassitude of the trail had reduced the beasts to little more than sunstruck wanderers, plodding along, heads swinging low.

Likewise, the trail had tolled on Bliss. She'd descended into a wretched state: saddle-weary, stuporous from exhaustion, cheeks sandblasted and flayed by galling wind, dark shadows smudging her dust-encrusted face beneath her eyes. Her lips were cracked. She rode, choking the saddle horn with numbing fingers, bindings of maguey rope gnawing at her wrists. A powerful thirst scathed her throat. She didn't know if she could talk, so long since she'd tried.

Her thoughts darted from one extreme to the other. At times, she judged herself unmercifully, saw the plague of miseries that now beset her as a foreseeable turn of events. Justice. For weeks, she'd been wondering what punishment God might inflict upon her and Harry for their sin. She always knew it was coming. *This must be it,* she thought. *Death preceded by humiliation and suffering. A fitting end. After all, I am a scarlet woman.* She wanted to cry for the pain she'd caused Marsh. He didn't deserve it, not any of it. But she had no tears left. Only a deep, dry ache.

At other times, she didn't feel an ounce of remorse for what she'd done. What did Marsh expect? Yes, she loved him. But not the way she loved Harry. She had always loved Harry. And he had always loved her. From the day they met until the day everyone thought he was dead, it had been Harry and Bliss, Bliss and Harry. They were meant to be together. Everyone knew it. *So how can that be wrong?* She would make no apology—not to anyone.

The sight of a couple of far-removed patches of ground vivid with color—purplish-blue and orange-red—excited her imagination. The first she took for Bluebonnets, the second Indian Paintbrush. Each in turn set her thoughts veering from the agony of the present to memories of the past, so far away from the heat and wind, the bite of the ropes on her wrists, the parching of her throat, that she almost forgot about them. She was with Harry at Blue Creek, wrapped in the old Navajo blanket, listening to the wind in the trees and the murmur of creek water.

But then she remembered the season for the blooming of wildflowers had long since passed and that realization jarred her back into the present. A whirlwind of dry-eyed anger erupted within her. Anger at everyone. Anger at Marsh for being there to assuage her loneliness in the last days of the war. *Damn you for coming home before Harry.* Anger at Harry for going missing. *Damn you for letting me think you were dead.* Anger at herself for her weakness, her betrayal, the sundering of her marriage vows. *How could I do such a thing?*

And yet, at the same time, she clung to a slender strand of hope that Harry would come for her. Or Marsh. Or the two of them together. Yes. They would put differences aside to save her. *Where are they? What's taking them so long?* She closed her eyes, listening for the sound of hoofbeats, gunshots, shouts, something. *Come soon. Please, come soon. We can work this out. I don't know how, but somehow we will. We're all good people.*

The scolding of an unkindness of ravens roused her from her reverie. She lifted her face and held her eyes steady on the feathered disparagers setting up a ruckus from their perch in a slouching shin oak tree. At that moment, she knew with unusual clarity that they were coming. It was just a matter of time before Harry showed up. Marsh, too. Whatever it took, fair means or foul, they would find her. They would be here . . . together. God knew what would come after that.

Behind her, Clayton tottered in his saddle, deep in a soporific languor. When he had the strength he peeked out from the overburden of hopelessness that was smothering him.

"Hey," he called to Catlett. "Hey. I thought you said we wasn't goin' too far. You said it was just a ways. You said we'd be at the river . . . or the road . . . or somewheres . . . by now. Steal a car, kick for Mexico, or somethin'. That's what you said."

Catlett ignored the sniveling kid.

"Billy, where're we goin'? How come we ain't there yet . . . wherever it is? I'm so tired I'm cross-eyed and I'm 'bout to die of thirst. And I ain't had no dinner. I got a real misery in my gut. Could be I got a case of the scours comin' on. Anything can happen out here, you know. Anything."

When whining and caterwauling failed to serve, the kid took a different approach. Clucking the bay forward, he reined alongside Bliss and faked lightheartedness.

"Hey, Billy," he said, making a sound stained with a mixture of laughter and crying. "My mouth tastes like I had dinner with a coyote. And, you know what? I'm hotter'n a fresh fucked fox in a forest fire."

He tried to laugh outright but couldn't. He furrowed his brow at Bliss.

"Pardon my French. No offense. Don't tell on me to Marsh, OK?"

Bliss ignored him. He called to Catlett again.

"Hey, Billy, you used to say that all the time, 'member? You'd say that fox thing, and I'd laugh. And you'd say, somethin' was redder'n a coyote's ass in hackberry season. 'Member? That's me. That's my face. I cain't see it, but I know it's red. I mean it now. And my bohunkus . . . it ain't no better. Feels like one of them damn baboon butts."

But humor and servile wheedling availed him nothing. So, he fell to pleading.

"Billy, please. I think I'm gettin' heatstroke. I know I'm gettin' it. I ain't in much shape for nothin'."

Catlett rode on.

"Billlllly, I ain't pissed all day. You hear that? Ain't pissed. That's gotta tell you somethin'. And I think I'm gettin' the awfulest carbuncle on my ass."

Catlett turned, murderous intent in his eyes.

"Your ass. Like anybody gives a shit about your ass. You want me to come back there and slap a hairlip on you? Why don't you put a lid on it?"

Receiving no sympathy from Catlett, the kid sought it from their hostage. "Bliss, I'm dyin' here. Ain't you? Ain't you dyin', too?"

She gave no sign she'd heard him.

"Bliss, I'm really hurtin'. Not a sup of water all day. I'd give my eye teeth for one. This is 'bout all the longer I can go. You all right? Tell me you're all right."

Still nothing.

The kid tried persuasion.

"I had to do it, you know. Had to go with him. I didn't want to, but I had to. Never wanted to hurt nobody. You know I didn't."

No response. Only the dull clop of hooves, clink of steel bits, slap of saddle leather, wheezing of jaded horses. Frustrated, the kid switched from innocent and childlike to malicious and remorseless.

"A damn chili picker that girl. So he raped her. What's the big deal?"

Bliss closed her bloodshot eyes.

"Bliss, talk to me, dammit. I'm dyin' here. I think I'm dyin'. Think I'm actually dyin'."

Bliss finally spoke in a dry-throated whisper.

"Clayton, we've got to get away. He's going to kill me. And he's going to kill you. He's got nothing to lose now. He already killed Woody."

"That's crazy."

"Stop it, Clayton. He told me himself. Bragged about it." Bliss looked hard at Clayton. "And you were there."

"But I didn't do nothin."

"Yes you did. You helped. Probably killed that poor farmer, too. Billy's going to the electric chair if he gets caught, and he knows it. All he's keeping you and me alive for is cover in case Marsh and Harry come after us."

The mention of Marsh and Harry arrested the boy. He checked his backtrail.

"You think they are? You think they're really comin'? Right now? Oh, God. No tellin' what they're gonna do to me. Oh, God."

"They're not your problem," Bliss said. "Billy is."

"I don't know. I don't know."

"Yes, you do. He's the one you should be worrying about."

The kid reined up his mount. He flashed a wide grin, stood in his stirrups and pointed.

"Look. Lookayonder. A tank. I see a stock tank out there. How far you make it?"

Bliss looked out through heat shimmer. For a moment, her spirits soared, too. But as soon as they rose, they fell.

"It's not a tank."

"Yeah. Yeah it is. I see it. Look. Right out there."

The kid became giddy with excitement.

"It's a tank, by God. A tank. I believe we're saved."

"It's not. It's a mirage. Optical illusion. Not real."

Clayton glanced at Bliss. When he shuttled his gaze to the front again, nothing in sight hinted at water, no tank, no shallow sink, no marshy seep, nothing. He rubbed his eyes and looked again. Still nothing. Crestfallen, he dropped back behind Bliss.

Failing horses, entrained head to tail, slaved on. For them and for the riders on their backs time crawled. Wind bit into them. Dust blew. All continued to weaken. The kid rode loose in the saddle, half asleep. After a spell, he roused himself for further complaint.

"Billy, Billy" he yammered in a squeaky voice, kicking his mount forward. "Billy, I gotta stop. I'm near give out. And I need water bad."

Bliss called up the last of her strength and rasped, "We have to stop. Clayton's gonna die on you if we don't."

Catlett hauled rein on the gray and jerked the animal toward Bliss.

"You shut up. When I want your opinion on somethin' I'll ask for it. You hear me?"

Bliss returned his hard gaze.

"This is good practice for hell, don't you think? Hope you like it, because that's where you're going to be by the end of this day."

Catlett squinted into the yellowed waste from beneath the brim of his sweat-stained hat pulled low on his head. His eyes settled on something in the great distance, call it three quarters of a mile away. He alerted himself in the saddle, raised an arm and extended it.

"There. Looks to be a house. Should be a well. We can wet our throats there."

Bliss strained to see. When her vision focused, she cast a scornful look at Catlett.

"That's got to be a fifty-year-old soddy. You are something, you know that? You think you're so smart. You don't bother to check the gas in the car. You don't take any water or food. And now we've ridden these poor horses to death. You're a fool is what you are."

"Shut up, you. Don't press your luck. I'm liable to jerk you bald-headed."

"You don't scare me."

"Hey, I'm the one with the whip hand here, honey. I could teach you a thing or two about respect."

Bliss snorted. "Respect? Not likely."

Fed up with insults, Catlett fetched Bliss a hard lick across the jaw. She pitched over and tumbled to the ground.

"Billy, no!" Clayton shouted.

"Quiet!" Catlett raged at the kid. He turned back to Bliss, rolled onto her side. "I've had it with you. You think you're a real hellcat, don't you. Well, it's time you found out different."

His fury stoked, he started to step down from his horse to rough her up some more, but the kid rode up and grabbed his arm.

"No, Billy, wait. We need her. Said so yourself. She's our ace in the hole."

Catlett yanked his arm free, eased up. The kid dismounted, staggered to Bliss, helped her back into the saddle. A bluish mouse already rising under her right eye, she blinked back tears, determined to deprive Catlett of the pleasure of seeing her cry.

They headed for the soddy. Drawing near, they sat looking at the woeful structure sited against a nubbin of hill. The upper half of the three exposed walls were planked with lumber hewn from meager timber the land must have yielded in a bygone era. The lower half was formed of mounded dirt, sodded over. A collapsing porch ran the length of the front wall. Gone to seed, the whole shebang. Roof fallen in. Windows shattered, snaggletooth remnants of fractured panes poking from rotting sills. Door hanging antigoglin within scantling jambs, yawning in the wind. Whited bones of a milk cow strewn in the yard.

Nearby, a dilapidated windmill stood with gust-bent blades rusted and frozen in place. A couple of outsheds, both weather-grayed, leaned to the north. A well-aimed boot heel would render them into jack-strawed rubble. Farther out, lay a gaunt field of what had once been plow-broken ground. Now brushy and brittle, it had surrendered to sand burrs and goatheads and broomweed.

The kid, stiffened to the saddle, climbed down from his mount and fell to the ground. The quivery-legged bay nearly fell, too. Hard-used, it took all his strength to shiver his hide or switch his tail to shoo a fly. The animal lowered his muzzle to the ground. Spasmodic gasps from winking nostrils raised puff clouds of stale dust but revealed no decent graze.

Clumsy from fatigue, the kid floundered to the windmill trough. Peering into it, he found a cactus that had taken root in the rusted-out bottom. He swabbed a fingertip around the inside of the spigot. Bone dry. He turned the valve wheel. Nothing. He swayed like a drunk where he stood.

Catlett let his eyes travel across the shamble of cast-off equipage scattered everywhere. A drawerless bedroom bureau, an overturned rocking chair, its rush seat long since rotted away, shards of crockery, rusty bundles of twisted bailing wire, disintegrating truck tires, oxidized bed springs, a broken-down oxcart. He dismounted and, weaving his way through the detritus, fetched himself onto the warped slatwood that answered for a pauper's veranda. He forced the wonky door open and beneath a shower of dust descending from caved-in roof beams slouched inside the low-vaulted dwelling. The puncheon floor creaked under his weight. At the rear, where it had collapsed, dank air emanated from the ruins of a cryptlike root cellar.

Catlett stepped back outside and sagged against the wall. "Stupid honyockers," he groused, lowering his rear to the rough planking. Bliss sank down at the far end of the porch. The kid flopped his torpid carcass beside her. All swooned and drowsed.

Pursuit

Harry cut for sign. Since leaving the Hightower place the tracking had been slow, dogged work. He'd pick up the trail, lose it, sometimes having to make a wide circle to regain it, often dismounting to inspect an uncertain hoofprint. Now, he'd lost the trail again and he feared this time it might be for good. Hopes rose when his eyes fell on what he took for hoof-broken ground. He stood down from his horse and squatted, examining the indentations. He poked at them with a stick. They were deep, sharp-cut. He'd struck the trail.

Harry remounted and put Rocky Red forward. The spoor led him to a sky island standing sentry over the horizontal plain. A monumental terrain feature for this tableland. Near the base of the mesa escarpment, the ground dropped away into a shallow swag. Beyond the subsidence a debris fan mantled the lower face of a tilted fortification wall. The prehistoric megalith was not wide or long but it was perfect for what Harry had in mind. He'd been keeping an eye out for high ground: a hillock, bald knob, any swell of land offering a long view of the country ahead. A foray to the platform surface would cost him some time and would wind his horses, but it would be worth it.

The surefooted Rocky Red and Blazer moiled their way across the marginal trough and stogged up the abutting rock scramble, tailings lapping their tiring legs to the fetlock. At the upper limit of the rockslide Harry put the horses to climbing in earnest. They followed a narrow switchback, rank with growth, so cramped and tangled it had barely enough width for one horse. At a narrow point of rock, where passage tightened, he had to drop the lead on the remount and allow him to trail untethered. With noble effort, the animals breasted the ramp and serpentined their way up the looming heights.

At the summit, Harry recovered the buckskin's dragging shank and dallied it to his saddle horn. He halted the horses to let them blow and shake. Afterwards, he pushed Rocky Red to the southern overlook, Blazer following on his lead. There, the earth sheered away and revealed a wide expanse of featureless plain below. The horses couldn't make it down the steep cliff face. He'd have to backtrack.

Harry raised his battered old felt hat and held it aloft to shade his eyes, blotted his brow with his forearm, put his hat back on. He unbuckled the straps of his near side saddlebag, pulled out his binoculars. Through the prisms of the glasses he could see the ruins of a rude half-sod shanty in the distance. Frazzled horses stood hipshot at the tie rail. He leaned forward in the saddle and trained the telescopic lenses on the soddy, fingered the focusing wheel. Two reposing men came into sight. And a woman. Bliss.

Catlett had caught a few snatches of sleep, slumped on the hovel's narrow porch, his back against the ruinous wall, stolen long gun cradled in his lap. He roused, and his blurry vision delivered to his muddled brain an image of an undulating dark shape on the brim of a flat-topped promontory in the distance. He blinked hard, knuckled his eyes. Now he could make out three rippling forms against the sky. Pronghorn? He squinted, shaded his eyes from the glare of the sun. No. Horses. And a rider. Maybe two. It had to be Harry True. Or Marsh. Or both of them.

"Shit."

They'd be armed, Catlett knew. Could have backup. He could sit tight, try to pick them off coming at him across open ground. But he didn't like the odds, didn't have a bottomless supply of ammunition, didn't know how many of them there were. Better to make a run for it.

He battled his way out of his stupor. "Come on," he yelled to Clayton. "Mount up. We're gettin' out of here. Move, you son of a bitch."

Insensate as a corpse laid out on a cooling board, the kid lolled supine at the far end of the stoop, arms crossed on his chest, toes pointing upward, hat propped against his forehead. Bliss sat next to him, knees drawn up, arms resting on them, chin sunk to her chest. Her windburned cheeks looked like they'd been scrubbed with a wire brush; bracelets of blood-raw skin encircled her still bound wrists.

Catlett clomped down the porch and rousted the kid with a kick to the upright sole of his left boot.

"Come on, dammit. Put it in the saddle."

Catlett grabbed Bliss's arm and jerked her to her feet.

"You, too, sister. Move it."

"What?" For a moment Bliss didn't know where she was. Then she did. "Let go of me."

Catlett dragged her to her horse, heaved her aboard. He grabbed the mare's headstall and snarled at the kid again.

"Get up, you sorry sack o' shit. Step on it."

Shocked back into semiconsciousness, Clayton straggled to his mount. He labored onto the horse's back.

"What's wrong, Billy? You see somethin'?"

Focused on sorting reins and leads, Catlett didn't answer.

"Bill-lly, did you see somethin'?"

"Sure did."

He rifled an arm toward the distant mesa top. At that moment, Harry was wheeling his horses about. Catlett and Clayton both saw the billows of dust jumped up by shifting hooves.

"Yonder they come. Time to haul ass."

Bliss scoured the barren landscape. *Please, let it be Harry.* But she saw nothing.

Catlett stepped into his saddle. He dug heels into the weary gray's slats, kicking him into a steady trot, ponying Bliss's mount. He shot a glance over his shoulder to the distant promontory, empty now. Knowing what that portended, he pummeled the straining horse with his heels again. He had no more than a dim notion of where he was going, but he was hell-bent on getting there.

Bliss considered trying to break away and run for it, and would have done it if she knew for sure someone was coming. But she didn't. *Soon,* she told herself. *Just hold on. You can do this. Stay calm. This will all be over soon.*

Harry scrabbled down the bald. His horses' gouging hooves churned the natural talus creep, sent rock splinters clattering along the winding gullet. All the way Harry sat Rocky Red tight, leaning back in the saddle, giving the horse a loose rein, telling him to keep his feet under him, telling himself to keep one leg on the right, one on the left, and his mind in the middle.

Near the lowest part of the chute, he barely managed to avoid being unhorsed when Red's hindfeet slipped under his belly and he sat down like a dog. He plunged the last twenty feet or more of the downslope on his hindquarters. After he'd come to a skidding halt and found his feet, Harry shortened up on the reins. When the animal felt solid he spurred him up and gave him his head, calling on him for more. And Red delivered.

Not far from the soddy, traversing what was for him terra incognita, Catlett dropped into a grassy draw where he calculated he could get out of sight and make good time. Bliss and the kid followed. At the end of the narrow course they lurched into a sandy-bottom arroyo. Dutiful beasts did their best to follow their riders' commands for speed, tried to answer the call to give and give again. For a while, they succeeded. But soon they faded, slowed.

"Git up, you son of a bitch," Catlett bawled. "Git up, dammit."

He scourged away with the tag end of the reins, but the horse beneath him was already taxed past endurance. No punishment would make him go faster. So, too, with the other scrub-horses.

Meanwhile, Harry plugged along at a smart pace, his mount hammering out an expectant drumroll with staccato hoofbeats. He'd caught a glimpse of the dust boiled up by the fleeing horses' hooves, a sure sign he was closing in.

As long as he could, he would keep to the flat. He knew the nature of these hydra-headed dry washes with their barbed tributaries and blind canyons. All had been countersunk over centuries by episodic rainfall and runoff, cutbanks rising in places as high as the hat brim of a man on horseback. He feared that if he dropped into one, he might get cut off and fall behind by hours. And he knew that before long Catlett would have to get back up on open range.

Better mounted, Harry decided to chance a wide swing to the west on ground where there was decent going. He was betting on being able to head the runaways off on the far side of the narrows. He still had a good horse under him; time to lather him. He brought up spur rowels and goaded Rocky Red into an all-out run. At top speed, he blasted through stands of shintangle brush, navigated all manner of obstacles, flew over skinny gullies. The horse stumbled a time or two, but always managed to right himself.

Before long, Harry could feel Rocky Red tiring. When the earth flattened and he found himself on an unobstructed trackway, he checked the winded horse to a short lope and brought the led horse abreast on his right. Without breaking stride, he flung himself out of the saddle and onto the sleek, wet coat of the relief mount. Draping the lead rope across the fresher horse's neck, he held both sets of reins in his right hand and with his left reached across and lifted the saddle gun from the scabbard. Carrying the rifle crosswise of the bareback horse's withers, he dropped the reins of the Red horse, let him slow and peel away. Riding light, Harry urged the unwearied Blazer full out.

Marsh had taken up the trail, too. Buckshot was holding up well and he could follow at speed. When he raised Harry's dust far across the sagebrush flat, he slid his Winchester from the saddle boot and jacked the lever, lowered the hammer. Patting his mount on the neck, he touched spurs to his sides. "OK, Buck, let's go."

The dry watercourse Catlett and his conscripts were following curved and boxed off without warning. Lathered horses pulled up hard. Danced a sluggish jig, snorting and slobbering, lungs heaving.

"Dammit," Catlett raved. "Son of a bitch."

"Now what, Billy?" the kid cried. "Now what do we do?"

"I don't know. I don't know."

"Cain't we turn ourselves in? Tell 'em we're sorry about everything?"

"You damn nitwit. Them sumbitches bird doggin' us'll have us by the short hairs in about three minutes if we don't get outa here."

"Can we go back the way we come? Give 'em the slip? Outrun 'em?"

Catlett searched for a way out. He pointed to a cut in the vertical bank of the sandy wash some twenty yards off to his right; it angled up to the eyebrow scarp of a narrow bench that preceded a sandstone ridge. On the ridge's upward lift a succession of transverse creases formed rugged stairsteps; a narrow defile no more than two axe handles wide tracked from shelf to shelf. The climb would be treacherous, but if they could make it all the way up and over the hump they'd be back on flat ground, open country ahead.

"There. That's it."

"We cain't go up there," Clayton protested.

"The hell we cain't. It's our only chance. If you want to live, you best get your ass in gear. Let's go."

Catlett gigged his mount. The gray struggled up the washout wall, grappled over the scarp to the narrow bench, and from there fought his way up the precipitous headland. Bliss followed. Clayton brought up the rear. Answering gaffs and profane commands, the horses filed up the scrabbly gradient, fragments of rocks scaling away with every step. About halfway up, the kid's cayuse faltered. Done in by the climb, his forelegs gave out and he dropped to his knees as if to pray. He lowered his muzzle to the dirt and groaned. Raspy breathing told the kid what was coming. He bailed off to the high side and grabbed an outgrowth of bitterbrush just as the horse caved, legs crumpling and snapping like kindling sticks under him. He leaned downslope and when he reached the tipping point, tumbled. Logrolled to the bench and over the scarp. He lay stone dead in the dry wash before the dust settled.

Catlett pointed to Bliss's mount. "Lay holt of her tail. Let her pull you up."

The kid seized the mare's scraggly tail and held on tight. In tow, he gained the ridge crest, followed the horses over it and down the reverse slope, more falling than walking. Where the drop-away reached a small tract of level ground, the pegged-out broomtails stood trembling. They'd made it out of the maze, but there would be no reprieve. They had to move. The kid shinnied up the mare's backside to ride double. Bliss tried to shoulder him off. Clayton raised a hand to hit her but lowered it when she cringed.

"Let's go," Catlett called out.

And go they did, but they didn't go far, for Harry had their lead. Before he'd gone twenty feet Catlett glimpsed Harry exploding out of a concealment of trash timber at his right. Choosing not to risk a rifle shot into a scramble of horses and riders, Harry charged forward on Blazer, reining hard to the right at the last moment, ramming the buckskin flank-on into Catlett's mount. Amidst a violent wreck and traumatic expulsion of equine breath, the gray toppled and rolled with Catlett still in the saddle when an enormous rolling pin of horseflesh flattened him against the ground, knocking him senseless. The horse whinnied, kicked, regained his feet and bolted.

Blazer kept his feet, but horse and rider parted company. The impact vaulted Harry into the air, arms outflung like a circus acrobat reaching for a trapeze. He landed hard.

The horse Bliss and Clayton were riding slammed on the brakes and reared up, forelegs flailing, letting out a near human cry. Clayton and Bliss slid off her back and went tumbling. The riderless mare slipped and fell backwards herself, missing her riders by inches. The fall left her a cripple, right front forelimb twisted and bloody, ivory cannon bone protruding through skin and hair. The mare struggled to her feet, her entire body quaking, hobbled away three-legged and folded.

The crushing weight of the rolling gray left Catlett lying on his back, fighting for breath. Recovering his wind and awareness, he cast about for his rifle, found it and skittered away into the brush. Nearby, Clayton sat up, disoriented, and crabbed away after Catlett.

When Harry had shaken off the effects of his gut-twisting fall, he spotted his rifle and clawed his way to it. He stood and saw Bliss lying motionless on her side. By the time he reached her, she'd managed to sit up. He knelt, held her by the shoulders, swept the drapery of hair from her face.

"Bliss, are you all right? Bliss, look at me. Are you OK?"

"I think so."

Harry cut away the fetters on her wrists. Swept dirt and grass from her cheeks.

"Harry, they lynched Woody," Bliss whispered hoarsely.

"No, he's lying low—"

"No, Harry. They killed him. Billy told me."

A bullet whanged. Harry pulled Bliss down, covering her, jerked around and saw Catlett, rifle at his shoulder, in the bastion rocks that bordered the clearing on the north side. Harry spotted a shallow gully a few feet away, pushed Bliss into it and lay his body over hers. A second shot roared. Dirt jumped where the bullet scalloped the ground. A ricochet screamed.

Staying low, Harry peered over the gully's rim. He spotted Blazer about fifty yards away stamping and groaning, his reins entangled in a thorny mesquite stump and spiny undergrowth at the edge of the *brasada*. The buckskin appeared to be in good shape despite the collision and his agitated state. Harry crouched again.

"You gotta get outa here," he said.

"Not without you."

"No, you have to go. Take my horse. We'll work our way down this wash and make a run for him. Get mounted and go west. When you come to a road swing north. Find somebody. Tell 'em where we are."

"Come with me."

"No."

"Harry, please. Leave Billy and Clayton here. They can't go any-where."

"Can't chance that. There are two horses out there somewhere."

"Then let them go."

"No. They took you. They killed Woody."

Harry raised himself and threw two quick rounds from his Winchester in Catlett's direction. He grabbed Bliss's upper arm and pulled her to a crouch.

"Let's go."

Moving in a bent-over run, they scrambled a hundred feet or so down the dusty channel, getting as close as they could to the bareback horse without breaking cover. Harry squeezed off another shot, lifted Bliss over the gully's lip and hustled her to Blazer, freed his reins, stead-ied him, heaved Bliss onto his back and thrust the reins into her hands.

"Go!" Harry said and whacked the horse on the rump.

Holding a clutch of mane in one hand, the reins in the other, her body flattened over the buckskin's neck, Bliss broke through the brush and gave the horse his head. Harry took cover and watched her ride away.

The air flush with lead, Catlett had stayed low. By the time he raised up again, Bliss had made her escape. He spotted her in the distance, heading west and knew he'd played out his string.

Harry caught a glimpse of him in the rocks and sent off another shot. Catlett ducked. Clayton had disappeared. Both concealed somewhere in a fortress of boulders. Harry would have to get around and above them to flush them out.

Like the others, Marsh had stopped at the soddy to blow his horse. After tying up at the hitch rack, he stood on the porch, sheltered from the sun, sipping water from his canteen. Picking up distant riflefire, he stared into the bleakness of the scrubland, steeling himself for the confrontation to come. When the report of the second storm of bullets reached him, he got a fix on it and mounted up. Resting the Winchester across the saddle tree, he ticked his horse with a spur and rode to the sound of the guns.

CHAPTER 33

Crucible

Harry reloaded his rifle and headed for the boulders. There, he commenced flanking and climbing. If he could out-coyote the black hats, get around and above them without being seen, he might get the drop on them, put Catlett down at range. No Code Duello, just a bullet at center mass, front or back. Then he'd deal with Clayton. He knew the kid had no stomach for gunplay; he might talk him into surrendering. He wouldn't kill him unless he had to.

Catlett and Clayton were also on the move, zigzagging upward among the boulders.

"Where we goin', Billy?" Clayton said, when they paused to scout the way ahead.

Catlett pointed.

"Up there? Why?"

"Because Harry True's breathin' down our necks. He's gonna kill us both if he can. We got one chance. Lay for him. Draw him in. Shoot first."

With Clayton stumbling along behind, Catlett kept going until he found a place suitable for an ambush: a slim, sandy-floored gunsight pass that opened into a small cleavage about the size of Harry's round pen at the Bar T. A pair of sandstone fangs standing about chest high atop an overlooking salient on the far side would provide good cover and concealment for a pair of bushwhackers. Catlett wagered that, in time, Harry would be coming through the narrow outlet. He'd bait him with plenty of identifiable tracks.

After thinking out his gambits, Catlett gave Clayton his orders.

"Listen up. See that eyetooth-looking rock up yonder on the left? That's yours. Get behind it."

"Then what? Then what are we gonna do, Billy?"

Catlett grabbed him by the shirtfront.

"Dammit. Do what I tell you. Now drag your butt up there. I'm gonna get behind that other tooth and we're gonna catch Mr. True in a little crossfire. When he comes through this break and shows hisself, we'll let loose on him from up there. Follow my lead. Don't do nothin' till I do."

"You mean you want him dead?"

"Do I want him dead? Hell, yes, I want him dead. Graveyard dead."

Catlett forced the side gun into the kid's hand.

"You got the balls to use this?"

"Uh . . . I don't know . . ."

"You don't know? Hell, boy, fat's in the fire now, you better—"

"Sure, Billy, sure. I can do it."

Catlett shoved Clayton toward his post. The kid scrabbled his way up and hunkered down behind the serrated spike. Catlett took cover behind the sister rock a dozen strides away. They waited.

Marsh continued to push his mount, homing in on the sound of gunshots. In the distance he saw a rider ripping across the sage flat, heading northwest. Pale hair flourishing in the wind told him who it was. He put rowels to his mount and gave chase. Heading her off, he waved his arm and called out, "Bliss! Bliss! Hold up."

At first, not knowing who might be coming for her, she kept riding hard. But when she saw Marsh she pulled up.

"Marsh," she cried. "Oh, thank God. Harry's out there with Catlett and Clayton."

"Are you all right?"

"Yes, yes. Thirsty."

Marsh pressed his canteen into her hands, watched her drink. She wiped her mouth, handed it back.

"No, keep it."

"Marsh, Harry needs your help."

Marsh sat back in his saddle. "Well, that's a damn shame, ain't it."

"Marsh, please. You can't leave him out there alone."

"Oh no? Watch me. I'm takin' you home. You're my wife and I'm takin' you home."

He reached for her reins. She moved away a few feet.

"I'm not going home with you, Marsh. Not now. Not ever, if you don't help Harry."

"The hell you say."

"Marsh, please. It's Harry we're talking about. Your brother."

"My brother? He ain't my brother. He ain't even my friend. He's the guy who's tryin' to steal my wife."

Bliss looked at him wearily. "He didn't steal me, Marsh. You know he didn't."

Marsh felt the sting of truth.

"I love you, Bliss. You know that."

"I know, Marsh. And I love you. But . . ." Her eyes welled with tears. "Marsh, please. You can't let Harry die."

Marsh didn't bend.

"OK then. What about your real brother? Do you care about him? Clayton's out there, too, and Catlett will kill him first chance he gets. You know he will."

Marsh grimaced. When the next bullet sounded, he shook his head. "Dammit."

He pointed to the northwest.

"Get out of here. Go that way. You'll hit a road."

"Marsh—"

He reined his horse around and galloped off.

Harry continued to flank and climb, keeping tight among the rocks. As Catlett had predicted, he came in time to the inviting crevice. When he saw the tracks he knew he was closing in on his quarry. From higher elevation, Catlett sensed a flutter of shadow in the narrow passageway and cocked his rifle, put the stock to his shoulder. Harry started to follow the tracks in the sand, but when he noticed the citadel rocks ahead of him he hesitated, knowing he couldn't get a good view of what lay behind them without exposing himself to fire. He watched and waited. Nothing moved. But he didn't like it. He backed away, made another flanking move to the west. And climbed.

Catlett lost sight of Harry. Now he didn't know if Harry was in front or behind, above or below. He hunkered down, waiting for his stalker to make a mistake and give himself away. At the same time, Harry was ascending an upward fold of earth, working his way to a shoulder-high turtleback boulder that would make a likely observation post. Reaching it, he removed his hat, flattened his body against the gritty surface, and pushed himself up until his eyes topped the rock line enough to take in the topography ahead. There before him lurked Billy Catlett, crouching behind a gritstone obelisk, within easy rifle range.

Harry held dead still, studying his mark. With cool deliberation, he braced himself on his elbows and brought his rifle to bear. Training the sights on Catlett, he slipped his finger inside the trigger guard and with his thumb set the hammer at full cock. Hearing the two metallic clicks, or feeling the sear of predatory eyes, Catlett whirled around and stood up straight. He brought the Hightower Winchester to his shoulder and fired. But he'd rushed his shot and it went wide. Harry returned fire. The slow-aimed bullet took Catlett in the chest. He dropped where he stood. Lying face down in the dirt, he didn't move again.

Harry wriggled down the shielding rock and side-stepped around it. Holding his Winchester waist-high, he levered a live round into the rifle's chamber. To his right, Clayton Stone came out from his hiding place behind the flanking eyetooth rock. Shaking from head to toe, the kid raised his gun-hand.

"I wouldn't," Harry called out, lifting his shoulder gun. "Catlett's done for. Nobody else has to die."

Three deafening shots rang out to Harry's left. He and Clayton crouched and pivoted to see Marsh, rifle in hand, standing on a rock just below them that gave him an unobstructed view of Catlett's body and his friend and brother facing off.

"Hey up there," Marsh called out. "You stupid sonsabitches knock off that damn shootin'. We don't need no more killin'. Clayton, get your ass down here."

Terror paralyzed the kid. Muddy tears scoring his face, he protested in a timorous garble.

"But . . . but . . . this bastard'll gun me in the back."

"No, he won't. Harry, give it up. I ain't gonna let you kill my brother. You know that. Now come on down here. Both of you. This bullshit's over."

After a few moments' hesitation, Clayton stood upright, lowering the pistol to his side. Harry watched him and, judging that the kid had no fight left in him, decided to stand down. He lowered his rifle, turned and began the descent to level ground. Clayton followed, took two steps and slipped on surface gravel. Losing his balance, he let out a shout. Harry spun around, rifle at his hip. Down on his backside, convinced Harry was about to shoot, Clayton raised his pistol.

From below, Marsh saw it all as if in slow motion.

"Nooo!" he yelled, shouldering his Winchester.

Two shots rang out.

CHAPTER 34

The Gravedigger

Marsh had a grave to dig. Berserk from reverberating gunfire, his horse had bolted and he had no way of transporting his brother's body to town and no idea when help might arrive. Flies were buzzing about; coyotes were lurking in the distance. Later, a proper Christian burial could be arranged, but for now he'd have to settle for an interment that would keep scavengers away, at least slow them down.

The only implement he had for digging was the Marine Ka-Bar Combat Knife he carried sheathed on his belt. With its stout blade he could hollow out a shallow pit, shovel loose dirt with his hands. He could cover the body with a shroud of prairie soil and stack rocks on top of it. The work ahead would be slow and arduous, but he had it to do.

He got down on his knees and attacked the dissonant earth with the Ka-Bar. Hack and scrape, hack and scrape. Garner the spoils. After a time, depleted of energy, he paused. Through parched lips, cracked and bleeding, he purged his lungs of air. He stripped a soiled bandana from his forehead, wiped tendrils of muddy sweat from his face. Pained by the cautery of the oven-hot claypan on the bend of his legs, he willed himself to rise. Resting his eyes on the seared ground, he sighted a bleached-out buffalo skull on the leeward slope of a low wrinkle of ground not far away. Frenzied yellow jackets swarmed over and within the vacant, chalky cranium, passing in and out through sunless orbits. Insect heirs to the crown shed by a long-forgotten monarch of the plains.

Marsh turned his eyes to the arching blue above. A flight of turkey vultures patrolled the sky, watching and waiting. Bone pickers. Eye pluckers. In time they'd be taking their due. The sorrowful reality that all that had happened had led to this, that bugs and prairie wolves and carrion feeders would be the victors, diminished him further. Lacking even the strength to cry out in protest, he surrendered.

You win. It's all yours. Every bit of it. Take it and be damned to you.

Marsh leveled his gaze. In the distance, he could make out amidst waves of brutal heat the low-circling embryo of a dust devil. He knew the ever-widening gyre of rasping air would soon take shape, transforming itself into a full-blown hell wind. *Common as pig tracks in these parts,* he told himself. *Wind. More damn wind. That's all.* But doubt seeped in. *Could be it's somethin' else this time. Could be it's more than dust and air. Maybe it's death itself, as old-time Indians might say. So be it.*

With no alteration of posture or mind, Marsh witnessed the phantasmal tempest complete its evolution. It stood upright. Rotating at high speed, abrading the earth's rind, sucking up sand and scoria, engorging itself with anything in its path. With the zeal of a righteous avenger, the contrary wind came straight for the gravedigger. *Ahh. I was right. You are the reaper. And you're comin' for me.*

Marsh returned to his labor. Time after time, he tied into the mineral soil with his sheath knife, graded up burnt-over loam with hands and forearms. Hours on, the sun fell away to the horizon. Western sky turned blood red. In failing light, he finished the grave—a new portal to the hereafter, long enough and wide enough to admit the body of his slain brother . . . but only partially. As he expected, an overlay of stones would be required.

Turning in a slow circle, he still saw no one. This time, his gaze fell upon a great horned owl lodged on a juniper limb a short distance away. The tortured scrag, clad in a skin of alligator bark, had a misshapen, malignant appearance. It sagged on one side, giving it the shape of a landslide in profile. From his post in the tree's meager foliage, the feathered observer held still and silent. The sole witness to the ritual taking place before him: Cain committing the lifeless body of Abel to Mother Earth, a murderer invoking for his fallen sibling the inevitable destiny of ashes to ashes, dust to dust. Detached and unmoved, the nightbird sat, as if in judgment, watching with perfect stillness, save languid blinking of amber eyes.

Night fell. By the light of the rising moon, Marsh scuffed to his brother's corpse lying nearby, toes up. He knelt at his head. Face waxen. Eyes open a crack. Mouth ajar as if a whisper had just breathed through. At the level of his heart, his shirt bore a small, bloody hole—the place a bullet had entered. *I killed my own brother. Shot him dead. Mama. Oh, Mama.*

Marsh burrowed his hands beneath Clayton's shoulders. Taking him by underholds, he leveraged his rigorous cargo to the threshold of the grave, dragging it across *tabula rasa,* inanimate extremities in tow, following heels leaving parallel tracks. He lowered his brother into the crude trench, laid him out full length. He knelt, folded Clayton's arms on his chest, masked his brother's face with his own bandana. Under the scrutiny of the owl in the juniper, he chucked his hands into the spoil bank like shovel blades, commenced blanketing the body with raw dirt, evened out the low mound and set to gathering stones.

When he'd completed his task, Marsh lingered on his knees at the grave. Rising, he raked back his head and entreated the lordly moon . . . as if for pardon. The full, perfect orb, magnificent in its reflection of the absent sun's radiance, transfixed him. The longer he stared at it, the more unmistakable the human features in the vast expanse of the lunar surface became. There, in the mottled gray, he discerned a face. Not kind, not at all merciful. A prosecutor, who would demand pitiless justice.

"It's finished. Forgive me. Please forgive me."

In the stance of a prisoner at the bar, he slumped before his luminous accuser. Arms hanging limp, body too insubstantial to fill out his clothes, eyes glassy like those of some moribund mongrel unable to howl or whimper. He knew he'd been tried and found guilty. And he knew his sentence was just. He could do nothing but remember and regret, imagine how things might have been. Unlike the moon, he should have been better. He should have been more.

When at last he spoke, his own voice was rust.

"All right. It's time."

He put his brother's pistol to his head, the muzzle pressing against his right temple. Withdrawing into profound blackness behind sealed eyelids, his quivering finger searched out the trigger and embraced its steely curve. A shot obliterated the silence, sent the owl flapping away.

Silence folded in again. The moon remained in place. The owl resettled. Coyotes yapped a lupine threnody. And in the east, thinning darkness foretold the onset of day. Indifferent to the passing of yet another mournful human being, the sun would soon rise.

Harry, flat on his back, began coming to. Flutter of eyelid. Twitch of cheek. He opened his eyes to windstill darkness. Felt a shiver of cold. *I must be alive.* How long he'd been unconscious he had no way of knowing.

He gazed with filmy eyes at a vast strewing of stars in the firmament. Struggling upright, he found himself afflicted with the stiffness of a centenarian and the torment of pulsating pain in his head. He put his right hand to his temple. An inch above it, he found and explored with his fingertips a shallow but bloody furrow left by the bullet that had skimmed his skull.

Looking around, Harry saw no one. No movement. A stark absence of sound broken only by the drumbeat in his head. When he judged he had it in him, he got to his feet. Raised a heavy foot to take a step, but halted, putting out his arms for balance like a man wading across a rain-swollen creek. When his vision clarified he beheld in close proximity what he took for a grave mounded with rocks and a body crumpled beside it.

In lagging steps, he made his way to the burial cairn, crowned at one end with Clayton Stone's hat. Within an arm's reach lay the body of Marshall Stone, his skull shattered and bloody, right arm flung out, gun resting in his open hand. Harry fell to his knees before his best and oldest friend. *Why?* But he knew why. He hung his head and tried to think of some words to say. All he came up with was a line from Euripides, something his mother used to quote at funerals—"Light be the earth upon you."

Kneeling, Harry watched the darkness lift in layers. He heard soft nickering. Marsh's horse, Buckshot, had wandered in. Harry stood, made his way slowly to the gelding, caught him up and, summoning the last of his strength, managed to heave Marsh's body up and drape it over the saddle. He lashed his flaccid limbs together with a rope passed under the horse's barrel. That done, he put his back to the risen sun and set out on foot, leading the horse, bearing northwest, following in Bliss's tracks. After a while, he came upon a little-traveled county road, turned due north. Around midmorning, he saw a car approaching in the distance, a flashing red light on the roof.

Haggard and filthy, weakened by pain and thirst, he waited in the middle of the road. The car became two cars. They came near and stopped. At the wheel of the front car sat D. C. Grubbs with Sheriff Dutch Mackey beside him.

The sheriff and Grubbs stepped out, wearing looks of disbelief. A moment later, the doors of the second car swung open and Doris Ann and Bliss appeared. Bliss gazed at Harry. At the horse he was leading. At the burden the animal carried. Harry heard a faint cry escape her lips. Escorted by the sheriff, she came to Harry and stood before him.

The sheriff gently loosened Bliss's hold on his arm, trudged to the body on the horse and identified who it was.

"What about the others?" the sheriff said, turning to Harry.

The two men stood facing each other.

"I said what about the others?"

"Dead."

"Catlett and Clayton?"

"Both of them."

Bliss went to Marsh and laid her hand on his shoulder. She leaned her head against her forearm and wept.

The sheriff removed his hat, held it to his chest. He panned the barrens, the set of his shoulders flagging.

"My Lord. My Lord."

He traced the edge of a finger along the crowfooted corner of each eye. He put his hat back on.

"You know we're gonna have to talk about this."

Harry nodded.

The sheriff took Bliss by the shoulders and led her back to the car.

Part Seven

CHAPTER 35

Penitents

As the sheriff and D. C. Grubbs were going about the grim business of transferring Marsh's body to the back seat of the police cruiser, Esau and Polly were burying their son in the Black Flats cemetery. The following morning, head still throbbing, wound cleaned and bandaged, Harry gathered his strength and courage and made his way to the Coats residence. He eased out of his truck, made his way slowly up the porch steps and knocked on the screen door, hat in hand.

Esau answered his knock, stood behind the rusty screen, a spectral image. He did not invite Harry in. Harry thought for a moment his old friend might shut the door in his face.

Frowning slightly, Esau stepped out onto the porch. The two men stood facing each other. Neither extended a hand.

"Mr. Coats," Harry said. He couldn't help thinking Esau looked ten years older than he did when he last saw him.

"Mr. True."

"I'm sorry for not coming by yesterday," Harry said, touching his bandage.

Esau nodded, said nothing.

"Polly?" Harry said.

"In bed, crying."

"Please give her my deepest sympathies. And . . ." He searched for the right words. ". . . My warmest regards."

Esau showed no reaction.

Unsteady on his feet, Harry sat without invitation in a porch rocker. Esau sighed, pulled the matching chair an arm's length away and sat down facing him.

Harry hunched forward, fingering the brim of his hat.

"The men who . . . did that to Woody, at least one of them, is dead," Harry said.

"Catlett," Esau said. "I know. Sheriff told us. Said he was gonna investigate further." Esau looked down, grunted. "I wouldn't put no money on that."

Harry nodded.

"Dutch tell you about Bliss?"

"He did."

Harry hung his head. "I didn't know, Esau." Harry looked up again. "God's honest truth. If I'd a known . . . ."

Esau remained cold-jawed and silent.

"That it?" he said finally.

Harry nodded.

Esau rose. "Here's what I know," he said. "My boy is dead. You could have prevented it, you and Miss Bliss, and you didn't. When you shoulda been comin' forward and standin' up to do the right thing you was hunkerin' down and studyin' on how to keep your secret."

Before Harry could even attempt an apology Esau rose and went inside, closed the door.

Sheriff Mackey conducted his investigation. It didn't take long. Speaking to Harry and Bliss, one at a time, he managed to piece together the timeline of events that came to their bloody conclusion in the *mal país*. Harry was the sole survivor of the crucible in the boulders and there was no reason to question his account. An examination of the three bodies and the conditions at the temporary gravesite supported Harry's description of how Catlett and Clayton had died and confirmed that Marsh had buried his brother, then killed himself. After consulting with the County Attorney, the sheriff closed the book on the whole tragic affair. No criminal charges would be brought.

Likewise with the lynching of Woody Coats. Sheriff Mackey could identify the men who demanded he release Billy Catlett from jail, but he couldn't identify the man who hurled the rock that put his lights out. Or the men who mauled him and stole his gun after he fell. His efforts to identify the men who helped put the noose around Woody's neck and winch him into the air also led to nothing. No one he interviewed could say who'd done it or abetted it. When it came to giving names, an epidemic of lockjaw seemed to strike the entire population of Serafina.

Hat in hand, the sheriff delivered the news to Esau and Polly on their porch.

"That cain't be," Polly said, sobbing. "There won't be no justice for my boy? That cain't be."

"I'm sorry, ma'am."

Esau put an arm around his wife, pulled her close.

"So them men that murdered Woody gets off scot-free?" he said.

"It's a sorry piece of business, I admit. It just is what it is."

"Naw, it ain't," Esau said, holding his weeping wife against his side, his eyes overflowing. "My boy never hurt nobody. He died because of who he was, a young man of color. Some white folks got a bad case of lynchin' fever. That there's the straight of it."

Esau walked his wife back into the house. The sheriff, his hat still in his hands, took his leave.

It took Bliss the better part of two weeks to recover enough to tend to the burial of her husband and brother-in-law. With her gratitude and blessing, Doris Ann Mackey and Mildred Brett handled the arrangements.

The day of the funeral, the church was packed. Outside the chancel rail, on a homemade wooden catafalque, lay two caskets. Same style, same bronze color, both closed, one draped with an American flag. At the appointed hour, with somber organ music playing, Dutch and Doris Ann escorted Bliss into the sanctuary, sat beside her in the first pew. Harry, and Ruth who'd taken charge of Harry's care during his convalescence, sat a row behind. Reverend Snowy Evans officiated. Ned Brett, Cal Barton, Elvin Sweeten, Oscar Tomlinson, Wilford Beck, D. C. Grubbs and six able hands from the Stone ranch served as pall bearers.

A simple graveside service followed at Oak Lawn Cemetery, where Marsh and Clayton were laid to rest in the Stone family plot.

Esau and Polly didn't attend either service. They had only recently buried their son and had no stomach for accepting condolences from members of the white community who had caused Woody's death, or at least failed to prevent it.

After the burial, family and friends gathered at Marsh and Bliss's home to share a late lunch provided by the ladies of the church. Numbed by grief and exhaustion, Bliss spent most of the afternoon ensconced in an armchair in the living room, accepting condolences from those in attendance and, from the church ladies, cups of tea. The bruise on her right cheek where Billy Catlett had struck her was still faintly visible. Her wrists, where the ropes had scored her skin, were still red.

By late afternoon, with the sun throwing long shadows, the crowd began dwindling. Dutch and Doris Ann Mackey said their goodbyes and Harry walked with them to the sheriff's car.

"What do you reckon Bliss will do now?" the sheriff asked Harry.

"Don't know. Too early to say, I guess."

"What about you, Harry?" Doris Ann asked bluntly. "What will you do? Go back to California? You and Bliss?"

Harry stared at her. "Thank you for coming," he said.

Ruth Blaylock was standing at the kitchen sink washing dishes when Harry came back inside. He grabbed a dish towel and started drying.

"Bliss has a hard road ahead of her," Ruth said, handing him a plate.

"I know."

She turned to him. "No you don't," she said. "You think you know but you don't. You can't."

Harry colored. *I do know,* he wanted to say. *Remember? I lost Bliss.* He took in a deep breath, calmed himself.

Seeing she'd wounded him, Ruth softened.

"I'm sorry, Harry. That was harsh."

"It's OK."

"Bliss is full of grief," Ruth said. "Not just sorrow, but grief. She's strong, though. We both know that."

Harry nodded.

"And I'll keep an eye on her after you're gone."

Harry looked at her.

"You're leaving," Ruth said. "You haven't told me yet but I know you, Harry." She smiled sadly. "I always knew I'd lose you someday. I just didn't know how or when. Now I know."

She dried her hands, took off her apron and laid it on the back of a chair.

"Time for me to go," she said.

She gave Harry a hug.

"Good-bye, Harry. Take good care of yourself, will you? Maybe send me a postcard once in a while to let me know you're OK?"

He touched her cheek. "I will."

Harry stayed until everyone else had left. He busied himself gathering drink glasses and emptying ash trays as Bliss sat in her armchair staring at nothing. Now, with dusk falling, she rose and went to the living room window, stood with arms crossed against her chest, gazing out at the ocherous layer of light smeared low across the indigo sky. Harry joined her.

"Do you know what line of poetry I've been repeating to myself all day?" Bliss said, not turning from the window. "'How do you like your blue-eyed boy, Mr. Death?'"

"E.E. Cummings," Harry said.

Bliss shuddered. "I can taste the anger in the words."

She turned to Harry.

"I went to see Alejandra Flores and her mother."

"You—When?"

"I went with Dutch. He didn't want me to go, but I insisted. They've been through so much. I wanted to be there when Dutch told them what had happened, make sure they understood they didn't have to be afraid anymore. They cried and thanked us. Thanked us. Can you imagine?" She shook her head. "It's not the same as seeing Billy Catlett brought to justice, but I think it helped them to know. I hope it did."

Bliss turned back to the window, watched the dregs of the day's glow drain over the edge of the visible world.

"And . . . I went to see Esau and Polly, too."

Harry waited.

"It was the hardest thing I've ever done," Bliss whispered.

Harry said nothing.

"They told me you'd been there. I'm glad."

"What did you say? What did they say?"

"I just apologized. It was the only thing I could do, really. I said I was sorry for what happened to Woody, sorry for not coming forward when I should have, sorry for being a coward, sorry for not being there for them the way Polly had always been there for me." Bliss was in tears now. "I said I didn't expect them to forgive me. Didn't know if I'd ever be able to forgive myself. I told them I love them and that all I can do is try to atone. I don't know if that's even possible, but I have to try."

"How did they respond?" Harry asked.

Bliss's hand went to her heart. "With such kindness, Harry. Such unbelievable strength and kindness. At first they just listened. Then Esau thanked me for coming. 'I know it wasn't easy for you,' he said, 'and we appreciate it.' He said if I saw you to thank you for coming, too."

"Did he."

"And then Polly hugged me and we just cried in each other's arms." Bliss wiped the tears from her eyes.

"Let's sit down," Harry said. "I have something to tell you, too."

They went to the divan, sat facing each other.

"I'll be leaving Oklahoma, Bliss."

She sat upright.

"I'm closing up the house. Selling the livestock. I've started making arrangements. This isn't home for me anymore. I need to start over somewhere else."

"Where? Where will you go?"

"I'm not sure. California, maybe. Tejon." He took her hand. "I'm hoping you'll come with me."

"California," Bliss repeated longingly. "I used to dream about seeing the ocean someday."

"You can still see it. Come with me. Please. Say you'll come."

Bliss withdrew her hand, shook her head. "No, Harry . . . I can't."

"But why? Why can't you—"

"I have work to do here, remember? I have amends to make . . . if I can. I promised Esau and Polly." She looked down. "I promised Woody."

"But what will you do?"

"I'm not sure. Help rebuild Black Flats. Change the name of that place to something more respectable. Raise money for a new school. Maybe teach there if they'll have me. Start a committee to build a new clinic. Get those horrible 'whites only' signs taken down for good."

Harry straightened himself and sighed.

"I can't stay, Bliss. Not after—"

"I understand, Harry. And I can't go with you."

Silence.

"But you should go," Bliss said softly, marshaling her strength. "Go to California. Make a new start if you can."

Harry's heart fell. He felt Bliss drifting away from him.

"Do you want me to stay with you tonight?" he said.

Another silence.

"Bliss?"

"No, I don't think so. I think—"

She started to tremble, had trouble finding her breath, bent forward at the waist and wept silently, holding herself and rocking, tears coursing down her face.

Harry reached for her but was afraid to touch her.

After a few moments she righted herself, took a deep hitching breath, wiped her eyes. Showing the faintest hint of a tender smile, she put a hand to Harry's cheek.

"Oh, Harry. My dear Harry. It seems the world has no place for us. We searched for it so long, but we never found it."

"Maybe it's not a matter of finding it. Maybe it's a matter of making it."

"Either way, we failed, didn't we. We wanted so much to believe that somehow things would work out in the end. But some things don't work out. Some stories aren't meant to have a happy ending, I guess."

"I love you, Bliss. That hasn't changed."

"And I love you. But how do we go on now? After everything we've done, everything that's happened." She shook her head. "We can't. We don't deserve to. Not now. Maybe not ever."

"So we just go our separate ways? I ride off into the sunset and you stay here? We just set each other free?"

Bliss was silent.

"You can't be serious. Just break it off completely? No calls, no letters . . . ."

"That's probably for the best," Bliss said.

Harry was stunned. "For how long? A month? A year? Forever?"

"I don't know." Bliss was crying again. "I don't know. I don't know. I'm sorry. I love you, Harry. I'll always love you. But you need to leave now. Please go."

Harry drove home to the Bar T, trying to work out in his mind what might come next, trying to imagine a future for himself without Bliss. But he got nowhere with that. He knew his feelings for Bliss had not changed; they never would. Until today he had believed her love for him was just as immutable. Now he didn't know. She had cast him out, possibly for good. On this dark night, he felt like a shipwrecked sailor washed up on the shore of an uncharted island. Lost, alone, and short on hope.

Three days later Harry pulled up stakes. On his way out of town he steeled his nerves and stopped by the Coats place again to say goodbye to Esau and Polly. When he arrived at their house, he got out of the truck and waited. Esau came to the door and stood behind the rusty screen. He stepped out onto the porch. Harry came forward as Esau descended the steps, cackling yard fowl scattering at their approach. The two men stood a few feet apart.

"I . . . I wanted to pay my respects before I go," Harry said. "I'm leaving Oklahoma."

"For good this time?"

"Yes. Selling the livestock, putting the ranch on the market."

"Cain't say I'm surprised. Cain't say I wish it wudn't true."

Harry absorbed the blow.

"Where you figger on lightin' out for?"

"West. How far, I don't know. Maybe back to Tejon. Some place where people don't know what happened here."

"West," Esau said wistfully. He hooked his thumbs in the galluses of his bib overalls, looked off in that direction. "Folks say a man can still make a new start out yonder. Course a man can make a new start in his own country, too. If he has what it takes."

Harry looked up into his old friend's weathered face.

"You ever think about it, Esau? You and Polly?"

"About what? Leavin'?"

Harry nodded.

"We considered it. After they kilt our boy. Talked about mebbe carrying him down to Texas, settlin' there. Problem is, our other two babies is buried here. And my daddy and mama, and Polly's daddy and mama. Cain't leave 'em. No, suh."

Harry bent his head, toed the dirt, looked up again.

"I'm sorry, Esau."

"Uh huh."

Harry took a deep breath. "I'm sorry about everything. Sorry I didn't stick up for Woody when I should have. Sorry I wasn't there when they grabbed him. Sorry I let you down. Sorry for so many things. I don't know where to start."

"Sorry," Esau said, sighing. "I do believe you are sorry. Don't change nothin'. My boy's still dead. But it's somethin', I guess."

The two men stood silent.

"Polly . . . ." Harry said, looking past Esau to the house. "Do you suppose I could . . . ."

Esau shook his head. "Best not, I reckon."

Harry nodded.

"Well, I'll be going then. I'll let you know when I get settled in case you need to reach me about anything, not that I expect you will."

Harry offered his hand.

Esau considered it a moment before taking it. His grip felt bony and had a tremor in it. But it was still strong.

As Harry was turning to go the screen door opened and Polly stepped out on the porch, arms folded across her chest, eyes red and overflowing. Harry looked at Esau. Esau nodded and Harry slowly ascended the steps, stood in front of the woman who had done so much for him, meant so much to him, gazed into her eyes, dark and swimming with love and pain.

"Polly, I . . ."

Harry's grief rose up then, overwhelming him, and he broke down. Polly opened her arms. Harry came into them and they held each other and cried. Finally, Polly released him. Patted his arm. Turned and went inside.

Harry came down the steps to Esau, put his hat back on, adjusted it, touched the brim with a finger.

"Good-bye then, Mr. Coats."

"Good-bye, Mr. True."

Harry got into his truck. He drove north to Route 66 and turned west.

CHAPTER 36

El Cuartelejo

Harry packed light. The sole remnant of the past he took with him, other than the memories burned into his heart, was the singed photograph of Bliss he had carried during the war, the one he had saved from the fire at the last moment. Now, as before, he kept it tucked away in a pocket over his heart.

Homeless and kinless, more wanderer than traveler, he drifted west, knowing only the company of strangers and haunted by regret. In time, Harry found himself at Tejon Ranch. His old friend J. T. Branum welcomed him back, no questions asked.

Harry asked J. T. to put him to work as a line rider. J. T. hesitated. They both knew what the job entailed: roaming the margins of the ranch on horseback, checking for breaks in fences, turning wandering cows back to their home range, rousting interlopers, checking grass and water levels. He'd be working an unshorn area Anglo ranch hands called the west forty and Mexican *vaqueros* called *el cuartelejo,* the far quarter.

"You sure?" J. T. asked. "You know what it's like out there. By yourself for days on end. Most cowboys don't roll in here and ask to ride line. They try to avoid it. I kindly gotta make 'em do it."

"So I've heard."

"Line riders have been known to come down with a touch of what folks in Oklahoma used to call prairie fever. Go a little crazy. You know that."

Harry did.

"I could use you right here, you know. I'm gettin' on in years and stove up more every day."

"No thanks," Harry said. "I'm a line rider. It's where I should be."

J. T. studied him. "You want to tell me what's brung you to this? I'm a pretty good listener, don't talk too much."

Harry didn't answer.

"I'll take that as a no. Well, OK. Pack your gear. You know where the Lone Wolf Creek line camp is. Smack dab in the middle of nowhere. Come in every couple three weeks to report and get a hot meal, a shower. If I don't see you I'll have to come alookin'. That would inconvenience me."

Harry headed west and after two days' ride arrived at his assigned outpost. The line camp consisted of a dingy one-room, south-facing shack not much bigger than a barnstall, jerry-built with unpeeled log construction, clay chinking, gabled roof and rough-cut shake shingles. All of it old and weathered. No electricity, no running water, packed-clay floor. Bullseye lantern for light. Double-hung windows flanked the door. For forting up, should that become necessary, there were stout board and batten shutters inside the sashes: hinges on the right side of the frame, slide bolt lock on the left. At the door, iron brackets could hold a two-by-four serving as a crossbeam lock.

The shack was furnished with an army surplus cot with metal springs and a thin GI tick; it stood against the east wall. On the opposite wall stood a crude stone fireplace outfitted with a chimney crane for a cooking pot. A trestle table hosted a blue enameled washbowl and pitcher, one battered ladder-back chair. Two plankwood shelves lining the north wall made a proper larder for a stock of staples: coffee, beans, salt, sugar, air tights of various kinds. And a few personal items: shaving gear, comb, toothbrush, mirror.

A good distance from the shack stood a one-holer outhouse, a crescent moon carved in the door. In the yard, there was a small gated corral, a slant-roof feed shed with enough room to provide protection from the elements for his saddlehorse and, from time to time, a pack animal. Next to it a tack shed. A vein of live water flowed nearby. Harry did his own cooking, drank creek coffee.

Every day he rode off in a different direction, alone. A monastic way of life. He could go weeks without seeing another human being. Some nights he slept out under the stars. Some days he idled away hours reposed on his bedroll, saddle for a backrest, mesmerized by campfire flames or the great expanse of green hills and indigo sky before him. He'd lost everything he loved and, at times, a deluge of tears overtook him with the celerity of chain lightning. Half-crazy with loneliness, he sometimes became so despondent at the certainty that his soul was irredeemable, he would take his government .45 from his saddlebag and go over in his mind the relief, and the justice, a bullet to the head might bring. Only the fear that death wouldn't be sufficient to the task of extinguishing the pain in his heart restrained him. His misery might follow him to the afterworld.

Every few weeks he'd take a break from riding fence and wander in to the ranch headquarters to report to J. T., catch a night's sleep in the bunkhouse, get a shower, eat a hot meal. He'd pick up what little mail he got about ranch business, return a call from his realtor, Rex Holmes, refuse another offer.

Ruth wrote on occasion at first, chatty letters filled with news from home. The violence and killings in Black Flats had sent shockwaves through the Black and white communities. She'd expected more violence after Woody's lynching but for the time being people seemed to have had enough. There was some good news to report. The WHITES ONLY signs had finally come down. The Black Flats school was being rebuilt. And the Men's Club had voted to make minstrel shows a thing of the past. Harry found Ruth's letters painful. He saw Bliss's hand in all of it. Ruth stopped writing when he didn't answer.

Bliss never wrote. Harry would lie on his bunkhouse cot or on his bedroll under the stars, wondering where she was at that moment, what she was doing, what she was thinking, whether he ever crossed her mind. Come morning he would saddle up and ride off to the high lonesome. Always alone. Always surprised when he'd made it through another bunkhouse visit without succumbing to the gnawing desire to call her or post the letters he wrote by lantern light confessing his sins, professing his love. He rode out, always an outlander, trailing feelings of guilt and longing that ran marrow deep, and for some reason he didn't quite understand, persevering against the load. He asked himself why, but the only answer he came up with was habit.

Back at ranch headquarters one Saturday afternoon his second spring season at Tejon, Harry lay on his bunkhouse cot perusing a Leddy's catalog when he heard the wall phone ring in the hallway.

"True. Hey, True!" one of the cowboys called out. "Phone call."

Had to be Rex Holmes with another offer on the Bar T. Rex was the only one who ever called. They both knew how the conversation would go.

It's a good offer, Harry.

I'll think about it.

The guy was persistent. Harry had to give him that.

"Hey, Harry," the cowboy called again. "The cord don't reach that far. You're gonna have to drag your lazy ass over here."

Harry drew himself up from the tick. He drudged to the telephone, took up the receiver that was hanging by its cord and put it to his ear.

"'Lo," he said.

No response.

Odd. He sensed someone on the other end of the line.

"Hello . . . Rex?"

Silence. And then a familiar voice, thin, whispery.

"Harry?"

He was imagining things. Had to be. His mind was playing tricks.

"Harry?"

"Bliss?"

"Harry, I . . . ."

Within an hour Harry had drawn his time, said *adiós* to J. T. and taken his leave of *Rancho El Tejón*. He worked his way east on Highway 138 to Cajon Pass, turned north on Route 66. At Barstow, he veered east on a journey of more than a thousand miles. The way he figured it, he could make Serafina by noon of the third day. The Mother Road would carry him home.

ACKNOWLEDGEMENTS

Many people had a hand in bringing *Blue Wild Indigo* to life. I owe a debt of gratitude to them all. My longtime editor and loyal friend, Gini Wallace, for her wise counsel, tireless effort, and stellar wordcraft. Barbara Benton for capturing the tone and feel of BWI with her loose brushwork cover art. Charles Salzberg, Tim Tomlinson, and Ross Klavan, leading members of the New York Writers Workshop and award-winning authors, for their early reading of the BWI manuscript, their guidance and encouragement. Claire McKinney and her Plum Bay team, including Sonya Dalton, Jeremy Townsend, and Barbara Aronica, for opening new doors to the publishing world and for having faith in BWI. Dr. Clif' Warren, the visionary behind the University of Central Oklahoma's writing program, for being the founder of the feast. And most of all, my late wife Vicky for all the dancing days, past and future.